HOW

Clarissa Burden

LEARNED TO

Fly

HOW

Clarissa Burden

LEARNED TO

Fly

Connie May Fowler

GRAND CENTRAL
PUBLISHING

NEW YORK   BOSTON

Grand Central Publishing
Hachette Book Group
237 Park Avenue
New York, NY 10017

www.HachetteBookGroup.com

Printed in the United States of America

First Edition: April 2010
10 9 8 7 6 5 4 3 2 1

Grand Central Publishing is a division of Hachette Book Group, Inc.
The Grand Central Publishing name and logo is a trademark of Hachette Book Group, Inc.

Library of Congress Cataloging-in-Publication Data

Fowler, Connie May.
    How Clarissa Burden learned to fly / Connie May Fowler.
        p. cm.
    ISBN 978-0-446-54068-1
    1. Self-realization in women—Fiction.   2. Psychological fiction.   I. Title.
    PS3556.O8265H69 2010
    813'.54—dc22

                                                                        2009030659

For Bill, My Moon Whisperer

$$E = mc^2$$
Albert Einstein

HOW

Clarissa Burden

LEARNED TO

Fly

On June 21, 2006, at seven a.m. in a malarial crossroads named Hope, Florida, the thermometer old Mrs. Hickok had nailed to the WELCOME TO HOPE sign fifteen years prior read ninety-two degrees. It would get a lot hotter that day, and there was plenty of time for it to do so, this being the summer solstice. But ninety-two at seven a.m., sunrise occurring only three hours earlier, suggested a harsh reckoning was in store for this swampy southern outpost. The weight of the humidity-laden situation pressed down on nearly all of the village's inhabitants, including its sundry wildlife—squirrels, raccoons, possums, rats, deer, and one lone bobcat—each of whom, immersed in its particular brand of animal consciousness, paused (some even in slumber), noses twitching, tails snapping, all steeling themselves against the inevitable onslaught of the day's hellish heat.

Hope's only living being to appear unfazed by the rising mercury was Clarissa Burden, a thirty-five-year-old woman who'd moved to the north Florida hamlet six months prior with her husband of seven years. Trapped as she was in a haze of insecurities and self-doubt, and being long divorced from her animal consciousness, she peered out her opened kitchen window into her rose garden and felt an undoing coming on that was totally unrelated to the weather. It was as if her brain stem, corpuscles, gallbladder, nail cuticles, the mole on her left shoulder, the scar on her knobby shin, the tender corpus of her womb—the whole she-bang—were about to surrender. But to what, she did not know.

She watched her husband—a multimedia artist who dabbled in painting, filmmaking, sculpture, pottery, and photography as long as his muse wore no clothes—alternately sketch and photograph a sweating young woman. With the exception of a silver ring piercing her belly button, the woman stood in the bright light of morning amid Clarissa's roses as naked as the moment she was born.

Clarissa leaned windward to get a better look. Barefoot and still wearing the clothes she had slept in—a rumpled T-shirt and dirt-stained shorts—she tapped her finger on the screen's dusty mesh, wondering what it felt like to be her husband's muse. Was the young woman racked with insecurity, fearing the artist was casting judgment with each stroke of his charcoal pencil? Or was she empowered, fully aware of the spell that flesh cast on weak men?

Her husband, Igor "Iggy" Dupuy, paused from his sketching and wiped perspiration from his bald pate and big face. "You have beautiful skin, even when you sweat." Clarissa took in every lyrical syllable her husband uttered. And while unhappy with their intent—even if it was a harmless observation—Clarissa had never grown tired of her husband's accent. South African by birth, of Dutch ancestry, and American by choice, Iggy was actually born Igor Pretoriun but changed his last name, favoring a French influence, to distance himself from his birth country's racial past. She appreciated that in him. It was something they had in common, both coming from a land of racial sins and both feeling it forever necessary to let people know that the old politic was never their politic. He was a tall, strapping man with hands twice the size of Clarissa's. It was one of the things that caused her to fall in love with him eight years ago, this stature that far outpaced her own.

Unwilling to continue to spy—that's what it felt like to her, but only because Iggy wanted her nowhere near him while he worked—she floated her attention past her husband and the young woman, beyond the towering magnolia with its opulent white flowers that Clarissa so loved, to the field south of the rose garden. There, hidden amid tall blades of grass, a black snake shed its skin. The snake, nearly finished with the process, soaked up the sun's early heat, enjoying the sensation of warmth on freshly minted scales, while all but two inches of its old self draped behind in the grass like a dull transparent cape, an afterthought.

If she had known the snake was out there, Clarissa's sense of imminent implosion might have lifted, because, while not stupid, she was superstitious and believed that the presence of a snake meant she was going to come into money. Without good cause except for a writer's ingrained insistence on avoiding clichés, she had long overlooked the importance of shed skin and what that might predict. She batted at a fly that had been pestering her ever since she'd put on the coffee. If it weren't so hot and if her husband weren't out there with a naked woman, she would have gone for a walk. They owned ten highly treed acres, and she was taken with it all: leaf and petal, blade and stamen. The north Florida landscape reminded her of abundance; it was such a far cry from the south Florida, palm-tree-stuttered trailer park of her youth.

She closed her eyes and breathed deeply. A cacophony of scents enveloped her, the floral high notes mingling with the musky scent of things dying. Clarissa was proud of her garden. It was becoming what she had envisioned the first time she'd stepped onto the property: her own private Eden, genteel and spilling over with rosebuds, jasmine, pendulous wisteria. Every time she tucked a plant's roots into the rich soil, she felt the distance between her adult life and her fatherless childhood grow ever greater. And that was a very good thing. She opened her eyes. The snake wandered into taller grass, leaving its former skin behind. Clarissa saw the grass sway but didn't think a thing of it. She was meandering through her garden's history: how she had, without her husband's labor or input, dreamed, planned, tilled, planted, sweated over, bled over, and adored her garden into existence. Wind rippled through the branches, bringing not a respite from the weather, but a mobile wall of heat. Clarissa tightened her ponytail, shimmying it up a tad higher on her head, and decided that she hadn't wanted his help. Not really. Her husband ignoring dirt, and plants, and compost was, she knew, the least of her matrimonial worries.

Iggy's big voice cut through the humid air. "Aye, Christ, this heat!"

"But when you sweat," his model said, "sex is the best."

"*Fowking* A, sweetie, *fowking* A!" That's how he said "fuck," as if the vowel were an *o*; stupid man. Determined to ignore them, Clarissa scanned the far boundary of her yard, where the regimental hand of her design gave way to the exuberant chaos of an oak grove. She watched a pileated woodpecker on those long wings with their lightning bolt patches of black and white dart through the cloud-free sky, and she considered the possibility that the malaise her marriage had slipped into was (a) inevitable; (b) temporary; and (c) possibly fatal. The woodpecker zigzagged over the treetops, cawed raucously, and then disappeared into the swamp's verdant green veil.

Batting again at that annoying fly, Clarissa thought, Iggy's art is his kingdom, but I am not his queen. He had many queens, models all: She was very clear about that issue. And also this one: He had not touched her—not so much as a peck on the cheek, an arm around her waist, a caress amid dreams on a warm night—in nearly two years. His amorous intentions had not stopped like a switch being flipped. They had slowly — over a period of... Clarissa wasn't sure, maybe four or five years — evaporated. Maybe, she thought as she scratched at a raw mosquito bite on her elbow, this is normal; maybe all men lose interest in their wives; maybe the whole "seven-year itch" thing should be renamed "24/7, 365 days from the get-go" itch.

As she stood there, looking at her garden teeming with hidden but complex activity — grubs eating tender roots, parasites sucking precious sap from nimble stems, mole rats digging underground labyrinths — she thought back to the first time they had met. They were both living in Gainesville. She had taken a visiting writers gig at the University of Florida, and he was an artist everyone in town wanted to know, because in those days he was funny and expansive; he didn't constantly bitch, and the whole foreigner thing was in.

A mutual friend who taught in the History Department, Jack Briggs, had invited a dozen or so people over to watch President Clinton's televised address regarding an alleged tryst he'd had with a White House intern. She and Iggy never saw the president speak, because not long after Jack introduced them in the kitchen, they wandered onto the back porch, where they settled into a couple of rocking chairs and talked for a good three hours.

Clarissa had been immediately struck by Iggy's otherness — his height, his big-boned frame, his Afrikaner accent that, she would discover, grew thick and impenetrable when he was angry or drunk. He was sixteen years her senior, and because she'd never known her father, she'd decided an older man in her life might offer stability.

Standing in June's webbed heat, thinking about that first meeting, Clarissa felt her heart swell with love and hate. She remembered gazing up at him, thinking he had the most amazing imperial blue and to-drown-in eyes, when he said, "I *fowking* hate the Afrikaners and what they did to the country. All the whites should leave, including my family. It is not their land. It is the black man's. Every last drop of white blood should leave the continent."

He placed his immense hand on her shoulder and squeezed. His touch thrilled her, as did his passion. Still young and inexperienced in the art of seduction, she tried to appear slightly bored, because boredom—she thought at the time—was an interesting, artsy conceit. "So, your family is still there?"

As men are wont to do with their facial hair, especially when it's the only hair they have, he stroked his beard, which, she decided, made him appear thoughtful, smart, and I'm-too-sexy-for-my-politics in a Marxian sort of way. "They will never leave," he said, leveling his eyes to hers. "They love their money and their land too much." He swirled his Scotch, studying it, and then leaned in very close to her. She could smell the oak-and-oat aroma on his breath. "But it's not their land. They stole it and delude themselves into thinking God gave it to them." He tapped his temple. "My parents don't deserve me to be their son. My sisters and brothers don't deserve to breathe the same air as I." He shot her a smile that was a nearly irresistible mix of self-deprecation and ego. "Racist bastards!"

As he spoke, his Dutch face, which seemed to Clarissa to be impossibly long and redolent with the hint of shadows, reminded her of someone Rembrandt would have painted. And at that moment, she had wanted him to kiss her. She found the very idea of him disowning his family on moral and political grounds to be courageous. Blinded by the hormones of early love, she did not see that it might also indicate a man who easily divorced himself from loyalties and truth. She did not ask, "If a man walks away from his mother because he seriously disagrees with her politics, how deep is his allegiance to a wife?"

Clarissa picked at the mosquito bite until it bled. The fly

settled on the window's top sash, and from there, the scent of her skin and faint suggestion of blood enveloping him, he watched her. Though a mere insect, the fly had a complex existence, full of near death experiences and matters of the heart. With a life span of only fifteen to thirty days—and that was *without* humans swatting at you—he lived in a perpetual state of pregnant urgency, as if each moment might be his last. He was well aware that he was in love with this human who, he thought, with her fair skin that often carried the scent of ripe apples, was the most beautiful creature in his world. At that moment, while she searched her yard for reasons he didn't grasp, the fly wanted nothing more than to light in her blond curls and never leave.

Oblivious to his intentions (how could one ever know the hidden desires of insects?), Clarissa ignored him. Her gaze drifted from the fringe of lesser oaks and skinny towers of bald cypress to the sprawling backdrop of a giant sentinel oak whose trunk was of such circumference, she believed it would take ten people, arms outstretched, fingertip to fingertip, to encircle it. This is where the swamp began. Jake's Hell was a gator-and-mosquito-infested expanse of fetid water that led, as far as she could tell, to absolutely nowhere. But the oak was beautiful; its widespread crown was home to a heron couple that rose daily into the dawn sky, squawking as they ascended, and returned at dusk—one behind the other—still squawking. In her six months here, Clarissa had grown attached to the birds and their noisy pronouncements. They were a real team: hunting, gathering, loving. And she found herself, even on this still young and fragile June solstice, hoping that the herons portended change: a wild turn toward passion in her marriage. This morning she had missed the birds; dawn had come earlier than she had expected. As she turned away from the window and the garden where her husband was asking his model to look toward the wisteria vine, and yes,

yes, lower her chin just a bit, Clarissa concluded that the detour in her routine—not seeing the birds take wing at first light—was the reason for her unease.

She stepped into the center of the room—no chance to watch her husband from there—and decided she needed something to keep her unsettled mind occupied. Perhaps she should be a couch potato for the day. Watch TV, turn on CNN. The war in Iraq—the casualties, the lies, the misery delivered on the wings of ineptitude, the casual quagmire of it all—infuriated her, and she wondered why Americans, including herself, hadn't taken to the streets, demanding an end to an immoral war. It was as if the entire world, in the early years of a new century, had given up believing in higher callings. Peace, love, and understanding felt like quaint ideas proffered by naive people. She absentmindedly rubbed the back of her left calf with her right foot's big toe and took in her farmhouse kitchen—its marble-topped oak island where she kept her mixer and rolling pin and food processor, the Marilyn Monroe cookie jar that was stuffed with pink sugar substitute packets (the fly lit on the tip of Marilyn's nose; Clarissa shooed it away), the jadeite dishware stacked in pale green heaps behind glass-front cabinet doors—and she decided that the new century didn't feel new at all. It felt overwhelming, as if change were out of reach and stagnation all the rage.

Clarissa tapped her fingers on the marble—it was still cool to the touch—and noticed that quivers of dried rosemary littered her Spanish tile floor. Yes indeed, the floor needed a good cleaning. Her ovarian shadow women (that's what she called the exuberant chorus of voices that swirled up from, she supposed, the depths of her unconscious and did their best to alternately ease her rising anxieties and inflame them beyond all reason) clucked and twittered, but she could not understand a damn thing they said.

She grabbed her broom and began sweeping, gathering the

rosemary quivers into a diminutive, spiky pile, when finally, one voice — it sounded suspiciously like Bea Arthur — broke through the chaos and asked, "Don't you have a novel to write?"

Then they all chimed in, prattling among themselves that, yes, she surely did, whatever was she thinking, it was high time she stopped procrastinating, sweeping up rosemary wasn't going to pay the mortgage.

Clarissa shoved the broom into the space between her fridge and the wall. "Oh, be quiet," she said, exasperation cooling her tendency toward long vowels. Noticing that the coffeepot was still on, she flipped it off. She knew the ovarian shadow women were correct, but she also felt helpless to remedy the situation. Clarissa Burden, author of two highly acclaimed and best-selling novels, had not written one decent sentence in over thirteen months. The longer the dry spell dragged on, the greater her fear of facing the virtual blank pages of her word processor. And the fear on that June morning was enough to inspire in her a slew of mundane tasks — sweeping, dusting, vacuuming, dishwashing — all designed to prevent her from laying even a single finger on her keyboard.

She pulled her T-shirt away from her body — she was finally beginning to succumb to the high morning heat — and thought about closing the windows and cranking the air-conditioning, but if she did that, she wouldn't be able to hear what was being said in her garden. Besides, in these past few weeks she had learned just how challenging it was to cool a circa 1823 home.

She retrieved the dustpan from its hiding place behind the door and, using her hand, pushed the rosemary into it. As she walked over to the trash can, she considered the advantages of hygiene. Maybe she should shower and dress and put on makeup. This was not like her, to sloth around in dirt-stained shorts, a T-shirt reeking with the sleep-stink, her face not yet washed; but she had awoken to the solstice, fully convinced that nothing interesting was going to happen on this clear, hot day, so therefore there was no need for pretense or the appearance of hopefulness. She attempted to dump the herb pile into the can, but the wind gusted, scattering the rosemary.

"Shit," she muttered. Even the wind was conspiring against her. On a normal day, Clarissa would have tried again, but being addled, she simply gave in, returned the dustpan to its hiding place, walked over to her sink, washed her hands, and wiped her hands on her belly as if she had no manners whatsoever.

As she leaned against the counter, considering her next move, music, faint at first and then more vigorous, wafted into the kitchen, but she couldn't tell from where. Tilting her head, she tried to zero in: a fiddle swirling a strange and lovely melody. Two nights prior, she had drifted up from a deep sleep, feeling guided and tugged by a similar tune. She had dismissed it as dream music—syncopated, foreign. But here she was, wide awake, and it was back.

She walked into the central room that, architecturally, was your typical shotgun affair (you could shoot a gun through the front door and the bullet would, barring impact with a human being, a hound dog, or ill-placed furniture, zip straight through the house and out the back door). But the large space with its gleaming French crystal chandelier and gracious curved staircase left no doubt that this house had little in common with typical southern shotgun shacks; unlike Clarissa's home, they appealed solely by virtue of their simplicity.

Clarissa peered out of the wavy, thick glass of the double doors that led onto the back porch and into the garden to see if her husband had brought out the boom box. Her red geraniums, planted in terra-cotta pots, lined either side of the railing. In the halcyon light of the morning sun, they appeared too perfect to be real. She did not see a boom box or any other sort of music-playing apparatus but was aware that her husband had just touched the hard edge of the model's jaw with his index finger and angled her face to the light. She was also aware that the model closed her eyes—probably against the glare—and that when she did, the music faded altogether.

The ovarian shadow woman who sounded like Bea Arthur said, "You have got to get away from those idiots in the backyard."

"Yes, yes, I do," Clarissa said, standing beneath the chandelier, not noticing that the fly had lit on one of its lower crystal prisms. She wanted to feel sunny, bountiful, in control, not jealous and ticked. Her hands itched to dig in dirt. Dirt, without a doubt, made her happy. And then she thought, Of course! Flowers! Cut some flowers; the front yard is chock-full of them. But before she could get to her pruning shears, which she kept in the laundry room situated down a hall off of the kitchen and to the right, or to the front door and outside to the rosebushes she'd planted five months ago by the porch steps, she heard Iggy instruct his model to spread her legs wider.

At that very moment, under the soft changing light of the chandelier, Clarissa Burden wanted her husband dead. She stomped through her kitchen, down a hallway (the house, like her brain, was a maze of hallways leading to rooms that she frequented so rarely, they sometimes surprised her), into the laundry room, a realization washing over her that would, in due course, change her forever: Not only did she want Iggy dead, she spent at least 90 percent of her waking hours and a good portion of her dreamtime fantasizing about said death. Oh, my God, she thought as she reached for the shears she kept on a hook to the right of the dryer, it was true. And disgusting. Contemptible. Obscene. She gripped the shears, unlocked them, and said, "Holy shit." She'd gone from being a writer who spun whole worlds from her imagination, populating thousands of pages with stories people wanted to read, to being a discontented wife consumed with spousal death scenarios.

There was no denying it. These send-him-to-the-grave vignettes welled up randomly inside the withering fields of her imagination, devoid top to bottom of literary merit. She searched her laundry basket for that pair of gardening gloves she'd washed just yesterday. Could it be, she wondered, sifting through underwear and tees (the fly now perched on the dryer door), that these death dreams were consuming every last drop of her creative energy? Were these negatively charged fantasies the source, the cause, perhaps the very nexus of her block? In an instant—blink, blink—what had the makings of a lengthy self-interrogation came to a whiplashing halt as she, with no will or discipline, tumbled straight into the dark heart of a death scenario rerun—one of her most popular, judging by how frequently she tuned in. She continued to search for her gloves, but in action only; in her head, she was on the scene of a grisly tragedy, one that changed little from episode to episode.

Clarissa saw herself with twenty-twenty clarity: Wearing a yellow sundress and black strappy sandals, she stood at the edge of the cane, cotton, and sorghum fields that lined the two-lane blacktop leading into town. Why she was by the road in the middle of an agricultural area, she didn't know. But she didn't need to; this was a fantasy, not a novel. Enveloped in the stench of manure and pesticides, she shaded her eyes with her hand and watched her husband, who had just left the house to attend to whatever affairs a multimedia artist must attend to, zip by in his green Honda Civic with the Monica Lewinsky bobblehead doll grooving on the dash. The sun was so intense, the asphalt appeared unstable, as if Florida's legendary heat had transmuted the road into a river of molten black lava.

She saw, with the aid of God's omniscient eye, her husband squint into the shimmying distance, lower the sun visor, and with his right hand spin the radio dial. He did not like American popular music, and given that the state of radio had declined since his youth (a splendid childhood spent on the family farm in the foothills of the Witzenberg Mountains), playing nothing but pop (which he could put up with only when he was in one of his rare generous moods) and country (which he loathed, claiming it gave him migraines and lower intestinal turbulence), he flipped off the radio and—steering with his left hand—reached under the passenger seat to retrieve a CD.

The road was narrow and winding; if a person allowed his focus to wander, or if he was unable to stop multitasking, or if he was impaired by drink or smoke or a desire to hear Howlin' Wolf wail "Smokestack Lightnin'," could not an accident easily happen?

Clarissa found the gloves at the bottom of the basket. She grabbed them and the shears, walked into the kitchen, opened her cupboard, retrieved a drinking glass, filled it with tap water, and nodded her head yes. In fact, she believed any number of fatal endings could result, but on this day, as the solstice sun slowly rose higher and higher in that heat-blanched sky, her continuous loop fantasy offered only one thing: Her husband did not realize that as he groped for a tune he could live with, he had crossed the double yellow lines. His only clue, a blasting horn, came too late. Three seconds before impact—in that zone where time takes on the all-knowing, all-penetrating, boundary-free quality of God—he grabbed the steering wheel with both hands, held her steady, and slammed the brakes. His face went slack with what was perhaps amazement as he realized that the last thing he would see in this old world was the love bug–splattered grille of an eighteen-wheeler.

Clarissa downed the water in one huge gulp, as if it were whiskey. She set the glass on the counter and wiped her mouth with the back of her hand. Seized with guilt (she didn't really want her husband dead, did she?), she attempted to steady herself by focusing: her glove's quaint blue daisy pattern, the brain-drilling buzz of that fly, the shadow of the Marilyn Monroe cookie jar wavering like mutant ink on her tile floor, the rosemary quivers scattered like ash. She opened the sink cabinet in search of a plastic bucket she'd stuffed there several weeks ago.

As she reached into the dark, humid abyss, a black widow spider that lived in the top right corner watched her giant arm approach. The spider twitched her legs, readied her fangs, prepared to defend her egg sac if necessary.

Oblivious, Clarissa waded through Drano, Raid, Goop, Mr. Clean, Tilex, Windex, Pine-Sol, Clorox spray, plastic disposable gloves, ammonia, baking soda (she was unaware that she had all the ingredients to build an explosive device), and a package of roach bombs before laying her hand on the rim of the bucket (it had fallen on its side in the far nether reaches, behind the bomb-making ingredients). She lifted it by the handle, tearing a small hole in the black widow's web.

An icy surge of venom filled the spider's fangs.

Clarissa pulled herself upright (relieved that the giant arm was retreating, the black widow withdrew and began repairing the hole in her web) and—dizzy-headed but determined to try to make something of this moment in June—filled the bottom third of the bucket with water. Her blue eyes bright with the excitement that comes with a decision well made, she grabbed the gloves and shears and ferried everything, water sloshing, to her front yard, far from Iggy and his model, where she would immerse herself in the business of cutting roses: peach-colored roses with thorn-studded stems and thick, serrated, crimson-tinged leaves. Their citrus-and-velvet scent would clear her mind. She would stop thinking about ways her husband might die. She would map out her novel and make a mental list of funny, smart, despicable, and fascinating characters. She would find joy in the satisfying snap the shears made with each angled cut. Come hell or high water, she would find a way to love this day. That's what Clarissa Burden told herself, her imagination stirring with possibilities, as she stepped out of her house and into the bright heat of this long morning.

Ouch!" Clarissa was on her knees, her bucket filling slowly with roses, elbow-deep in foliage, when she got snagged on the healthy, beautiful, sharp point of a curved thorn. She pulled off her glove and examined the petite wound. Her punctured finger bled lightly. She put it to her lips and sucked; for some reason, this took away the sting.

Smelling of sweat and roses, she stood, swiped the dirt from her knees, surveyed her bushes, and decided she needed to move on to those on the right. As she reached for the bucket, that strange music welled up again. Was someone down the road playing a stereo too loudly? And by down the road, she meant a couple of miles, because Hope was bordered on all sides by swamp and forest. She walked to her front gate and tried to figure it out. Carl Washington, a man whose skin was the color of strong coffee, approached from the east on a blue bike.

"Good morning, Carl." Clarissa waved. His handlebar basket brimmed with tomatoes and greens.

Carl slowed the bike. "Morning, Clarissa. Hot enough for you?" Carl might have stopped and chatted were he not on a mission, because he liked Clarissa Burden. She was pretty, but not in a trashy way, and did not appear to be afraid of him like so many other white women in these parts. But his mother was sick, and he was on his way to her house to fix her a proper meal.

Clarissa wanted to ask what he was doing with those tomatoes. She loved homegrown tomatoes, and from her vantage point, they appeared to be just that. What she wouldn't give for a thick-sliced tomato with basil, salt, pepper, a bit of lemon, and mozzarella. But he was on the move, obviously busy, so as she stepped into the road she simply said, "Yes, sir, it's going to be a scorcher." He waved, the bike bobbled, he brought it straight again, and Clarissa watched him pedal hard, westward bound.

She leaned forward, craning her neck first to the left, then to the right, unable to determine what direction the music was coming from. Her tanned skin glowed—a peach glow—in the lucid, shady light. In the distance, she saw the WELCOME TO HOPE sign but could not read the thermometer because the sign was poised on the outskirts of the town, on the far end of the village green. But if she'd been able to, Clarissa would have taken note that at half-past seven, it was nearly ninety-five degrees.

Clarissa loved the small-town feel of her new home. Comprising a smattering of old houses and single-wide trailers—a quiet oasis amid the north Florida wilderness—Hope existed because cotton had once been king in these soft rises. Some of the old plantations still existed, now owned mostly by wealthy northerners who came down with their well-heeled buddies to hunt quail. Clarissa, barefoot (soon the asphalt would be too hot to walk on, and Chet Lewis, the man who owned the house catty-corner from Clarissa's, would wander into the street, egg in hand, and fry it just for the bragging rights), walked toward the crossroads where Bread of Life Way intersected Mosquito Swamp Trail. She didn't know why it was called Mosquito Swamp since it wound its way through Jake's Hell. She looked to the east, toward the green, listening to the music fade in and out, and decided that perhaps a good Christian in the county road department objected to putting the word *hell* on a county sign, especially since it intersected the Bible-inspired Bread of Life.

Past the crossroads, on the right, stretched the village

green, where each year Hope held a town fair, replete with a dunking tank, homemade pies, and beauty queens, the proceeds going to restore old Mrs. Hickok's house for use as a community center. Mrs. Hickok, dead for fifteen years, was part Seminole Indian, part Irish, and—blessed with a knack for midwifery—had delivered several generations of Hopians, as she called the locals.

Shortly after Clarissa moved to Hope, the mail lady told her that the legendary Mrs. Hickok had suffered a stroke in her front yard and that she'd been discovered by the then postmistress, Mrs. Auden, who was the great-great-grandniece of John Milton, Florida's Civil War–era governor. A rabid secessionist (he shot himself in the head to avoid submitting to Union occupation), Milton presided over a state whose total population at the time Florida joined the Confederacy in 1861 was 140,424 souls. Nearly half of them—over 61,000—were slaves. Included in that number were 15 of Carl Washington's ancestors, a fact he never mentioned.

The mail lady, however, mystified by life's unpredictability, took a lot of nerve pills and was therefore perpetually confused, forever misdelivering mail and getting the details of local lore wrong nearly every time she attempted to share.

In actuality, Mrs. Hickok had died of heatstroke immediately after nailing that thermometer, using all her seventy-eight-year-old might, onto the WELCOME TO HOPE sign on a day nearly as hot as this one. And she was discovered not by Mrs. Auden, but by the circuit court judge, old Judge Revel, with whom she'd had a twenty-two-year affair. If Clarissa had dug a little deeper, if she weren't so preoccupied with her palsied marriage, she would have known these things.

Still, as she walked along the oak-dappled road, picking up her pace because the asphalt was growing hotter, Clarissa thought, Maybe there's a story here somewhere. "A Florida backwoods, half-Seminole midwife is falsely accused of murder and..."

And then what? Clarissa couldn't think of anything. Her mind, as it was wont to do when she tried to think about writing, simply went blank. Shaking her head, Clarissa said, "I'm a hopeless Hopian."

A squirrel that had been watching Clarissa from the boughs of a pecan tree scurried across an electric wire, and a pickup truck driven by a young man with wild red hair slowed down. He waved and smiled as he moseyed past, and Clarissa returned the greeting. She remembered him. He'd tried to talk to her back in May at the fair. Charmed by his attention but weirded out by the wolfish glint in his eye, when he had offered to buy her "a cold co-cola," she'd refused.

The other thing she remembered was that she had eaten a cumulous cloud of pink cotton candy. It almost made her sick, all that sugar. And also, Iggy had declined to accompany her. "*Boknaai*," he had said, dismissing her invitation, slipping into his native jargon's word for "bullshit." That's what he'd said; that's what he thought of most anything she wanted to do. But she'd enjoyed the carnival despite the cotton candy, and she was quite taken with how many folks had ventured out of the woods and into the village, making it appear for one day as if Hope were a thriving hamlet.

At the corner, an old woman in a sky blue Bonneville puttered along, ignoring the stop sign, ignoring Clarissa, favoring the road's right-hand shoulder. She can't see squat, Clarissa thought; she must not have anyone to help her, no one to run errands or get groceries or take her to the doctor. I hope I never get like that, Clarissa fretted, and by "that," she meant alone.

She scanned the green: not a soul in sight, not even a mockingbird, much less a man. A fire tower, rising one hundred feet into that infinite sky, dominated both the three-acre plot and the village itself. Clarissa eyed the lookout station but saw no one. Besides, how in the world could the music—which she no longer heard; she wasn't sure when it had stopped—waft such a great distance? For nearly a full minute, she stood in the deep heat, protected from the sun by a shady oak, and studied the tower, an idea taking shape. Perhaps if she got to know the fire ranger, he would let her climb to the very top (could she make it?) and see for herself what her world looked like from on high. The view must be tremendous. She'd even be able to enjoy a bird's-eye gander of that sentinel oak. And then she thought, Uh-oh. From way up there, a fire ranger and his buddies could see into her backyard. A pair of binoculars, and boy, oh boy! Voyeur city. Clarissa looked over her shoulder to her house and again to the tower. There goes my reputation, she thought. If folks here knew what her husband did right under their noses, they'd be run out of town on a rail.

An ovarian shadow woman, adopting Christiane Amanpour's sartorial tone, mocked from the depths, "Author Clarissa Burden was arrested today for having a bevy of naked women in her backyard. Her husband was also taken into custody, in shackles."

"Nudity is not a crime," she whispered, and then, without having solved the music mystery, she turned and headed home, but this time she stayed on the grass.

Clarissa unlocked her gate, swung it open, heard the metallic clunk of the latch reengage, looked at the rose-filled bucket, and thought she needed just a few more stems when someone behind her cleared his throat and said, "Well, hello there."

Startled, she spun around. Outside the gate stood a short, muscular man, maybe her age, with bamboo-colored dreadlocks that ran past his waist. He wore a plaid shirt and blue jeans. He was missing his right arm. The one he did have was draped in rope. Where had he come from? Clarissa wondered. Other than

Carl, her redheaded suitor, and the old lady in the Bonneville, she hadn't seen a single other soul on Hope's main drag.

"Can I help you?" Clarissa stayed where she was. From three yards out, she decided there was something shifty about him.

"No, but I think I can help you. Name's Larry. Larry Dibble." He smiled, showing off a set of chompers that didn't fit him; they were too white, and nothing about him suggested he was the type of man who would indulge in the expense and time it took to whiten teeth. He stuck out his only hand.

Clarissa did not want to shake it. But she also didn't want to appear rude, so she reached for the bucket and pretended to be busy with the roses.

Little things didn't get to Larry Dibble, especially small sins committed by a trifle like her. So he rested his hand on the gate and massaged a sore spot in the wood.

For a man, he had unusually long fingernails, but what was even stranger was that he appeared not to notice the battalion of ants traversing the mountainous terrain of his knuckles.

"May I come in?"

Was he crazy? Clarissa wanted to send this fool packing. And what was up with the rope? She remembered the southern superstition about the devil: When he takes human form, he's always missing a body part and always asks for permission before coming onto your property. Not that she believed in such things, of course not, but there was no way she was going to let him step one foot into her yard. "I'm sorry, but I'm very busy."

He nodded his head in the direction of a tree that was taller than the house, and Clarissa detected movement in his woolly hair: more ants. "That water oak, there? Needs to come down. It's rotten on the inside. I can take her down for you. It's what I do."

Clarissa looked at the tree. It seemed fine to her. "How do you know?"

He tapped the side of his nose. "I can smell it." He flashed her that bright smile again and winked. This guy was giving her the heebie-jeebies. "In fact, you got a world of trouble in the tree department. At least half a dozen are close to dead. Water oaks do that, rot from the inside out. And that big feller you got back there, the live oak? That sucker is sick. I don't know who or what has been gnawing on it, but that's one embattled tree." He shook his head, and his certitude, Clarissa decided, made him appear arrogant. She could not have known that he looked that way — all full of himself — when he wasn't telling the entire truth.

"How do you know about the tree in the back?" Clarissa set the bucket of roses by her feet, just in case she had to run.

"I get around. Walk a lot. And like I said" — he tapped his nose again — "I specialize in putrefaction. I guess you could say it's a blessing and a curse." He paused as if he expected her to say something, but she was, in fact, speechless. "The issue is" — he adjusted the coil of rope, draping it over his shoulder, and Clarissa wondered how on earth a one-armed man could climb a tree, much less take one down — "that there water oak will succumb to a hard wind or a heavy rain, and there ain't no guarantees it will get blowed on your fence instead of your house."

This was a hard sell. No gleaming smile now; his spooky green eyes darkened, and his narrow face reflected impassive concern.

Clarissa feared, even though she didn't like the guy, that he was right. "You'll need to come back and talk to my husband." Not wanting him to think she was home alone, she added, "He's here, but he's busy."

"Oh, I've already talked to him." The smile was back. "I stopped by yesterday and took a good hard look at just about everything."

Clarissa literally felt her jaw drop. "Well, then, why are you asking me?" He must have come by when she was at the grocery store, and Iggy hadn't bothered to tell her.

"I need permission from the lady of the house. That's what your husband said. Well, sort of. I'll be by tomorrow to get some of the weight off the big'un in the back, but he wanted me to talk to you about them others. Evidently"—he winked again—"you control the purse strings."

Clarissa was pissed. "I don't want you touching that sentinel oak."

"Lady, it's too heavy. You gotta shore it up or it's gonna drop."

Clarissa didn't know if the guy knew what he was talking about or not, but she hated being railroaded. "No one touches the tree."

He shrugged, wrapped his fingers with those long nails around the rope as if he were caressing a lock of his own hair. "Ma'am, sounds like you're the one who needs to talk to your husband. You have a good day." And with that, his dazzling smile lighting his sharp-angled face, he walked away in the same direction Carl had gone.

An urge to cuss out the little two-pint, one-armed jackass surged through her, but Clarissa rarely lost her surface cool. Only below, in the deep and strange recesses of her mind, did she kick and holler. She walked to the gate and watched.

He seemed in no hurry. He ambled down the road with good posture, grace even, despite the missing limb.

What Clarissa could not see and did not know was that the precocious angel named Larry Dibble had to force himself not to laugh out loud. He knew he'd gotten her goat and gotten it good.

⌐◦

*B*etween the heat and the tree cutter, Clarissa was just about ready to faint. She looked at the rose bucket. She'd cut fifteen stems before being sidetracked by first the music and then that Dibble fellow, and that would have to do. But before she reached the top step, pail in one hand, shears in another, gloves stuffed in her back pocket, she heard a car engine and looked up to see a red Camaro pulling into her drive. Behind the steering wheel sat a pretty young blonde. Now what? Clarissa stood on the steps and waited for the woman to get out of the car. She was leggy and wore a thin cotton dress that covered only about an inch of thigh. A slim gold bracelet encircled her wrist.

"Can I help you?" Clarissa tried to keep the acid out of her voice.

"Hi!" the woman-child said with what Clarissa deemed was inappropriate enthusiasm. Her voice was squeaky, high-pitched, and Clarissa wondered if this was her real voice or something she had adopted. "Are you Iggy's housekeeper?"

"Housekeeper?" Clarissa reeled. What on earth was this person thinking? Housekeeper! She hugged the bucket close to her body — a shield. "No, no, I'm not."

The woman-child giggled. "Well, is he here? I'm modeling for him."

This, evidently, was a great honor. How much talent did it take to stand around naked? "Yeah, just go around the back. He's out there."

"Cool! See ya!" She turned on her thin little sandals and headed to the backyard. "Iggy! Where are you?"

Clarissa barreled into the house. She didn't have time to be upset; she had roses to trim, a vase to stuff. Housekeeper indeed! As the screen door banged behind her, she caught a glimpse of herself in the pier mirror that faced the base of the stairs. Her face was smudged with dirt. Her hair was coming out of the ponytail. Her T-shirt was torn and filthy. Her arms were scratched and bleeding from the thorns. She looked absolutely mad. *The Mad Woman of Hope.* Nice title. She'd clean up later.

In the kitchen, she ran water into the sink and tossed in a tray of ice cubes. She transferred the roses, a stem at a time, into the water. She refused to look outside, but she sure could hear them out there, giggling, chatting. "Oh yeah, perfect. Put your arm around her....Good. Good. Mind if I shoot some video later? The two of you, ya know, sexy play, a little edgy."

Again the giggling girls and then the insistence by one of them that they move their little party: "I'd love it! But can we do it at my place? I'm just dying to show you my new apartment. You promised me last week you'd come by."

Clarissa's gaze drifted over to the wall where her knives, on a magnetic strip, gleamed. Should she kill just him or all three of them? Before she could decide, her mind faded to black and she found herself wading waist-deep in a particular spousal death episode that would normally, in summer, fall, winter, and spring, tear her from whatever swamp-bottomed novel she was trying to write (she'd once abandoned a novel called *Breathing Room*—a coming-of-age tale with a protagonist who was a budding sculptress who, to everyone's dismay, gave up her art and joined the Sisters of Mercy—for *Dimitri's Big Day*, an inane little number about a five-foot-two Russian spy who meets the love of his life on Match .com, ick). Seated at her cluttered desk in her cluttered studio in front of a computer that droned like a buzz saw when kept on for more than three hours, she, above the hard drive's din, would find herself rustled from the uninspired sentences that collided and split like a road map composed exclusively of dead ends by the even louder drone of the John Deere riding mower, which was, it seemed to Clarissa, one of her husband's most prized possessions.

Except today he wasn't on the mower—he was out in the garden communing with a couple of naked bimbos. So why was she descending into John Deere episode three? Was she getting sicker? Closer to actually killing him?

She didn't know. All that seemed certain was that other than pursuing—for art purposes only, of course—women who couldn't

seem to keep their clothes on, Iggy divided his time between surf-
ing the Internet and mowing their gentleman's farm, which lay
fifty-seven miles east of Tallahassee (Florida's capital and, oddly
enough, a town riddled with hills and rises). On a normal day,
Clarissa would look up from the computer screen and spy him as
he headed into the pecan grove. Out of habit, she would hit the
save command (was there a limit to the number of blank pages she
could save? she really wanted to know) and then watch him grow
smaller and smaller until he eventually disappeared into the grove's
shadowed world of leaf mold, wood rot, vermin, and snakes.

But this day was not normal. It was the solstice, and Clarissa
was becoming undone, and though she was unaware of this fact,
there were spirits afoot. It didn't take much for her to snap. So
she wasn't in her studio and the computer wasn't buzzing and
the John Deere wasn't droning. She was simply standing in her
kitchen, annoyed, envisioning episode three, blow by delicious
blow. She adjusted the TV set in her brain and watched the star
of the show putter into the distance on his beloved John Deere.
The sound track switched from happy-go-lucky to something out
of a Vincent Price horror flick, signaling that violence, capri-
cious or otherwise, was imminent. If there had been a bowl of
popcorn handy, Clarissa might have actually enjoyed a fistful as
she watched her husband remove his ball cap and swipe sweat off
his brow with a forearm glistening with yard grime. She studied
his face—how sweat-drenched, hollow-cheeked, and Dutch it
appeared. She knew he was desirous of a beer and, therefore, not
concentrating on the mechanics, however dull, of safely operating a riding mower. This was a shame, really, because just as with
the Civic and eighteen-wheeler episode, all it took for tragedy to
strike was one or two seconds of preoccupation.

As her husband fiddled with seating the hat back onto his
head (for some reason, this required both hands), the John

Deere hit a stump. The impact was of such force that he — having had both hands on his ball cap — went flying as if he were a gigantic rag doll tossed by a petulant and unusually strong child. Airborne, his big face collapsed into a puzzle composed of O's: the widened eyes, the opened mouth, the nostrils stretched from oblong to round. And then everything — his mouth, his eyes, and for a nanosecond his nostrils — slammed shut as he landed *ka-lump!* on a snag of fallen branches.

He was unconscious but breathing, and for a moment Clarissa decided he had a chance. But then, in a sick, implausible turn of events, the mower vibrated off of the accident-wreaking stump, kicked itself into forward motion, and headed straight at him. The mower blades were so sharp, so coldhearted in their efficiency, that her husband never had a chance. Nevertheless, Clarissa imagined herself running into the yard, cell phone in hand, dialing 911 even as she performed CPR on his mangled body, even as the John Deere puttered into the distance, coming to rest beneath the soft shade of a dogwood stand, the tattered remains of her husband's T-shirt trailing like a humongous rattail in the soft gray dirt.

Clarissa reached for a rose, clipped an inch off the end, and shuddered as she thought of the media coverage. News of the freak accident would become fodder for such FOX television hits as *At Large with Geraldo Rivera*. Stories would be printed in newspapers as far away as Miami: AUTHOR'S SPOUSE KILLED IN TRAGIC MOWING MISHAP. If things got heated enough, consumer advocates nationwide would call for a congressional hearing to look into the safety of all riding mowers, John Deere and otherwise, and the thought of having to get on a plane and fly to D.C. and testify before a panel of well-heeled, oily-palmed politicians terrified the bejesus out of her.

The ringing phone pulled Clarissa out of her grim reverie. She was of no mind to talk to anybody. But being a naturally curious woman, she checked the caller ID. Well, what do you know! Leo Adams. A terrific young writer—published thus far in regional presses, but she felt confident that would change—he'd become friends with Clarissa when he took a workshop she'd taught in Atlanta. She'd been drawn to him immediately. But who wouldn't be? He was easygoing, funny, smart, and self-effacing, not to mention sexy. And they were, as he'd told her the last time she'd seen him (was it Santa Fe or Portland? she couldn't remember), simpatico (his word). They were at a hotel bar and had removed themselves from a clot of other writers. He'd slipped what she'd decided was a brotherly arm around her shoulders and said, "You and me, baby, we're what they call simpatico," and she had thought, Oh, if you were a little older and I were a whole lot less married.

She grabbed the phone. "Hey. Adams!"

"How'd you know it was me?"

"The miracle of cell phone technology, silly." She laughed and fiddled with the roses. "What're you doing?"

"Actually, I just gassed up in Cocoa and I'm heading your way."

"Really." She gazed up at her ceiling and watched a housefly walk upside down as if he were Fred Astaire in *Royal Wedding*. (The fly was happy that she was back and smellier than ever.) "Business? Pleasure?" She hoped she didn't sound eager. The last thing she wanted was for him to think she was coming on to him. She must have had ten years on the little hunk of burning love and hadn't heard from him since he'd drunk-dialed her on her birthday three months prior. Her reptilian brain lit up, red and pulsing, and reminded her that she was married to a man who had sixteen years on her.

"I'm doing a reading tonight in Tallahassee. At the library downtown. Can you make it?"

She paused and hated the fact that she suddenly felt so

hopeful. There was no way she'd ever have an affair, not ever. And then she heard herself say, "Absolutely. Need a place to crash? We've got plenty of room." She squeezed shut her eyes. Fuck, why did she have to go there—the whole "place to crash" thing—especially so fast?

Clarissa heard Green Day on his car stereo: "He steals the image in her kiss / From her heart's apocalypse..." "Cutie-pie, I'd love to, but they're putting me up at some fancy B and B close to the shindig."

"Oooo, big-time! Who's the sponsor?" Clarissa walked into the chandelier room, as she liked to call it, sat on her third step, and gazed out her screen door at the sky.

"I dunno, darling. A bunch of well-meaning old ladies, I think."

"I'm sure you'll charm them."

"Yeah. Well. The theme is something about up-and-comers. That would be me."

"Not for long. You mark my words." Clarissa was surprised at how airy her voice sounded, especially given the snit she'd been in much of the morning.

"I'm only doing it because I need to get used to standing in front of people and reading my shit. And, well, I thought I might get to see you."

"Aw. Aren't you sweet! And everyone thinks you're such a hard-ass." She watched a blue jay dart by and wondered why the sound of Adams's voice made her dangerously happy.

Sounding like a chorus composed of Peggy Lee clones, her ovarian shadow women rose up in unision: "Fever! Fever in the morning..."

Clarissa silently finished it for them: Fever all through the night.

"So, drinks first? Say about six?" She heard a horn honk and then Adams yell, "Jerk, stay in your own lane!"

"Perfect. Just call me when you get in." She wiggled her toes. They looked great; she'd polished them the night before. Ten sexy beauties. Harlot red—her nickname for Chanel's deepest red lacquer. She wondered if Iggy would want to go. Did she want him to? Why did she feel as if she were stepping into a matrimonial foul zone?

"Later, baby," Adams said. "Traffic's bad." And he was gone.

She stared at the phone. Wow, he'd called her baby. And darling. And cutie-pie. She knew the terms of endearment were a manifestation of Adams's machismo and were not personal. Still, she couldn't help but smile head to toe. Sometimes, she thought, rising to her feet, a girl just needed to feel appreciated.

Brimming with what she thought was undeserved happiness, she stretched her arms over her head, yawned (the heat was making her drowsy), and told herself that she really ought to try to write that day. But then again, without a plot what was she supposed to do? Adams probably never experienced writer's block. At least not for more than a day or so. He was probably one of those charmed writers—the kind who write Nobel Prize–winning shit wearing blindfolds and earmuffs. A bad-boy poet in a prose writer's disguise. Who knew? Maybe word anemia was a fatal condition. *Here Lies Clarissa Burden, a Good Woman Who Died of Writer's Block.*

She walked across the room to the thermostat and turned on the air. She shut the front door and then paused to wipe off a cobweb that had gathered—an elfin cloud—on the bottom right corner of a nearly four-foot-long shadow box that dominated the entry wall. It housed Iggy's pride and joy: a rifle. Allegedly, an ancestor in the 1838 Battle of Blood River had used it to great effect. The Boers massacred three thousand Zulu warriors; only three of the white men were slightly wounded. Iggy had special-ordered the shadow box from Pretoria. It was, Clarissa admitted, beautiful, hand-carved from pink ivory wood, one of the world's rarest woods and native to South Africa. But it was also sacred to

Zulus. All of this confused Clarissa: her husband's disdain for his Afrikaner heritage, his rejection of them having any legal claim to the land, his pride over his family having taken part in the massacre, and his apparent unwillingness to see the cruel irony of displaying a weapon used to kill an indigenous people in the very wood they held sacred.

One night not long after they'd moved in, over a dinner of shrimp pilau and avocado soup, she had tried discussing this with him, including broaching the subject that, according to her research, it was doubtful that this rifle even existed in 1838. But he'd successfully shut her down, accusing her of once again displaying her American stupidity and arrogance. He'd speared a shrimp and, before popping it in his mouth, said, "You are young and stupid, Clarissa. You need to listen to what I tell you."

Clarissa wiped the bottom lip of the shadow box with her bare hand. It needed dusting. A fly lit on the glass, and she wondered if it was the same one that had pestered her earlier — the little winged Fred Astaire — and if not, where all of them were coming from. The shadow box was positioned on the wall above a C-curve rolltop desk. Curious, Clarissa opened the top right drawer. They were still there: the bullets Iggy had special-ordered for the single-shot rifle. Three years prior, before he'd encased it in glass, he'd shown her how to use it. He'd slipped a bullet into the breechblock, said, "That's a sound a man can love, eh?" and then he'd done something that rattled Clarissa to this day. He'd aimed the rifle at her, said, "Boom!" and laughed. Clarissa picked up the box, shook it, wondered why he had bullets for a rifle he couldn't get to, set them back down, closed the drawer, looked at the long-barreled weapon, and thought, I wish to hell he'd never displayed that thing.

Phone in hand, she decided she'd best start closing windows before she air-conditioned the whole neighborhood. This wasn't an easy task, because the old wood tended to swell and stick. First she tackled the two in her library. With its wall-to-wall built-in bookcases, corniced ceiling, and marble-framed fireplace, this was a room she loved. It was the one place in the house where she approached something akin to feeling at home, because Iggy didn't go behind her back rearranging everything the way he did in the rest of the house and because here she was in the company of books. Long ago she had learned that all of her hopes, dreams, and potentialities could be defined and refined through the reading of good literature and even pulp fiction of dubious quality if the hero had enough oomph.

After a brief struggle, she managed to shut both windows. She checked the clock she kept on the bookcase reserved for poetry, plays, and her Zora Neale Hurston collection. Eight-fifteen. Nine hours and forty-five minutes until six p.m. Thanks to one surprise phone call, the longest day of the year was turning out to also be the slowest. But she had more windows to close; it was a sixteen-room rambling house, for goodness' sakes. And those roses were summoning her. No time to write! She had to finish trimming the stems, had to find the tall, cut crystal vase. *Stunning!* The word surged through her. The arrangement would be absolutely stunning!

She headed out of the library but stopped at the stairs because she heard laughter coming from the second floor. Surely Iggy didn't have a naked woman stashed in his office. For one horrible moment, she flashed on an image of him romping in the guest room with that skinny blonde. Was she, Clarissa worried, becoming certifiable? First the music from nowhere, now this ebullient laughter and fantasies of him cheating right under her nose? She gripped the carved oak newel post and looked up at the landing; the laughter stopped, started, trailed away. She gained the stairs, determined to throw an absolute fit if Iggy was carrying on with one of his bimbos in her house. The phone rang, startling her.

She dropped it, and, ringing all the while, it tumbled two steps down. She grabbed it, checked the caller ID.

Oh God. Cookie Manx, her agent. Was it a mortal or simply a venial sin not to take your agent's call? She wasn't sure, but she couldn't risk piling up any more bad juju, especially where her career was concerned.

She flipped open the phone and brought it to her ear. "Hey!" she said, forcing a bouncy enthusiasm into her voice.

"Hey, sweetie! I'm not interrupting, am I?" A woman on a perpetual mission, her agent never called just to chitchat.

Clarissa continued up the stairs, the phone pressed hard against her cartilage. The fly, the one head over heels for her, the very same one that had trailed her all morning, followed. "Actually, I was, um, just taking a break." She hated herself when she lied, hated the warble and hesitation—they gave her away. She paused at the landing window, which was closed, and looked out. Yep, all three of them were out there. The blonde was naked and sitting in one of the Adirondacks. The brunette was holding a rake and staring dead-eyed ahead. *American Gothic in the Nude*. How charming. "So, how are you?" Clarissa turned her back to the window. She must have been wrong about the laughter. It must be the house settling; it was an old house, and old houses creaked.

"Good, good, just got a thousand things going. Listen, I don't want to pressure you. That's not what this call is about..." Clarissa felt her gizzard crack. "But I need a really, really honest idea of when you think you're going to deliver the novel. No pressure. Just asking. Your publisher is planning the catalog."

"Soon," Clarissa said, "really soon." A chunk of her gizzard broke off and lodged somewhere, maybe in the concave curve of her left kidney. The fly flitted past Clarissa's head and then zipped over to the north-facing window, where it was cooler.

She thought she heard her agent—a very nice woman who

understood the publishing business with the same acuity that a bulldog understood the sweet spot of a butcher's bone—groan. "Well, I'm not sure I know what 'soon' means."

During the ensuing pause, whatever was left of Clarissa's porous stone gizzard flaked away to parts unseen, and she pondered if she was brave enough to confess. Or was confession simply the yellow-bellied flag of a quitter? And once she admitted that she'd been unable to write more than two or three sentences in a row that amounted to more than squat, what else might issue forth? Why, no telling what might come out, and there was not one living, breathing human being on the planet—especially Cookie Manx—who had time for such nonsense. And what were the subtle gradations separating, say, yellow-bellied cowardice and saffron-jaundiced professionalism? The phone felt as if it weighed a thousand pounds.

"Sweetie, are you okay?" Cookie Manx asked.

"Of course. Yes, yes, I'm fine. I'm just, working out some problems in the novel. I think I need about another six months." Where was this coming from? Six months? What? Was she crazy?

"Okay. That's good. That's all I needed to know."

"It's really..." The sound of a clay marble rolling across the pine floor vaguely caught Clarissa's attention. Indeed, she stepped over the marble, it just missed the crown of her big toe, and the little ghost boy who rolled it—Heart Archer—giggled and scrambled like a crab to retrieve it from its eventual resting place against the baseboard. Every time the big man was in the yard with ladies who wore no clothes, his mother sent him to his room. But he, without her knowing, spied on those naked ladies. It was fun.

"The book is going well. The process, you know, always surprises."

"Are you still calling it *Breathing Room*?"

"No. Uh-uh." She wandered into the guest room. Why was

her agent driving her mad, forcing her to lie, asking questions she couldn't possibly answer? She noticed, to her relief, that all the windows were closed.

Heart Archer, holding the marble in his tiny hand as if it were the most precious of possessions, followed her in. He was barefoot, too, and he marveled at how much blacker his skin was than hers.

The bed with its wedding ring quilt was lumpy. Iggy must have taken a nap up here. She put the phone on speaker, set it on the nightstand, and, as she drew the quilt tight and smooth, said into the air, "I'm thinking of calling it something edgier. Something like *American Gothic: The Nude*."

"Great!"

Cookie Manx really did sound enthusiastic. Or maybe what Clarissa was hearing was distortion courtesy of the speaker function. What would a book with that title be about, anyway? Naked farmers? Swinging suburbanites? Clarissa took the phone with her as she walked to the front window, where the fly had fallen into a momentary slumber, and looked out at her oak-shaded front yard, and its azaleas that were in need of a good trimming, and the roses that, from this vantage point, appeared nearly decimated. Jeez, she had cut more than she had realized. "That's just for now. It'll probably change. But I'm working hard."

The ovarian shadow women, having traveled to her cerebral cortex, sounded like a gang of mean schoolchildren as they hissed, "Liar, liar, pants on fire!"

Heart Archer scrambled onto the bed and jumped up and down. The squeaking bedsprings woke the fly. Being prudent, he flew over to the rocking chair and from his perch on the bottom rung watched Heart watch Clarissa. Outside, a red-tailed hawk flickered through the oak canopy. The mold on her white picket fence crept like mutant kudzu made slow and tiny by an unexplained kink in its DNA.

"I know, and like I said, no pressure."

"None taken." Clarissa heard that laughter again, but this time it was closer. This time it was right behind her. She spun around. The double wedding ring quilt was kerfuffled, as if a child had been playing, jumping, squirming, as children were prone to do on beds. What in the world? The stress; she was simply under too much stress.

"How's hubby?"

"Fine," Clarissa said, still staring at the bed, adept at deflection and denial. "He's in the yard. How's Richard?" The laughter was infectious. It rang with the kind of joy one hears only from children who know they are loved. Or maybe the rat family in the attic was having one hell of a good time. Or maybe it was the laughter of the child she and her husband never had because he didn't want children. Maybe that should be the name of the novel she couldn't write: *Maybe Maybe Maybe*.

"Okay, sweetie, I have to get across town for an appointment. I'll talk to you later."

"Thanks for calling, Cookie. Have a great day," Clarissa said, faking it, all sunshine and zest.

She flipped the phone closed. The laughter stopped. The fly flew to the doorjamb. Clarissa walked to the bed and pressed her hand against the quilt. It felt cold, even though the upstairs was hotter than downstairs. It was as if the quilt had absorbed all of the house's air-conditioning from the day before and held it.

Heart Archer sat very still on the edge of the bed, afraid he'd made her angry. He held the clay marble close to his chest. She smoothed the quilt again. I'm losing it, she fretted, absolutely losing it. Her intention had been to straighten the quilt, but she'd gotten preoccupied with her agent's call. And the laughter wasn't laughter at all, but wind rattling through the eaves. Something like that. Just like the music, the laughter didn't exist.

But whether it did or didn't, the mere thought of a child reawakened in her an old ache: the baby ache. Iggy had said it to her many times: "See how miserable women are who have kids? We don't want the snot-nosed little *fowkers*. They only screw everything up."

For reasons Clarissa could not fathom other than it felt right, she kissed her fingertips and touched them to the quilt. Then she left the room, thinking, Of course, he's right; he's always right. She couldn't even write a book; how could she raise a child? She headed down the stairs, and the fly followed, leaving Heart Archer alone.

The little boy, no longer afraid, slid off the bed, sat on the floor, shot the marble — it skidded left, hooked back to the right — and waited for his mother.

———

*C*larissa was halfway down the stairs when she noticed that someone was standing at her front door, knocking. Holy moly, if this is another naked bimbo model, heads are going to roll, Clarissa thought, fed up; and she better not confuse me for a housekeeper.

She threw open the door, fully prepared to tell the girl who appeared to be not a day over twenty that Iggy didn't live there. "Hi, can I help you?" With her wire-rimmed glasses, notepad and paper, and a skirt hem that fell below her knees, she appeared bookish, innocent, not Iggy's kind of gal.

"Ms. Burden?"

"Yes." Clarissa wiped at a dirt smudge on her cheek but succeeded only in smearing it from her nose to her ear.

"I'm Jane Boyer with the *Aucilla Chronicle*."

Jane Boyer. *Aucilla Chronicle*. Nothing clicked.

"I'm here for the interview. I'm sorry that I'm a little late. I got lost." She pushed her glasses up the bridge of her nose.

"Oh! Oh, yes," Clarissa said, wondering how on earth she could have forgotten and wanting nothing more than for a sinkhole to swallow her whole. Not only was she filthy, she stank. Really stank. During the ensuing three seconds that dragged on for what felt like three years, she could think of no way to tell this girl to go away, that now wasn't a good time. So she pushed open the screen door, her heartbeat slowed by dread. "Come in. Welcome!" She offered her hand, but it was so grimy, she withdrew it. "I'm sorry, I was working in my garden and time got away from me."

"That's okay. I just love your books. I've read them both three times. So far, *Listening for Light* is my favorite, but *Blue River* is really fantastic, too. When the paper said I could interview you, first thing I did was call my mom and she got so excited that she started crying." Jane smiled, revealing a mouthful of braces.

Clarissa smiled back and said, "Why, thank you." She was, relatively speaking, new at being in the public eye, and though she instinctively liked this young woman, she was shy in the face of enthusiasm. "Would you like something to drink? Some lemonade?"

"Sure." Jane stood in the middle of the chandelier room, eyes wide. "Wow. This is some house."

"It's an oldie," Clarissa said, shuttling her into the kitchen as quickly as she could. The last thing she wanted was for the reporter to see the backyard activities. "It's got some real history to it, which I'm just starting to get into." She hurried over to the window—no time to close it—and pulled the blinds.

"Look at those roses! They're beautiful."

"Aren't they gorgeous? I grew them myself." Clarissa, mortified by her appearance but knowing it would be crazy of her to make the reporter wait while she went and showered, said, "I'll be right back."

"Sure. Mind if I look around?"

Panicked, Clarissa had to think fast. There was no way she was going to let her get caught up with her husband or even go into the living room, where his paintings of giant crotches covered the walls. "Actually, why don't you wait here and I'll give you a tour when I come back."

"Okay." She pulled a stool over to the island and sat down. "Can I look at that magazine?" She pointed at an old copy of *Gourmet* that Clarissa had left out on the counter.

"Absolutely." Clarissa handed it to her and noted that nothing much seemed to bother Jane. "Back in a jiffy."

She shot through the chandelier room, down the hall, and into the half bath. The fly flew in dizzying circles above her head and dipped into the bathroom just before she slammed the door. Clarissa spied the fly, looked for something to kill it with, but came up empty. She washed her face, patted down her hair, and slipped on some Apricot Breeze lip gloss that she kept in the vanity drawer. Iggy's blue denim shirt hung from the door hook. She pulled it on. The thing swallowed her; the shirttail came down to her knees. But it hid the T-shirt.

As she made her way through the house, the fly in tow, she saw that Iggy and the models had moved onto the back porch. Great. Just great. There goes even a truncated tour.

Jane stood at the kitchen door, looking out into the side yard. "You sure do have a lot of cars."

"My husband has…" Clarissa paused, trying to find the right word. "Visitors." She walked over to the refrigerator and pulled out the lemonade pitcher. Jane reminded Clarissa of herself at that age: a little pudgy, nerdy, even the braces. "Do you write? I mean, fiction?"

"I try. But I don't think I'm very good."

"You read a lot?" Clarissa poured the lemonade and then walked over to the pantry in search of shortbread cookies.

"Oh, yeah. I'm a big reader. My mom is, too."

"I tell you," Clarissa said, spying the cookies behind a jar of pickles, "reading is the best favor a writer can do for herself." She grabbed the cookies and pulled a jadeite plate from her cupboard.

"No cookies for me," Jane said, and pointed at her braces.

"Ah, I see." Clarissa set the bag on the counter. "You know, I had braces at about your age."

"You did?"

"Yep. I had jaw surgery. Born with a defect, I guess you could say, and we were so poor, nothing could be done for it when I was a kid. But when I got older, I had it taken care of." Clarissa sipped her lemonade, silently marveling at how adept she was at sanitizing history.

"So, you grew up real poor?" Jane flipped open her stenographer pad, poised her pen at the ready.

"We didn't have much."

"That's what I thought," she said. "Just like in *Listening for Light*." She scribbled something and, still writing, asked, "In the book, Laureena doesn't know her father. Did you know yours?"

"No." Clarissa pulled Iggy's shirt more tightly around her. "He was long gone by the time I was born."

Jane stopped writing, looked Clarissa directly in the eyes, and said softly, "I'm sorry. That must have been very hard on you."

A maternal blush stirred through Clarissa. This little girl is far more confident than I was at her age, she thought. "Hard? I guess so. My mother was a little crazy. Maybe that's why he left. I don't know. But, hey," she said, massaging that old chip on her shoulder, "at least it makes for interesting reading."

"Your mom? She still alive?"

Clarissa was beginning to wish she'd told her to come back some other day; there were things she still didn't like talking about. She sipped her lemonade, traced its water circles. "No, she died a long time ago."

"How old were you?"

"I don't know. College. Eighteen...nineteen? I don't do numbers." A pause ensued—sort of like an intermission in which only the very hardy or very bored return.

A woodpecker pounding on the kitchen siding broke up the silence. "Can I see your library?" Jane tapped her pen on the pad and, not waiting for an answer, headed for the door, engendering a new surge of panic in Clarissa.

"Don't go out there!"

"I read an article about you and they described it—I can't remember what it was in—but I thought, That sounds really nice."

"Don't you want to finish your lemonade first?"

Jane shrugged and wrote something down.

How could Clarissa tell her no? She was enthusiastic, and young, and bright. Eager, even. Iggy was simply going to have to cooperate, even if it made him mad. "Sure. Hold on one second. Just stay here."

Clarissa walked into the chandelier room, took a deep breath, opened the back door, and without sticking her head out said, "Iggy, I need to speak to you."

"Iggy!" The blonde's squeaky voice unfurled across Clarissa's raw nerve endings. "Your housekeeper wants you!"

Why, you little impudent cretin, thought Clarissa. In an instinctive move to protect her heart and deflect anger, she withdrew into her imagination, where a wholly new death scenario played out, one in which she was the star. In her mind's eye, she ran into the kitchen, grabbed a wineglass from the dish drainer, broke it on her counter as if she were a galloping babe in a Wild West flick, and sprang forth not as a victimized wife, but as a superhero hot babe named Super Dame. Dressed in a red jumpsuit and cerulean knee-high boots, she fearlessly pursued her mission to defend all women who'd been wronged by all hussies throughout all known history, or at least ever since women had been keeping count of the sins and digressions of their husbands. She flew out of the house (Jane was in awe, a female counterpoint to the traditional cub reporter), into the yard—the glinting edge of the broken glass transformed itself into a laser beam—and back onto the porch, where she buzzed her husband and the squeaky-voiced model with all the efficiency of a bombshell fighter pilot.

"Fuck you, you little whore!" she screamed, but Super Dame's voice was so loud, so otherworldly, that the words came out distended, flaccid, loosey-goosey. It sounded as if she'd hollered, "Fwuk u u liho!"

Words and their meanings didn't matter, though, because she was Super Dame—a woman who was more action than talk. Her laser beam pulsing, she took aim at her husband's foolish, arrogant, dysfunctional, anemic, mean-spirited, necrotic, cheating little heart. First she'd off him and then both models. She paused, midair. A text bubble formed over her head: "Perhaps less drastic measures are in order."

"What do you want, Clarissa? I'm busy." Iggy's giant frame filled the doorway, his words and presence slamming shut her fantasy. He wiped sweat from his brow with a white towel and was, she thought, working hard to avoid making eye contact. The heat and humidity were causing his beard to frizz.

"I'm sorry. But there is a reporter here interviewing me and I don't want her to see them."

"Them who?" He stared at the ceiling. He was sunburned. She'd told him a thousand times to wear a hat.

"Those two girls. I don't want the reporter seeing them. Naked and all. She wouldn't understand."

"Jesus *fowking* Christ, Clarissa, I don't care what the stupid little twat sees." He looked toward the models. Clarissa couldn't see them, but she heard them whispering, giggling.

"Don't use that language with me. And get them out of sight. Go down by the barn or something. I don't care where, just get them out of here." Clarissa surprised herself. She didn't have that sliding-down-the-slippery-slope feeling she got every time she was about to cave.

Iggy walked away, swiping his hand through the air in dismissal. Clarissa watched him go, and a horrible possibility took hold. Maybe the nitwit thought Clarissa was the housekeeper because that's what Iggy told her. No, not that, please not that, she thought, watching them parade into the yard.

Clarissa went back into the kitchen—Jane was writing furiously—and peeked out of the blinds. They were prancing out of sight, down by the dogwood grove. Now was her chance to close the window. She opened the blinds, said, "We'll go see the library just as soon as I close this," gripped the base of the windowpane, and pushed, but it didn't yield. She tried again; it slid halfway down, shimmying to the left. Jane stood at the island, paying no mind to Clarissa, reading over her notes. Clarissa hit the side of the pane to try to get it to even up in the casing, which it did, but she still couldn't get it to slide a hair farther, so she turned around, thinking that if she pushed with the base of her hands, she'd exert more strength. Her arms shook from the effort. A fine dappling of sweat broke out along her hairline. Just as she was about to give up, the window hurtled shut like a guillotine blade, catching her shirttail and trapping her at a preposterous angle because more of the left side of the shirt was jammed than the right. She couldn't stand up straight. She looked like Quasimodo.

"Do you need help?" Jane asked, flipping pages.

Clarissa felt as if she had been sucked into an old *I Love Lucy* show. Except because it was happening to her, it wasn't funny, at least not at the moment. "No, I'm okay." She pulled, but the shirt didn't budge.

Jane held her pen aloft and looked at the ceiling, her eyes dreamy. "Do you write at night or during the day?"

Clarissa tugged as hard as she could, grunting involuntarily. "Day." She felt the left shoulder seam begin to give.

Jane nodded as if that were fascinating information. "Longhand or on a computer?"

"Computer." Clarissa gritted her teeth and heaved herself forward. She got only as far as the fabric not jammed in the window would allow.

"Do you have a favorite place you like to write?"

Oh, my heavens. Jane was, unknowingly, ticking off the list of the most asked, most useless questions thrown at writers. "My studio." She put her hands on either side of the shirt and yanked. The shoulder seam ripped wide open, but nothing else gave. She had no choice; she was going to have to slip out of the shirt. But that wasn't as easy as it sounded, since thanks to the angle at which she was trapped, she was in essence straitjacketed. Sweat dripped down her cheeks to her chin, forming a clear, tremulous goatee.

"Your husband is African, right?"

"South African. Afrikaner." Clarissa twisted to the left and tried to free her right arm, but her torso was bent at such a crazy tilt, she couldn't wiggle her arm out of the sleeve.

"Afrikaner?"

"Yes. The bad guys. I mean, he's not bad, but, you know, the apartheid crowd."

"Oh." Jane's lips settled in on themselves, grim, tight. "Sooooo, he hates black people?"

"No, no. It's not like that at all. He didn't agree with apartheid, so he left."

"Whew! I was getting worried for a minute." Her face brightened.

Clarissa decided that she'd pull one last time, and if that didn't work, she was going to have to ask Jane—who appeared oblivious to the seriousness of Clarissa's predicament—for help. She grabbed the shirt on either side again and gave one desperate heave-ho.

"How did y'all meet?"

The ovarian shadow women piped up. "Harder!"

The scratchy sound of denim tearing filled the air as the shirt ripped along the fault line of the jam. Clarissa tumbled forward, fell, and hit her head on the floor. It really, really hurt. This is the worst interview of my life, she thought. She looked at Jane. "We met at a party."

"And then what?"

"What do you mean?" Clarissa rolled over and sat up. She swiped at the sweat on her chin with her shirtsleeve and felt her forehead, fearing the possibility of a goose egg. That would keep her butt at home tonight for sure.

"Hmmm. I mean, what caused you to fall in love?"

An innocent question, delivered straight from the bowels of hell. "Well..." Clarissa grabbed the corner of the island and pulled herself to her feet. She rested her forearms on the marble. "He was a lot better to me than the previous boyfriend, who beat me, and a lot better to me than my mother, who also beat me. In fact"—Clarissa pushed away from the island, suddenly grateful for the question because it stirred in her long-forgotten recollections of things past—"come with me."

Clarissa headed for the library, looking out the back door as she passed, happy that not a soul was in sight. She stepped into the room, Jane at her heels with pen and paper in hand.

"Cool beans!" Jane said, her eyes drifting over the bookshelves. She walked over to Clarissa's collection of Floridiana: chalkware busts of male and female Seminole Indians, a timetable for the Florida East Coast Railroad, a heavy brass key from the long defunct Alcazar Hotel, a machete with a hand-carved wooden handle that had once been used to cut sugarcane on a plantation in the Everglades, and a box made of magnolia that was studded with tiny white seashells. "Wow!" Jane said, her hand lingering on the machete handle.

"See this?" Clarissa picked up a framed photograph. "This is Iggy and me at my first book signing down in Gainesville. *Listening for Light* was under contract when I met him, but it wasn't published until after our wedding. He was real helpful back then."

Jane studied the photograph, and that dreamy glaze returned to her eyes. "Aww. Your life is perfect!"

Clarissa placed the photo on the shelf, her finger lingering on the image of a smiling Iggy—an Iggy who hadn't yet shut her out—turned to Jane, and said, "You know, my husband doesn't make much money—what artist does?—but in the early days, he was supportive and that meant the world to me." Clarissa settled into the planter's chair that faced her red fainting couch. "That's off the record, of course." And she should have stopped there but couldn't. She felt a need to protect this girl from that world of mistakes waiting right outside the library door. "It's important to be with someone who celebrates you rather than resents you, Jane. Remember that." She picked at a rough spot in the chair's cane weave. "And sometimes, resentment? It comes on slowly."

Jane nodded; her eyes looked even bigger in the library's soft light. Or perhaps Clarissa had simply said too much, revealed more than she should have. "It's good to be loved," Jane said.

"Yes, yes, it is."

They spent the next twenty minutes talking about writing and books. Jane had never heard of Zora Neale Hurston, so Clarissa gave the girl her own copy of *Their Eyes Were Watching God*. "No Florida writer should be without that one," Clarissa said. She signed a copy of *Listening for Light* to Jane's mother, April, and *Blue River* to Jane. At eighteen years old, the girl seemed a little starstruck, which

Clarissa found endearing. And when, upon leaving, Jane asked if she could take her picture—for the weekly *Aucilla Chronicle*, no less—Clarissa did not have the heart to say no despite her dirty tee, the ripped denim shirt, and the serpentine chaos of her hair.

Jane retrieved her camera from her gray Mazda 323, and Clarissa stood on the front porch, holding copies of her books, and that was what Jane shot: Clarissa standing on the worn planks of the 183-year-old house, hardcover books in hand, surrounded by hanging baskets of bougainvillea, sumptuous thickets of roses, wild sprays of azaleas, and the bright comet of one remarkable ghost.

*Jane's visit had perked up Clarissa, made her feel nearly like a writer again, as though, while optimistic, six months to write her book might be within the realm of possibility. She'd never know if she didn't try. What had she just told Jane? You have to keep your butt in the chair because novels don't write themselves. So she waved good-bye to Jane and then hurried into the library, shelved the books, and checked the time. It was approaching ten a.m. If she started writing now, she'd have plenty of time to get some work done, fix supper, and make it to Adams's reading.

She went into the kitchen (Iggy's shirttail hung from the window like a flaccid blue tongue), fixed a cup of tea, and headed for her studio, which was connected to the eastern wing of the house via a deck. If she ran into Iggy and the girls, she'd simply ignore them. After all, housekeepers were under no requirement to be nice.

The fly, which if he'd been human could have been arrested for stalking, waited on the ceiling in the chandelier room, and when Clarissa exited the kitchen, he flew in circles, keeping pace with her forward motion—a laborious process given that he could fly much faster than she walked. Still, when she stopped abruptly at the back door, he bumped into the wall, nearly knocking himself out.

Clarissa peeked through the blinds she'd hung from the door just the week prior. The coast was clear. She pushed open the door, dashed to her studio, spilling some of her tea in the process, and ducked in.

The fly, exhausted, set a straight course for a poster nailed to the facing wall. It featured Clarissa holding the paperback edition of *Listening for Light*; blurbs of praise from other authors filled the foreground. The fly lit on the gray-tone ridge of Clarissa's cheek.

The studio was steamy. Its old walls had no insulation and it was so poorly sealed that among the animals that came and went as if it were a Ritz for wildlife were frogs, lizards, snakes (Clarissa once opened the door and down from the top jamb fell a four-foot-long rat snake—thud—who, upon landing, slithered into the wall), mice, rats, and even the occasional pine skink.

"Good God, it's an oven in here," Clarissa said, turning down the thermostat to sixty before flopping into her office chair. She set the tea beside her monitor and closed her eyes. Her former optimism evaporated now that she was in the presence of her computer; no siree, she did not want to face that blank screen. From the sidelines of her brain, Cookie Manx, sounding strangely like Bobby Knight, yelled, "Six months!"

Christ. How was she going to pull this off? It was as if she'd removed her brain and stuffed it in the freezer.

"Six freaking months!" Cookie Manx screamed.

Okay, okay. Failure was not in her lexicon. Or was it? She opened her eyes, straightened her spine, and hit the on button. Her old computer sputtered and quarked and finally came to life.

The din that resembled the low growl of a wounded wildcat — the one that usually didn't start up until about three hours in — filled the studio's wretchedly hot air.

Clarissa decided it was best to jump right in, without a plan, a plot, a character, a pot to pee in. Maybe a miracle would happen. She typed: "The girl."

Fuck. What girl?

Whose girl?

How old of a girl? She pressed the delete key until the page was blank.

Then she typed: "The moon wept." Delete. What was she, a freaking poet? Like *that's* really going to help.

"The girl with the long blond hair broke her husband's easel into one thousand and eighty-six jagged pieces." Delete.

"It was a dark and stormy night and the girl was pissed." Delete.

"It was a dark and stormy night and the girl with the long blond hair was so pissed she broke her cheating, no-count, double-crossing, flat-assed Afrikaner husband's most expensive camera (Leica?) into one thousand and eighty-six jagged pieces. She tossed them into the air. Their sharp edges scratched the sky. The moon wept." Delete.

"How come I'm a talentless hack who deserves to have her fingers chopped off?

"How many letters fit on one page?

"How many capital M's? Lowercase i's?

"Do Chinese characters take up less or more room than the English alphabet on a Korean-made computer? Can my computer type in Chinese and, if so, why can't I speak Chinese?

"How many times could I strike randomly at the keyboard before stumbling onto a string of consonants and vowels that lined up in a logical sequence of more than three words?

"Where is Jack Nicholson in *The Shining* when you need him?

"Motherfucking Stephen King *never* gets fucking writer's block. And if he did, he has so much money he could pay someone to (a) unblock him, and (b) write the book for him while he drank mojitos on a nude beach in Puerto Rico.

"Stephen King naked—yuck.

"If one sat in front of a computer long enough, slapping out words, and more words, and more words, how long would it take for a novel to eventually form all on its own?

"Isn't that how Kerouac did it?

"How many vowels, on average, are in a typical novel? A typical short story? A typical laundry list? A typical..."

Her work-stalling questioning was broken by laughter wafting in from outside. Iggy and his bimbo models were back. Clarissa looked up from her screen, which, if one wanted to be positive, was no longer blank.

The girls were voguing, using a white silk kimono embroidered with golden cranes as if it were a cape. That kimono belonged to Clarissa. A cherished possession, it had been given to her by a fan from Japan. How could he? And look at him, straddling that stool, painting wild stripes of color on a small canvas, saying, "Yes, yes, that's it!"

Bile jettisoned up Clarissa's windpipe: jealousy, bitterness, and anger glowing acid yellow. The fly lit on her shoulder. The brunette dropped the kimono in the grass and lay on top of it, buns up.

Clarissa, her face pinched, her eyes narrowing, hit the X key and did not let up. She filled several pages with the letter X. "X marks the spot. *The X-Files.* The X Girl has X-ray vision. Pressing the X feels X-tra good. X-tremely good." As her virtual blank pages accumulated one X after another—XXXXXXXX—forming a chorus line of stacked V's, Clarissa attempted to conjure her superhero self, now named X Girl; but the stubborn little thing refused to don those cerulean boots or kick ass in any way. Clarissa let up on the X key. She turned off the computer. When it prompted her about saving the file, she clicked No.

Iggy's voice wafted into the studio. "Tonight I'll make contact prints of the shots I got of you two in the barn. Lunch tomorrow, perhaps? You can pick out what you want prints of."

Well, ain't he just got himself one dandy life, Clarissa bitched silently. She imagined him out there in his darkroom, mixing unstable chemicals in order to produce platinum prints of naked women—many of whom didn't even know Clarissa's name; hell, evidently he'd told them she was his house-fucking-keeper—when the unspeakable occurred: *Death in the Darkroom*, episode two.

There he was—a very, very old-looking fifty-one (he had not aged well)—moving with the herky-jerky intensity of a giant rodent in the haunting red glow of the safe light, mixing elements, practicing a relatively recent form of alchemy (it wasn't as though he were creating fire from two sticks), producing one-dimensional objectified paper images out of three-dimensional hot-blooded bodies.

Careless, as was his way, he reached out his rodent hand and grabbed the wrong brown bottle. He poured it into a steel canister that already had some sort of chemical elixir in it. With the sure movements of a bartender who enjoyed the process of turning gin into a rickey, he shook, shook, shook, inadvertently concocting a poisonous brew. And although it was a total accident, the result was the same as if Clarissa herself had gone out there under the cover of a new moon and relabeled all the bottles. Just as with Jeremiah de Saint-Amour's death in *Love in the Time of Cholera* sans the suicide twist, the photo chemicals—fine on their own but nuclear when coupled—sent forth an invisible cloud of murderous fumes...the scent of bitter almonds. And then, just as if life were nothing more than a sigh stirring the air of a windowless room before evaporating without a trace into the heavens, her husband—while placing an image of a giant crotch in the stop bath with the aid of a pair of old wooden tongs—collapsed, not recognizing his own stupid mistake, onto his rubber-matted floor, dead as a poisoned house cat.

As Clarissa fanned herself with an empty file folder marked "Story Ideas," a realization forced itself on her with the same shame-mongering vigor as those spousal death scenarios. Maybe her death fantasies had nothing to do with her writer's block. Rather, was the block a symptom of her wanting not to succeed? Or to put a finer point on her mind's restless pencil, if she faltered, would she be doing her husband, and therefore their marriage, a favor?

She spun her chair away from the window. The fly flew to the desk and lit on the tab of a very fat manila folder that was tucked under a stack of half-baked novel attempts (Clarissa printed everything out). The tab, which was the only visible part of the folder, was labeled in black Sharpie "House History Dossier."

"Fuuuuuck, I'm finished," Clarissa said to the room, not knowing exactly what she meant yet understanding it was true. She stamped her foot three times—a tiny tantrum disturbing the heavy air—and no sooner had the ball of her foot tapped thrice than Olga Villada, a woman who had been dead since 1826, brushed a cobweb out of her way and entered the studio through Clarissa's south-facing wall.

Olga Villada was a handsome woman, and if Clarissa had bothered to look through the dossier, she would have known that. Shortly after she bought the property, she'd traveled to the state archives in Tallahassee and paid for duplicates of everything they had in their files about the house; but she'd been so busy staring, dumb-faced, into her blank computer screen that she'd not gotten around to reading through the inch-thick stack of photocopies. The Realtor had told her the house had been built by a woman, but how much stock could you put into what a Realtor said?

If she had simply flipped open the file, she would have seen—because the librarian had put it on top, a frontispiece, as it were—a copy of an engraving rendered by an anonymous artist who'd cast Olga Villada as a young woman of modest height, abundant bosomry, and corkscrew curls that seemed inspired more by the area's ubiquitous Spanish moss than reality. In the illustration, she stood beneath a large, canopied live oak, holding a bullwhip in one hand and a map in the other. She did not appear to want to indulge the artist—no smile, no precious posing. Rather, her raised eyebrow, direct gaze, and pursed lips would have led Clarissa to believe that Olga Villada had been a busy woman with better things to do than stand still while somebody drew her likeness.

In all honesty, the artist had captured Olga Villada's beautiful curls with fair accuracy. But she was prettier than in the engraving. This was possibly because Olga Villada, having been the daughter of one of Spain's most beloved and successful flamenco guitarists, Federico García Villada, moved even in death with a dancer's rhythm and grace.

She glided across the room, her booted feet echoing against the heart pine floor, but it was a sound only she and the fly heard. The onetime mistress of the Spanish governor of Florida, Olga Villada knew about emotionally unavailable men and broken hearts. She also knew about good men, which was one of the reasons—other than Clarissa being the only person who ever lived in the house capable of telling her story—that she had taken a personal interest in the young woman. Life was too short, the ghost knew, for a woman to waste it on a man who did not know how to love.

Olga Villada was entering dangerous territory. Prodding Clarissa into writing their story and inspiring in her the will to mend her passionless marriage violated the family's number one dictum: Do not interfere with the living; no funny business, no helping out, no causing harm. Olga Villada noticed how Clarissa sat hunched over her computer, staring hopelessly at its black screen, and how she clenched and unclenched her fists as if preparing for a fight that never came, and how unkempt she was: hair stringy, complexion sallow. The poor thing was a wreck, in need of the kind of encouragement only a woman as seasoned and wise as Olga Villada could provide. She would simply have to tread lightly—no direct intervention, just some mild jabs to get her started. No one would have to know. Olga Villada moved aside Clarissa's long curls and began, with a mother's tenderness, to massage her neck.

Clarissa, unaware that there was a ghost in the room, closed her eyes, sat very still, and tried to will her womanhood back, sensing that if she was successful, the world—and therefore her novel and maybe even her husband—would open up to her again. Her soul's numbness, her heart's unease, her mind's white noise: It would all be replaced by a new and vigorous awareness that either would allow her to care not one whit about what was going on out there in her garden or would give her the tools she needed to do something about it; and either way, this changed perspective would reopen her creative vein. This was what she told herself.

But nothing came to her. Nothing. Even her ovarian shadow women sat silent, unseeing, unhearing, like those horrible little know-no-evil monkeys for sale in import stores. But at least some of the tension in her shoulders and neck was easing.

Olga Villada, seeing that the fly was sipping Clarissa's tea, whipped out her fan (she was a very sexy woman) and shooed it away.

Clarissa opened her eyes and reached for her cup, not knowing that the fatigued little fly had indulged. She could not write under this pressure, under these circumstances, with her husband out there cavorting. Again. And it wasn't so much the cavorting or the painting and drawing or even all the nakedness. More than anything, she struggled with the reality that her husband was consumed with the joy of being with other women—naked women, all confident and booby and young—to the total exclusion of herself. He was chattering, laughing, whispering, and saying, "Yes, yes"—all sounds he'd stopped sharing with her years ago.

My, oh my, how she wanted him dead! She drank her tea (Olga Villada rifled through her desk), and as the sweet, cream-heavy liquid coated her tongue, the present moment dissolved into a rerun of episode six: Michael Douglas and the Voodoo Dude, based on a movie she'd seen ages ago.

Although the real title forever eluded her, the plot—adjusted to suit her needs—never did. Douglas's sweet, good-natured wife died while using an electric mixer, because unbeknownst to her, the dishwasher had sprung a leak and there was something about standing in water while using an electrical device that could kill a person. With her out of the way, the evil voodoo priest spent the rest of the film seriously screwing with the dead woman's hapless husband.

In Clarissa's revisioned film, she was the doting wife who was busy cleaning the face of their cherubic little boy while the family dog jumped and barked and wagged his tail. Iggy was trying to fix the dishwasher. He was impatient and, of course, careless. While the water rose up his pant leg—the rising level determined by the voodoo priest posing as a gardener—he touched a live wire. The rest was history. Clarissa—mother, wife, and brownie maker—heard the electric hiss and immediately hid her son's face in the soft folds of her skirt. Iggy let out a surprised, anguished, voltage-filled yelp and then fell flat over, big blue eyes wide open, giant hand seared to the — *zzzzzz!* — sparking wire.

Quick as that, Clarissa was a widow, and even as she stood there, her son in her arms, his face hidden from the tragedy while she wept a widow's tears, she knew that she and her son would go on, that somehow they would find a way to live abundant lives without Daddy. The voodoo priest would prove to be no match for maternal love. Cue the sappy, heart-lifting music.

Clarissa shook her head, releasing the fantasy. The words *You do not really want to kill your husband* floated through her brain. The bimbo models and Iggy were chatting. Clarissa refused to look. She reached for the remote control, turned on the TV, and scrolled through the channels until she found CNN. Olga Villada, immediately taken with this glowing box and its talking heads, walked over to the TV, her long skirt swishing, and pressed her face against the screen. The picture bounced, sputtered, faded, and bloomed into snow. Olga Villada jumped back and moved to a safer distance, next to the desk.

"Stupid cable!" Clarissa said, turning the TV off and then on again, just in time to catch a report from Stonehenge. Several thousand pagans and other assorted revelers had descended on the ancient site, braving cold temperatures and intermittent rain, to celebrate the solstice.

"The clouds broke right at dawn, man, and there was music and singing and dancing. It was awesome," said a bearded guy with a Southern California accent and dilated pupils. His nose and cheekbones were painted in yellow and green stripes. He wore shorts and what appeared to be an animal skin.

Weirdo American, thought Clarissa, you're embarrassing all of us. Freaking caveman wannabe.

Olga Villada thought he looked quite fetching, a warrior. She imagined herself in his arms, her locks flowing across his chest. But she stopped there. She was in love, after all.

"On a more serious note," said the anchorwoman, who looked just like the reporter from the previous story but was not. "According to the Defense Department, a disturbing milestone has been reached in the Iraq war. Twenty-five hundred American troops have now died in action."

They rolled a clip of Tony Snow, the president's press secretary, skipping not one guilty beat as he replied to a reporter who asked if the president had any reaction to the new figure, "It's a number, and every time there's one of these five hundred benchmarks, people want something."

"Jesus H. Christ," Clarissa said, not believing her ears. Just a number! How about just twenty-five hundred souls. Just children. Just husbands. Just sons. Just daughters. How dared he! The whole world, from Stonehenge to Iraq to Washington to her rose garden, was unraveling, perilous thread by perilous thread. Just a number!

The anchor said, "Democrats on the Hill are not happy and are threatening to withhold future funding and are pushing for a timetable for withdrawal from Iraq. Today, the junior senator from Illinois, Senator Barack Obama, delivered a stinging indictment from the Senate floor."

They ran a video of a handsome young African American man, looking fine in his suit and tie. "As one who strongly opposed the decision to go to war," he said, his eyes reflecting, Clarissa thought, a determination and clarity she was unaccustomed to, "and who has met with servicemen and -women injured in this conflict and seen the pain of the parents and loved ones of those who have died in Iraq, I would like nothing more than for our military involvement to end."

"Barack Obama, Barack Obama." Clarissa liked this guy and wanted to remember his crazy-assed name. She switched channels. MSNBC was covering the president's G-8 meeting in Vienna—nothing more than a photo op. The reporter said no one knew if Bush had been briefed on the updated death toll— that's right, the entire country knows, but not the president. Great; now ignorance is his number one defense.

Disgusted, she punched the mute button but couldn't pull herself away from the image that flashed across the screen. A woman who appeared to be in her early to midfifties, her face tear-streaked, was handcuffed and flanked by police. The caption revealed that she had attempted to jump off the 110-story Sears Tower to protest the Iraq war. Briefly, before returning to the footage of the woman being shuttled out by far more law enforcement than seemed necessary, they showed stock footage of the skyscraper, its top floors obscured by clouds. Clarissa could not help but think back to the horror of 9/11 and the people who had chosen to jump to certain death and how their reflections must have flickered against the glass—human birds plummeting to earth. Why, Clarissa wondered, would someone believe that leaping from the Sears Tower would help stop the war? And how did it feel to fall through the sky? Did God render mercy, filling their minds with blind grace? Or were they on their own, their only company fear and a change of heart? Clarissa couldn't take any more. She turned off the TV, but her brain kept going: Do you have to bend your knees to leap or do you just fall forward, rigid and bright? She closed her eyes and imagined herself on the Sears Tower roof, among the clouds.

Noticing that the House History Dossier file was buried beneath a stack of manuscripts, Olga Villada decided that this was her chance to exert a little direct action. While Clarissa rested her eyes, Olga Villada quickly fished the dossier out of the pile and placed it on top.

A door slammed. She and Clarissa glanced out the window. Iggy was alone, flipping through his sketchpad.

Clarissa leaned forward and peered past the rose garden. The models were nowhere to be seen. Perhaps they're in my house, defiling my toilet, Clarissa thought. She closed the blinds.

Olga Villada nodded her approval; she was not a woman who suffered fools.

Perhaps, Clarissa mused, Jane had been on to something with her sophomoric questions. Maybe she should try writing in long-hand. Maybe the act of actually putting pen to paper would thaw her frozen brain. She searched the cluttered desk for a pen, look-ing under magazines, manuscripts, empty and overstuffed files, a spine-broken and dog-eared copy of Aleixandre's *Destruction or Love*, the House History Dossier folder. Funny, she did not remem-ber it being on top of the stack. Hadn't it been buried for weeks under the manuscript pile? When had she pulled it out? Holy moly, more evidence that she was going mad. Or there was always the possibility that her desk was such a mess—a helter-skelter mass of papers, files, and missing books—that nothing was really visible. She looked at her computer and then the folder.

Olga Villada considered moving the file a hair closer and then thought better of it. She wanted her to read the material, not be so frightened that she stopped coming into the studio.

Clarissa fingered the bottom edge of the file. Maybe, she pondered, if she read up on the house's history, she'd feel more at home, more like the place was hers, no matter that her husband went behind her back, rearranging everything she touched. Take the time to read this; do something nice for yourself, she thought. What's one more day without writing going to cost? Five months and twenty-nine days?

She grabbed the folder. She could spend the rest of the morn-ing in her library, laid out on her fainting couch, reading. What a nice idea. Besides, now was her chance: The naked models were disposed, somewhere. And if she ran into them inside the house, she held the power; a clothed woman in her own home trumped naked bimbos in search of the bathroom any day. Folder and teacup in hand, feeling uncharacteristically courageous, she hurried out the door.

The fly rode the wake of Clarissa's scent, intoxicated by the faintly acidic odor of her sweat.

Olga Villada, satisfied that she was finally getting somewhere with Clarissa, stepped into the backyard and gazed at the sentinel oak that rose, majestic and powerful, at the edge of Jake's Hell. The herons pierced the sky above the tree, twin arrows on their way to what? Even she did not know.

The wind blew, and Olga Villada, despite all these years, caught the stench of charred flesh. If she tried hard enough, she could still hear the voices of those men, those wicked, wicked men. And her little boy crying and asking, "Why are they doing this to us, Mama?" Olga Villada stood on a patch of ground she had inhabited for 183 years, and that old, stark sadness took hold; she wanted to double over from the horror of it but was too proud. Even as a ghost, she refused to show the depths to which she hurt.

Her husband emerged from the shadows of the tree, a rusted shovel in hand. She knew what he'd been doing. Unless the tree died — its cells having absorbed the violence perpetrated against Olga Villada's family — they would never be released from this place. The pain, the cruelty, the fear, were crystallized in the tree's sap; until that energy was destroyed, the souls of the three victims would remain trapped, and they would be forced to wander through their ghost lives in the same location they had been murdered, unable to ascend the horror. Olga Villada's husband had spent thousands of hours trying to damage the oak's root system, slashing open fresh runners, exposing them to insects and disease. He'd doused the tree with gasoline, set it on fire, driven an ax deep into its bark. He'd prayed — not knowing if

God existed—for a lightning strike. Nothing worked. For 180 years he'd been trying to kill it. Olga Villada searched the tree; scanned its crown, its limbs, its trunk, looking for signs of canker; and then—shocking even the fly—she disappeared.

Clarissa, her heart thumping, unable to breathe in the fire pit of the midmorning heat, paused on her way to the house. Her husband, consumed with the sketchbook, had not noticed her.

"Hey," she said.

He glanced up. "Oh, hey."

"How's it going?"

"The shadows on their skin are fantastic." He removed a pencil from his shirt pocket and began to refine his line drawing.

"Great, but..." She tried to shut up and couldn't. "You know, they aren't going to last." She wasn't sure if her trivia-clopedic knowledge base was going to help or hurt in this situation, but the chunk of coal forming in her belly gave her a good idea of the outcome.

He rested the sketchbook, which looked small in his big hand, against his thigh. "What are you talking about?" He did not look at her when he asked the question.

"The solstice. The sun will reach its northernmost point for the whole year by noon. For a few moments, our hemisphere will be shadow-free." She wiped the sweat from her eyes. Could she say nothing, do nothing, to impress him?

He shook his head, snorted, and returned his attention to his sketchbook. "I'm busy, Clarissa."

Despite his full-frontal rudeness, she reverted to her tendency to try to make everything A-OK. "You need anything? Water or something?"

"No. They've gone to Natalie's car. She's got a cooler out there. She's bringing us something."

"They don't have on any clothes."

60

"One slipped on her dress. The other one is wearing your kimono," he said, punching each word. He shot her a brief smile, which she interpreted as a smirk.

A cocktail—one part anger, one part humiliation, one part pain—singed her veins. *Motherfucker. On top of everything else, he's mocking me.* And she could not call him on it, could not risk having an argument in front of the models. That's all the gossip circuit would need. Clarissa didn't know what else to do other than take the high ground, which meant acting as if her head were simultaneously up her ass and in the ground. "Well"— she held up the folder and smiled—"research for me."

"Is that my *fowking* shirt?"

"No," Clarissa lied, and before Iggy could protest, a squeaky voice wafted through the heat.

"This Tazo tea is terrific!"

Clarissa bolted through the door so swiftly that she closed it before the fly, who was a seasoned aerial acrobat, could sweep in. He buzzed, looking more like a mad little bee than a fly, at times throwing himself against the glass, risking serious injury to his thorax. He was just about to zip over to the kitchen to seek an opening there when, in his frenetic circling, he noticed a herd of mosquitoes enter the house through a gap at the top of the door.

"Bingo!" the fly would have said, swirling on stationary wings, if he could have talked.

∾

*L*arry Dibble sat in the crown of the sentinel oak, getting the lay of the land. Now he knew why the tree was in trouble. That crazy black guy had been hacking away at it for nearly two centuries. Unlucky bastard. As for himself, Larry didn't understand why he, being an angel who favored mischief and mayhem over all that goodness-and-light bullshit, had been sent to this stupid little village named, moronically, Hope. What did the big boys think he was going to do? Learn a lesson? Was this one last chance to prove he deserved those wings? Did they even have the balls to kick him downstairs? He stroked his beautiful long dreadlocks, picked an ant from his hair, and ate it. Who was the lucky one? He was. Those were some fine-looking lassies cavorting amid that snotty bitch's roses.

~

*C*lutching the manila folder, Clarissa began to thread her way back to the library and got as far as the half bath when she was stopped in her tracks by voices inside her house.

"This rifle was used by my great-great-great-grandfather in the Battle of Blood River. Ncome River, we call it. My people defeated the mighty Zulus. It was one hell of a fight," she heard her husband say, his Afrikaner accent fully engaged.

Christ.

"South Africa must be so beautiful," said the model who did not squeak, the brunette.

"Every part of the country is beautiful. I mean, the kind of beauty that poets and artists spend their entire lives trying to capture. But it's not our country. God rest my great-great-great-grandfather's soul. He was a legendary warrior, a true hero. But in history's great ebb and flow, we have to get back to what is right. The *fowking* white man should leave the entire continent. Racist bastards!"

Clarissa dropped the folder. She was shaking. So their first conversation, the one that happened eight years ago at a party thrown by a mutual friend, had been nothing more than his version of a pickup line? She knelt down, fought back tears—she would not cry over his sorry ass—and began gathering the dossier's scattered pages.

"You are so brilliant," Squeaky said, and then Clarissa heard the back door open and slam shut.

Dingbat, Clarissa thought, and what an asshole husband! Do not let it bother you, do not let it bother you, do not let it bother you, she chanted silently as she made her way to her library, where the fly lit on the handle of her machete, and she checked the clock: ten forty-five. Only six hours to go before she'd see Adams. She revised the sentence to *if* she saw Adams. *If* Iggy truly did intend to spend the evening in the darkroom, she wondered *if* she could—despite the horrible way Iggy was behaving—muster the nerve to go alone. Despite all that she had accomplished in her life, she was not a woman accustomed to doing things on her own—a fact about her basic nature that she loathed. It was turning her into a goddamn doormat. Independence, from her perch, was a scary but intoxicating proposition. "One day," she whispered, looking at the clock, "I'll be an independent woman and he'll be sorry for the shit he's pulled."

She heard that laughter again—one fine trill—and then the sound of bare feet running across a pine floor. They sounded like short steps, the kind a child would make. She ducked into the chandelier room and gazed at the ceiling. The sounds ceased. Now all she heard was Iggy, those girls, and a bird, probably a mockingbird, chirping. It was hopeless. The old house was full of strange noises. There was no laughing child, no running child; the idea was absurd. She stepped back into the library and remembered that she still had roses in the sink. Oh well, no harm. They were in water and could wait.

The library was a good two or three degrees hotter than when she'd left it less than an hour before. She wondered if the air-conditioning was working at all. Perhaps global warming was descending even faster than all the scientists in the world (with the exception of one jackass holdout) were predicting. Eschewing the practicality of the library table for the comfort of the red silk fainting couch, upon which, predawn, three moths had feasted (a fact that, if she had known it, would have piqued her anger because she loved this couch, as it reminded her of how very far she'd traveled from that trailer park).

Determined to not care what her husband was doing, she stretched out—a human ribbon unfurling—wiped a fine film of sweat off her neck, gathered her long curly hair into a single tail, and braided it with nimble fingers. As she wove one strand over the next, she felt the morning settle into her bones. Sunlight filtered through her Irish lace curtains, and if she had stared at it—which she did not—she would have seen billions of bits of swirling dust, and this might have made her feel even more insignificant than she was already feeling that day; so it was her good luck that she faced away from the solstice light.

The fly zigzagged across the room and then lit upon the couch's curved arm.

Clarissa opened the folder and was immediately taken by the engraving of Olga Villada. There the woman of the house stood, under the sentinel oak in Clarissa's backyard, a map (of La Florida, Clarissa assumed) in one hand and a bullwhip (cows, snakes, what else?) in the other, looking defiant, brilliant, beautiful.

"Fantastic," Clarissa whispered into the hot, hot air, her heart's molecules rearranging themselves into a pattern reminiscent of love. She felt the shift just to the left of her breastbone and then a small quake. It rippled through her, head to toe, but she was so entrenched in refusing even the smallest of pleasures that she did not recognize that she might have just fallen head over heels. We're talking platonic, of course. But did it matter? What was love if not an idea—abstract as wind, concrete as rain—an invisible homily so powerful that it propelled even the meekest souls to hold dear what they feared most?

She set the engraving on her chest and flipped through the folder, finding that it contained scholarly examinations (including an unfinished doctoral thesis written by a certain Rosa Pigot), land grants, newspaper articles, and a plethora of sundry scribblings—some in Spanish, some in English, some in shaky translation. She searched her memory bank about her day at the archives. While the librarian made photocopies of what Clarissa assumed would be flimsy documentation, skewed through the dusty lens of history, she had searched for a daguerreotype of anything pertaining to her house and had come up empty. She hadn't known about the engraving until this moment.

She scanned pages quickly, trying to get a broad overview before she delved into details. Olga Villada, the daughter of Spain's most beloved flamenco guitarist and New World mistress to Florida's Spanish governor, had apparently journeyed to a land of swamps, snakes, mosquitoes, and wildflowers just because she could. At least, that's what the opening paragraphs of the thesis led her to believe.

The thesis, supported by other documentation, established that Olga Villada was at one time the largest landowner in what was to become Aucilla County. Under Spanish law, women were allowed to own land, something their sisters living under U.S. rule could not do. In her time, she owned hundreds of acres of fertile earth that—thanks to greed, ignorance, and curses cast by slaves whose hands bore scars inflicted by cotton's mighty thorns—would be mismanaged by subsequent owners, becoming nothing but dust, depleted of its nutrients, in need of the care twentieth-century planters would eventually provide. But before the earth went dry and Florida became a slave-owning U.S. territory, Olga Villada raised crops and cattle and owned two sawmills. She also, with the help of her common-law husband,

Amaziah Archer, designed and built the very house Clarissa called home.

Notes accompanying the thesis, scrawled in a left-leaning cursive script, claimed that Olga Villada's husband was a free black man (free as in he had *never* been enslaved) who had once taught math in a one-room schoolhouse in Haiti and who, in Florida, enjoyed the benefits of living in a society that allowed Africans and people of African descent to be free, to buy their freedom if they were unfortunate enough to be enslaved, to own land, to sue people and businesses, to sit on juries, and to live — compared with what their brethren and sisters were experiencing in the U.S. territories — with dignity.

Clarissa sifted through the pages, reeling. One hundred and eighty-three years ago, her yard had been tilled, planted, and nurtured by Olga Villada. Her house was built on land that Olga Villada had tamed. Perhaps somewhere on this sprawling property — maybe in the attic or out in the barn — she would discover the woman's bullwhip. She placed one foot on the floor. Even in this heat, the planks were cool to the touch. She imagined Olga Villada and Amaziah Archer's strength, fatigue, and joy as they hewed the trees, planed the wood, and locked the house together via the very neat trick of tongue and groove. The very floors she walked were hewn from pine trees harvested on a patch of earth where the house now sat. But they had not touched what would have surely yielded the finest wood: the sentinel oak. Even back then, Clarissa mused, it must have been a grand tree.

Overwhelmed, she closed the folder. She couldn't wait to get outside, in her yard, and explore, now knowing that she was walking in the footsteps of Olga Villada, a woman of fierce independence and obvious charm. Clarissa wanted to be just like her: businesswoman, snake tamer, lover to a man who knew what to do with a saw, a hammer, a nail. She laid her head on the couch and sighed. The happy and distorted sound of Iggy and the models talking swirled through the library, but soon their voices wafted farther out and finally could not be heard. Maybe they're dead from heat prostration. If so, they could just lie out there and steam for a while. But seriously, Clarissa decided, as soon as the models left, she would reclaim her yard for herself and her new long-dead heroine. Clarissa shut her eyes and drifted. As her mind floated into a nonsensical state of ease—as is the case with time and planets—the light moved, rearranging the room's shadows.

In the kitchen, the heat took its toll on one rose. Older and less vigorous than the others, the flower turned brown at its edges. In the future, near midnight, unseen by any human eye, the rose would drop three petals.

Change was happening everywhere. In the yard, the solstice sun edged ever higher, pulling the shadows from the earth, leaving the models more exposed than even Iggy liked, prompting him to pack up. The girls slipped on their clothes and headed to their cars and town, taking with them small bundles of roses Iggy had cut for them (it was fortuitous that Clarissa did not know this, because it would have only made the soiling of her kimono all the more egregious). Olga Villada wandered upstairs and played marbles with her son, who wanted to know when Papa would be home. The fly spied a few crumbs on a side table—the long-forgotten remains of a shortbread cookie. He snacked even as he stood guard over Clarissa. With no naked women to ogle, Larry Dibble grew bored, flew from his perch in the oak, and, whistling a melody whose words he'd long forgotten, wandered the streets of Hope, his new godforsaken home.

Perhaps it was the stress from the morning's events or a prescient gift in light of what would transpire that day, but Clarissa, uncharacteristically, fell into a deep slumber, and immediately the fly, sensing this was his chance, lit on her cheek and then disappeared into her hair. Although her sleeping brain led her to believe the abandonment dream she was about to have lasted a very long time (hours, perhaps), that was not the case. In reality, the dream unfolded—omniscient and playful, like a wind that caresses as easily as it kills—in Clarissa's subconscious in a matter of three seconds.

She stood in dream light at the kitchen sink, her hand trapped in the cavity of a plucked, ready-to-be-popped-in-the-oven hen, and gazed out the same window through which she had watched her husband and his models that morning. She leaned forward to get a better glimpse of the world. Her head touched the window, and the walls evaporated.

It was just Clarissa and the sink and the outdoors, and this seemed normal to her. She looked around. Exotic animals from various continents roamed her property: giraffes, ocelots, dingoes, polar bears, ruby-assed baboons; a bevy of water buffalo took mud baths where her rose garden grew. A fly flitted aimlessly through her hair. She was unfazed by these animals, and they, for their part, reciprocated her disinterest; many of them could have torn her to smithereens, but they didn't so much as glance in her direction. Perhaps she was invisible.

And there was this curious fact: If an interloper wandered into her dream, he would have been surprised, it's safe to say, that she didn't give a whit that her right hand was permanently stuck inside the chicken (for all intents and purposes, her hand had become the hen's giblets and the hen had replaced her palm and fingers as her primary appendage, rendering her lifeline obsolete). But phooey: All she cared about was her husband. When would he come home? Where was he? What was he doing out there, somewhere she could not imagine?

It felt to Clarissa as if aeons had passed since she'd last seen him. She waited and waited, ignored by man and beast, longing for some sign of that green Honda Civic, knowing that first she would hear music blasting because he always turned up the volume full-tilt. She hated that. How could he think straight with all that noise? That's why he wasn't returning home: He wasn't preoccupied with an endless string of naked models; he was simply confused by that ever-pounding bass line.

After standing at the sink for a few thousand years, she took three steps back, and when she did, the sink crumbled into a pile of steaming manure. Her head became a giant screen door. She pushed it open, bruising the hen's thin, pimpled flesh in the process, and stepped into the yard. A giraffe bumped into her and then walked through her. The animal smelled like tangerines and that made Clarissa hungry, but she knew that if she ate the giraffe, unpeeling its orange rind and tossing it in the air, she would die.

She raised her chicken hand to her brow (her face had returned; the screen door was the size of a thimble, and it resided in the center of her forehead: a third eye) and scanned the tree-stitched horizon as if she were a sailor searching the blue yonder. It had, after all, been so, so long since last he had held her or slid his hand over the swell of her hip or whispered her name into the soft, wild curve of her spine. But her effort was in vain. She stood there, the chicken pressed bravely to her forehead, for three hundred years. The Honda never arrived, yet she — unable to imagine a different life — remained tied to that spot, in the sun, her chicken hand bulbous and grotesque, waiting, watching: nothing.

Clarissa did not like this dream — it had a narrator and story line, neither of which she could control. She struggled up through the layers of swift sleep, determined to put it all behind her. On her journey toward wakefulness, she heard that fiddle music — wild and syncopated, with hints of Africa and Spain.

When she opened her eyes, the first thing she saw was the fly; it was perched on the tip of her nose, mesmerized. "Uhhhh!" Clarissa mumbled, batting at it with both hands.

The fly scooted to her desk lamp. Its shape was definite and stark against the polished brass shade.

"Stupid fly!" Clarissa said, and then she yawned, stretched, and rather than feeling refreshed from her nap or rejuvenated by the discovery of Olga Villada's story, she could think only that nothing was right. The room was too hot, the fly too forward, her husband too removed.

Clarissa looked at the fly. He stared back, his orbital eyes bursting with fresh pressure, which was as close as flies came to crying. That's right. The woman's beauty moved the little fly to tears.

The floorboards upstairs squeaked once, twice, and then she heard that familiar shuffle, shuffle, pause cadence. Ahh, Iggy. He was in his office, pacing. Shuffle, shuffle, pause. Shuffle, shuffle, pause. What did he have to worry about? she wondered.

The fly rubbed his front legs together, giving him the air of a greedy cartoon banker, but really he was simply enjoying the taste of her; it lingered on his legs and thorax.

Her skin still held the bristled memory of the disease-carrying pest tripping the light fantastic through her arm hairs, the tip of her nose. The memory, coupled with the sensation of everything being outside her control, made her shudder. But then, as life sometimes affords, she sensed an opportunity.

In her peripheral vision, she saw a folded, creased, and perfect (for her purposes) copy of the *Tallahassee Democrat*. Its butt end was extended like a handle from one of the chairs pulled up to her library table. Her husband must have left it there; perhaps he also had been engaged in battle with this fly. Had the fly tasted him, too? She suddenly hated the little cretin. It felt good, this hate. It was the kind of hate she could do something about.

She imagined the fly's little insect grin, all gummy, self-satisfied, mocking, its orbital red eyes gleaming. Is the little bugger taunting me? Is there no one in this house who respects me?

The fly knew what was happening yet was helpless to delay the inevitable. For him, love equaled sacrifice; what a great journey this was, to give himself so selflessly to his one great amour! He watched as Clarissa wrapped her hand around the newspaper and wanted nothing more than to taste her delectable skin, especially the soft inner curve of her elbow. He heard Section A crinkle as she tightened her grip. He considered India's sacred cows and how they viewed humans as little more than pests. The news of divine bovines had first been relayed in 1898 by an Indian fly that had made the journey to America in a valise made of crocodile hide. As global travel became more commonplace, tales of the nonstop banquet the cows afforded India's flies spread wing to wing, coast to coast, and generation to generation with all the continuity of a narrative-born genetic marker. So, too, did the news of how the cows viewed the worshipful humans. If sacred cows had thumbs, the fly mused, they'd take swatters to every idiot who dared approach them with a lantern smoldering with incense. The whole sacred thing had rendered their lives meaningless, had forced them into an unnatural state of grace. He twitched his wings, unable to get past the irony that one person's deity was another's pest. Here he was, adoring this goddess of a woman, and all she held for him were murderous thoughts. If he were a writer, the fly decided, he would pen an opus titled *Of Pests and Gods.*

Clarissa was grateful that her husband had—for whatever reason—fashioned a club. She steadied her heart and grip, kept her eyes on the insect prize even as she pulled on her cerulean boots with her free hand and stood upright—her superhero breasts perky, hard, Buick-proud.

The fly stayed very still for her, sad beyond all measure but thankful that he had had this day, thankful in the way of the hopelessly lovesick that he was allowed to sacrifice himself on the altar of her dysfunction. He did not close his eyes, not even when Clarissa shouted like a good warrior, "Fwuk u u liho!" because that would have dishonored this moment and her need. In the face of death, he was full of ardor.

With one mighty, well-placed blow, Clarissa smashed the god fly, her accidental suitor, into a blood-and-guts, peanut-buttery mash.

"Hmpf!" Clarissa said. She tossed the paper to the floor, a casual but triumphant act. She smoothed her T-shirt, which her subconscious fancied was a gold lamé second skin, threw back her bouncy hair, and took a deep, deep superhero breath.

And all the while, Clarissa *domestica*, who'd taken cover in the buried cave of Super Clarissa's dermal layer, felt slightly embarrassed about the thrill she'd experienced in killing her tormentor. As she struggled to the epidermal surface of her life, she fretted over where her inner Buddha (she was certain she had one) had fled. Was he that fickle? Was she that unworthy? Had he simply decided to leave the killing to her so that he could then enjoy life untainted by guilt or insect? Was the Buddha a student of *The Art of War*? She did not know.

Leaving the dead fly where it lay, all the Clarissas in her body walked into the kitchen and headed for the fridge. She was hungry and was certain Iggy was, too. The man had a mammoth appetite. Three burgers or a whole chicken at one sitting was a normal meal for him. A possible new title: *Iggy: The Great Blue Ox*. She threw open the fridge door and pondered what to fix for lunch. Her eyes wandered over a package of thawing chicken breasts, a bouquet of parsley still on the stem and stuffed into a tumbler of greening water, an unopened package of hoop cheese, a giant can of Hansa pilsner sent by a school chum from Johannesburg, a half-full bottle of Pinot Grigio, and a loaf of nine-grain wheat bread. She thought about Jane and how she'd declined the cookies because of her braces. Clarissa knew full well what an annoyance a mouthful of metal could be. But that was nothing compared with going through life with a severe case of catty-whomped teeth. Clarissa reached for the Pinot, uncorked it, and took a slug, and as the wine cooled her throat, she found herself mercilessly stumbling backward into the dark heart of her childhood.

Knuckles and bones, marrow and tendon, skin and vein — the entire all-suffering, Christ-like body of being Mrs. Burden's daughter rushed at her. She saw little Clarissa, one of the many Clarissas whom she found embarrassing, whom she could not love, standing on her tiptoes, gazing into the cracked medicine cabinet mirror in the small, dimly lit bathroom that, in all honesty, appeared to be a divine indulgence given the size and modesty of that single-wide trailer.

Her mother towered over her, swirling her bourbon and Tab in a plastic tumbler and flicking her cigarette that was poised all jaunty and absurd in its stop-smoking plastic filter. To Clarissa, her mother resembled Ava Gardner in her boozy role in *Night of the Iguana*, which was for some odd reason her very favorite movie on the entire planet, and she was happy that Channel 13 sometimes ran it on Saturday afternoons. But she was also bitter that there was no Richard Burton or Deborah Kerr or dying poet to save her and her crazy mother.

Little Clarissa brought her hand to her mouth and pressed against her teeth — those teeth that stuck out at demonic angles, those teeth that were an object of derision and shame.

"Push harder," Mrs. Burden ordered, her red lips releasing each word in a tiny, invisible, bourbon-scented barrel.

Clarissa pressed her fist against her buckteeth with all the force she could muster, so much so that her face shook. Her hand shook. Her lips — flushed with blood — grew warm and the tips of her knuckles blazed white. Her eyes widened in tandem with the bubbling pain.

Her mother grabbed Clarissa's chin, tilted the girl's head to the hard light of the naked bulb, and inspected her daughter's profile. "They haven't budged a hair." She let go with a shove. "Have you been doing this three times a day like I told you?"

Clarissa did not answer. Her job was to keep pressing those teeth, forcing them into pretty-girl alignment, because being bucktoothed all her life was out of the question. But so was paying for braces. How many times would her mother have to tell her that? "No goddamn braces! We have no goddamn money!" As Clarissa applied more pressure, she became snagged in her mother's reflection, which dodged like a punch-drunk prizefighter in the cracked mirror.

Mrs. Burden grabbed her daughter by the hair and yanked. "I said push!" Then she gripped the doorjamb and propelled herself out of the bathroom, away from the fractured image, and down the hall. "Don't stop until I say you can stop," she shouted, slurring, from the front room—although shouting to be heard in the confines of this aluminum can with wheels was unnecessary. And despite the fact that she mumbled her next words, Clarissa took note of each syllable: "Stupid child."

Clarissa's hand was tired; that's why she brought both fists to her mouth and pressed with double strength. She pressed so hard that her body, not just her face and hands, shook. She heard herself grunt. She willed her spirit into a dark, still room and swore she would not let it out until her mother's cure worked.

"You have to become a girl with perfect teeth or else you will die." That's what she told the little girl in the mirror.

Clarissa shoved the wine bottle back into the fridge, and as she recorked it, she knocked over the parsley-filled tumbler. It fell in slow motion, or so Clarissa thought, toward the floor, pulling Clarissa back to the present moment. It twirled end over end, brushing the air with a green, feathery swath. In its descent, the tumbler seemed Newtonian, determined to obey gravity no matter how much Clarissa tried to intercede. As if there were two of her — one who was real and one who simply went through the motions of life — Clarissa saw herself mouth the words *Oh no* and heard in exquisite, symphonic detail the high-pitched stutter of glass shattering against tile. Shards, both infinitesimal and large, sliced the air, settling in a pattern that appeared loose and chaotic but actually followed the laws of physics.

Iggy's voice swirled from on high, plump with irritation. "What's going on, eh?"

Clarissa tested the point of a large shard with the ball of her right foot. "Nothing."

"What broke?"

She eyed the distance between herself and the broom that she'd tucked into the narrow space between the fridge and wall. Could she lean that far? She picked up the large shard and slid it against her thumb. She watched a strand of blood curl slowly down her hand.

"*Kak!* What do you mean, 'nothing'? I heard..." Her husband's voice ushered in — close, surprising.

She looked up.

He stood at the base of the stairs, staring into the kitchen. He must have been using the hole punch; a paper dot was caught in his beard. "Shit, Clarissa, why didn't you say something?"

"I didn't want to bother you. Don't come in here without shoes." A drop of blood spiraled downward, landing on her big toe. She couldn't differentiate between her blood and the nail lacquer. Perhaps harlot red was the wrong name. Slasher red — now, that was more appropriate. She had to fight back a wild giggle.

"You're bleeding all over the floor."

"It's no big deal."

He rolled his eyes. Clarissa concentrated on his height — was he twice her length?—this helped her ignore his omnipresent disapproval.

"What's wrong with you? You should have called me, eh. What were you going to do, stand here all day and bleed to death? *Fowk!*"

Maybe, she thought.

He barreled to the doorway. "Where's the *fowking* broom?"

"Just bring me my flip-flops. I'll take care of it."

He shrugged. "Whatever."

She watched him walk away—clop, clop, clop. He wore a size nineteen shoe, something that wasn't easy to find. She wondered what it felt like to take up so much space on earth. He stopped in the chandelier room and looked under the sideboard. Why would he think she'd leave her flip-flops there?

"They're on the porch." She turned on her toes and caught a glimpse of herself in the mirror that hung beside the door leading into the dining room. No cracks. No Ava Gardner mom. No buck-teeth. Just the unremarkable face of a pretty woman. Magic.

"Here."

She spun back around.

"I really wish you'd learn to be more careful," Iggy snapped from his renewed position in the doorway, heaving the shoes with the sudden resentment of a four-year-old. "Sometimes, I swear to God, you're such a *fowked*-up mess. You remind me of my mother. *Jou dom stuk kak!*"

"Do not call me a stupid piece of shit. Or any other kind of shit, Iggy. It was an accident. They happen." His hard-angled nose grew longer. She saw it sharpen into a beak. He was a bird. A big, fat, pooping bird. She hoped everyone in South Africa hated him. Clarissa tried to separate herself from his words by concentrating on the trajectory and landing of the flip-flops. They skidded and swirled, reminding her of tiny bumper cars, stopping near enough that she managed, by twisting each ankle in opposing directions, to slip them on without risking the mine-field of broken glass.

"Thank you."

"Sure you don't want any help?" He uttered each word as if they were random sounds.

Clarissa studied him. Joy, disgust, pity, love: Nothing betrayed his steady features. She thought it probably took a great deal of energy to shunt all of life's emotions into an interior space no one could get to. She tucked her hair behind her ear. "No, I'll take care of it."

Again he shrugged and turned away. "I've got paperwork to finish, and then I'm running into town," he said, retreating.

"I was about to fix us lunch."

"I'm meeting Yvette and"—he sighed; it was a buying-time technique she'd often seen him use—"umm, her boyfriend for lunch."

"Who's Yvette?"

"The brunette from this morning. Her boyfriend wants to meet me." He said this as if some schlub wanting to rub shoulders with him was a big deal. "I suspect Natalie will also join us."

Liar. He didn't know that she'd overheard his suggestion that they shoot some "edgy" video and that Yvette had begged him to film them at her new apartment. Omission, you son of a bitch, is the same as lying. "Lunch, is it?"

"Yes, Clarissa, lunch. Do you even know how to spell the word?"

Clarissa ignored the insult; it would be too easy to go hysteri-cal on him right now. But her ovarian shadow women screamed, "Can you spell asshole, asshole?"

She studied a strand of hair for split ends—a nervous tic—and said, "Leo Adams is giving a reading in town tonight. I told him we'd go."

Iggy shook his head as if he'd just been told to eat cow balls. "And you're just telling me this now?"

"I'm sorry. He called this morning. You know how Leo is. Everything is spur of the moment with him."

"Well, that's too *fowking* bad because I've got about thirty rolls of film to develop. I don't have time to go to a reading. Besides, Leo bores me." He studied what she hoped was an infection on his hand. "He ought to bore you, too."

Clarissa decided she hated the big, pooping bird standing before her. She saw herself standing atop the cloud-shrouded Sears Tower, without her cerulean boots to give her wings. She felt her calves tense at the thought of jumping. "Well," she said, "I guess I'll just go alone."

He rubbed his hand over his bald head and scratched at his beard as if deep in thought. "Clarissa," he said in the exact tone fathers use with unruly toddlers, "the truck doesn't have brake lights. You can't drive a truck at night that has no brake lights. You realize that, don't you?"

And how many times had she asked him to get them fixed? And the gas gauge? And to haul away the trash in the bed that was threatening to turn the truck into a toxic dump on wheels? But she was afraid to point out these issues, so instead she said, the cold Chicago air buffeting her, "I'll just take the Civic."

He turned away. His big feet clomped against the old pine. She heard him loud and clear as he ascended the stairs, "And what am I supposed to do, Clarissa? What if I need a car while you're gone? I don't think so."

Seething, she had to fight an urge to run after him. Beating on him, screaming at him, demanding better treatment: None of it would amount to a hill of beans. She imagined him in the doorway, suddenly keeling over from what—heart attack?—landing with the force of a giant log (the bigger they are, the harder they fall), slicing his throat on a thick blade of broken glass. There was nothing anyone could do about a slit jugular.

She stepped gingerly, careful to avoid shards that could puncture her rubber soles, and grabbed the broom. She had to sweep up the mess. Every sliver. Not one thin dagger could be left behind to puncture an unsuspecting foot. Some things you just had to put your mind to. Cleaning spills and adjusting one's attitude: They were ordinary chores in an ordinary day.

Her cut throbbed. She was the only one in the house who was bleeding. She reached for her dish towel and wrapped her hand. A deep self-loathing coursed through her. How could she expect her husband to be attracted to her with her obvious belly and butt and breasts?

Clarissa swept like a good soldier — intent, vigilant — searching for pieces she feared she'd never find.

⌒

*B*ut still there were the roses. And the garden out back that she wanted to ramble through. And the insistent need that this day not be lost. Clarissa slid the vacuum into her cleaning supply closet in the hallway — the broom, she'd decided, wasn't sufficient for the task at hand — and spied the cut crystal vase on the top shelf, behind a shoebox filled with needles, thread, a dead spider, and one sterling thimble. She pulled down the vase, ferried it to the kitchen, and in short order transferred the rose stems. Her thumb no longer bled, nor did she give it another thought. She stepped back and admired her handiwork. Lucky for her she'd stopped cutting when she had, because the vase was packed as tightly as she dared stuff it. The blossoms — such a lovely shade of peach — had started to open. They bore tiny white centers — star-shaped and soft. She brought the roses to her face and inhaled. What an intoxicating bouquet, something out of a movie! Wasn't it wonderful, this capacity to grow things! It was a talent that until moving to Hope she never knew she possessed. She didn't have to think long about where to put them: on the sideboard in the chandelier room. That way, each time she passed through the house, she would see them.

Holding the vase in both hands lest she drop it, too, she carried the flowers out of the kitchen, placed them on the white lace runner in the middle of the sideboard, and fussed with two stems that had shimmied below the others. She heard Iggy stomping around upstairs but felt under no obligation to tell him what she was about to do.

Satisfied that each rose was perfectly situated, she flung open the back door as his slammed shut and hurried down the porch steps.

Dear God," Clarissa said, fanning herself, breathing hard, threading her way through the winding path of her butterfly garden that hugged the rear of the house. She rubbed her eyes, which stung with sweat and grit. It must be close to one hundred degrees, she thought, and she was not far off.

Larry Dibble had made his way to the edge of town and, though unaffected by weather, was still impressed when he saw that the thermometer nailed like a cross to the WELCOME TO HOPE sign reflected a climate more suited to the underworld: a round, voluptuous, even-numbered 102 degrees.

The mail lady drove by in an SUV that had 156,000 miles on it and three worn shocks, the fourth soon to follow. She saw Larry Dibble standing by the sign and, though naturally suspicious of strangers, was immediately smitten with the one-armed, dreadlocked man who shot her a dazzling smile.

He sniffed the air. Oil. The fetid gal had a leak. As he watched her stop at Hope's first house on the right and open its mailbox with a long, hooked stick, he pondered the advantages of helping her out with her car problem or tending to her libido with a bit of afternoon fallen angel love. He tapped his index finger on the sign; his long nail clacked against the wood with curious intent.

Unaware of the intrigues plaguing greater Hope, Clarissa noticed that her butterfly garden was holding up to the scorching weather with aplomb but that the yarrow she'd planted two days prior next to the house and studio needed water. The cilantro had gone to seed, and caterpillars were sucking the life out of much of her parsley, but that was okay. She'd planted extra just for that purpose—some parsley for her, some nutrition for the future butterflies. She wandered through the rose garden, not realizing that Olga Villada was also there, admiring a white rose named Moon Dance that smelled of raspberries.

Determined not to let the models' presence linger in any way, Clarissa walked past each bush, subconsciously laying down scent (little wonder she couldn't shake the image of a snail leaving a trail of glimmering dew), sometimes touching a leaf, a petal, a nascent bloom.

Clarissa, in her short six months on this gentleman's farm, had planted an exuberant garden: hybrid teas, floribundas, David Austin English roses. And so many colors: reds, lilacs, peaches, pinks, creams, yellows. While she loved the roses, she abhorred most of their names. So as her scent settled amid the foliage, she decided to give them new ones. The pedestrian-named Outrageous Floribunda, an orange rose that smelled like cayenne, honey, and citrus? Clarissa pinched a fiery petal and said, "From here on out, you're my Hell Hath No Fury Floribunda." The Peace Rose could keep its name, as could Black Magic, Moon Dance, and Wildfire. But the Ronald Reagan Rose definitely needed to get out of politics. "I name you Red Hot Mama Rose." Clarissa laughed and was amazed that she had not yet been mosquito bit. She did not know that aphids—glutinous monsters that resembled tiny woolen commas—were multiplying in alarming numbers on the cool, dark undersides of the leaves.

But Olga Villada did. She walked behind Clarissa, running her hand over each bush, the scent of sorrowful death killing the sap-sucking insects. And if Clarissa had looked closely at the ground, she would have seen hundreds of dead mosquitoes; the little bloodsuckers fell like Satan's snowflakes when they flew within fifteen feet of Olga Villada.

Clarissa stepped out of the rose garden and into the clearing. She walked right past the snake's shed skin, totally missing it, and stared up at the sky, studying the sun's zenith. Olga Villada ventured near, smelling of swamp, stinkweed, verbena, and magnolia. Clarissa breathed in the scent and decided that this was a good day, despite her decaying marriage. She pushed her hair off her face, exposing it all—cheekbones, forehead, chin, and neck—to the full measure of the sun. Then she remembered what she had told her husband. Could she be lucky enough to have wandered outside at just the precise moment? She gazed at the thick grass carpeting the earth where she stood: green blades dotted here and there with tiny black mosquito carcasses. She looked to the sky and then again to the earth. She waved her hand, shook her foot. Nothing.

"Woohoo!" she said, flinging her arms. She possessed no shadow. None at all. The solstice sun was a shadow stealer. She spun—once, twice, three times. She wondered how many people on the planet were aware of their brief, shadowless existence. And, she wanted to know, was her body chemistry, her cellular road map, her blood pressure, altered by being, for only a few moments, relieved of the burden of carrying the weight of one's own shadow?

Olga Villada watched her spin and thought that with a little training, she could be a fine flamenco dancer. She had the legs for it. If circumstances were different, she would teach her. Inside her self, which in death looked like an infinite hall of mirrors, Olga Villada heard her father playing *alegrías*. She danced one full bar; she swirled her foot, threw back her head, showed some calf. She still had it, by golly.

Clarissa spun once more, this time slowly, in an orbit all her own, marveling—degree by degree—over the fact that there were no shadows. Not even the sentinel oak cast a likeness. Its branches stretched from its central trunk for, Clarissa guessed, twenty or thirty feet. It was ancient, already hundreds of years old, by the time Olga Villada bought this property. Clarissa searched the canopy and spied where she thought the herons nested. Whole worlds, universes just out of her reach, thrived— in the roots that traveled underground like giant, twisting muscles; in the thick trunk that was the center of gravity for all that grew from it; and in the tender new shoots that fringed the tree's crown. No way was she going to let Larry Dibble mess with this baby. She placed her hands on the trunk. The bark was rough and textured. An ant scurried across her hand and did not sting her. Life was cooler under the tree. She pressed her finger-tips into the cobbled bark and, without knowing it, dug two nails on her left hand into the tree's soft pulp. As the whitish insides of the tree's flesh met the half-moon curves of her fingernails, a shot of pure terror flashed through her. Pain crackled her bones; she feared they were snapping. She crumpled to the earth; had she just been lightning struck? She turned her palms faceup, facedown. Her knees sank in the soft, mosquito-laden earth. Of course not. It was a cloudless sky.

As she scanned the field and distant tree line, images of a crime she did not yet know about flashed through her mind: ropes, torches, bullwhip, one wild eye, a man's forearm rippled in violence, a black man's hands reaching through a space empty but for smoke, a little boy clinging to a woman's long skirts, a clay marble clutched in his tiny hand.

Clarissa turned again to the tree, struggling to gain her footing. She rose first to all fours, animal-like and grunting. Something yanked her by the hair. She stumbled backward and felt the sinewy, rough braid of a noose tighten around her neck. She twisted away and ran. Gruff, mocking laughter—not a child's laughter—trailed her. As the distance between her and the tree grew, her shadow re-formed—gathering its weight in darkness—inch by wavering inch.

Olga Villada stood twenty yards out. In the far distance, where the dogwoods gave way to pine and hickory, she saw her husband walk toward her, an exquisite fiddle in his left hand, a horsetail bow in his right. She hurried to greet him. There was nothing she could do about Clarissa, especially not with Amaziah watching. The young woman had, through an act all her own (or perhaps it was simply a function of her heart's long desire to be of the world again), opened herself to a fissure in time's wide scrim, unwittingly making contact with men of evil intent, men Olga Villada hated with every invisible drop of her gossamer soul.

⁓

By the time Clarissa made it to the house, her shadow was back and her husband was gone.

Son of a bitch, thought Clarissa, anger subsuming fear. She grabbed the hose by the back porch and twisted the faucet. Water gushed out in a hot torrent, but she drank from it anyway. He hadn't even the decency to say good-bye. Furthermore, he was fully assuming that she'd be waiting for him—dutiful and obedient—when he returned. She had no idea what had happened out there on the swamp's edge with the sentinel oak; must have been heatstroke. She bent over and let the water cool her neck; she could still feel the sting of that imaginary noose. She splashed water on her face and thought about the engraving of Olga Villada—a woman equipped with a bullwhip and map. Hell, yes. That's what she needed. Clarissa "Bullwhip and a Map" Burden. Symbols were powerful tools in times of crisis. She turned off the faucet and looked to the western end of her property, where the red Dodge truck sat, moldering. It was probably full of roaches, rats, snakes, not to mention new life-forms. A mockingbird flew directly over the truck bed and pooped. Great.

Clarissa imagined it was she, not Olga Villada, in that engraving: powerful, no-nonsense, a get-'er-done kind of gal. What could stop her from seizing this day?

"Nothing," chirped the ovarian shadow women (if Clarissa could have seen them, she would have been struck by how much, at this moment, they resembled the joyous figures in Matisse's *The Dance*). "Absolutely nothing."

"Damn straight," she said, clarity blooming. Bullwhip and map indeed. She wiped her face with what was left of Iggy's shirt and headed back into the house. She grabbed her gardening gloves off the kitchen counter and went into her laundry room (the one room in the house her husband never went into) and nabbed a pink bandanna from the laundry basket. She shoved them into her back pocket. She fished out her purse—the one she used most every day—from behind a box of tools her husband didn't know she had and which she kept stashed in the bottom cabinet so that her husband wouldn't rifle through it (Clarissa had a few secrets of her own). She shook her purse, heard the keys jangle, and thought, I can do this.

She left the way she came in: through the back porch. Once she was within ten yards of the truck, she caught a whiff of the stench. They lived so far out in the country that they did not have trash pickup. But instead of hauling their garbage to the county dump weekly, her husband had decided that the best thing to do was let it accumulate. In *her* vehicle. She eyed the baking, fermenting heap. Rotted garbage wine: Now that was a million-dollar idea.

What a mess, she thought, meaning both her life and the transportation situation. Here she was, stuck in the middle of the swamp, with no way out except for a truck that was itself a hazardous material. But she aimed to change that. She peered in the driver's-side window, checking to see if, say, a rat or squirrel was feasting on the upholstery or a snake was sunning itself on the dash. She took a mental inventory of the scattered trash: candy wrappers, tollbooth stubs, a half-eaten and hopefully petrified package of Twinkies, old coffee cups from Dunkin' Donuts, a six-pack holder, a stained edition of the *South African*, Budweiser cans, pop-tops, a torn and wadded-up photograph of de Klerk, a Kentucky Fried Chicken bucket, bleached bones that were hopefully from said bucket, a stone. The good news was nothing moved.

Just get in and don't think about it, she told herself. She opened the door, made sure there weren't any critters sleeping under the front seat or curled around the pedals, and hopped in. This became her mantra: Roaches can't kill you, roaches can't kill you, roaches can't kill you. She jammed the key in the ignition. After three chugging, gas-belching tries, the truck sputtered to life. Out of habit, Clarissa looked in the rearview mirror. There wasn't one. She checked the passenger-side mirror. Gone. Driver's-side mirror? Gone. She checked the gas gauge. Empty, but that didn't mean anything. The gauge had quit working two years ago.

She couldn't risk running out of gas, especially on these country roads. Her first stop would have to be the filling station, which was five miles away. Even on fumes, she might be able to make it that far. Then it was on to the dump and finally the car wash by the interstate near Dead Oak. Clarissa gripped the sticky wheel. She wanted to cry, to break down and have an I-can't-do-this tantrum. But an old kernel of strength, one that if the truth be told she was born with, still had a pulse. She put the truck in gear. Luckily, she had no idea that as the truck groaned forward, a nest of cockroaches that lived under the passenger seat scurried over and under and around one another, teeming like a boiling clump of winged evil. Unaccustomed to this sudden movement, the spider in the glove compartment lifted one of its eight legs and repositioned itself for the ride.

Clarissa worked hard at focusing on the positive. At least she had transportation, as meager as it might be. And by the time she was done cleaning this piece of junk, maybe, amid the rubble, she would find the courage to defy her husband, put on some pretty clothes, and take herself to town. She turned out of her driveway, onto Mosquito Swamp, and saw that the mail lady had pulled off the road in front of Chet Lewis's house and that the tree cutter was leaning into her window, using his one arm as support, chatting her up. Clarissa's hackles flared immediately; she felt a need to warn the mail lady about this Dibble fellow, but the woman was gazing at him starry-eyed and did not give Clarissa so much as a glance.

Surely the guy didn't fool her. Although Clarissa had to admit, there was something faintly sexy about him. She pressed the gas, tapped her brakes at the intersection, sailed on through, sped past the empty green and its empty fire tower, and took a left onto Tremble and Shout.

Though not a religious woman, Clarissa prayed the entire way to Dirty Dick's Interstate Stop, Shop, and Fuel. Dear God, don't let me run out of gas on this godforsaken road. Dear God, I have no idea how fast I'm going because the goddamn speed-ometer doesn't work. Dear God, what a piece-of-shit mess my life is. When she spied Dirty Dick's humongous sign that advertised cigarettes, gas, Skoal, and beer, she said, "Thank God, it's about time."

Considering the fact that she spoke good English, could read without stumbling over big words, and had all thirty-two of her teeth (a feat given what she had gone through to attain that lovely smile), it was ironic that a rush of embarrassment swept through her as she pulled up to the pump.

At the island ahead of hers, a woman who appeared to be in her fifties but was probably not a day over thirty-three looked at the truck, caught a whiff of the rotting cargo, cast a glance at Clarissa that was part horror/part curse, said, "Quick, get in the car. Jesse ain't had all his shots," and hurried her five children and one hound into a rusted, shock-absorber-needing, torn-landau-roof 1999 Buick LeSabre. Clarissa took note: It had both its side mirrors and a rearview; it did not stink.

I sure hope Jesse's the dog, Clarissa thought, turning off the engine and fishing a ten from her wallet. As she slid out of the truck, reeking (her skin and clothes were absorbing the stench), a man who appeared to be in his sixties, with a head of hair so wavy that it reminded Clarissa of ocean swells, leaned on the side of his 1969 candy apple red Corvette, laughed, and said, "Damn, girl, I'd take you for a ride, but I'm afraid you'd make me stop at every corner and pick up trash."

Clarissa wanted to smack that smirk right off his face; she wanted the gas he was pumping into his over-the-hill crisis to be so unstable that it blew him and his car to smithereens.

"Old man, even with that bulge of Viagra in your pants you couldn't keep up with me, trash or no trash." Clarissa didn't really say that. But she wanted to, and it felt good even to think it. In lieu of mouthing off, she pretended to be deeply involved in the gas-pumping procedure, as if it were as complicated as excising—under emergency circumstances—her husband's medulla oblongata.

Dirty Dick's did not take cards at the pump, so she'd have to go in and pay. She hated that. Human interaction: For reasons she could not identify, as her marriage wore on, she had grown fearful of it. But she'd rather have to interact with the station attendant than trust that perhaps her husband had been thoughtful enough to leave any gas in the tank. If she didn't have to wait for change, she could just slide the ten-dollar bill on the counter and slide on out, but she'd need to hit it on the zeros. She coached herself: When you hit nine bucks, pulse the gas in—one, two, three, like that.

The man with the Corvette shot her an Elvis sneer. "You need a man in your life, honey. What is somebody as gorgeous as you doing hauling trash?" He winked.

Her superhero self had an urge to stick the nozzle in a part of his anatomy that was unspeakable, but instead she put it in her tank, squeezed the trigger (the pungent scent of gas mixed with the stagnant aroma of rotting meat and vegetable pustulence), and tried to look as if she were not experiencing a total meltdown and that her toxic waste dump of a truck weren't emitting a noxious cloud of fumes that wafted over the entire station.

Two little girls in the backseat of a late-model something-or-other said in unison, "Pew!" and held their noses.

In less than four seconds the nozzle clicked, signaling the tank was full. Worried that she'd done something wrong (how hard could pumping gas be?), she tried the trigger again, and again it clicked. The gas pump total read thirty-five cents.

The wavy-haired man guffawed and slapped the top of his Corvette, apparently delighted by Clarissa's woes. "You sure you got yourself a full tank there, little lady? Wanna try for a whole forty-two cents?"

"Are you sure you have half a dick for a brain?" Clarissa reached in the cab and found thirty-five cents and a dead cricket in the beverage holder. She tossed back her hair and walked into the station, not knowing if she or her superhero had mouthed off. But one thing was certain: She liked the tap, tap, tap of those cerulean boots.

Inside, a long line of folks waited to get lotto tickets with their cold beers and Slim Jims. She wasn't going to wait; no back of the line for thirty-five cents of fuel. If you pump less than a dollar, the gas should be free. She slapped the coins on the counter. "Pump number three," she said, ignoring the stares. She turned on her heel and walked right out. Click, click, click went those boots.

As she waded through the blistering heat, feeling oddly more confident, she surveyed the scene. Mr. Wavy Hair Viagra Pants was gone. He must have prepaid. Six or seven men were standing around gaping at her truck, laughing. The asshole sifting through the trash in her bed backed off, pretending he was just walking by. The others looked away. In her soul, she dared the whole bunch of them to say one smart-mouthed word. She got in her truck and turned the key, grateful that it started on the first try. When she rolled onto the highway, she gunned the engine so hard, her tires spun. She cranked down the window, not believing herself. To hell with the heat. The wind felt good.

She barreled south on Tremble and Shout. Two miles or so from the interstate, it became a skinny two-lane blacktop that, if you followed it far enough, intersected with Poor Spot Cemetery Road, where, she presumed, one would find an actual graveyard. Or at least the remnants of one, even if all that was left were a few cracked headstones mostly swallowed up by leaf litter and loam. She passed a tractor-trailer that was moving too slowly and flipped on the stereo. Nothing. Not even the radio worked. Why hadn't he told her? Clarissa shook her head and tried not to care. But the litany kicked in: She provided the sole financial support in her household, and look at what she was driving. But whose fault was that? Sweat trickled down her face, her spine, the hollow of her breasts. The world shimmered in the solstice heat. She drove a little faster, uncertain if she was within the speed limit.

Sitting high in the cab, she sped down the winding, isolated asphalt ribbon that led, as far as she knew, to three destinations: deeper into the swamp, Poor Spot Cemetery, and the Southern Aucilla County Waste Disposal Depot, which lay like a bald spot on the edge of Lake Prohibition, the largest in a chain of lakes that included Morality and Reform, their Indian names long ago relegated to trivia contests conducted among history geeks.

She took a dogleg turn, leaned to the right, rumbled past a stand of cypress, and eased up on the accelerator as the depot came into view. The primeval music of bullfrogs and cicadas rose from the surrounding swamp. She thought she heard the hollow, low whomp of a gator. Her tires crunching and grumbling along the depot's gravel road prevented her from hearing a lizard traverse a stash of junk mail jammed behind her seat. She sat up a little straighter. Not having been here before, she didn't know what to expect. As far as she could tell, the depot was a ghost town and she was its only living soul.

"I do not like this," Clarissa said to the cracked windshield. Shadows darkened the gravel path. She leaned forward and looked at the sky just in time to witness a real-life cliché. Vultures, riding the thermals, circled lazily: black hats floating in a blue sky. "Perfect," she said, wiping sweat off her forehead with the back of her hand.

Not seeing anywhere to check in, she pulled alongside three giant trash bins designed to be loaded onto a flatbed truck and hauled to some other dump station. A girl could die in a place like this and never be found. She checked her cell phone. Just as she feared: no signal. Maybe this wasn't such a good idea. No wonder her husband had never emptied the truck: He didn't want to die. She thought about turning around and going home, the truck still stacked high and reeking. He'd want to know where she'd been. He'd laugh at her, ripping open her folly and weakness.

She turned off the ignition. Better to die with dignity than go home whipped.

Clarissa jumped out of the cab and, with a fervent desire to prove that she was capable of this mindless if unsavory task, got busy. She considered the three bins. Evidently, recycling was not an option. She fished the bandanna out of her back pocket, put it on bandit style to kick back the stench, pulled on her gloves, climbed into the truck bed, waded into the sea of trash, and started heaving four months of refuse into the bins. She hoped to God she wouldn't run across any rodents, living or dead. Maybe the living ones had leaped out of the truck when she first headed down the road. She smiled as an image of rats jumping ship bloomed.

She heard glass break when one of the bags hit its mark. Perhaps she should have also brought goggles. She paused, and as she struggled for a decent breath behind the bandanna, she wondered why she'd elected to do this on the hottest day of the year. Oh, yeah. Adams. She wiped the pooling sweat off her face, reached for another bag, slipped on a rot-swollen watermelon, and fell flat on her back. "Fuck!" she yelled, and struggled to her feet. Frustrated, she kicked aside a pizza box. The moment her toe made contact, out swarmed an insect version of the Red Army. Roaches rushed in frenetic waves over her feet, around her ankles, up her legs.

She screamed and danced the banshee dance, slapping everywhere she could reach, nearly knocking herself out. It was perhaps a miracle that while she hollered and yodeled and flailed and yelled epithets such as, "Die, you sons a bitches!" she heard someone behind her say, "Ma'am, why don't I give you a hand."

She spun around, slapping her legs, and attempted to make

a break for it, but her feet got tangled in the morass of bags and malodorous crap. She fell face forward, toward the wheel well. This was going to hurt. A bruise? Concussion? Coma leading to eventual death? She did not want to die amid trash and cock-roaches in the middle of a no-man's-land swamp. Sure, she had fleeting thoughts of suicide. Didn't everyone? But death here? Right now? No way.

As she attempted to twist her torso to avoid the wheel well in favor of a garbage bag that, unbeknownst to her, contained the jagged shards of a green glass bowl her husband broke when fer-rying it to a woman's house (he'd painted Elsa Sloan in the nude and had wanted her to hold the bowl in her arms, baby style), the young man who had offered his help bounded into the truck and caught her, moments before she would have surely cracked open her head.

Her chin planted in his chest, she yelped even as she noticed that his arms were long, lean, muscled, but not grotesque.

"Sorry to startle you, ma'am."

She grunted in single syllables, her blue eyes wide as they searched for more roaches.

"Don't worry. It's okay. I work here." He helped her to the ground, said, "If you don't mind," and then plucked a roach off her shoulder.

Clarissa heard herself moan. There was nothing worse in this whole world than roaches.

Trash Man, who Clarissa guessed was in his early twenties, pointed past the Dumpsters and was evidently worried that her reaction was because she feared him. "That's the office over there. See? The trailer."

"Are there any more on me?" Clarissa feared she might have dislodged her heart. She flapped the denim shirt, checked her arms and legs. He kept his eyes on her face.

"No, ma'am, I don't think so. They're nasty little critters, ain't they?" He glanced at the trash, took off his Aucilla County ball cap, wiped his brow, and said, "Really, I don't mind helping. Looks like you've got quite a load there." His blue eyes flashed in the bright light; he was sincere, Clarissa thought, a man who'd been raised right.

She peeled a rotted lemon rind off her shin. The sun beat clear and relentless.

"Whew! It sure is hot, ain't it?"

"Yes. Yes, it is," Clarissa said. He had broad shoulders. She liked broad shoulders. But she had come here on a mission. She looked to the truck bed and its wild tangle of yuck. In all honesty, the roaches hadn't hurt her one bit, the little bastards. And this was her chore, her goal. She could do it. Self-sufficiency without complaint: That needed to be her new motto. "Thanks for the offer, but I can manage." And she meant it. After all, it was just trash.

"All right." He repositioned his ball cap. "But if you change your mind, just holler. I'll hear you." He smiled. It was a nice smile. Pretty teeth. Not stained by cigarettes or chewing tobacco or hard-knock coffee.

"Thank you. But I think I'm okay." She felt herself smile in return; she hadn't meant to do that.

A dog—part pit bull, part hellhound—bounded up, barking, growling, snarling.

"Don't worry, Maggie won't hurt you. Come on, girl, come with me." He turned and headed toward the entrance. The dog fell silent and, wagging her tail, followed at his heels.

"Hey!" Clarissa called. He turned around, and the dog did, too. "Thanks for breaking my fall."

"No problem, ma'am. Couldn't let you hurt yourself. That would've ruined my day." And then he ambled off.

Clarissa found a brick nudged in the corner of the truck bed near the tailgate. She used it to smash to smithereens the remaining roaches. "Ugh, roach guts," she said, whaling on a particularly juicy one, but the truth was, she was happy she'd declined Trash Man's offer. If her husband was too good to deal with unpleasant chores, she was well equipped. What are men good for, anyway? she wondered, pausing to watch Trash Man in the distance gain the trailer steps, taking note of how well he wore his jeans. If not for physical pleasure, mental companionship, carpentry skills, culinary aptitude, or brute strength, why have them around?

Shit, she thought, lifting another putrefying watermelon (her husband had used them as props in one of his naked sessions), she could learn how to use a power drill. She tossed the jelly belly fruit through the air and turned to see if she could catch one last glimpse of Trash Man, who had paused before entering the depot office.

He turned around, placed his hands on his hips — they were fine hips, narrow and strong. "You sure?" His voice echoed across the wide expanse of gravel.

"I'm positive," she said as the watermelon hit a rusty radiator, releasing a spray of festering juice.

He grinned again, shook his head as if to say, "You are a marvel," and stepped inside the office.

Nice, Clarissa thought, very, very nice. I'm standing in a garbage dump thinking about fucking the trash man. She supposed it could be worse. At least he was thoughtful.

The pheromones that mingled with the stench gave Clarissa a needed energy boost. It took her all of twenty minutes to clear the four months of garbage — bag after disgusting bag, some of which had been torn open by possums, raccoons, rats, and squirrels. I'll be lucky not to die of typhoid, she thought.

Soaked in sweat, splashed with the decomposing liquids of various vegetable and animal matter, stinking like a whiskey still gone bad, her hair a mess of wet ringlets, a smashed grape stuck to her ankle, she stood in the empty truck bed and felt an unusual sensation wash over her: satisfaction.

Right before she jumped down, Trash Man (his blue eyes, she noticed, were the color of plumbago blossoms) sauntered by, all cock walk and charm, whistling. "Would you look at that!" he said.

Clarissa blushed and thought, He's at least twelve years younger than me. She pulled a strand of hair away from her face. "Yep, I did good, even if I say so myself."

He offered her his hand. At first she didn't know what he was doing. She giggled, felt something good surge through her veins, and then decided it would be rude if she didn't let him help her. She put her slimy hand in his callused one. He supported her all the way to the ground. She felt faint, happy. She and Trash Man had bonded. Maggie ran up and he caught her by the collar. "I think she wants to go with you."

Clarissa petted the dog. Trash Man smelled like aftershave and sawdust. "Maybe next time, sweetie." She made goo-goo eyes at the dog and then got in her truck.

As she drove away, her tires crackling over the gravel, Trash Man yelled, "Hey, wait a minute!"

She stopped, stuck her head out the window, and feared he might be about to ask for her phone number. "Yes?"

"You ain't got no brake lights. That's dangerous. Somebody rear-end you and a pretty little thing such as yourself could go flying through the windshield."

Glowing all over, she said, "Thank you. I appreciate it. I'll put it on my to-do list."

"Sure enough. You come back and see me." He winked. It was the second time in under an hour that a man had winked at her. Earlier Dibble had, but he didn't count. Must be the stink, she thought.

She waved good-bye like a beauty queen on a flower-studded float. "Have a good day."

"You too."

Again she pressed the gas harder than she'd meant to—she was having a hard time getting used to the truck's calibrations. Her tires spun in place, hissing against the gravel, kicking up a white, chalky cloud, and then the truck took off like a bat out of hell. "Don't forget to get those brake lights fixed," he yelled, his voice trailing in the dust.

Hoping to catch one last glimpse of him, she looked at where the rearview mirror should have been and then to the passenger-side floor, where her husband months ago had tossed it amid the Twinkies wrappers. "Damn it all to hell," she whispered. Trash Man was right: She could get killed driving this rattletrap truck. And then it dawned on her that perhaps that was why her husband had let the vehicle get in this condition in the first place. Perhaps he, too, was burdened with spousal death scenarios. "You first," she said, and then sighed at the pitifully optimistic thought that at least someone had flirted with her before she'd met her demise.

⟍⟋

In her temporary state of hormonal oblivion, Clarissa took a right onto Tremble and Shout, which meant she was heading away from civilization. She checked the clock on the dash. Five-fifteen. Was almost everything on this truck broken? She guessed it couldn't be much past one. She was sure her husband was with Yvette and Natalie and maybe even Yvette's boyfriend, and she had to push out of her mind fears that her husband might be, if truth be told, a pornographer.

She gazed at the swamp with its cypress hammocks and mallow and yellow-cupped bladderworts and thought, Hell, I've come this far; I might as well go ahead and check out Poor Spot Cemetery. It couldn't be more than a few miles away.

An egret flew low, across a ridge of bulrush, and she mused that wouldn't anyone, even a corpse, tremble and shout if her final resting place—for all freaking eternity—was Poor Spot Cemetery? She imagined a long line of skeletons dancing conga style as they made their sad approach to the grave. "Boom-shaka-shaka, boom-shaka-shaka," they sang, their bulrush skirts wafting in the breeze. Clarissa tapped the steering wheel in time to their zippy funeral march.

Her macabre musings skidded to a halt, however, as she realized that Tremble and Shout was narrowing, the swamp encroaching ever closer. She took stock: no cell service, alone on a wilderness road, and driving an unreliable vehicle. She eased up on the accelerator and searched the distance: no side streets and pavement too narrow to accommodate even a three-point turn. Not wanting to risk ending up stuck in swamp muck, she had no choice but to keep heading south.

"Enjoy the ride, girlie," an ovarian shadow woman said, her voice dry and crackly and eerily reminiscent of *The Wizard of Oz*'s Wicked Witch of the West.

Clarissa sped up again, pegged it at what she presumed was in the neighborhood of sixty miles an hour. Surely the road led somewhere. And despite her attempts at positivity, her anxiety level rose. Here she was, alone in the world, surrounded by a swamp filled with gators, water moccasins, bobcats, bears, and God only knew what else that could kill her. How much worse can things get? she wondered, and then decided that wasn't a question she should ask.

Out of the corner of her eye, she saw a red-winged blackbird approaching low and fast. She fought against her instinct to swerve. The bird hit the windshield. Clarissa screamed. One obsidian eye gazed at her.

With nowhere to pull over, she checked for traffic, stopped the truck, got out, and hoped the bird was dead. She breathed out hard and pulled it off the windshield. No such luck. Its beak was open; the poor thing was alive. She wrapped her hand around its wounded body. The bird struggled. Its feathers—black crowned with shoulder badges of yellow and red—gleamed iridescent; divine. She stroked its head and damned this moment.

"Everything is going to be okay, baby." She opened her palm, a futile gesture fueled by the hope that the bird might fly away. It did not. Clarissa knew what she had to do—allowing a creature to suffer was out of the question—but wasn't sure if she could. She remembered back to earlier in the day when she had killed the fly. But that was different. The fly was a nuisance. The fly did not inspire beauty or dreams. Why, it probably didn't even have a soul.

Clarissa cupped the bird in her hands. Killing it felt like a sin; not killing it felt like a bigger one. Perhaps some mercies—even though violent—were still mercies. She looked into the heat-bleached sky, whispered, "Please forgive me." In the hard and soft and sinewy places of her palm—in every cell—she pulled the bird's head away from its body and twisted. She felt its neck snap.

Just like that, in the span of one breath, the bird was gone. No more misery. That's what the shadow women, including the Wicked Witch, whispered: "No more misery."

Clarissa tried to not feel. She did not want a single emotion to drip like poison through her bloodstream. She walked to the swamp's edge, dug a depression in the muck with her heel, placed the bird in the hollow, and buried it. "I'm sorry. I'm so sorry."

She got back in the truck and put it in drive, the warmth that had been the bird's life searing her hand.

Two minutes later, she turned onto Poor Spot Cemetery Road, and the guilt over having killed the bird was subsumed by the surprised panic that overtook her as an insect horde engulfed the truck, turning her view of the blanched sky black. As she rolled up the windows and cranked the air-conditioning (at least *that* worked), a panoply of bugs splattered the windshield in such numbers that they created a tight netting of blood and guts, making it nearly impossible to see out. She hurtled down the road, damning herself for going for this ride. But she stayed steady.

As she barreled on, the swamp grew more substantial, morphing into a wet jungle shaded by cypress, pine, magnolia, sweet gum, tupelo, and oak. Without warning, the pavement ended and she found herself bouncing down a dirt path once considered a road. A fawn darted out of the dense growth, and a group of ghosts — all women and girls, some holding babies — emerged from the shadows and ran alongside the truck. They threw stones, sticks, pebbles, the button off a hunter's shirt. Clarissa, unaware, thought the wind was creating a debris storm. She slammed her brakes to avoid hitting the fawn; the smell of rubber grinding against metal filled the cab. The truck veered to the right, but Clarissa managed to keep it on the path.

The fawn disappeared back into the understory, but the ghost women with their children continued to crowd the truck, yelling, hissing, hurling whatever they could find. Even as ghosts, fear clouded their faces and fueled their mass tantrum.

Clarissa bumped along for half a mile or so, amid palmetto, marsh holly, wild azalea, and vines, until she reached a clearing that was also the end of the road. She knew she'd found it: Poor Spot Cemetery.

"Well, I'll be damned," she said, putting the truck into park. She jumped out of the cab and sank a couple of inches into the soft, damp, tangled earth. It was quiet here — no birdsong, no wind tripping through the canopy. What happened to the wind? Clarissa wondered. She grabbed a moss-covered limb, thrown there by one of the ghost children, off of her hood and tossed it to the ground. This place is indeed, she thought as she slapped at the mosquitoes descending upon her, a piss-poor spot to bury the dead.

The ghosts circled her; they had not expected a woman. Why was she not dead, too? One of the children, a little girl with blond braids, picked up a rock and started to heave it, but her mother, who was dressed only in a cotton nightshirt, caught her by the arm. "No, no," she said. "Not yet. Maybe not."

Wrenching herself from her mother's grip, the blond ghost child ran over to her friend, an African girl whose face was tear-streaked and who kept one hand on her mother's long, blood-soaked skirt. The blond ghost child whispered in her friend's ear, and they both clapped their hands over their mouths to stifle giggles. Three of the ghost women drew closer to Clarissa. Mosquitoes fell to the ground like black rain.

The air was thick and rank with decaying vegetation—a smell Clarissa had always associated with snakes. If something happened—snakebite, bear mauling, whatever—she was miles from help, and her cell phone was useless. But to hell with it. She was here now, and there were gravestones lying helter-skelter in the soggy soil just a few yards in front of her. Clarissa loved old graveyards. The headstone inscriptions were tantamount to tiny stories offering clues about the lives of the departed. And Clarissa craved stories the way drowning people craved dry land.

With halting steps, keeping watch for snakes and mud holes, Clarissa made her way over to the grave cluster. Even the earth that was solid enough to walk on felt mushy, leading her to believe that it didn't take much more than a heavy dew for Poor Spot Cemetery to be underwater.

The ghost women, their fear easing, drew closer. The children played. The babies fussed.

Clarissa knelt on one knee and wiped off a clump of red-tinged moss on the first headstone she came to. A wolf spider the size of her fist scurried from its perch on top of the stone, disappearing into the wet soil. Startled, Clarissa tumbled backward, lost her balance, and fell into a muck pit composed of ancient graves. Screaming, she struggled to sit upright, but the quick mud pulled her in. She heard the scuttling of what she thought were insect legs. Something scurried across her face. She tried to slap it off, but her hands were mired in mud that felt to her as if it were alive, as if its intent were to consume her, body and soul. Her breath escaped her the moment she imagined she was being eaten by swamp roaches. She attempted to flail, kick, thrust her way out, but nothing worked. As slowly as a feather falling through a milky sky, Clarissa Burden sank deeper. Oh, my God, she thought, the graves are eating me; I am being buried alive. She did not want to die with a mouthful of mud: This was her third thought. Her fourth was, Is this cosmic payback for killing—even out of mercy—the red-winged blackbird?

Of all the ways she did not want to die, drowning in quick mud—graves or no graves—ranked near the top. Something slithered through her hair. She yelled, "Oh, hell, no!"

The ghost women watched, wondering if that was why she had come here: to die. But no one had done that in a very long time. Most of the women had been murdered and dumped at Poor Spot.

Not, however, Melissa Jackson. She knew exactly what it was to die out here. A yellow-haired mulatto, she held her baby to her chest and fought the horrible, sudden urge to remember. But fighting an urge, she knew, almost always ended in failure. In 1853, four days after her baby was murdered (the church's fathers had decided that her mulatto baby would infect the village with evil and had slit, upon birth, the baby's throat and dumped her in an unmarked grave), Melissa Jackson had fled here under the good light of a three-quarter moon and slashed her wrists so she could be with her little girl. It was not a good place to die.

Mud oozed around Clarissa's kneecaps; soon it would fill her ears. Because the circumstances were so dire, her reactions evolved like a Darwinian dream. Panic morphed into fear, which flashed into anger; anger erupted into multiple flares of disbelief. This full-blown incredulity slowed her beating heart, thickened her blood. Ultimately, it steadied her; out of chaos came certainty. She would die or she would live; but she wouldn't give up. No way, nohow. "Help! Somebody help me!" she screamed, the mud seeping over her silver earrings.

Melissa Jackson knew the distance even a ghost had to traverse to save the white woman. She knew, as did all the ghost women, that souls carried weight and, therefore, could fall victim to quick mud. If this woman was to be saved, the children would have to do it.

"Cornelia! Jessamine! Quick! Hurry like little bees," Melissa Jackson said, addressing the blond-braided child and her friend. She chose them because they bore the least fear.

The mothers of the two girls exchanged glances. No one wanted another dead woman out here. "Jessamine, can you do it?" the African girl's mother asked.

Jessamine looked at Cornelia, and they, feeling invincible in death, smiled wide. "I think so."

"Soft step, Cornelia, like I taught you," her mother said.

Jessamine whispered into Cornelia's ear. Cornelia, eyes wide, nodded, whispered something in return, and then, holding hands, the two girls made their way out to Clarissa, who, even as she sank, refused to cry. No one would find her out here, and perhaps, given the absurdity of her life (a mother who did not love her, a father who did not love her, a husband who did not love her, a womb so empty she had no children to love her), this was a perfect way to go. And if that were the case, she'd succumb without hysterics.

Hysterics: That was the last word that spiraled through Clarissa Burden's mind before she felt herself, as if by playful and strong arms, being pulled—up, up, up—from the muck. She heard a tearing and then a sucking sound as the quick mud ripped off of her what was left of Iggy's shirt. The girls worked hard, grunting as they pulled. Clarissa, for a full ten count, felt as if she were a child on a summer's day, floating on her back in the Tangelo County municipal pool, staring at the sky. It was a lovely sensation, this miracle of ghost children wrenching her from their grave. She got one knee on solid ground and scrambled with the agility of the spider that had gotten her into this fix in the first place.

Cornelia and Jessamine joined hands again and ran back to their mothers. The ghost women surrounded them, showering them with kisses.

"She felt hot!" Cornelia said.

"Hot as fire!" Jessamine added.

"The living are much warmer than we are," Jessamine's mother said, stroking the girl's hair.

Weak but grateful, Clarissa clung to the first fixed object she found. She did not realize it, but as she hugged the headstone of Florida Lee Bessamer, she was the happiest she'd been in years. A voice in her head whispered, "I am so happy to be alive."

Clarissa said, "Me too."

As she sat there trying to regain her bearings in a forsaken cemetery, awestruck at being alive, covered in grave muck, having just been rescued by ghost children, having almost suffocated to death in a mud pit, clinging to a moss-laden headstone, she stumbled through what had just tripped through her mind. Me too? Me too? Who the hell am I talking to?

Amid the dead, Clarissa tried to untangle the voices that

crowded her brain: the reasonables and the hysterics; the ovarian shadow women and the fwuk u u liho superheroine; the wise ancients and the girl who could—for a few moments—fall in love with Trash Man. She pressed her cheek against Florida Lee Bessamer's headstone and tried to understand who they were and if she needed psychotherapy. As a dusting of dead mosquitoes fell into her palm, the simplest and most honest of answers came to her: All the voices—each and every one—were part and parcel of who she was. They weren't independent beings. They weren't manifestations of a sick mind. They were different facets of a writer's being, real as the mud under her nails. And she needed to love them. Somehow, this was essential if she was ever to conquer the frightening landscape composed of white space on her computer screen. With a mud-caked hand, she ran her fingers over the headstone's inscription.

The ghost women, who had been watching from a few feet away, their curiosity getting the best of them, circled closer. Having accepted their fates long ago, they watched Clarissa without anger or remorse, fully immersed in a need to know her story.

"What is she doing here?" asked a pretty, cinnamon-skinned woman with long straight hair. "This is no place for a living woman." Her flour-sack dress was ripped. Her cobalt amulet gleamed in the flickering sunlight.

Overhead, a screech owl suddenly changed its trajectory when it set its yellow eye on the ghost women, swerving hard to the left and out of sight.

"Child must be lost," said a black woman whose hair was hidden in a blue cloth and whose arms still bore the bruises of the beating she had suffered at her death.

"Lost or crazy," said a young, brown-haired white woman who cradled a silent baby.

"Florida Lee Bessamer, 1828 to 1845," Clarissa said, reading the stone. "May Jesus Accept Her into His Forgiving Arms."

She rose to her feet and, moving with light, tentative steps, made it to the next stone, which was smaller. She wiped off the grime. "Josephine Bessamer, 1845 to 1845, Infant Daughter of Florida Lee, Born in Sin but Loved by a Patient God."

Clarissa, urgency tugging at her bones, walked the line of headstones, reading quickly, making sure she stayed on solid ground. "Glorious Louise Johnston, 1827 to 1844, Cleanse Your Heart, So Sayeth the Savior; Cornelia Glory Johnston, 1843 to 1845, May the Child Not Know Hell; Rosa Maria Valdez, 1840 to 1855, God's Tears Cannot Undo What Satan Hath Wrought; Consuelo Luna Valdez, 1842 to 1855, Little Sister, Once Christ's Dove, Now Satan's Breath; Baby Valdez, God Save Her Soul; Jessamine Freedom, 1856, And It Continues."

What did this mean? And why did the inscriptions become more cryptic, ominous? There were, by her count, twenty-two bodies buried at Poor Spot, and although some of the inscriptions were eroded into oblivion, as far as Clarissa could tell, everyone interred was a woman. She wound her way back through the headstones, trying to make sense of this place, these brief inscriptions that led only to questions. Dead mosquitoes rained down around her. Maybe, she thought, standing in front of Consuelo Luna's headstone, Poor Spot was a yellow jack cemetery. But why no males? Why had, in death, the females been segregated and buried in a place so hellish that no one—especially no one trying to stay healthy—would visit?

The black woman with the blue head cloth whose name Clarissa did not utter because her headstone had been swallowed by the mud nearly a century ago, said, "What do you think would happen if she knew the truth?"

Three of the ghost women, including Melissa Jackson, in unison said, "Dead."

Clarissa looked beyond the ragtag line of graves that

surrounded her, feeling certain there were plots without head-stones, that at some point bodies had been dumped and aban-doned, that she was walking on the graves of women and their children who had been long forgotten. No one had tended these graves since the day they were dumped.

A sadness as thick as the sweltering air descended on her. These were her sisters, sisters who had been considered dispos-able, unclean, unworthy. Maybe it wasn't a yellow jack cemetery at all. Maybe it was a potter's field for women who spoke their minds, whose sexuality was considered too obvious, tempting, dangerous, evil — bad women spawning bad seed. Maybe she had stumbled onto her own private Salem. She would find out who these women were, and she would write about them, honor them; she would not let them be forgotten. If they were witches, she thought, I want to be one of them.

She knelt down, grabbed a fistful of dirt, sifted it through her fingers, knowing that come winter, when the heat and creepy crawlies had eased, she would return here — a stronger woman — and tend their graves. She would clean headstones, clear vines, rake leaves, haul limbs, and not fall into the quick mud. She would whisper prayers. Flowers would grow.

Feeling a twinge of the magic that blooms when words and narratives couple, Clarissa said, "God bless this place; God bless these women."

The brown-haired woman, raising her scarred arms above her head, said, "A benediction! Ain't no one ever said that over us."

"Yeah, well, don't you start crying," Glorious Louise Johnston said, shaking her head as if she'd seen the woman break down once too often.

Clarissa started back to her truck, the dried grave mud flak-ing off as she walked, and the ghost women followed. Cornelia and Jessamine ran ahead — ghost children, like their living counterparts, ran whenever walking would do—and clambered into the truck bed.

"Get out of there right this second!" Jessamine's mother said.

"You leave this place and go out there?" Glorious jabbed her head in the direction of Tremble and Shout, "And a world of trouble gonna descend on you, child!"

The girls jumped down, and when no one was looking except for Cornelia, Jessamine stuck her tongue out at her mother. The two girls giggled and shoved each other. The ghost women circled Clarissa's truck, and despite Glorious's admonition, the brown-haired woman began to weep.

Clarissa, thinking it was the dried mud that was keeping the mosquitoes away, got in the cab, her mind clearer than it had been in months. She turned the key. The engine sputtered, coughed, died. It didn't faze her. She did not panic. Nothing bad had happened to her out here. She had survived the quick mud, discovered a killing field, and had finally found something to write about. She tried again. The truck rumbled to life. Clarissa headed back down the path that led to sunshine.

The ghost women gathered in a knot in the clearing where they had been buried without ceremony or kind words and watched her leave. When they could no longer see her, they laced their arms, raised their faces to the dappled light, and became, once more, a gust of wind.

Back on Tremble and Shout, Clarissa headed north. She tried to remember where she had buried the bird but could not find it. This unsettled her, because she thought that surely a person should be able to remember where she had buried an animal— mercy killing or no—just an hour prior. As the distance between her and Poor Spot Cemetery grew, she thought that the road seemed less ominous now that she was returning to some semblance of civilization. When she passed the depot, she honked.

Sweet Trash Man! If he could only see her now, mud-covered, that gleam in his eyes might not sparkle quite so brightly.

Just as she whipped by a patch of swamp turnips whose trumpet-throated blossoms had been snuffed out by summer's heat, Clarissa spied an obstruction in the road. At first she thought it might be a mirage, but she couldn't take the chance. If it was a fallen tree and she hit it, she could flip the truck and end up drinking swamp water until something came along and turned her into dinner. She slowed down and thought, Gator? She checked her cell phone: still no signal.

As she drew nearer, the watery mirage froze, pixel by pixel, into something definite and real. When she was within twenty feet, she identified what lay ahead, and because humans are by design pre-disposed to at least two things—avoidance of pain, and survival—her heart beat faster. A rattler, maybe five feet long, was stretched out on the asphalt, a deadly ribbon absorbing the solstice heat.

Lucky for you, Mr. Snake, Clarissa thought, that I'm the person who has happened upon you; most anyone else would run you over—back and forth, back and forth, back and forth—as if overkill were a necessary component in roadkill.

Clarissa laid on her horn. Nothing happened. The horn, evidently, had lost its honk. She tried again. A spark sizzled like a shooting star up from the steering column, followed by the faint smell of burning wires, but still, no horn. This is not a truck; it's a disaster waiting for an accident, Clarissa thought.

The snake appeared content, as if sunning itself in the middle of a road were a rational act. Being a Florida native and having grown up in the subtropics before most of it was paved over, Clarissa was schooled in the ways of rattlers, gators, black widows, mosquitoes, and other creatures that if given half a chance could kill you or at least drive you mad. She did not want to get out of the truck. Snakes could strike half their body length (that knowledge — along with understanding that freshwater was mainly for fishing, not swimming, unless you were an alligator or water moccasin — was conferred on a certain generation of Floridian at birth), and given the fact that the snake would not tolerate her measuring distance, length, or trajectory, the cab was a safe space. She could try to drive around it but feared the moving vehicle would startle the reptile, causing it to slither directly under her rear tires. Maybe if she inched up, the snake would get the drift and mosey on. She slowly rolled forward.

He was a beautiful creature, with scales that glinted like tiny bits of polished granite; there was something archetypal about his form, something ancient and dangerous that made her afraid even in the midst of being awestruck. The front of the truck was within a foot of the snake, but he did not move. Maybe he's dead, Clarissa thought. As if reading her mind, he flicked his tongue.

She rolled down her car window and yelled, "Go! You're going to get killed out here." Nothing. And then she remembered that snakes, in addition to being stubborn, were more attuned to vibrations than to any sound that might trip the hidden cochlear chambers of their earless souls. So, ignoring her self-preservation instinct, she got out of the truck and, with the door as her shield, stomped and hollered on Tremble and Shout, grateful that no one came upon her, because Clarissa was sensitive about what people thought and surely she appeared insane. As she flailed, the mud from the graves fell in chunks and flakes, forming tiny dunes of funereal dirt at her feet. The snake ignored her.

"Hey, lady, what do you think you're doing?"

Clarissa spun around, and a voice in her head — which one, she didn't know — said, "Never turn your back on a snake."

A little towheaded, sunburned boy ambled down the road at the edge of a lily pond. He carried a long stick known by locals as a snake stick, named for what it was supposed to keep at bay. He carried a canvas bag over his shoulder; its strap ran at a diagonal across his chest. "You messing with my snake?"

"Your snake?" Clarissa shaded her eyes and saw that the boy was barefoot. "It's a rattler. Very poisonous. You need to stay where you—"

"Bubba, no! Lady, get in your truck." The little boy ran forward, waving the stick.

Unaccustomed to taking orders from a child, but sensing this one knew what he was talking about, Clarissa scrambled back into the cab just as the snake struck the front bumper. Her ovarian shadow women screamed. She thought one of them shouted, "Holy shit!"

"Bubba, stop that right this second or I ain't gonna give you any supper tonight!"

Clarissa saw something move in his canvas tote. Supper indeed. She craned her neck but could no longer see the snake. With her luck, the venomous reptile would find his way into a heretofore undiscovered hole in the floorboard.

"Now look at what you gone and done. Scared the pee out of the lady."

The snake slithered into view, undulating across the road, toward the swamp on the far side. He blinked his little slit eyes. Or was that a wink? Clarissa rolled down the window.

"Little boy, that snake can kill you. You need to stay where you are."

The child waved his stick at Clarissa. "That's my pet, lady. You're really lucky you didn't run him over."

"Children should not have pet rattlesnakes. Do your parents know?"

"Mind your own business, lady. Besides, my daddy give him to me."

"But..." Clarissa started to protest the entire idea of a pet viper but looked at the boy's obstinate, button-nosed face and realized she was in way over her head.

"Come on, Bubba, let's go home," he said. "Good thing I found you. No telling what that lady might have done if I hadn't come along." He turned his back to Clarissa, paused, looked over his shoulder, and said, "Lady, you need to be more careful. You got no idea what my daddy woulda done to you if you'd killed Bubba." The little boy spit once as if to reveal the depth of his disgust and then headed back in the direction he'd come from. The snake, sliding along in the low weeds near the road, trailed behind him—his motility fueled by what appeared to be magic.

Clarissa wiped her forehead with the back of her hand. Grave dirt smudged her face, and more of it swirled through the air, dusting the seat and floor. She carried the scent of the two dead girls but did not know this. And thanks to not having a rearview mirror, she had no idea how bonkers she truly appeared. She stuck her head out the window and watched the little boy grow smaller and smaller as he headed away from her. The snake was no longer visible. A truck zoomed up behind her. Its driver honked at the little boy, who waved in response. Clarissa was a sitting duck. She pushed her hazard lights button, but nothing happened.

The driver, a young, heavyset woman with her brunette hair pulled into a tight ponytail, slowed down, eased alongside Clarissa, and asked, "You okay?"

"Yes, I'm fine. I just stopped because a rattlesnake was on the road."

"Oh, yeah, that was Bubba." She rolled her eyes as if to say, "Snakes, what are you gonna do!" The girl looked in her rearview mirror—an act that Clarissa envied—said, "You have a good day," waved a hand adorned with glue-on nails painted what Clarissa considered to be screamin' eagle orange, and then drove on.

Clarissa put the truck in drive. *"Bubba, the Pet Rattlesnake,"* she said. "A children's story by Clarissa Burden." She stepped on the gas, intrigued and energized by the strange little swamp boy. The snake had actually tried to bite her. This observation made her feel wildly alive. So did surviving the quick mud. As she barreled down the road, she mused that perhaps life lived dangerously was the key to true happiness.

In the distance, she spied a cell tower. She checked her phone; she had juice but no messages. She wanted to talk to Iggy, wanted to let him know she was safe and ask what he was up to. She had, after all, taken the truck even though he had warned her that it was unsafe.

The phone trilled four times before he picked up. She heard a woman laughing in the background and people chatting.

"Yes, Clarissa?" He sounded annoyed. No, worse. His inflection dripped with boredom.

She thought about hanging up but couldn't. She'd catch hell later for something like that. So she plunged on, feeling stupid, hapless, powerless. "Hey!" She tried to sound casual. "I'm just calling to say hey."

"I'm busy." His voice was flat. In her mind, she flashed on her mother yelling at her as she cowered in a corner of the trailer, "You're dead to me!"

Clarissa hit the end call button and tossed the phone on the seat. If he did give her hell later, demanding to know why she hung up on him, she'd deny it. "I didn't. I was in a dead zone," she'd say. She sped up and felt two things: angry that she didn't have the courage to tell him to fuck off and empowered that she'd hung up on his ass.

The truck still needed to be washed, but she was ravenous, so she elected to take herself to lunch at the Treetop General Store. At Treetop's, they wouldn't care how she was dressed, how much mud caked her jeans, or how badly she smelled. And their smoked mullet was to die for.

As she traveled north, the land became higher and drier; in ten minutes she had left the swamp and entered the forest. Here the world gleamed dark and bright like a bird whose flickering wings balanced sun and moon in wavering measure. The high, sandy plane was home to dwindling populations of foxes, bears, bobcats, pileated woodpeckers, redneck farmers, black farmers, and old hippies. The only things flourishing were the coyotes. Welcome to the twenty-first century, she mused, where most everything is a threatened species.

A murder of crows winged out of the forest, cast frenetic shadows across her path, and spiraled into the sweltering dome of the solstice sky. She sped past miles of robust habitat, the giant oaks towering over an understory of magnolia, dogwood, cabbage palm, and loblolly pine, which in turn created a shelter for blackberry, deerberry, bracken fern, and more. Ten minutes in and the forest's dense complexity was replaced by the rigid geometry of a pulp farm: pine trees planted in regimental rows that supported no understory to speak of.

But the pulp pines, destined to become toilet paper, were in trouble. The columns of skinny, vertical trunks topped with exploding green fans were interrupted by large stands of dead trees, their remaining needles resembling rusted bones scratching news of their demise into the wide plank of the bleached sky. An infestation of pine beetles threatened huge swaths of the piney woods.

She slid her sweating palms along the circumference of the steering wheel. Everything is dying, she thought.

Ahead, someone driving a late-model camouflaged green Ford pickup pulled out of a side road and then crawled along, well below the speed limit. In under a minute, Clarissa was just yards behind the old man, who seemed content to mosey. Even though his speedometer probably worked and hers didn't, she—brimming with what the old man would most likely call the arrogance of youth—felt she had a better grasp on what constituted a safe speed. She hit the gas and zoomed past.

The dying pulp pines and her increased speed dragging against the old man's crawl served no purpose other than to pull her, as if by the hands of a petulant god, back into the morass of her marriage. In the swirl of motion, color, wind, and light, the recognition— while not new—that her marriage hung by a single tendril spun of stubbornness and fear kicked her in the spine. She tightened her grip on the steering wheel and bore down on the tough nut of her marriage. Their union had not always been fragile. Spousal death scenarios had not always hounded her conscious and unconscious thoughts. He had not always clung to the opposite side of the bed as if intimacy with her would give him smallpox.

She squinted into the heat-quivering distance and tried to focus on other issues, other ideas, other planets. Before she could chew hard on anything new, the Treetop General Store rose out of the heat, shimmering, distant, and real. She slowed, put on her blinker, but nothing happened (Jesus, this truck is falling apart before my eyes, she thought), waited for two cars in the oncoming lane to pass, wondered where Adams was and if she should call him. If she went tonight, what should she wear? She sat there, blinkerless, flipping through her mental closet: blue jeans, flouncy skirt, skinny black dress. She was just about to inventory her shoes when her meanderings were shattered by the cacophony of a honking horn and screeching brakes. The light inside and outside the truck shifted. She jerked her head to see what was happening, but of course, there was no rearview. She heard a *whoosh*—her heart pounded; she instinctively wanted to jerk the truck out of harm's way but had no idea what direction that would be. A commotion popped, definite and loud, on her passenger side. The old man in the Ford was on the shoulder, passing her. His full-moon eyes snapped with fear, anger.

"Get some brake lights!" he yelled.

She watched him rumble back onto the highway. She shouted, "I'm sorry!"

He stuck his gnarled hand out the window and flipped her off.

"Old fool!" Clarissa said, fully aware that the man had a right to be angry. Hands shaking, she pulled into Treetop's oyster-shell drive and parked beside a truck that had a FORGET HELL bumper sticker and a rear window vinyl graphic of a rebel flag. Jerk. Clarissa always appreciated assholes that loudly announced said affliction. A fully dressed Harley gleamed in the space nearest the door. She sat in her truck, in the record-breaking heat, trying to calm down. After damning herself for nearly getting hit, she damned her husband for a host of violations. Did she have to do everything? Cook, clean, earn their living, and get the truck fixed? Maybe she should take matters into her own hands and drive this piece of junk into a lake. Lake Reform. And then run away with Trash Man. Ha!

She looked at the signs plastered willy-nilly on the outside of the building. It didn't take much to know what Treetop sold. In addition to being part hardware store, part grocery store, customers could buy Skoal, ice cold beer, boiled peanuts, Sopchoppy night crawlers, fried oyster po'boys, and, of course, smoked mullet.

From the moment Clarissa stepped foot into Treetop's five months prior, she loved the store and its owner, the cocoa-skinned, sweetly freckled Miss Lossie. The authenticity of the place, the no-frills goodness of it all, helped her feel grounded, which, considering the precarious nature of her personal life, was needed. And right now, having fallen into quick mud, survived a rattlesnake, and almost been rear-ended by an angry old man who was probably legally blind, she was more than happy to be here.

Clarissa reached for the door handle. It came off in her hand. She tossed it on the floor and opened the door by unlatching it from the outside. She barely even cared. As she slid out of the truck and made her way toward the door, she clicked through a mental list of everything she knew about Miss Lossie. Her great-grandparents had been slaves on a cotton plantation just north of where the store stood. She claimed to be eighty-four years old but looked to be in her sixties. She was a wife (her husband was by all accounts still spry, but Clarissa had never laid eyes on him) and mother of ten (Clarissa had met her two youngest) and was taking an online real estate course. She said she didn't want to become a Realtor, she simply wanted to know how to outfox them.

Feeling better but hungry and needing to wash up, Clarissa first wound her way out back where there was a spigot and hose, an outdoor restroom, and three picnic tables. Four teenage boys, one with a Mohawk and the rest with crew cuts, ate sandwiches at the table shaded by a lone oak. They passed a brown bag–wrapped bottle. Miss Lossie sold beer and wine but not liquor. And she'd never sell alcohol to minors.

"What are you looking at, sweetmeat?" Mohawk asked. His cohorts laughed as if he were the wittiest fool on the planet.

Clarissa ignored them. Drunken males in groups scared her. She turned on the spigot and took the hose around the corner so they couldn't see her.

"Watch out," one of them yelled, "we might just come over there and get you."

"Yeah. Fuck you like you ain't never been fucked before." Their laughter battered the sky.

"Jackasses," Clarissa whispered. She ran the water over her hair and rinsed out the grave dirt. The water ran down her T-shirt, soaking it. She washed her arms, sprayed her tennis shoes, and then took a long drink out of the hose. A wasp dive-bombed her. She batted it away, tried to wring out her T-shirt, and walked again to the back of the store.

The boy sitting beside Mohawk chugged the bottle. Mohawk slapped his back, causing the kid to snort liquor out of his nose. As Clarissa bent to turn off the faucet, the boys whooped and hollered as if they'd never laid eyes on a female before. The shortest of the four threw the bottle into the parking lot. Mohawk already was passing another one. The scrawniest of the four pulled a blue plastic cooler from under the table, opened it, pulled out a pick, and began chiseling away at a block of ice.

Chugger stood up, grabbed his crotch, and yelled, "You want some of this, baby?"

"You'd have to grow up first," Clarissa said, trying to hide how addled she was.

"Bitch!"

Clarissa, having already had one hellacious, albeit fascinating, day, was in no mood. She spun around. "What did you say?"

"Bitch." Unsteady on his legs, he curled his lip and sneered. She thought the little idiot might puke at any moment.

That was it. She was done with this group of twerps. Clarissa tossed her hair and planted her fists on her hips. "Number one, son, there are no bitches present. Number two, you kids don't even know how to drink, forget about being of age. Number three, there is no amount of desperation in the world that would allow me to let a single one of you lay even a finger on me, you with your stupid racist bullshit plastered on your truck. Grow up! And number four"—Clarissa sighed heavily; the heat ratcheted up her irritation—"I'm going to go inside and call the sheriff on your no-count, scrawny asses." Clarissa marched toward the door, her wet T-shirt clinging to places she did not want it to. But there was nothing she could do, no self-conscious tugs or readjustments; she would not let the punks see even the smallest crack in her facade. She walked, head high, letting the catcalls, epithets, and jeers bounce off her like foam balls. Right as she passed the WE RENT VIDEOS sign, she tripped on the uneven concrete walk that lined the side of the building. She caught herself before she fell, but it was a definite win for the Punk Brothers.

"Have a nice trip?" Mohawk cackled.

"Come back next fall!" Chugger chimed in.

They laughed, and she could hear them high-fiving. Little no-brained, fat-necked cretins.

She grabbed the door that was adorned with a WE SHOOT FIRST AND ASK QUESTIONS LATER sticker, threw it open, stepped inside, was hit with a wall of cold air, and said, "Oh, my God, it feels good in here." She stood stock-still for a moment, letting her body sink into the cool temperature. "Like a different world."

Miss Lossie looked up from the TV that blared full-tilt the *People's Court* theme song. "Goodness gracious, will you look who it is! I thought somebody done stole you!" She hit the mute button, rose to her feet, walked with the wide stride of a man even though she was only five feet two, came out from behind the counter, and started to hug Clarissa but stopped. She crinkled her eyes and took two steps back. "Oh my."

"I know, I know, I stink."

She waved her hand in front of her nose. "You got that right. What on earth have you been doing, child?"

"Well," she said, pulling her T-shirt away from her curves and hollows, trying to think of a reason not to tell Miss Lossie everything but not finding one, "my husband has been using my truck as a trash can. I've told him to stop, but he ignores me. No matter how many times I've asked him to at least take the trash to the dump, he refuses. And no matter how many times I've asked him to fix something, anything, on the truck, he acts like he doesn't hear me. The thing is falling apart. I mean a-p-a-r-t! No mirrors, no gas gauge, no speedometer, no brake lights—I almost got killed out there thanks to the brake lights—no nothing. So I just decided that at the very least, I could clear out the trash my own self." She brushed her palms together as if wiping them clean. Wow, it felt good to unload. Dangerous and damn good.

Miss Lossie shook her head as though she knew intimately what Clarissa was going though. "You know what I say?" She had a pencil behind her ear, and Clarissa thought it made her look oddly coquettish.

"What?"

"You need to tell that husband of yours to get his ass in gear or find himself someplace else to stay. Look at you! You smell like you been living in the Dumpster." Miss Lossie fiddled with the belt that circled her tiny waist. She wore a pretty red cotton dress, buttons down the front, and white tennis shoes. "That was you that almost got hit out there? You running with no brake lights! What's that man going to do without you, you get laid up or killed?"

"I know, I know. You're right." Clarissa shook her head, feeling comforted by Miss Lossie's solidarity and guilty over talking like this about her husband.

"You bet I'm right." Miss Lossie sauntered back around the counter. "You'd best be taking control of some things. If he won't do it, find yourself somebody new. You ain't bad-looking. A pretty little thing like you!" Her face wandered from defiant to mischievous. "At least when you ain't been wallowing in the trash bin!" And then she proceeded to have a good laugh at Clarissa's expense.

Near the front of the store, a man dressed in white fishing boots, yellow shorts, and nothing else save for the sunglasses perched atop his head, laughed, too. He was tall and thin, wide-shouldered and long-armed, and was sifting through a pile of fishing lures. Even from where Clarissa stood she saw that the man, who was both tanned and burned, sported a silver-veined goatee and his shorts that hung low on his hips were staying put only through the power of prayer. She figured him to be around the same age as her husband, except he, from her vantage point near the register, appeared hard-bodied. Iggy, on the best of days, was soft in all the wrong places. A flutter rose and fell in her stomach. She dismissed it as sun poisoning. A dust bunny with a tiny spider trapped in it rolled like tumbleweed down the candy aisle.

"Oh, listen," Clarissa said, turning her attention back to Miss Lossie, "did you know those boys are drinking?"

Miss Lossie's eyes flashed. She snapped her head toward the door. "They're doing what! I warned them about that!" She marched over to the back wall, grabbed a broom that was tilted against a nonworking jukebox, and headed outside.

"Be careful, Miss Lossie. They're kinda mean and have been drinking a lot, and I made them mad."

"I'll show them mad," the little woman said as she stormed into the heat.

Clarissa started to follow her, but in a thick, north Florida drawl, the near naked fisherman said, "She can handle it. You'll just get in the way."

"But—"

"No but," he interrupted. "They will not mess with her." He held a lure up to the sun-filtered shadows and studied it. "You, on the other hand..."

Clarissa rolled her eyes, bit her tongue. Arrogant oaf, she thought. Know-it-all man. She sidled up to the door but for some reason heeded his words. From within the store's confines, she listened to the goings-on in the parking lot, fully prepared to run out and help if assistance was needed. Miss Lossie was so loud, Clarissa heard her every word.

"Jason! Bobbie! Eric Lee! Tommy Lee! Clean this mess up this very minute and do not come back here. If you do, I'm calling the sheriff and then I'm calling your daddies! But first I'm gonna beat you with this broom. Now get!"

The boys responded sheepishly in a jumbled chorus: "Sorry..." Surprised at their sudden compliance, Clarissa wondered why she had commanded such little respect from the two-pint punks.

Miss Lossie marched back in, wielding the broom. "Little devils. They think they're so tough, but you blow on them hard and they near about start crying." She tilted the broom back against the jukebox. "Good God, it's hot out there!"

"Sure is." Clarissa, feeling herself settling in, took a seat at the counter. "They say it's a record setter."

Miss Lossie nodded toward the window on the east wall. "One oh four according to the gauge. That's heatstroke weather."

"What did they do before air-conditioning?"

"Nobody complained because there wasn't anything we could do." She shrugged. "See, luxury makes us weak."

"I suppose that's true," Clarissa said. "But I'm still grateful for it."

"You and me both." Miss Lossie moved a thick book—*Florida Land Statutes*—from beside the TV to a desk under the east-facing window.

Clarissa's stomach growled.

"Sounds like you need to eat."

"Yes, ma'am." She watched as Miss Lossie slipped a bookmark on a page that had been dog-eared. "Any smoked mullet today?"

"For you, I sure do. Chester, you okay up there while I go get her a plate?"

"Take your time."

Miss Lossie disappeared through the swinging door into the kitchen. Clarissa helped herself to an RC out of the cooler and a bag of boiled peanuts. She was starving. She popped open three peanuts, sucked down their salty juice, and watched a commercial about a topical cream that could help ameliorate the ravages of feminine itch. Clarissa was mortified; she stole a look at the fisherman at the front of the store. Nope, he was immersed in lures. Thank God the sound was off.

Miss Lossie returned with a paper plate stacked high with smoked mullet. "Here you go, honey. And I put some coleslaw on there for you, too."

"Thank you so much. This looks fabulous." She pulled mullet meat off the bone with her fingers. "Mmmm, yummy." Strong notes of salt, hickory, and cayenne blossomed on her tongue. She reached for her drink. "Do you smoke the fish yourself?"

"Goodness, no. Mr. Strawder does it. He loves smoked anything. The man would smoke his britches if I'd let him." She retrieved a plastic pitcher from the end of the counter and poured herself a glass of iced tea. Clarissa was charmed by the fact that Miss Lossie always referred to her husband as Mr. Strawder, and she wondered if she called him that always, even in private, even when they were young lovers.

As Clarissa ate, her eyes drifted over the store's ephemera. She didn't have use for any of this stuff: moleskins, washboards, Jell-O molds. She remembered the "aspic" her mother made — red Jell-O with peas and carrots suspended like spiders in amber. She shivered; her mother had been a god-awful cook (mac and cheese baked in grapefruit juice) with the exception of her blackberry cobbler. It was Clarissa's favorite dish bar none. She'd spent her childhood wishing it were the only thing her mother cooked and her adulthood unsuccessfully re-creating it.

"What's that?" Clarissa pointed above the door leading to the kitchen, where what she surmised to be a four-foot-long length of wood hung in the curved grip of two rings, one end whittled to such a fine point that it reminded Clarissa of a vampire stake.

Miss Lossie followed the line of Clarissa's finger. "That old thing? That, my dear, is a worm-gruntin' stob."

"A what?"

"You know," Miss Lossie said, a hint of impatience creeping into her voice, "for gruntin' worms."

"Worm grunting?" Clarissa wanted to laugh, but Miss Lossie's brown eyes had turned a shade deeper, indicating this was serious business. "Is that anything like snake charming?" Bubba's owner's defiant little face gathered in her mind's eye.

The fisherman, still rifling through lures, his shorts still riding perilously low on his hips, snorted.

"Actually, it's close," Miss Lossie said. She moved aside a stack of random papers, cocked her head, looked at Clarissa as if she were sizing up whether the mullet eater sitting before her could possibly understand the intricacies involved in an activity as nuanced as worm grunting.

"Okay." Clarissa wiped her hands on a paper napkin. "The stob. What do you do with it?"

"Pound it into the ground," Miss Lossie said as if that were the stupidest question she'd ever heard, and then she demonstrated the proper movement, "so the worms wiggle up. But the stob has to be from a dependable tree. Black gum, tupelo. Like that." She held up her arms as if she were reaching for something. "It's got to feel good in the hand. That's primary. And it can't break on you, because you get hold of your iron—not the kind you use on clothes, but the kind that you can get a decent grip on—and you take that hunk of metal and you pound the stob into the ground." Bent at the waist, she made a pounding motion. "You follow? And then you glide that iron across the stob just as if it were a fine-haired bow and the stob were the sweetest fiddle."

Clarissa paused from shelling a peanut. "It makes music?"

"Prettiest music you ever did hear," the fisherman offered.

"No, not really," Miss Lossie said, batting down his comment.

"It does make a pretty, low-seated grunt that falls just short of a moan. But the worms can't hear, so that's not what gets them."

Clarissa brought the peanut and its shell, brimming with brine, to her lips. "What does?"

"The vibrations radiating underground," the fisherman said.

"Yes, sir."

"Really!"

Miss Lossie looked around. "I had an iron around here somewhere. Mr. Strawder must have taken it. You bang the stob into the ground and then you start playing it, as I said, like the sweetest fiddle — actually it sounds like an old, gassy donkey named Sarah Mr. Strawder and I once had — and next thing you know, up they come — hundreds, if you're living right — of the fattest earthworms you ever did see."

"Ew!" Clarissa pushed back her plate.

From the lure section, the fisherman said, "There ain't no 'ew' about it."

"That's right," Miss Lossie said.

The man walked down the canned goods aisle toward the counter, apparently at ease with the state of his shorts, three freshwater lures dangling from his thick fingers. Clarissa was dying to ask why he was buying fake lures when there were probably free earthworms right outside the door, but she didn't want to sidetrack the conversation. His face was sunburned everywhere but around his eyes — a cracker tan, some people called it, acquired by wearing sunglasses and little else. Clarissa had to gulp down a giggle. She saw him as her superhero's partner: Cracker Bandit!

He looked at Clarissa with the same skepticism exhibited by Miss Lossie. His left eye was milky white, the right cornflower blue. So, she mused, he's a one-eyed Cracker Bandit. Even better. "Do you know who you're talking to?"

Taken aback, unappreciative of his rude manners, Clarissa said, "Well, no, I don't believe we've ever met."

"Not us!" he said, adding several vowels to each word. His blue eye sparkled. His white one just sat there.

"Chester Maines, don't tell her all that," Miss Lossie said.

"I certainly will," Cracker Bandit said. "Take a look over there"—he pointed to the far wall—"at that photograph."

Clarissa eased off the stool, almost knocked over a life-size cutout of a racecar driver holding a can of Skoal, and examined the black-and-white image. "Oh, my gosh!" she moved in closer. "Is that you, Miss Lossie?"

"I'm afraid so." She sighed and shut her eyes as if she simply couldn't bear the weight of the past.

"What year?"

"Nineteen sixty-nine," Cracker Bandit said with such surety that it led Clarissa to believe that he had memorized all sorts of Miss Lossie trivia. "I give you Lossie Strawder, the 1969 Worm Grunting Queen."

"With a sash and flowers and everything," Clarissa said, studying the photo, lingering over the details: the old porch of a wood-frame shotgun house and Miss Lossie, who was wearing a pretty floral dress, sitting in a regal bent-willow rocking chair, her tiara askew. "Where's the king?"

"No king—although if there had been one, it would have to have been Mr. Strawder, but he is not the kind to go in for such foolishness. And the only reason it was me—"

"Six years in a row!" Cracker Bandit crowed.

"—is because no one else would do it."

"'Sopchoppy Worm Gruntin' Queen,'" Clarissa read the banner in the photo. "Sopchoppy?"

Cracker Bandit held his free hand to his forehead. His shorts slipped a hair lower. Dear God, no, thought Clarissa.

"You don't know Sopchoppy?"

Miss Lossie said, "She's from south Florida."

"Where at?"

"Don't know. One of those little orange grove towns, I think."

"Clewiston? I did some bass fishing down there last year."

"I don't think it was that far south."

"Hmpf," he said. He had a handsome face: chiseled, strong, and full of interesting lines. Clarissa wondered why they were speaking as if she weren't present.

"Sopchoppy," Cracker Bandit said, returning to the topic and adopting a professorial air, which was impressive given the state of his dress and sunburn, "is"—he drew an imaginary circle on the counter and tapped its equatorial midpoint—"the center of the universe."

"The worm-gruntin' universe," Miss Lossie said with a little giggle, her eyes merry.

"It used to be a doggone honorable profession. That is until that TV man..." Cracker Bandit snapped his fingers, apparently searching for the name.

"Kuralt." Miss Lossie spit the word.

"That's right. Charlie Kuralt. Well, everybody down there in Sopchoppy—"

Miss Lossie interrupted. "It's thirty-five miles southwest of Tallahassee on the Sopchoppy River in the middle of the prettiest forest you ever did see, except for the parts the paper company timbers."

"Her people are from there," Cracker Bandit said, helping himself to some of Clarissa's boiled peanuts.

"Actually, my distant people are from around here. After Emancipation, my great-grandparents slinked off into the woods over there a ways in Sopchoppy."

"Anyway," Cracker Bandit said, tossing back some peanuts, "at one time, all of Sopchoppy's finest people were worm grunters. Black, white, Choctaw." He stared into the distance, his jaw hard set, a peanut shell lodged between his teeth, as if he were remembering. The way he said "worm grunter" reminded Clarissa of the way an East Indian woman she'd gone to graduate school with said "fire-eater" and "rat temple keeper," as if they were sacred vocations.

"Okay," Clarissa said, trying to steer the discussion back three feet, "but what about Kuralt?"

Miss Lossie threw up her hands in disgust. "Oh, that man!"

"Ah, Kuralt! Well, he blows into town with his cameras and all and does this little piece for television about the worm grunters, about how you can walk to the ends of the universe and never find another community of them—how it's rare and honest work and all that." Cracker Bandit picked a wet shell out from between his teeth. "Well, hell, next thing you know, the poor, honest salt of their grandmamas' earth, never-bothered-nobody worm grunters had the tax man pounding on their doors."

"And those state regulators." Miss Lossie worked her lips back and forth. "Awful! They put us out of business. Like we were nothing but you know what on the bottom of their shoes. Sure, you can still make a dime here and there on your worms, but the government is going to take nine cents of it. And by the time you fill out all their paperwork, you're best off keeping your fanny on the couch."

Cracker Bandit shook his head as if it were a crying shame. "One cent outta ten. It ain't worth it." He shot Clarissa a dead-eyed stare. "You think?"

"No, no, doesn't sound worth it at all," Clarissa said, the writer in her wishing she had a tape recorder, but as it was she was simply going to have to rely on memory, clinging to every single last morsel of this conversation as if she were a starving woman and words were manna. "But I still don't understand," she said, picking on the mullet's backbone. "What's the big deal about these worms?"

"The big deal!" Cracker Bandit appeared stunned, his mouth agape, and Clarissa felt herself bristle at what she took to be his physical inference that she was ignorant. She really wished he would pull up his pants.

"Now, Chester, you can't expect everybody to know. She hasn't lived here a year yet." She turned to Clarissa. "Have you?"

"No, ma'am."

"Well, let me tell you." She pulled the pencil from behind her ear and pointed it at Clarissa. "The big deal is the Sopchoppy worms are like no other in the world. Are they?" She looked at Cracker Bandit.

"Ma'am . . ." He gestured at Clarissa as if he were about to try to reason with her. "May I call you ma'am?"

Clarissa dead-eyed him back. She was beginning to want the scoop without the nuts.

Cracker Bandit spoke slowly, to add gravity to his knowledge, Clarissa supposed. "Them *Diplocardia mississippiensis* earthworms, otherwise known as Sopchoppy wigglers, are the finest worms on God's green earth." He blinked for emphasis, and this time his milky eye wobbled as if it were focusing on worlds only he could see.

"Because, among other things," Miss Lossie said, tossing aside the pencil—Clarissa heard it roll—"they have twelve hearts. Count them. Not nine. Not ten. But twelve." She leaned across the knotted pine counter and whispered, her eyes twinkling with the knowledge of saints, "Twelve hearts so small only an angel can dance upon them."

"Twelve hearts?" Clarissa felt a twinge of wonder.

"Twelve tiny hearts, all just a-beating like crazy."

Miss Lossie's eyes filmed over with twin tears. Clarissa felt her own eyes do likewise. She had no idea why she found the notion of an earthworm with twelve hearts so moving, and if she'd been clairvoyant, she would have known that Miss Lossie didn't understand it, either.

Tossing the lures on the counter, Cracker Bandit said, clearly thrilled to have such a receptive audience, "You cannot buy a better worm."

"'Cause God don't grow no better worm," Miss Lossie said. "I don't have my glasses on. Are those the lures on sale?"

"One is, two ain't."

She twisted her lips as she thought. "Oh, heck, just give me six dollars."

"They're fat," he said, aiming his good eye at Clarissa. "The worms, that is."

Clarissa knew from the beatific look on his face that he was imagining one right then and there.

"Ruler long and finger fat," said Miss Lossie. "Gotta be with all them hearts."

"I'm telling you," Cracker Bandit said, pulling his wallet out of his back pocket, which helped ease the falling shorts situation, "they are the sumo wrestlers of the worm world. Biggest suckers, pardon my language, ma'am, that you will ever see."

He moved closer to Clarissa, apparently oblivious to how badly she stank, and winked his blue eye, which caused Clarissa both delight and alarm; she'd never been winked at by so many men in one day in all her life, and never by a one-eyed man. His voice turned warm, steamy, his words inflating with vowels that curled and plumped. "They've got themselves one hardy constitution."

"You got that right." Miss Lossie sounded like a backup chorus.

"The sun don't faze them."

"The heat don't faze them."

"Drought barely fazes them."

"This man knows what he's talking about!"

"They behave," Cracker Bandit said, his face gleaming like a slick cherry, "the way you *want* a worm to behave in the water." He nodded in agreement with himself.

Clarissa looked at Miss Lossie, who was nodding, too, and then back at Cracker Bandit.

The only thing Clarissa hated more than feeling stupid was looking stupid. But by now she was invested in these worms. "And how is that?"

Miss Lossie gasped. Evidently, even she was finally startled at Clarissa's low worm IQ. Giving each word equal weight, she intoned, "As if they have some pep."

"Yes!" Cracker Bandit said. "Thank you! Thank you! That's exactly it!" He slapped the counter.

Miss Lossie looked from Cracker Bandit to Clarissa and rubbed her eyes with arthritic fingers. "I have no idea why more people don't know about them."

"You know what the most beautiful thing about gruntin' is?" Cracker Bandit looked into the distance, the one filled with Ace bandages, wart remover, and hemorrhoid creams. Without waiting for them to answer, he said, "Go out there in the forest near Sopchoppy just around daybreak, when all is quiet in the world, and do yourself some gruntin' and then fall still." He cast his gaze directly upon Clarissa. "Know what you'll hear?"

Mesmerized, Clarissa shook her head no.

"Hundreds of worms rising up through the earth, outta the darkness, into the dawn, and then their pearly, pale bodies moving through the reeds, the grasses, the wildflowers." He paused and smiled at Clarissa, clarion and calm. "Ain't no wonder Darwin called them the most important critter in the history of the world. Everything depends on them: their rising and falling and aerating and pooping."

"Wow." Clarissa had never known that a person could get so worked up over a worm. "I want to go one day."

Cracker Bandit dropped his professorial-bleeding-into-evangelical facade and said smooth and slick, "Well, I'll be happy to take you, little lady. You just say when."

"Stop that, Chester." Miss Lossie wagged a finger at him. "She is a married woman. For now, anyway."

"Miss Lossie!"

The two women started laughing. Cracker Bandit shook his head in that way men have when utterly confounded by the opposite sex. He paid Miss Lossie with six crisp one-dollar bills, said, "Thank you, Miss Lossie. A pleasure as always," tucked his wallet back into his shorts—an action that caused them to edge south again—pulled his shades down over his eyes, and headed for the door, his white fishing boots squeaking as he went. Before disappearing into the sweltering heat, he paused, the sunlight cradling him in a head-to-toe corolla, and said, "April. Next year. You and me, little lady, at the Worm Gruntin' Festival."

Clarissa laughed. "Sure thing," she said. He headed out, and she took a long swig of her RC, embarrassed that she felt flushed from the attention. She was still drinking when Cracker Bandit stuck his head back in the store and asked, "That your Dodge sitting out here?"

She set down the RC. "I know; it needs a good washing. That's where I'm headed next."

"I don't think you'll be heading anywhere." He held the door wide and swept one arm to welcome her hither.

"Chester, what on earth!" Miss Lossie said, shuttling Clarissa outside.

The heat hit Clarissa as if it were an entity, solid, angry, evil. It took her breath away. She looked at the truck; nothing registered.

Miss Lossie said, "Lord God, them boys done ice-picked your tires."

Clarissa's stomach lurched; she felt the old, familiar acidic tide of panic begin to surge. She walked the circumference of the truck. Each tire was as flat as an old cow's tit. Freaking, fucking A. And forget four spares; she didn't own even one. She reached into her jeans pocket for her phone and then stopped: No, I will not call my husband. *I told you not to drive that thing! How come you're so fowking stupid!* She could hear his voice, spreading like mustard gas, coating the concave surface of her skull. The brake lights, the mirrors, the fuel gauge, the hazards, the blinkers, the door handle, and now this: four slashed tires. Freaking, fucking A indeed! She felt the muscles that tied her spine to her brain and belly curl and tighten. Her cells had turned into corpuscular vise grips. She kicked the tailgate; its rusted hinge gave way, and the gate fell off, landing by her feet on the oyster-shell drive. A tiny cloud of dust mushroomed.

Miss Lossie said, "Uh-oh."

Cracker Bandit adjusted his sunglasses and looked away.

Clarissa, not knowing what else to do, gave up. The entire situation with the truck was too absurd for anger or words. She started laughing, laughed so hard that she could not breathe. As she held her sides and doubled over, she wondered if suffocation were an option. *Here Lies Clarissa Burden, Who Died from Laughing.* And because unhinged laughter is, like yawning, infectious, Miss Lossie and Cracker Bandit began with a few tentative giggles and then roared at full boil.

"Lord God, I have no idea why we're laughing," Miss Lossie said between guffaws.

"Me neither!" Cracker Bandit chortled, his voice high and nasally with mirth.

"Because," Clarissa said, between hitch-kicking inhalations, "it's not like it was a flipping Ferrari." She wiped her eyes, and her words bubbled. "I think this piece-of-shit truck is finally done for. I should have just left it at the dump along with the rotten, festering garbage."

Cracker Bandit kicked one of the tires, his face crinkled with laughter, and said in a nonhelpful manly way, "Yep, I'd say these suckers are good and flat."

Like a song whose second verse no one could remember, amid the heat, their laughter slowly waned, until the three of them finally stood in silence, sweating, staring at the hobbled truck.

"Pitiful," Miss Lossie said, breaking the quiet.

"A damn shame." Cracker Bandit shook his head and closed his eyes, appearing to be all shook up, as if he had a personal relationship with the truck.

Clarissa gazed at the glimmering road, beyond words.

"Let's go inside out of this heat and call the sheriff," Miss Lossie said.

"We didn't actually see the boys do it." Clarissa picked up the tailgate and tossed it in the bed. It was surprisingly light. Piece of shit, she thought.

"Don't need to. Those boys been messing up all over the county. Sheriff's been wanting to nail them for a while."

Cracker Bandit opened the door. As they shuttled back into the store, the gravity of the situation bore down on Clarissa. "How am I even going to get home?" She knew she could kiss Adams's reading good-bye. And that her husband was going to have a grand time beating her up over this; it would be her fault, all her fault, because she was irresponsible and selfish and nonthinking. She could hear it now, even the way his Afrikaner vowels curled more thickly over his tongue when he got angry. But of greater concern was, How would she have any independence without wheels of her own? A death trap of a vehicle had been bad enough, but at least she knew if she really needed to get away from her husband and those naked women and his all-consuming disinterest, the truck would get her somewhere, if only to the closest gas station.

"Well," Miss Lossie said, getting three cold RCs out of the cooler and handing one each to Clarissa and Cracker Bandit, "let's just think on the bigger picture for a minute."

"I can take you home," Cracker Bandit said. "That's no problem. If you don't mind riding on the back of my Harley."

Fear tiptoed up Clarissa's spine. A one-eyed man on a Harley? She wanted to ask, "Isn't that like double-dipping into danger?"

"Hold on. I'm thinking." Miss Lossie held up her hand. She looked at Clarissa. "You got any money?"

"After I pay for lunch, maybe five dollars."

"I mean in the bank."

"I've got some in savings, but don't tell anybody." And then she thought she should explain that her husband spent pretty much every dime she made on antique maps of Africa that he kept in a safety deposit box, oil paints even though he worked in acrylics, limited-edition sneakers, French pornography (sex, she surmised, was a universal language), long-distance phone calls to someone in Europe whose name and gender he refused to reveal, three kilns—two of which he had never used—Tommy Hilfiger button-down shirts, a small batch of single-malt Scotch that he'd purchased from a broker in New York, real estate holdings (using her money, he had begun buying easements in hopes that he could flip them for exorbitant prices to developers), 1970s videocameras (he insisted their poor quality was perfect for his two-minute flicks), and an ever-mounting collection of military paraphernalia (medals awarded to some long-dead South African army general for a battle she could not pronounce was his latest acquisition), so in desperation she had started a secret account. Thus the need to hide her purse; it's where she kept the bankbook. But why tell them this? They didn't know her husband. And why the burst of guilt? She flexed her hands; a desire to wring the necks of those ice-pick-wielding juvenile delinquents rippled through her.

Miss Lossie picked up the phone and dialed. "How much you got?"

"How much what?" Clarissa was lost, tied as she was to the fantasy of strangling the four delinquents.

"Money, child, money."

"I don't know." Clarissa looked at Cracker Bandit, who put a sympathetic, long-fingered hand on her shoulder.

"Hello, Eva. This is Lossie Strawder."

Clarissa pulled away, walked over to the door—acutely aware that his warmth had left an invisible imprint on her skin—and peered out. Actually, she did know; she had eighteen thousand dollars in her secret account. But there was no salvaging that truck. She did not want to buy new tires. She did not want to be stuck with a reclamation project. She wasn't a grease monkey. Gears and pistons and the proper installation of rearview mirrors were absent from her gene pool. Why not do something proactive? Like burn the damn vehicle. She heard Miss Lossie exchange pleasantries with whoever this Eva was.

"Those Parker boys were up here at the store, acting the fool, and then they ice-picked one of my customer's cars," Miss Lossie said.

Clarissa turned around. Cracker Bandit held his palms up to the heavens, which Clarissa interpreted as his way of wringing his hands. "Like I said, I am more than happy to give you a lift home."

She had to fight an urge to scream something totally rude and obnoxious, such as "Getting home isn't the issue, asshole, even though I'm the jerk who brought it up!" But, electing prudence over irrationality, she simply ignored him and stared out the door into the blinding sunlight.

Miss Lossie tossed the phone on the counter. "The sheriff

will be here in a few minutes," she said. "Now, back to the real problem."

"The real problem is," Clarissa said, feeling the air go out of her just as if the boys had ice-picked her, "as crummy as that truck was, it was the one thing that let me pretend I had options." She slumped into an overstuffed brown armchair in the corner.

"What do you mean?" Cracker Bandit asked.

"I mean, having a car is important. It's..." Clarissa paused, watched a moth float over to a Dr Pepper sign. She didn't dare look at anyone. "Has either of you been to Poor Spot Cemetery?"

"There's no cemetery out there, child. Hasn't been for years."

How could she tell Miss Lossie that wasn't true? That it held the souls of women and children who'd suffered wrongs never rectified? "A car," she started again, "is freedom. You know? How do you get away if you don't have wheels?"

"What kind of credit you got?" Cracker Bandit positioned his sunglasses back on top of his head, and Clarissa—for a split second—mused he had an invisible working pair of eyes up there.

"My credit is just fine."

"Then why are you driving that piece of junk?" Miss Lossie asked.

"I guess..." Clarissa watched the moth float over to canned goods. "Well, I guess I was waiting for my husband to fix it or get me something new. Even though he is a kept man." She rolled her eyes. "How pathetic is that?"

Cracker Bandit rubbed his forehead and said, "Little lady, it ain't pathetic at all. You're just being a good wife."

"The hell she is," Miss Lossie said. "As if you, a man who's never been married, would know a good wife from a varmint. You and all your card playing makes you blinder than that bad eye does."

"Let's not go there." Cracker Bandit held up a hand, stopping the flow of potentially hurtful words.

Miss Lossie jabbed her head toward Clarissa. "It's called being a human doormat."

Cracker Bandit shrugged, as if conceding the point, and then Miss Lossie aimed her wisdom at Clarissa. "Child, it's your money, your life. You've got to take care of you. Nobody else is going to do that."

"But it's still the two of us making the decisions." Clarissa put her head in her hands. "I can't go off on my own and do anything I want."

"Clarissa," Miss Lossie said, "how many times have you told him the truck needed to be fixed?"

Clarissa stared down the shadowy tunnel of the dry goods aisle. "More than I can count. I've been asking since we moved here."

"You asked. He didn't do squat. Now what do you think you should do?"

Clarissa looked at Miss Lossie, six-time Worm Gruntin' Queen. She thought about what she'd learned that day about Sopchoppy earthworms. An image of twelve tiny hearts beating side by side in two vertical lines floated through her consciousness, effortlessly, like the moth that was lighting on a box of Borax. Maybe that's what she needed—the constitution of a Sopchoppy earthworm, wiggling through her own private, subterranean labyrinth, unseen but worthy, propelled by a dozen angel-dancing hearts. If she were an earthworm, she'd have spares: no tires, but spare hearts. She looked at Cracker Bandit and wondered why he didn't have anything better to do but stand around in a general store. Maybe it was his day off and he was doing exactly as his single, one-and-forever-only heart desired. Oh, to hell with hearts. She erased the earthworm from her mind. What she needed was courage. And a plan. As is sometimes the case with life—especially one in crisis — as soon as the word *plan* wafted through her brain, a solution — simple and pure — took root. If she verbalized what she suddenly knew, she felt certain there would be no going back. Sitting in that general store, drowning in a torrent of informed despair, mulling over the merits of her still hatching plan, she again considered what life would be like atop the Sears Tower, the earth obscured by cold white clouds.

"What I need to do," she said, her steady voice having nothing in common with her jitterbug brain, "is...is..." She watched the moth take to the air.

"Say it," Cracker Bandit said.

"That's right. Come on." Miss Lossie and Cracker Bandit trapped her in their mutual gaze.

"What I need to do..." She started over and felt her face and hands go clammy, as if — body part by body part — panic were slowly curdling her. "Is go buy myself a car."

"Bingo!" Cracker Bandit punched the air with his fist. Clarissa was certain his crack was showing, so she looked away. In her tender state of sexual deprivation, no sight — however base — was immune from catapulting her into arousal.

"Now you're talking with some good sense." Miss Lossie nodded her approval. "Good sense!"

Brow creased, grim-lipped, she appeared but did not feel determined. "And I'm not going to care what he thinks about it."

The moth floated out of dry goods, came within an eighth of an inch of getting tangled in Clarissa's hair, and then lit on the back of her chair. She did not notice. In her mind, she had made it to the edge. "Do you think that's a good idea? I mean, really, do you?"

She looked downward, into the clouds, knowing their answers didn't matter, knowing she had no choice. Before Miss Lossie or

Cracker Bandit could respond, she jumped. In her soul, she saw the Sears Tower fall away. The air was brilliant. Brilliant and cold.

***

*A*fter the sheriff took her statement, lectured her over the condition of the truck ("If I'd seen you on the highway in that thing, I'd have been obliged to ticket you, miss"), and had her sign various police-related documents, none of which she paid much attention to because her mind was locked down in a state of free fall, Cracker Bandit perched her on his Harley and drove her to the nearest car lot.

But first, Miss Lossie sent Clarissa into the kitchen with a bar of soap. "Child, you have got to wash some of that stink off before you go out in public."

Clarissa did as she was told. Using an old kitchen towel, she scrubbed her arms and belly and legs and face and neck and did not stop until her skin bore fewer traces of garbage and grave.

When she returned to the store's inner sanctum, just as she was about to say, "Well, I guess we should get going," Cracker Bandit, who was leaning on the counter, much of his left butt cheek exposed, said, "Ma'am, I have a proposition for you."

She eyed him, steely, wanting to say, "For the love of God, pull up your pants!" But instead she offered a careful, "What?"

"I'll give you five hundred dollars cash right now for that truck sitting out there on four flat tires."

"You're joking, right?" Clarissa scrunched her face, stayed steady by grabbing the counter with one hand, and dismissed the offer as his sorry attempt at humor.

"Nu-uh," Miss Lossie said. "Chester does not joke. Not at cards, not at life."

"That's right. I don't. At least not where vehicles are concerned."

Three moles dotted the skin just to the left of his navel: a tiny crescent moon. Her pelvis suddenly crackled with warmth, burnished as it were by the notion of a man's pigment forming a celestial body. Clarissa damned her libido. "But it's not worth five hundred."

"It is to me."

He was serious; she could tell that by the steady bead he had on her. His blue eye was pretty—the deep blue of a storm-scrubbed sky—and his white eye wasn't so bad, either, Clarissa decided, well aware that her mind's wheels weren't on the track. "I think it's in both our names, my husband's and mine."

"Don't matter. You can still sell it to me. You don't need his permission." Cracker Bandit blinked one time, slowly.

I don't need his permission? This was becoming the theme du jour, although every time it reared its independent head, she was startled.

"You can just leave it here overnight. Can she just leave it here overnight?" he asked Miss Lossie without taking his eye off Clarissa.

"Of course she can." Miss Lossie moved a stool to the counter and sat down with an exhausted sigh. "She can leave it here all week for all I care."

"So, we go buy you a car and tomorrow you meet me back here and we'll do the paperwork. In the meantime..." He paused, pulled out his wallet—an action that this time had no effect on the precarious position of his shorts—opened it, removed five one-hundred-dollar bills that were so pristine Clarissa wondered if they were real, and placed them in her palm. "So you know I mean it."

Clarissa, stunned, looked at the green pile of money and then at Cracker Bandit's face, etched, one-eyed, and handsome in a John Wayne kind of way. "How do you know I won't back out and keep this?"

He tapped the tip of her nose. "Well, I don't think that truck is going nowheres."

Miss Lossie started laughing. "You got that right. Child, you better take that money and sell him that heap. He's doing you a mighty favor. Besides, that's poker winnings; he's got to do something good with it."

Clarissa had an urge to hug him, but he stepped away and it was at that moment she knew he was not just a good man, but also a softy, someone who'd been hurt. "Thank you, Crac... Chester. Thank you so much."

He looked over her head. She could see that he was both pleased and embarrassed. "Ain't nothing. Been needing a truck like that for a good long while."

"Like a hole in the head," Miss Lossie said. The bells on the door jangled and in walked a gaggle of construction workers, all of them complaining about the heat. "You two better get on out of here if you're going to go car shopping."

Miss Lossie pecked Clarissa's cheek, told Cracker Bandit to behave, to which he responded, "Me? Always," and Clarissa, watching the moth float amid the shadows, thought her ovarian shadow women were chattering again. She couldn't hear them clearly, but she was pretty sure they were urging her on.

⌒

*P*erched on the back of his Harley (having, at his insistence, donned his helmet — she needed help securing the chinstrap — and an extra pair of sunglasses, and after slinging her purse diagonally across her chest, and then having no choice but to steady herself by placing one hand on his shoulder as she wobbled onto the cycle with all the poise of a three-legged donkey), Clarissa stiffened in both fear and anticipation as Cracker Bandit settled himself onto the bike. He was surprisingly graceful: the Lone Ranger mounting Silver. Except he was nearly naked. And his crack was showing. And he wore a single silver earring: a skull, which she'd noticed only after she'd felt his body heat rush over her.

What, Clarissa fretted, tracking a constellation of freckles on his lower back that resembled the Big Dipper, was proper lady biker etiquette? Was she supposed to use Cracker Bandit as a human handle? Did gravity naturally nail her ass to the seat? Or did the helmet make her top-heavy and therefore vulnerable to flipping over, as if, weight-distribution-wise, she was part Jeep, part road dart?

Cracker Bandit walked the bike into a forward-facing stance. This gave her a full-eyed view of the mystery of his shorts. How did they manage to stay on—not on the bike, but on his butt? Perhaps, rather than prayer, it was hip bones; they acted as hangers. If she wanted to be generous about it—he was being awfully kind to her—his ass crack wasn't bad as ass cracks went. It was dead-on centered and from this vantage point appeared to be free of rash and hair. He looked over his shoulder. "Ready?"

"I think so," she said, and with that, a series of bedazzlements ensued: the intimacy involved in being a passenger on a motorcycle; how much she enjoyed the feel of nine hundred pounds of chrome, leather, and steel between her legs; the curious facts that she had said yes to any of this and that except for one brief moment she did not care what reaction her husband would have to her adventure (if she ever bothered to tell him); how she instinctively and almost without shame grabbed Cracker Bandit's waist, even though gravity did indeed nail her to the seat; that he smelled of cinnamon and something else, something so familiar, something from her garden...aha!...lemon verbena (this delighted her even as she grew embarrassed at how the scent of garbage—despite her attempt at cleaning up in the kitchen—still faintly perfumed her skin); and above all, the unexpected, delicious vibration whistling through her womb into her ovaries, with their shadow women now dressed in chaps, up the storybook ladder of her spine, into the hard knot at the base of her neck, and through the switchbacks of her brain—a brain that glowed the moment Cracker Bandit turned the key and pushed the starter button.

As they sped eastward, Clarissa tightened her grip on Cracker Bandit's waist and noticed that his head metronomed left and right, left and right, as he steered them to a town named Dead Oak. She assumed the bobbing was a result of his compromised peripheral vision and, swathed in his scent, was grateful that he cut such a confident, assured path.

A half mile down the road, in front of a cell phone tower she had never before noticed, her reptilian brain—fueled by ecstatic nerve endings—segued into an erotic fantasy: she and Cracker Bandit writhing in ecstasy on the back of his bike. Gone were his white crabbing boots and loose shorts, her stinky T-shirt and filthy jeans. They were naked and thrusting, akimbo and bouncing.

Clarissa being Clarissa, however, overcame the reptile, deleted the X-rated images almost as soon as they bloomed, and returned to her cerebral core, contemplating the idea that some people equated riding a motorized bullet called a Harley with freedom. In her sensually battered condition, however, freedom was yoked to a sense of dynamic mortality. Hurtling down the highway on two wheels, she felt death's presence; not a fallow, one-dimensional, life-robbing death, but a force steeped in smoke and bone, breath and blood, flesh and flower. Duende. Yes, that's what seized her as she balanced her wild heart on the back of the Harley, inhaling Cracker Bandit's cinnamon-and-verbena scent: the Spanish notion of a creative force antithetical to the muse—a death dancer spinning a flamenco composed of carnality, sadness, and passion. As the world rushed by, she thought, To hell with the muse; where is my duende?

That Sears Tower tumble ventured again into her mind, and she wondered, Is this what it feels like to jump? The pavement rushing at you, the wind holding you, the speed—the awesome speed— made headier by the imminent possibilities of both life and death?

She closed her eyes and took it all in. The sensation of charging through time and space free of the constraints of seat belts and car doors and passenger compartments led her to venture that angels preferred flight to heaven.

~

A-One Auto Sales was located on the corner of Main Street and Robber's Roost Way in Dead Oak. She wanted to ask Cracker Bandit if the location of a used-car lot on Main and Robber's Roost was intentional, ironic, a warning, or delicious dumb luck but was afraid his answer would take longer than the time they'd spent getting there.

As he pulled up to the intersection and stopped for a red light, over the rumble of the pipes, Clarissa said, "You can just drop me off. No need to stick around. You've done too much already."

He looked over his shoulder. "You sure? I don't mind hanging out. I know a thing or two about reliable rides."

"I think I've got this one. But thanks." Clarissa patted his back, enjoying too much, she thought, the physical proximity to a man who was for all intents and purposes a stranger.

Cracker Bandit eased the Harley over to the curb. This time, she acted on her impulse. She slipped her arms around his shoulders and hugged him. "I cannot thank you enough, but I've got to do this alone," she said into his ear.

"All right, then. Do it your way," he said, shutting down the bike. "You working gals always do." He dismounted and helped her off. Bugs splattered his bald pate.

Clarissa hit the pavement on legs that felt jelly-filled. She took off the helmet and shook out her hair; her house and the trash truck and the disapproving husband seemed a continent away. She looked at Cracker Bandit, who stood smiling down at her, and she was suddenly overwhelmed by his kindness. She knew what her mother would have said: All of his care and generosity had simply been a ploy to get laid. Clarissa refused to believe it. She handed him the helmet and noticed that on the back it sported a LA-DI-FUCKIN'-DA sticker. This delighted her beyond all measure. "Thanks for your help. I really mean it."

"It's nothing, little lady. Just be sure you tell them I sent you. You'll get a better deal."

"Chester?"

He cocked his head and seemed to be waiting for a question he knew was coming. His blue eye was patient; his white eye she couldn't read. "Why haven't you ever been married?"

He rubbed his hand over his sunburned face. "Well," he said, "it's like this." He stared down at the pavement, then over his shoulder at the traffic whipping by. He made a sucking sound and turned back to her. "Sometimes, we love too damn much. People can't handle it. And when that's the case"—he remounted the bike and slipped on the helmet—"it's best if you just ride solo." He turned the key and pressed the starter button. The Harley rumbled to life, more beast than machine.

"I'll see you tomorrow with the truck title," she yelled.

Cracker Bandit waved in acknowledgment, but his focus was on the road ahead. He shot down Robber's Roost, never looking back, his butt crack gleaming, leaving Clarissa as she had requested: alone and without transportation in a town full of strangers.

⸻

*T*he Dead Oak State Bank's sign flashed the temperature in digital glory: 106 degrees. Clarissa felt her purse to make sure she had her cell phone. Perhaps she should call Iggy, tell him where she was, how hot it was, what her plans were. Nah. That made about as much sense as playing peekaboo with Bubba the pet rattlesnake. Cars zipped past. The words *independent, alone, positive,* careened through her head like neon flash cards. She gazed down the street at the jumble of signs: McDonald's, BP, Dollar Store, First Baptist Church, Hardee's, Big Top IGA. Dead Oak was a busy little town. No one gave her a second glance. She ran through her options: fall down and cry, hitch a ride home, call the son of a bitch and beg for mercy, buy a car.

It was a no-brainer. She made her way around a boxwood hedge and into the steel-and-chrome world of the car lot. A handsome Latin man—tall, thin, wild curls, and broad almond eyes—wearing jeans, a striped tailored shirt, and a yellow tie appeared instantly, as if by used-car-salesman magic.

He said something to her, but his accent was thick and Clarissa was overwrought. "I'm sorry?"

After shooting a brief suggestion of a smile, he repeated himself.

Clarissa still did not understand. Maybe the heat was baking her brain cells. "I need to buy a car. That's all." She noticed his plain gold wedding band. What else was she going to buy at A-One Auto? Idiot, she thought.

"My name is Raul." He held out his hand, the one without a wedding band.

She shook it. "Clarissa."

"Hello, Clarissa. You have"—he leaned to the left and looked behind her—"trade-in?"

"No, not really. I'm...well, I have a car, it's just that it's... it's just so screwed up. These kids, they were drinking and, it was really a junk heap before they...but it runs if I get new tires, and I own another car, but sort of. I mean, it's my husband's. But it's in my name..." She drifted off. She realized that she wasn't speaking English as well as he was.

He appeared to really be listening to her, even though she wasn't saying anything that a reasonable person would discern as comprehensible.

She tried again. "The truck is a piece of junk. I can't even get it here. All the tires are flat."

"Money?"

He certainly had a way of getting to the point.

"Yes," she said. "Actually, I do have money."

"Good!" He clapped his hands once. "You want little car? Save gas. Or big *bu-bbbbb bu-bbbbb* car?"

"I want..." She looked over the small pond of used cars and trucks—this was no acre upon acre of glistening new vehicles, dealer showroom type of place—and started to perk up. She listened to the plastic triangle-shaped flags in all their primary color glory flap and snap in the hellish breeze. This A-One Auto was its own little land of opportunity. Possibilities on four inflated wheels dotted the lot, hither and yon.

She took notice. Being in the middle of farmland, it had a lot of pickups. And old-lady cars that fit the cliché to a T: They had probably been driven only to church and back for thirty years. But surely there was something else...something a little more... she tried to put her writer's finger on what exactly that itch was: adventuresome.

"I want," she said, feeling taller than when Cracker Bandit had dropped her off, "something with a little zip. I want to feel jazzed every time I get behind the wheel."

She closed her eyes and listened to the thick flutter of the plastic flags; she thought that if it got any hotter, they might melt in this wicked wind and then all the cars would need new paint jobs. They would look as if giant birds had pooped on them in Technicolor. She opened her eyes and turned a complete circle, hoping to see the very car that would suit her whim and cure her ills. When she faced Raul again, she said, sensing he would understand, "I'm tired of being bored."

"Ahhhh!" This time he really smiled. He had nice, white, pearly, straight chompers. "Let me show you something that came in yesterday. It is"—he inhaled as if he were sniffing out the right word, as if each letter of the alphabet had its own special scent—"how you say..." He lifted a slender finger to the wind, paused in thought, and then said, "Cherry!"

"I don't want a red car."

"You aren't going to get a red car," he said, conviction lighting his fine features, and then he turned and walked away. He had a nice ass. Yes, Clarissa thought, I am an ass gal.

She followed him to a line of cars closest to the building. A Buick Riviera, an F-150, a Jeep Cherokee, a Civic (that would never do), another F-150, a Dodge Ram, a Ford Escort, a Ford Ranger, a GMC Sonoma, an F-350, a Chevy Silverado, a canary yellow El Camino. That's where he stopped. At the El Camino. It was long. Lean. Beautiful. Spotless. Gleaming. Cherry.

He turned to her, put his hand on the hood, and rubbed it the way, she imagined, he rubbed his wife's thigh. "Watch you think?"

She felt herself smile. She walked the length of it. The sun glinted off all its surfaces, just like the flash of a bird's wings. A black roof and two black racing stripes that ran the length of the hood highlighted the yellow paint job. Chrome rails—she supposed for tying stuff down—stretched like long, gleaming hyphens down either side of the bed. El Camino SS. Yes indeed. She did not want to appear eager. Whatever you do, she lectured silently, do not touch the automobile; do not let your hand linger longingly over its yellow hip of a fender.

But Raul, she feared, had the type of instincts all successful salesmen possessed: He could smell her desire. He opened the driver's-side door. "Go for a ride?"

She shrugged, hoping to sound bored. "Sure." She caught a whiff of his aftershave as she slid in. Old Spice. Of course he would wear Old Spice: solid, out of fashion, and unapologetic. The car (or was it a truck? she wasn't sure) had a rearview mirror. And side mirrors. She bet that the gas gauge worked. And brake lights? Oh yeah. The keys were in the ignition. She looked at him.

"I took it out a few minutes ago," he said, blushing. "This is my kind of car."

He slid onto the passenger seat. Something other than Old Spice was in the mix: autumn and leather. She wanted to ask what it was but feared that he'd misinterpret the question as a come-on. She turned the key and said, "Whoa!" There was power under that hood.

"Top of the line—1970 Chevy El Camino SS." His eyes softened as he ran his hand over the dash. "This little beauty," he said, descending into motorhead-speak, a language Clarissa did not know, "has a 350 V8 engine, Holley 650 double-pump carburetor, Edelbrock duel-plane low-rise intake, Crane Saturday Night Special, solid lifter cam with roller rockers, bored .060 over Dome top 11 55:1 compression pistons, Edelbrock Performer aluminum heads, a four-bolt main with a steel crank, Hooker Headers running into Aero Chamber Mufflers with a three-inch exhaust out the back, a Hughes TH-350 transmission with a 4.11 posi rear end, power front disc brakes, power steering, factory a/c, Alpine AM/FM/CD player, and 46,333 original miles." He recited the stats as if he were a sports announcer providing the star player's performance stats. He didn't miss a single one of his r's—he rolled them all. Then he shot her that beautiful grin, leaned back expansively in his seat, and said, "Cherry, yes?"

"Perhaps," Clarissa said, hearing the flirt and confidence in her voice, and she laughed. She put the car in drive and glided off the lot, down Robber's Roost, which became a country road after three blocks, and pressed the accelerator, watching the needle tick higher and higher until it pegged at ninety miles an hour. The windows were down. Her back itched. She wanted to fly. She drove for a good ten minutes, in silence. Raul seemed content to let the hot wind tousle his hair. Finally, she couldn't help herself.

"How much?" Clarissa asked above the thrum of the engine, the wind, the tires.

"Sixteen two," he shouted, his fingers dancing along the window's chrome trim.

Clarissa slowed the car, flipped on the blinker (what a beautiful sound), and turned into an abandoned roadhouse. The gravel crunched like a lover's sigh as she brought the El Camino to a halt. She wiped a swath of grime off her face, listened to the sweet idle of the motor. She was very aware of Raul's presence. It was masculine, dominating, nonviolent, patient. This El Camino, she knew, was about a whole lot more than simply securing transportation. "You're married?"

"Yes."

"Children?"

"A baby boy, seven months." He pulled his wallet out of his back pocket and flipped it open.

Clarissa took it from him, stared at the Walmart photo of three humans smiling, the wife with the big-eyed baby on her lap,

Raul sitting behind them with one hand on her shoulder and the other on the baby's leg. Picture-perfect.

"How beautiful!" Clarissa said, her heart aching for the family she did not possess. "Your wife is very pretty." And she was: petite with black hair that reached her waist.

Raul took the wallet, returned it to his back pocket, and said, "I am a very, very lucky man."

"Indeed." Clarissa looked in the rearview, which reflected a long stretch of open road. "Sixteen thousand two hundred dollars?"

Raul nodded, kept his sights straight ahead.

Clarissa popped the car into drive, pulled onto the road in the direction from which they'd traveled, and gunned it. Empowerment, she mused, should not be so fleeting. Above the engine's full-throated growl, she shouted, as if she were a woman with nothing to lose, "I'll give you ten grand cash and finance five. Not one dime more."

Raul's fingers resumed their dance. They were graceful fingers, tanned, and still bore the calluses of a man who used his hands to make a living.

Clarissa wondered how long he had worked at the car lot and if he missed whatever it was he did that earned him those calluses. Maybe he understood the secrets of oak and pine, citrus and tomatoes, drywall and nails.

He looked out the passenger-side window, watched the world go by, his handsome face crinkled in concentration.

"Why you want this car?" he asked. He turned to her. "I mean"—he tapped his index finger on the dash—"*this* car."

"You're supposed to be selling me. Not interrogating me."

"You a lady. This a man's car."

"Then why did you show it to me?" Deep inside, Clarissa felt as if her imaginary fall from the Sears Tower were about to end on a positive note.

He laughed. "That's right. I show it to you. But you want it. I mean *want* it, the way a man wants. Why?"

Clarissa looked at him—his face was open and beautiful—and then back at the road. Dead Oak lay just ahead in the scintillating distance. She knew the answer, and the knowledge made her light-headed; it was the same feeling she experienced in the old days when she was writing and writing well, when she knew the next word she typed would be not simply an okay word or a good word, but the only word in all the English language that would do.

Still, she took her time, not answering immediately, allowing herself the luxury of experiencing the totality of the El Camino, feeling the engine's power radiate up through the drive shaft, the steering column, the tiny bones of each finger, the hard orbs of her wrists. She listened to the truck's pitch-perfect rumble the way a jazz aficionado listens to Coltrane's "A Love Supreme." She saw the yellow-and-black-striped hood gleaming, a few stray clouds reflected in its polished shine, and thought that there was nothing mundane about power and utility combined. In her mind, she sat at the keyboard and began typing, clicking the letters that would form the perfect word. Click, click, click: Everything—the alphabet and all its sounds—lined up as if they were charmed and she were their wizard.

She knew Raul was watching her, and she liked that. She looked over at him. His brown eyes were patient, intent, hungry. Hunger for a woman, for air, for life—that was something she hadn't seen in her own husband in years. Raul was the kind of man, she knew, who would impale himself with guilt and shame if he ever did cheat on his wife. He might even confess, and Clarissa hoped that if any of that actually happened, his wife would forgive him.

"You want to know why, really why?" Clarissa asked.

"*Sí.* Yes."

She caught a glimpse of herself in the rearview. She was sweaty. Dirty. Unafraid. Maybe, she ventured, even beautiful. "Freedom," she said.

⁓

*A*maziah Archer stood on the front porch of the house he had built—nail by hand-forged nail—and played the fiddle while Olga Villada patted her leg in time to the whirling rhythm. Their son, Heart Archer, standing an arm's length away from his mother, bounced up and down in that odd way children have of dancing. Amaziah had crafted the fiddle back in 1825. Hewn from the wood of trees he had felled on the western boundary of their property, in both appearance and tonal quality, it was an exquisite instrument. In deference to the surrounding swamp's wildlife, he had forgone the scroll's traditional circular motif in favor of a heron's head. Each of the four tuning pegs was a hand-carved replica of the bird. Because of the nature-inspired scroll and pegs, it was easy to imagine that the fiddle's neck—which was practical and necessary—also paid homage to the great bird.

Later on during that long, hot solstice, Clarissa would turn again to the material from the archives and learn that Amaziah was in his time known as a craftsman of the highest order. His fiddles produced melodious sounds so sweet that slave-owning white men as far away as New York sent emissaries to purchase this free black man's instruments. Clarissa presumed that in the early nineteenth century, commerce and politics—on both sides of the divide—were perhaps more pragmatic than in the early twenty-first century yet equally complicated and ethically anemic.

Discovering that Amaziah Archer was a first-rate fiddle maker led Clarissa to fantasize that she would discover, in a forgotten corner of the attic, both fiddle and bow and that she would display them in her own shadow box by the front door of the old, lovely house. She would even allow herself to imagine that her husband's rifle displayed in a case of sacred pink ivory would end up in his office, out of sight. And because it suited her daydream, she would decide that she was not hearing the wind whip through the eaves but that it was actual remnant scraps of music, still alive in the atmosphere, played by Amaziah nearly two hundred years ago. The truth—that she was under a spell of her own casting (sometimes soul-gnawing need reprises itself as practical magic) as she trundled down the path of possibly becoming a writer again and, as part of this process, was privy to the sounds and sensitivities of the resident ghosts—was too logical for her to entertain.

Amaziah stopped playing as he caught sight of Clarissa rolling up to the house in a long beast of a yellow car. He lowered the fiddle. "What do we have here?"

Olga Villada's face lit up. "Isn't it beautiful!" she said. "Look, Heart, at the big crazy horse." Amaziah and Olga Villada referred to all cars and trucks as crazy horses, and they often mused about what their lives might have been like—how different their fates—had such contraptions existed when they were living.

Heart ran into the yard before Clarissa had come to a full stop.

"Let her at least get out of it first," Olga Villada called, feeling a tinge of pride, wondering if her presence—however spectral—was actually having a positive influence on Clarissa.

Unaware of the three spirits, Clarissa slammed the heavy door and headed toward the back entrance of the house, her head spinning with trepidation. What would Iggy do? How would she explain? She paused before rounding the corner and looked at the truck, which, according to the owner's manual, was what it was. Not a car, not an open-air station wagon, not some strange retro hybrid: simply and quite extraordinarily a truck.

Olga Villada, hurrying toward her son, spied fear in the tense angle of Clarissa's jaw and fledgling independence in the flickering light of her eyes. She wished she could sit with Clarissa, have a cup of tea, tell her about her life (how wonderful a life it had been right up until those awful, final moments), share with her things about the house she would never come to on her own, warn her to tread wisely when it came to defiance. She had watched the way Clarissa's husband interacted with the naked women (oh, how she wished that would stop; poor Heart, always being sent to his room so that he wouldn't see the goings-on in that yard). And, perhaps more important, she had seen the way he treated Clarissa, with indifference and disdain. The woman needed to know what it felt like to be loved by a confident, generous man. Oh, what she would give for the chance of just one conversation, one breach in the living-and-dead divide.

Amaziah stepped off the porch, watching his wife. "Olga," he said.

"What?"

He put his arm around her. "I know what you're thinking. But you can't."

"I know, I know! But look at her. She needs my help."

"She needs," Amaziah said, squeezing her shoulders, "to live her life without us meddling in it."

"Mama! Come play!" Heart called, running his tiny hand over the shining door latch. "Daddy, can we get inside it?"

Amaziah and his wife exchanged glances.

"It's up to you," Olga Villada said.

Amaziah looked at the gleaming mechanical beast and felt deep down, in a place that he would not share with even his wife, that he had been cheated. The twenty-first century should have been his time, his day. He'd seen Clarissa's computer—how images and words flew across the screen like a rush of wings—and had heard the people who lived in that thing called a television talk about satellites and rocket ships. Just think of the fiddles I could have crafted, he mused, if I'd had power tools.

"Daddy!" Heart tugged on his father's hand.

Amaziah looked at his son and then the El Camino. "Oh, why not!"

During the most profound heat of the day, the three of them—bemused, excited, and riddled with longing—wafted through the steel body of the yellow crazy horse, Heart in the middle, Olga Villada in the passenger seat, and Amaziah behind the wheel. The Civic had only mildly interested them, and the pickup, once it began to reek, was off-limits. But this gleaming yellow Minotaur of a vehicle with its long black racing stripes and chrome flourishes was a seduction even a man like Amaziah could not resist.

"It seems dangerous to me," Olga Villada said, pressing her face close to the windshield, trying to hide her fascination with the idea of mortals moving faster than the wind.

Amaziah ran his hands over the steering wheel. Heart kicked his legs and tried to make a rumbling sound, imitating the engine. "If we'd had one of these," Amaziah said, his eyes wandering over the instrument panel, his feet testing the accelerator, "we would have been able to escape."

Olga Villada looked at him and made the "Hush, you're scaring the baby" face, but Amaziah let it roll right off him.

As for Heart, he followed his father's lead. "Yeah! And we would have shot them dead! Bang! Bang! Bang!"

Olga Villada ran her hand over her son's head. "Now, sweetie, we don't talk that way. Okay?"

Heart studied his mother's face and nodded his agreement, even though he had no idea why he should not express his hatred for those men. After all, he remembered in perfect detail what had happened: the men and the beatings and the smell and the pain and the scorch of the ropes. He knew the terror he felt if he ventured too near the sentinel oak. But mostly, he thought as he reached up and patted his mother's cheek, he remembered how much he was loved.

⁓

*L*arry Dibble sauntered down the road, satisfied with himself. He had waited until the mail lady had misdelivered most of Hope's mail before nailing her in the back of her SUV. She would not remember it, of course. He wasn't that much of an asshole. He had ethics, even if the big shots didn't think so. He knew the gal would have felt guilty over having sex with a tree cutter in the middle of the day, a man she'd just met, a compromised angel. So he'd pleasured her but stole the memory, leaving her to wake up alone amid U.S. mailboxes and third-class junk mail, parked behind an abandoned single-wide on Bread of Life Way, a vague sensation of happiness overtaking—for a few moments—her perpetual confusion.

He headed down Mosquito Swamp Trail and thought he might stop by that snotty bitch's house again. He was strangely drawn to the place and not because of the sick trees (he really was a tree cutter; it was a skill he'd picked up to kill the boredom of eternity) or that big fucker's slew of naked babes (although what a delightful and unexpected perk, especially since the big boys had banished him to Nowheresville). As he nodded to a black guy who passed by on a blue bike (pity his mother wouldn't make it to the next full moon), Larry Dibble considered the wonderful possibility that the powers-that-be had given up on him falling in line and, thus, stuck him in a place where he could do no harm. Ha!

Up ahead, on the right, some fella was cracking open an egg on the road. "Hey there, mister. What are you doing?"

Chet Lewis tossed the broken shell in the grass and pointed at the sizzling egg. "Hungry?"

Larry Dibble laughed.

"That there," Chet Lewis said, "is proof of global warming. Yes siree. Damn, it's hot."

Larry Dibble wiggled his nose. He hated the smell of fried eggs. It reminded him of burning flesh, and that was the one stench he could not abide. "You got some tree work for me?"

Chet Lewis stood and smoothed his yellow-and-pink plaid shirt. "Maybe. You reasonable?"

Larry Dibble bit down on a little clump of ants he'd tucked into his mouth after leaving the mail lady all spread-legged and satiated. Chet Lewis assumed it was chaw.

"Oh, you have no idea."

"All right. I got stuff I gotta do today. Come back tomorrow. We'll talk."

Larry Dibble gave him a sloppy salute. "You bet." He walked across the road, toward the snotty bitch's house, and thought that if he were in a good mood tomorrow, he'd do something about that man's gout, which had been misdiagnosed as a pulled shoulder muscle. A little tree trimming, a little gout curing; that wouldn't be a bad day's work.

He stepped up to the gate, spied a fine-looking automobile that had not been parked there that morning. And then he saw them, the three of them in the front seat, chattering away. It was the black guy he'd seen earlier who'd been out there by the swamp, wounding the tree with an old ax Larry Dibble wanted nothing to do with. But the boy? And the woman? Who the fuck were they? Why did the very sight of them make him want to rip this suit of skin right off his hollow bones? Something was wrong. He'd been tricked. Why the hell did he feel as if his wings were on fire? He hit the gate with his open hand. "Son of a bitch!"

Larry Dibble ran down the road, flapped his burning wings, tried to take flight but couldn't. The bastards had grounded him.

⁓

*B*efore Clarissa had steered the big yellow car-truck into her yard, before she heard the heavy door slam shut with a no-nonsense and deeply satisfying thud, before the three ghosts had slipped unnoticed into its passenger compartment, before Larry Dibble had run down the road with his wings on fire, Clarissa had journeyed homeward, ebullient about her new purchase and terrified regarding her husband's reaction.

When she pulled into the crossroads called Hope, the radio blaring squeeze-box-laced Tejano ballads courtesy of the Latin station Raul had tuned to, she checked old Mrs. Hickok's thermometer. The mercury hovered a hair below 107 degrees. At that moment, above all the things she loved about the El Camino, Clarissa was grateful for its air-conditioning. Close behind was the fact that everything worked. The car had, in working order, all its knobs, mirrors, gadgets, gauges, blinkers, tires. Everything was big, solid, and the vehicle went really fast. How could her husband not be happy for her? How could he not be even slightly amused that his wife had brought home a big American muscle car? Surely his heart would ease toward her. She'd even taken on the job of trash hauler. What more could he ask?

Still, her hands shook, her pulse tripped and raced, as she turned onto Mosquito Swamp. She had to get her story straight before facing him. And she had to be calm, because he could read her; if she let her nerves show, he'd go for the kill. Buying the El Camino was all about safety. That's what she would tell him. The mail lady approached in her SUV that was belching smoke. She flagged Clarissa down.

Clarissa flipped off the radio and lowered her window. See, more evidence that she'd done the right thing. She'd tell Iggy about the poor mail lady and her broken-down car and her all alone on a country road. He was surly, but not stupid. Of course he wanted her in a reliable vehicle. "Car problems?"

"What do you mean?" The mail lady's face was plastered with a ridiculous grin, and her brown hair was all undone.

"Your car. It's smoking."

"Oh, that!" She laughed hysterically. Her pupils were dilated. Clarissa wondered if she was on drugs. "It's nothing. I just wanted to say hello."

The engine was about to blow up and she stopped to exchange pleasantries? Was she nuts? Clarissa felt a need to warn her about that Dibble fellow, but she really didn't have anything solid on him. What was she going to say? "There's something not right about that one-armed tree cutter." She sure hoped the mail lady, whose husband had passed three years prior, to hear her tell it, wasn't taking up with him.

"You know"—the mail lady tossed her hair and fluttered her lashes; this was not the mail lady Clarissa knew—"I've been wanting to say something to you, and I just haven't had the nerve." An awful ping sounded in her engine.

Clarissa noticed that the woman's blouse was unfastened to just below her bra line. Her right breast cupped in pink lace was clearly visible.

"I just wanted to say," the mail lady started up again, tapping her gas in an attempt to keep her car idling, "I think you are the nicest lady, but that husband of yours is the rudest man I've ever dealt with. Why, he doesn't even say hello."

Clarissa could not believe her ears. She was astounded by the mail lady's unabashed gall. But her urge to take up for Iggy was trumped by the relief at having affirmation, no matter the source, that he was truly a jerk.

"He's South African," she said. "They aren't always the friend-liest folks on earth." Clarissa knew this was untrue, but it was all she could come up with in a pinch.

"Mmmm," the mail lady said, a polite, closemouthed grin revealing that she did not buy Clarissa's explanation. "Well, gotta go before this old car blows up on me." She blew Clarissa a kiss as if she were some country club debutante and drove away.

Clarissa watched her turn onto Tremble and Shout in a cloud of noxious smoke and hoped the woman would make it home. Perhaps she has sons, Clarissa thought, pressing the accelerator, who know how to work on cars.

Up ahead, in the vicinity of the fire tower, someone stood in the road, waving a red caution flag; from this distance it appeared to be a child. Perhaps there had been an accident. Per-haps Iggy had been drinking all afternoon with his little models and, bombed out of his mind on sickeningly sweet piña coladas, flipped his Civic just a few blocks from the house. Would he be sprawled on the pavement—bloody and dead—or would the Jaws of Life have to wrench his decapitated body from the wreck-age? Would Clarissa, like the dutiful and devoted wife she was, be pressed once more into saving his life? What would she wear to the funeral? Something Jackie-O-ish.

As she slowly eased forward, she saw that the flagman wasn't a child at all, but a midget in need of a shave. The road in front of the green was blocked. A giant trailer with a phantasmagoric painting of a snake-eating man—a short man, a really short man; the snake was three times his height—emblazoned across its alu-minum siding was backing up onto the green. Traveling conces-sion stands plastered with pop art images of popcorn, lemonade, cotton candy, candied apples, foot-long hot dogs, grilled corn, funnel cakes, hot pretzels, and snow cones were lined up north-bound on Bread of Life Way. All of this paled, however, against the forty or fifty midgets—mainly men: rough-looking, tattooed, carnie midgets—who ran hither-skither, an army of two-legged ants, laughing, cursing, order-shouting, beneath the tall, shin-ing, phallus-reminding fire tower. The bucolic village of Hope, population seventeen (this was an optimistic but government-sanctioned estimate and didn't include the folks who populated the forest and swamp just outside the city limits), had, in Cla-rissa's brief absence, become a bustling carnie town filled with cigar-chewing short people, none of whom could have reasonably convinced anyone but a shit-faced deaf, dumb, and blind man that they tipped the height scale anywhere close to five feet.

Clarissa, now at a dead stop, nodded at the sweat-drenched midget who was directing traffic.

"Nice car," he said, wiping the side of his face with his T-shirt sleeve. "Sixty-nine?"

"Nope. Seventy."

His whistled; it was a long, low, seductive, dirt-bag whistle.

"What is all this?" Clarissa asked.

"The All-American Dynamite Dwarf Carnival. Ta-daa!" He struck a pose, arms extended and waving. It was as if all four feet three of him were composed of flourish and pomp. He winked at Clarissa, which caused a shiver composed of hot and cold neurons to glitter flashbulb-style the length of her spine. She was just about to go where she had never gone before—that there was something wildly sexy about midgets—when he pulled on the end of his nose as if it were full of dust and snorted. He put his hands on either side of her window, which Clarissa did not like, but he cut her off before she could say, "Hey, get your grimy paws off my vehicle."

"It starts tomorrow," he said—his voice sounded like buffed rust—"and lasts through the weekend." He winked again and rapped his knuckles on the top of the El Camino. He had to reach high to get there, and she wondered if he was on his tiptoes. She started to look but stopped, not wanting to appear rude. She felt her ovaries tingle. They always did that when she met a man brimming with confidence, whether said confidence was justified or not.

"A whole carnival of midgets?" She supposed Hope was so small that only a midget carnival would fit. He smelled like pepperoni. She spied the tendrils of a tattoo curl from his chest and up into the wrinkles and grime of his neck.

He grimaced. It looked as if he hadn't shaved in three days, maybe more. A chewed stogie sat perched like a bloated pencil behind his left ear. "Not midgets." He spit the m-word the way one would spit out a mouth full of maggots. "Dwarfs. We're dwarfs. Big difference, lady."

"Sorry!" Clarissa hadn't meant to offend. Just as her reptilian brain awoke and whispered in her ear that the guy was an asshole, a dog shot in front of the car.

The dwarf yelled, flapping his little, tattoo-covered arms (a buxom blonde, a red heart, a bare-breasted hula girl, a flourishing "I love Mom," a pair of black-and-white dice, a silver-nailed crucifix, a bicep-bulging Popeye—all of them miniature versions of traditional tats). "Money Dog, you're gonna get smashed. Get back up there in the trailer where you belong!"

The diminutive Money Dog looked like a chow chow that had been left in the dryer too long. And with his crooked front teeth (his bottom canines jutted up over his lip) and black muzzle, Clarissa decided he bore a striking resemblance to Ernest Borgnine.

Money Dog wagged his proud foxlike tail and then bounded onto the green. He ran an obstacle course of legs, tents, and traveling sideshows. He paused at the fire tower, peed all about its perimeter, and, satisfied that it was sufficiently marked, jumped into a red, white, and blue trailer that announced it was the home of Rocket Dog and Nicolai, the World's Smallest Human Cannonball. Painted across the trailer's side was a wild-eyed rendering of the shrunken chow chow, replete with crimson cape, flying into the arms of a dwarf in a silver jumpsuit. In the background, a golden cannon gleamed.

Clarissa wondered if the dog liked being called Money Dog better than Rocket Dog and if he responded to both or ignored people when they called him by the one he didn't prefer. And then she thought, Surely they don't shoot that dog out of a cannon, and if they did, surely she would call the ASPCA.

Just as she was imagining picking up the phone to report that the dwarf circus was being cruel to what appeared to be a dwarf chow chow, the truck pulling the Snake-Eating Man trailer, which had nearly cleared the road, backfired, causing Clarissa and the traffic-directing dwarf to jump.

"Hey, get a tune-up, you freaking knucklehead," the dwarf yelled, flipping off the snake eater.

From what Clarissa could tell, the snake eater was also a dwarf. Just as she slipped into a mental meandering about what special equipment the truck that towed the trailer came with in order to accommodate a man with legs only two feet long, it rolled forward, clearing the way for her to proceed.

"Maybe I'll see you tomorrow," she told the dwarf, sliding the El Camino into gear.

"If you're free tonight, come on by. I'll buy you a beer." He winked at her again, and Clarissa, being polite, flattered, dumbfounded, shot him a wave ripe with feminine, mail lady flourish, then rolled up her window, flipped on the tunes, and watched the dwarf and the carnival's attendant commotion grow ever smaller in her splendid rearview.

As she neared her house (Iggy wasn't dead after all—no EMS units, no Jaws of Life), her resolve to be firm about why she'd bought the El Camino waned. Maybe he wouldn't be home and she could put off having to explain. Despite the El Camino's unapologetic air-conditioning, fear forced a cold sweat to break out along Clarissa's brow, chin, breastbone. What had she done? What if he flew into a rage, forcing her into that trap of believing she was nothing more than her mother's child? Maybe she should drive around the block and phone him, prepare him. Too late. Her timing sucked. The Civic was approaching from the opposite direction. Feeling cursed, she checked her phone. It was 5:17. He'd spent the entire day with his freakin' models.

Asshole. What on God's earth was she going to do? She actually had a mental image of herself jumping out of the El Camino, abandoning it in the middle of the road, claiming it was someone else's fine car. She scanned her inner play yard: Nobody was home. The ovarian shadow women were hiding behind her hip bone. Super Dame was long gone, probably throwing a party in her brain stem at Clarissa's expense. The pessimist in her was gaining strength. Her husband was not going to like what she had done, and she'd better be prepared for him exhibiting his displeasure in shattering detail.

"You must be tough, Clarissa. This is not the time for pussies." Deepak Chopra's oddly handsome face flickered and then held steady in her ever-running mental movie. He wore big red eyeglasses studded with beautiful ruby rhinestones. That took balls, she thought, wearing those Liberace glasses.

"Listen to me. Courage is not born; it is seized. Seize your courage, Clarissa. If you don't, you will regret every day of the rest of your life."

This made-to-order Deepak inspired in Clarissa a reexamination. This was her vehicle, and above all else, she'd bought it because she'd *wanted* to buy it. It was her money, her work, her life. This was not Iggy's decision to make. If he didn't like what she'd done, he could pout all by his lonesome. She wasn't going to care or apologize or accommodate.

"Go, baby, go!" Deepak adjusted his glasses and gazed at her, mirthful, curious.

"Yeah, right," she said, slowing down, letting Iggy turn in first. He didn't glance in her direction. He was in his own world as usual, that smug half-smile teetering on an otherwise impassive face. He was too big for that Civic, like a sausage in a casing. An awful notion took hold: What if the opposite happened? What if he claimed the El Camino for himself? Clarissa was sure he didn't realize it was *her* behind the wheel. So she drove a quarter mile past the house to give him time to go inside and her time to try to get a grip. She would not let him steal her car.

Three minutes later, when she pulled into the yard, she glimpsed in her peripheral vision a flurry of shadow and light. She turned and looked. All she saw was one leaf falling, a whirlybird without anchor. It landed in the cradled branches of a camellia. Stay steady, she told herself, shifting into park; you have the right to buy a car, a truck, a goat, a barrel of whiskey, or a boatload of orphans if that's what suits you.

"He can only take it from you if you allow it," Deepak said, and then he took the slightest nibble from a pink-frosted chocolate bonbon.

She turned off the ignition, got out of the truck, cursed the heat, tried to push out of her mind all fantasies involving a bonbon-eating New Age guru, and noticed that under the shade of the oaks, the El Camino's yellow paint took on a deeper hue. Thinking there was a scratch on the door, she rubbed it with her T-shirt; it was only a shadow. She imagined herself becoming one of those obnoxious people who set safety cones around their cars in parking lots. No, I'll never get that bad, she thought. Besides, those people were begging to get keyed. She walked to the rear of the house, felt her heart beat too fast, and went in through the back door. She slipped into the laundry room and stashed her purse back in its hiding place. In the dim glow of the chandelier room, she closed her eyes, counted to ten, and then went for it.

"Hey!" she yelled. "Where are you?"

The floor upstairs creaked. He had headed straight to his office. She walked to the foot of the stairs. She could simply let him discover the El Camino all on his own. She didn't have to say a thing. But now, having already started down the path to confrontation, she felt almost heady about his possible reactions. "Hey! Watcha doing?"

"Busy," he shouted. She heard him open and close his desk drawer.

"Well, take a break. I've got something to show you." That felt good—and dangerous.

He groaned. Her life—all of its molehills and detours—she realized, was an enormous annoyance to him.

"I told you," he said, stepping into the oval of light that defined the landing, "not to take out the truck. And what do you do?" At this angle, his ears looked bigger than his head, or maybe she was hallucinating—the whole heatstroke theory again.

He hurried down the stairs. His long limbs and torso moved like a baby rattle—loose and disjointed. She wondered if his penis flopped around as much as his arms did and if that was an enjoyable or encumbering sensation. His face was blotchy—red dots on a pale canvas. His skin always got blotchy in the heat. His beard was tangled—nearly matted—and she decided not to ponder how it got in such a state.

Her spine burned. *Stay strong, stay strong.* "I had to go out. Didn't have any choice."

"You could have waited until I got back." His bald head was baboon red. He was sunburned. Good. I hope it blisters and peels and maybe even rots, she thought.

"You were gone all day."

"I had business to take care of." He looked past her, boredom lengthening his face.

"And you don't want me taking the Civic."

"I don't care if you take the Civic, Clarissa." He hit the c's too hard, a hiss and a threat. "I care if you take it without asking. I have meetings, people I have to see. You know that. I can't walk into the yard and find that I have no transportation, now, can I?" He had not yet looked directly at her.

Clarissa always grew confused, as if her brain filled with nettles, when he spoke to her in his you're-an-idiot tone. Why didn't she lay it on the line? Why didn't she tell him that lunch with his models was not "business," and that she knew he'd been over at Yvette's apartment filming them doing only God knew what, and that the Civic was in both their names but purchased with her earnings? Something prevented her from speaking her mind, something she had learned as a girl when her mother was browbeating her over her figure or her moral character or her tendency to hide behind books. "Why do you read all the goddamn time?" She wanted this conversation to go well, even if it meant playing along with his lie.

"Did you have a good lunch?" she asked.

He waved off her words and stormed into the kitchen. "Lunch was fine. It was business." He gave equal and exaggerated emphasis to the last three words, opened the refrigerator, withdrew a beer, slammed shut the door, twisted off the cap, and said with his eyes closed, as if what he was about to utter caused him such distress that life was barely worth living, "On the way home, I stopped at a new gallery. Downtown near the Capitol." He took a swig, then stared at the floor as he spoke. "I was showing the *fowking* woman my book, just about had her convinced to host an installation of my nude wire sculptures, and suddenly she stops and says, 'Oh! You're Clarissa Burden's husband!'" He snorted, his free hand clenching into a giant fist. He glared at Clarissa, his lips spreading into a grimace, as if the encounter were his wife's fault. "I was so *fowking* mad at the *fowking* whore I walked out right then and there. I refused to show her one more image."

Clarissa did not know how to respond. How troubled should she be, she wondered, that his resentment ran this thick? "I'm sorry that happened to you."

He studied the bottle's label as if it were the most fascinating read on the planet. "No big deal. The gallery is a shithole. She'll be out of business before Halloween." Once more, he leveled his gaze at Clarissa. "The owner whore is a stupid cunt."

The words hit Clarissa like a whip. He was baiting her. But she would not bite. Her ears started to ring; she needed the world to leave her alone for one day, one week, one month. That was the solution: run. But to where?

"Courage, Clarissa. Born or seized?" Deepak was frowning.

Clarissa forced a smile. That's how you don't take bait. You ignore it. "I've got a really great surprise for you. Come with me." She walked ahead of him and said over her shoulder, surprising herself with how careless she sounded, "You're not going to believe it!"

"I've got a lot of work to do, Clarissa. I told Yvette and Natalie I'd have proofs for them tomorrow."

Lovely little Yvette and Natalie. "Are they coming back out?"

"No. I'm going to..." He paused, and in those three seconds, Clarissa perceived the pulsing vulnerability of yet another lie. "Um, meet them in town."

"I see." Clarissa threw open the front door. "This won't take long."

They stepped onto the porch. "Goddamn, this heat!" he said.

Amaziah, from his position behind the wheel, saw Iggy and Clarissa and sensed trouble. He put his hand on his son's head. "How about we go for a walk?"

"Yes, yes, yes!" Heart kicked his little legs. His face beamed.

Olga Villada took one look at Clarissa and knew that if it weren't for the presence of her husband and son, she'd stay put and interfere. The young woman looked absolutely vanquished, as if the man she had married were stealing her soul. Quickly she pecked her son's cheek. "What a good idea!"

Hand in hand, the three of them tumbled through the hot wind until they reached the hardwood grove behind the barn, a safe distance from the sentinel oak and the El Camino.

"What do you think?" Clarissa asked. Her instinct to stay safe propelled her into the yard and out of reach.

Iggy remained on the porch. He stroked his beard as if deeply contemplating the situation. Without warning, he spun around, slapped the porch rail that Amaziah had hand-carved, and yelled, "What the *fowk* did you do, *jou teef?*" He pounded each word.

Jou teef. You bitch. "I…" Clarissa looked down at her feet. She felt every shred of that day's happiness float away. "I bought a car."

He snorted. "Well, that's obvious. How badly did you get taken? How many miles does it have?"

"That's the thing. This old guy in Dead Oak owned it. It was like his hobby car. He barely drove it."

"How many, Clarissa?"

"Only forty-six thousand."

"Yeah, right. Forty-six thousand after they *fowked* with the odometer. What other bullshit did they feed you, eh?"

Clarissa did not say another word because she couldn't. Fury, pain, and embarrassment had frozen her thought processes, rendering her mute, immobile. It was the same feeling that overcame her when her mother beat her and called her a stupid fat whore. None of those three words had any basis in fact. But Clarissa took them in one by one, like poisoned slices of an ancient apple; she swallowed, every time.

"What did you do with the truck, Clarissa?"

How could she explain that its tires had been ice-picked and that a one-eyed man she'd just met whose name was Cracker Bandit who loved Sopchoppy earthworms with his whole heart had given her five hundred dollars cash for it? Five hundred dollars—it wasn't worth that much money—and the junk heap went away. She didn't have to think ever again about the stupid truck or how she would get to the grocery store or how she longed for the illusion of freedom. And she had five hundred dollars in her pocket—her lucky day. And a couple of thousand in her secret bank account. She wasn't going to tell him squat.

"Listen to me." He paced, pulled his rolled-sleeve Tommy Hilfiger shirt away from his long, wide torso. Clarissa stood silent, feeling stupid, a blind anger building. He stopped at the very edge of the porch, looked out over the yard as if he were a king surveying his fiefdom. Surely he was enjoying this, taking his sweet time before delivering his edict. He wiped his giant hand over his face in a gesture that suggested he was struggling with Clarissa's idiocy. And then the king spoke, that half-smile planted like a cockroach. "You're going to take this piece of redneck *kak* back to where you got it. *Ne?* Do you understand?...Clarissa?"

She stared at the dirt. An acorn, perfectly formed—as if it were the idea of an acorn rather than the real deal—landed by her left foot. She thought about Poor Spot Cemetery and the souls who rested there, how they had been powerless in life because of their gender.

"I don't want to see this monstrosity in my yard again. And

then you're going to get the truck back and bring it home and keep your stupid, fat American ass in line."

Both the little girl and the middle-aged woman Clarissa would soon become looked up at him, wondering who in the hell he thought he was speaking to. Fury, frustration, fear, and a host of other words that began primarily with *f* (*fucking motherfucker* led the way) coursed through her. She could feel tears rising, but by God, she would not give him the satisfaction. She would, however, no matter the price, find her voice. The words popped, the staccato rhythm creating tiny holes in the hot breeze. She was unaware of everything except her pain as she screamed, "You will not tell me what to do. Not now. Not ever. Never!"

He threw back his head and laughed.

"Don't laugh at me," she screamed through gritted teeth.

Arrogance lit his features as if he were made of crystal and ice. "Take the car back, Clarissa. I'm not going to tell you again." And then he turned and sauntered into the house, calm as dust, as if he'd done one fine job of scolding an impertinent child.

In her mind's eye, Clarissa fell to her knees and wailed as her mother and husband laughed, taunting her.

"You little fool," she heard her mother say.

"Have you always been such a dimwit?" her husband chortled.

Clarissa, standing under the oaks, the heat searing her T-shirt to her skin, said to the memories, "No, no, no!" She would not allow the past, her mother's meanness, her husband's arrogance, to define her. She had no idea how she would step out of this wasteland riddled with her mother's bones and her husband's resentment, but she was determined to find her way.

She was off to a fair start. For instance, she did not consider for even a moment following her husband's orders. "No way," she said at the thought of taking the El Camino back to A-One Auto.

As she wiped lifeless mosquitoes off the hood, her unhinged

self-pity morphed into something she had control over. Standing in the blistering heat, she understood there would be no slinking back into the house and asking for forgiveness, no crying, no trying to make things right with Papa Bear. She giggled. Papa Bear was a perfect name for him.

She waited by the El Camino for what she thought was two or three minutes—enough time for him to get settled again into his office. Then she went inside, retrieved her purse from its hiding place, fished out her cell phone, and flipped it open.

Bingo! Adams had called. She walked into her bedroom, called him back, checked the time, told him she wouldn't make it to his reading because her day had gotten a little crazy and she was running late, but that she'd meet up with him at the B and B. They'd have drinks. Get caught up. There would be other people around. She'd enjoy herself. She wouldn't worry about getting home before midnight. Papa Bear could go fuck himself. She decided all of this in the span of a thirty-second conversation.

"Can't wait to see you, baby." That's what Adams said to her right before they hung up.

⌐

Despite the day's searing heat, Clarissa took the hottest shower of her life. She needed to rid her skin, her hair, her soul, of all of the day's stink and gunk and funereal dust. The water pooled around her feet. She wiggled her toes, admiring the harlot red lacquer. It had not yet chipped or flaked. She shaved her legs, exfoliated nearly every inch of skin, washed her hair twice, and conditioned it with a cream that smelled of lavender and thyme. The water rushed over her hair, head, breasts, belly, hips, thighs, legs, tender feet. The shadow women, muttering in the soft light of her ovaries, relaxed amid the steam.

Happiness, serenity, and well-being, she told herself as she scrubbed between her toes, was a decision. A goddamn simple decision.

That's right, Clarissa. Just make up your mind: Be happy. Do not dwell on your fears. Do not let someone else's insecurities fuel your own. Do not be a pussy. Do not think about bliss. *Be bliss...* I can't hear you! The voice in her head had taken on the tonality of a Parris Island drill sergeant who had a thing for Deepak Chopra platitudes and spike Prada pumps.

She reached for the faucet knobs, turned off the water, grabbed the towel that she'd slung over the top of the door, and stepped out of the shower. Thinking that a vigorous drying would stimulate blood flow (and perhaps slough off dead cells, the benefits of which were innumerable) and knowing that healthy circulation helped ward off anxiety and stress (those little demons), Clarissa proceeded to rub herself with her towel—forehead to foot—so enthusiastically that a mole on her left calf began to bleed. "Holy shit," she said when she noticed. She dabbed off the blood and rubbed Chanel No. 5 moisturizer (*"Pour le corps,"* she said in a shaky French accent) on the length and breadth of both smooth legs.

Feeling as if the day's heat were a minor annoyance rather than a life-threatening record breaker, she stood in front of the bathroom mirror, combed through her long curls, and plotted. If her husband tried to stop her, she'd simply say, "Too bad!" And if he began to deride her, she'd—without emotion—gather her things, drive the hour to town, and finish dressing in the restroom of, say, that McDonald's on the parkway. Life was suddenly full of solutions. Optimism wasn't such a slippery slope, after all. Besides, there was no way he was going to get what he wanted. Not this time.

She combed conditioner through her hair and imagined him up there in his office, sifting through his favorite porn sites (she envisioned him as a giant fly, his right front leg tapping Enter, his compound eyes glowing in the screen's reflection, his thorax bloated with beer), and then she told herself that it was unfair to assume such a thing. Perhaps he was perusing Dick Blick Art Materials, where he could order online anything from paint-brushes to lead-free glazes. Or checking his e-mail. Or reading the *Times*. Why was she so suspicious? It was one of her worst traits. Just because he suffered from a porn addiction did not mean that he was whacking off upstairs. Besides, she thought she heard him pacing. Could one whack off and pace simultaneously? Absolutely not. He wasn't coordinated enough.

She secured her hair with a green ribbon and moisturized her face. Rather than slopping it on as usual, she took the time to massage in the thirty-five-dollar-a-tube goop with her fingertips, using smooth, concentric motions just as the nineteen-year-old Shisheido counter girl had demonstrated.

Olga Villada wafted in, looked at Clarissa's arsenal of beauty products, and felt a quick stab of regret; what she wouldn't give to be alive — young and pretty — and trying all those little pots of color for herself. She watched Clarissa bend into her reflection, her image blooming in a mirror Olga Villada had once primped in front of. But that was all over. When her life was taken, her reflection went with it. Bitterness, that old poison, mushroomed through her spectral veins, and she decided it was best if she stayed away from Clarissa's tantalizing gels and powders and sable brushes and a mirror that for her held only the image of other women: never her own, not ever again. She tossed back her head — she was a proud woman — drifted out of the bathroom, through the bedroom, and down the hall in search of strength; where were her husband and son?

Clarissa studied herself in the mirror, searching, angling to catch a purer light. Jaws. Cheeks. Mouth. Teeth: straight and unremarkable. Thanks to the surgeon's scalpel and drill and five years in braces, she only slightly resembled the Clarissa of her youth. No one would ever guess that she'd once been disfigured ("deformed" was the word that rose in Clarissa's mind), that her mother's often shouted order to "push harder!"—an impossible solution for the wrong problem—bedeviled her like an aural haunting, a maternal curse. For the last fourteen years, she had lived with an ordinary face: no underbite, no overbite, no buckteeth, nothing to prevent her from operating in the world as if she had every right to be treated with the same respect as any other person. On that hot solstice day—one that had already proven to be extraordinary for Clarissa—she gazed into Olga Villada's unblemished mirror and realized that the person she was in her head was not the person whose reflection stared back at her.

"Interesting," Clarissa whispered, surprised by a sudden sense of loss. Would she ever be able to meld the two—the pre- and post-surgery Clarissas? Would she ever rid her consciousness of the Clarissa her classmates had dubbed Bucky? Did she really want to? If she banished Ugly Clarissa, would her life be different in ways noticeable and not? Would she be a better person? Would her husband finally love her? Clarissa closed her eyes and, understanding she had no answers, forced all the images—mental pixel by mental pixel—to dissolve. As her world faded to white, she heard the laughter of a woman and child and decided it was her heart song. Nothing more. She stood quiet and still, nearly a solid minute, enjoying the nothingness. But because life is not composed of dearth no matter how comforting, an image of those peach roses in their cut crystal vase took shape, obliterating her mind's cool white canvas. How lovely, she thought, how very, very lovely. She opened her eyes.

"Tonight, you are beautiful," she told the mirror, a cold fury steadying her. "Tonight, you will do whatever your heart desires." She loved this strange new sensation, loved how it was directed exclusively at her husband. Leashed anger.

She stepped into her bedroom and rummaged through her closet, amazed at the clarifying power of being profoundly yet calmly pissed off. She sifted through her collection of jumpers—oversize numbers that hid her curves and suggested that middle age was a lonely, horrid Sahara desert bereft of plant life, chocolate, and sex.

"Fuck that," Clarissa said. She turned her attention to her jeans, searching for a specific pair—skintight with a poppy embroidered up one thigh—she'd bought on a whim two months prior but never worn. She pulled them off the hanger and held them in front of her. Dubious but tempted, she thought, If you can buy yourself an El Camino, you can certainly rock these jeans. She folded them over her arm and tried to feel comfortable with this newfound recklessness. It made her nose itch. She sneezed. Fear and something akin to exhilaration boiled through her.

Despite the sex-kitten jeans and her emerging resolve to allow her real self to come out of hiding, Clarissa reverted to habit, drifting over to her sizable collection of long-sleeved, elephantine tunics. This urge to hide her body was nearly pathological. It had taken root in her early years when her mother prattled nearly nonstop about the evils of men and the need for Clarissa to cover up. To add salt to the old wound, here she was, married to a man obsessed with flesh as long as it wasn't her flesh. No wonder she felt like a mop. She stood there, holding the slinky jeans to her breasts, wondering if she had the nerve to wear a top that showed off her cleavage, her tight waist.

She went back into her bedroom and waded through her chest of drawers. She was the owner of a collection of chemises she never wore, unless she hid them under something big and blousy. There was one in particular she had in mind. It was coral—a good color match with the poppy—and had thin lace straps. She dug like a dog hunting down a lost bone, tossing silky little squares into the air. They floated, landing silently in a shimmering butterfly pile. Finally, at the bottom of the last drawer, she found the one she wanted; it was balled up like a lonely fist. She unfurled the chemise and held it to the light. "Perfect."

Other women showed their bodies. Other women were confident and saucy. Her husband — the painter, ceramicist, sculptor, multimedia madman, and photographer of butt-naked women — did not like it when she revealed that she was a woman with fair contours. *All the more reason, my dear, all the more reason.*

She laid the jeans and chemise on the bed, arranging them the way one would on a mannequin, smoothing and poufing. She stepped back, studied the ensemble, and felt hope's thick sap rise. But she could not identify what the hope was pinned to. What good was hope if it remained nebulous? Hope was one of those abstractions, like love; for it to be meaningful, it had to be hitched to something real — like a car or a can of good tuna or a decent man.

Clarissa stepped back into the bathroom and once more faced the antique walnut-framed mirror. She had discovered it in the barn underneath a pile of old lumber. She did not know, of course, that the mirror had once held the reflection of Olga Villada and that a spark of that woman's energy remained, a faint shine, all about the beveled edge. Indeed, when she thought about it at all, Clarissa attributed the mirror's suggestion of a sparkly outline to the light cast by the bathroom's pink, frosted-glass chandelier that hung from the ceiling like a frozen, three-armed octopus. Clarissa leaned in close to the mirror and applied two coats of mascara. She rifled through her lipsticks in the vanity drawer and chose a pale coral gloss, betting it would snap up the blue of her eyes and the slow burn of her blond hair that was naturally streaked with tones of amber and red. Because the gloss was a soft hue, she knew it would not compete with the deeper coral of the chemise.

All made up, she returned to the bedroom, pretty, adrenaline flowing, vibrant, and bubbly. She eyed the jeans and knew it was now or never. She sighed, stretched her arms over her head as if she were warming up for a marathon, remembered a girl she went to high school with who bragged that she stuffed herself into her too-tight jeans by lying on her bed, sucking in her stomach, and pulling up the zipper with a pair of pliers. She would not resort to that. No. Not ever. Life should be lived one leg at a time, she thought, grabbing the jeans and pulling them on, an idea of what she wanted to look like plastered in her brain.

As was the case with most women, the idea—fed by a fashion industry intent on glorifying skeletal chic—was far more anemic than the opulent reality. She zipped up—without the aid of pliers or any other hand tool—half squatted to stretch the fabric, and then looked at herself in the full-length mirror nailed to her bedroom door, front and side and three-quarter rear. The horror of actuality versus the folly of hope slammed her down. She had a butt. A real butt. An I'm a Woman with Ample Hips for Loving butt. The Some Men Hate It and Others Can't Get Enough of It butt. The Size Two Is for Fools and Starvation Victims butt. The Here I Am and I'm Not Going to Go Away No Matter How Much Artificial Sweetener I Ingest butt. The Why Couldn't My Mother Have Been Twiggy butt. The Could You Please Slide over a Little Bit More butt. The I Clear the Dance Floor Because I'm the Only One Out Here Bopping with a Big Butt butt. The I Shed Tears and Curse the Gods and Feel Deeply Ashamed over My Big-Assed Booty butt.

There it was, sheathed in denim as if it were a peacock in full bloom announcing to heaven and hell that it had a sex drive. Holy shit. She could not go out like this. What on earth had she been thinking!

Deepak, a new and growing voice in her consciousness, having lost his drill sergeant edge, turned on the light in her brain, waved his Prada clutch in her face, and said, "Embrace the butt, my friend."

Embrace the butt? Embrace the butt?

"Yes, yes! Embrace it, for it is like a beautiful flower your soul sends out into the world for the glory of all the universe."

Oh, shut up, Deepak. She closed her eyes, then reopened them, hoping something had changed. Nope, it was still there, celestial and proud.

"There is no other butt in the world like it. Yours is unique. It is what makes you you. Imperfection is the key to beauty." Deepak's voice reminded her of incense, wind chimes, and bullshit.

She ran her hands over her hips. In eighth grade, Danny Davis, a kid on whom she'd had a monstrous crush, told her that if she were tall, she wouldn't be fat. What did he know? He'd flunked out. Didn't make it past eleventh grade. Jerk. She could be six feet tall and she'd still have a big ass. Maybe little Deepdeep had a point. Other women rocked their butts. Why couldn't she?

"Exactly! You just have to get used to seeing it," Deepak said. "A hidden candle offers no light."

Jesus, where did her brain get this guy? But she was going to try. If no one liked her butt, they didn't have to look at her butt.

"Just a little confidence goes a long way!"

That's enough, Deepak Platitude. You've convinced me. Hoping she would not regret it later, Clarissa committed to the jeans. She reached for the chemise and pulled it over her head. She wasn't sure if she dared look or not.

"You must. You are a real beauty," Deepak said. Like five other men that day and possibly one snake, he winked at her and then dotted a smudge of mascara off his upper eyelid.

Clarissa surprised herself. She sort of liked what she saw.

Maybe Deepdeep had a point: It was all about confidence. But she wasn't used to this woman in tight jeans and a flimsy, flirtatious top. In fact, she was embarrassed. What if she looked like a cow, but her brain was playing a trick on her? What then? What if she walked into a bar or restaurant or wherever she and Adams might land and people started laughing, looking away and whispering? Just like before her surgery? What if Adams was embarrassed to be seen with her? She stared hard at her reflection.

"You've come too far to start in with all this negative thinking," Deepak said, buffing his nails. "My mother always said it is a wise woman who does not backtrack."

"Shut up!" Clarissa said, only slightly worried that she was talking back to a figment of her imagination. She stared, shoulders slumped. "I'm a fucking disaster."

Deepak paused from his buffing, looked her up and down, one perfect brow arched, and then started swiping again. "You know, good posture is one of the five keys to happiness."

"Oh yeah, and what are the other four?" Clarissa muttered, pulling the chemise over the slight rise of her belly. "Always sit like a lady? Don't curse? Never pass gas?" She huffed, trying to dispel her agitation and self-revulsion. "No backtracking," she whispered to her reflection, and then—pretending her head was attached to a string and God was pulling on it, stretching her taller, forcing her shoulders back and her head high—she addressed the fact of her poor posture.

"Ah! And now, only four more to go." Deepak shot her a catty, drag queen smile.

She turned away from the mirror, shut the door on Deepak, and headed back to her closet, muttering, "Maybe. Maybe I can do this." She flicked on the light and surveyed her shoes. Closed-toed, open-toed, sandals, sneakers, high heels, flats, babushka clompers with lots of support. Sensible? With this outfit? Not.

She opted for a pair of sky blue, open-toed suede pumps with a three-inch heel. Gorgeous.

Once dressed, in a ritual that she could trace to her girlhood when she stood before the cracked mirror in the tin bucket trailer and tried on her mother's glitter-and-paste Woolworth's earrings, Clarissa donned her jewelry. She began with a silver charm necklace that held talismans of different sorts: a solid silver frog from Mexico bought at a flea market, a leaping dolphin procured at a roadside tourist trap, a scarab given to her by a former lover, a baby ring she found in the trash outside an apartment building she once lived in, a Tibetan prayer box containing an image of the Dalai Lama she purchased on eBay, a simple sterling silver disk she decided symbolized renewal, a St. Christopher's medal because she felt like a traveler even in her own home. Then came her earrings: silver hoops—big ones because she liked the sizable circles they formed on each ear, fancying that the space within the twin spheres held all of life's possibilities.

Finally, on each arm she stacked sterling bangles—some plain, some engraved, some pierced, some wide, and others deliciously narrow. They chimed *shh shh shh* as she walked.

Her jewelry was her armament; goddess protection designed to help hide and protect her heart, a trick that forced the male eye away from the breasts, the cleavage, the full lips. As she separated out the charms on her necklace and studied the smooth belly of her lucky frog, she thought that these pieces of silver were the only things that made her feel feminine anymore, little trinkets deflecting pain, flashes of light signaling that her life as a sensual being was not over even while they redirected—at least for a moment—the forever roaming male eye.

Clarissa shook her arms and delighted in the bangles' music. She tossed back her curls and squared her shoulders. She didn't know the woman in the mirror.

"Yes, you do!" Deepak said. "Embrace not just your butt. Embrace all of the sensual you."

Clarissa rolled her eyes. She really needed to do something about her inner monologue. She turned away from the mirror and reached for her tote, which still smelled of the truck rot.

Deepak smacked her on the behind. "Take my clutch, silly girl. It's much sexier."

Clarissa rummaged through her box of handbags until she found the purse Deepak wanted her to take. There was just enough room in it for her lipstick, cell phone, compact, and keys. What more did she need? She looked in the mirror one final time. "Thanks, Deepdeep," she said.

She walked through the house, her bracelets clinking, clutch and keys in hand, stinky tote over her shoulder, terrified that Iggy would come down from on high. But she did not have the nerve to simply waltz out. That would make her, she feared, a bad wife. So, as women in her predicament were wont to do, she struck a coward's compromise. After hiding her tote in the laundry room, she stepped into the kitchen, out of sight of the upstairs landing, and yelled, "Hey, I'm leaving!"

She heard a scraping of a chair against the floor and thought, No, no, no, don't come out here.

"It's too late for you to take it back tonight. Do it tomorrow," he shouted. And though he whispered what came out of his mouth next, the words tumbled through the heat, spiraling downward like autumn leaves, landing on Clarissa's waiting eardrums: "Dumb ass."

The words entered her as if delivered by a flame-tipped arrow. For a moment, she imagined her sky blue pumps had morphed into those sexy, superhero cerulean boots. She heard her superhero cape flap in the imaginary superhero breeze. She reached through her skin, wiggled her hand past cartilage and bone and into the pulpy mess of her heart. She withdrew the flaming arrow and snapped it in two. Keep your voice steady, she thought. "I'm going to Adams's reading. I'll see you when I get home."

She closed her eyes, hid her face in her superhero cape as protection against his response. But none came. She stood alone, dressed up, her sky blue pumps pinching her toes, waiting for him to say something, anything — go to hell, good-bye, you can't go, have a nice time. For the second time that day, she heard what sounded like a marble roll across the floor.

Olga Villada swirled in, amazed at Clarissa's star shine. She was glad that Amaziah was upstairs. Death had not extinguished Olga Villada's jealous streak.

Standing underneath the crystal chandelier, looking beautiful and confident (two things she did not feel), Clarissa realized that her husband had chosen, in his calculated way, not to respond. There she stood, shut out again. She felt that anger — still controlled, still leashed — rumble through her. "You have no idea," she whispered, her words furling like smoke but not rising high enough for her husband to hear, "how independent I can be."

"Brava!" Olga Villada said. "Brava!" She clapped twice in her flamenco way. Her black ringlets bounced. She, too, in the early evening light, though spectral, looked beautiful.

Clarissa went into the library. The ghost followed. The research dossier was on the fainting couch, its pages a messy jumble. The newspaper Clarissa had used to kill the fly was still on the floor. Clarissa picked it up and tossed it into the wastebasket in the corner. The fly's carcass remained stuck to the weapon's wide, blunt blade.

Olga Villada, again violating the family rule, thinking it would be more noticeable to Clarissa if it was on the library table, reached for the file.

Clarissa turned away from the wastebasket and swept it up

before Olga Villada had it in her hands. She tapped the file on the table, straightening the papers. She couldn't wait to share with Adams what she'd discovered about her house.

I'm more powerful than I know, Olga Villada mused as Clarissa left the library, crossing into the chandelier room, dossier in hand.

Clarissa, refusing her urge to offer one last good-bye to her husband, walked out the front door and closed it gently.

Olga Villada stood at the window and watched Clarissa slide behind the steering wheel of the giant steel-and-chrome crazy horse. She saw her place the dossier on the dash. In the early evening light, Clarissa and the El Camino glowed.

The closest Clarissa could park to the bed-and-breakfast was a block north, within walking distance of the old state Capitol and its red-and-white candy-striped awnings, under the vacant glare of a streetlight. She turned off the ignition, gripped the steering wheel, closed her eyes, and decided she did not have the strength to go through with this. Maybe she could just drive aimlessly in her splendid new car-truck for an hour or so, head home, and lie to her husband about what a wonderful time she'd had.

"Are you nothing but a big chicken?" Deepdeep piped up. "A chicken—bwaak! bwaak!—and not a woman?"

"Deepdeep," Clarissa said, fully annoyed, "you're not even real. You wouldn't even exist if it weren't for me." She opened her eyes, reached for the rearview, paused because she was afraid she'd break it off, and then gingerly tilted it toward her. There she was, in the solstice's slow fade: Her face, the one that after fourteen years still felt like a stranger's, reflected back at her. "I am not a chicken," she said. "I can do this."

She smiled. Everything was fine. No lip gloss–smudged teeth, no clumped mascara, no raccoon eyes. She was good to go. But still she sat, afraid to open the door. Afraid to step into the world alone. Afraid to gallivant down the street on her way to see a man who was straight, single, talented, and gorgeous. She could simply scurry back into her solitary marital existence and not see an old friend who just happened to be a male. There was still time. Adams would understand. Hell, maybe he'd prefer it: out on the town alone, without the encumbrance of a married woman. But he had asked, and she had given him her word. It was a professional relationship—one writer to another. And she had not lied to her husband; he knew where she was going. Even on the off chance that Adams was willing, Clarissa Burden would not cheat. Maybe flirt, but sex was not on the table. Ever. Evidently not even with her husband, she thought ruefully. Yep, she'd keep her vows even if they and all her sex organs were moldering from profound neglect.

Clarissa took in her new car; it was all jazzy with gleaming knobs and gadgets she didn't know how to work. Its cream-colored leather upholstery was cool to the touch. The windshield was wide and crack-free. She opened the glove box and peered in: just the manual; no telltale ephemera from the previous owner. She pushed a button on the dash, curious as to what it was for. Nothing happened. She loved this car.

"There is nothing you cannot do," Deepdeep whispered. And for moment, amid all that chrome and steel, Clarissa decided to believe him.

"Just give me the strength to get out of the car," she said. She straightened the rearview, stuffed the dossier out of sight under the passenger seat, grabbed the blue silk clutch, dropped her keys into it, opened the El Camino's heavy door, and pushed herself into the night. Feeling impossibly underdressed, overdressed, miserable, beautiful, grotesque, and a tad A-OK, she wondered how she could even walk given the conflicted condition of her heart and mind.

She opened the clutch and checked the time on her cell phone: 7:58. Daylight still shifted through the oaks, their burled limbs laden with curling trails of Spanish moss. The slow-building dusk had brought with it little relief from the day's swelter. It remained so hot that the evening birdsong was labored, stifled. She cut across the street and headed west, hoping she didn't look like a streetwalker, fearful that her makeup was going to experience a Salvador Dalí meltdown, thankful for the double dose of deodorant she'd wisely swathed on. At the next intersection, she hung a left. The B and B was moments away. She decided that breathing was no longer involuntary; she had to think about it. Do not panic. Even though you fear you look like Tony Curtis in *Some Like It Hot*, again, do not panic. Adams was just a friend. Nothing more. Ever. He wasn't interested in her sexually or romantically. He knew her husband; they'd met twice before at readings. He was an honorable guy. She was just doing her duty: mentoring a young writer.

The Old Florida Magnolia Inn was on a corner lot—a rambling, aged jewel of a structure set amid oaks, camellias, azaleas, palm trees, and jasmine so fragrant that Clarissa imagined herself rubbing a bouquet of tiny white blossoms on her wrists, shoulders, temples. Before crossing the cobblestone street, she paused, struck by how much the place looked like her house, only larger, with a more manicured lawn. It was beautiful. Even the porch's gingerbread scrollwork was identical. So, too, were the glass-and-paneled front doors topped with narrow transoms. How odd, she thought, twin houses.

She stood alone in the slow-waning light, the thick heat, the jasmine wind, contemplating the day. For the first time in her marriage, she had defied her husband, and he was so self-absorbed that he did not get the significance. Come morning, she thought, when he realized the El Camino was not going anywhere, perhaps he'd finally begin to understand the depth of her discontent and stop ignoring her.

An abundant hedge of yellow roses hugged the length of the B and B's picket fence. What a wonderful idea, she thought. Come fall, she would do that: line her fence in yellow roses. She stepped into the street, her blond curls blowing in the soft, hot wind, her mind pondering a hedge flush with bright blossoms. Halfway across, a stone's throw from the hedge, her sky blue heel caught firmly in the uneven bricks. She tried to wrench free. She looked toward the Capitol. A car was barreling down on her. She slipped off the shoe, knelt, and tugged as hard she dared, cognizant that if she pulled too hard, she would snap the heel. Despite the oncoming vehicle and the knowledge that she was laced in dusk's shadows, she could not abandon the shoe. How could she go through the night wearing only one blue pump? Surely the idiot would stop.

"Boo!"

Startled, she jerked her body toward the sound but lost her balance. In the crab crawl that ensued, she tumbled off her one shod foot, landing on her ass. The car slowed but did not stop. The driver honked.

"Jesus, I'm sorry. I didn't mean to scare you."

Clarissa looked up and saw Adams standing over her, wearing an ear-to-ear grin, a taut, pearl-buttoned rockabilly shirt, and jeans that fit real, real well. The car—another freaking Civic, thought Clarissa—skidded to a stop. The brakes squealed. Again, the driver honked.

"Hey, buddy, give it a rest. Can't you see I'm helping my lady friend here?"

Adams offered his hand, which Clarissa accepted, and he

pulled her to her feet. Feeling like a three-hundred-pound moron in a single shoe, while silently cussing Deepak (she felt the need to blame *someone*), she dusted off her jeans and studied the distance between herself, the shoe that was jammed in the cobblestone, and the car that had almost hit her.

The idiot in the Civic laid on his horn a third time.

"Mister, if you honk that horn once more," Adams said, calm and cool, as if he were discussing the vitamin content of a watermelon, "I will personally shove that steering wheel up your ass. Now just give us a second."

The moonfaced, bespectacled Civic driver, who sported a comb-over that started below his right ear, appeared stunned that anyone would say something so rude, even in the wake of his insistent honking. But he kept his hands away from the horn.

Adams walked over to the trapped sky blue shoe and with one firm tug freed it. He headed back to Clarissa and said, "Sweetheart, I've always wanted to do this." And with that, he picked her up.

This was, at the risk of pointing out the obvious, a literal manifestation of sweeping her off her feet, but Clarissa, given how stunned she was, did not think of the obvious, the sublime, or even the ridiculous. She experienced solely, and unfortunately for her burgeoning heart, a flood of overanxious gratitude.

Adams carried her the remaining width of the street, deposited her on the sidewalk, bent down, and slipped the sky blue pump onto her bare ruby-toed foot. Deepak whispered, "Nail lacquer: It is a girl's best friend." Her ovarian shadow women were fanning themselves in a collective swoon.

The Civic sped by, its driver grimacing at the couple. But he did not honk.

"Thank you!" Clarissa said, breathless, off-kilter, an insane happiness tapping the pulse points of her wrists. She pulled the bottom edge of the chemise even with her hips. "You are quite the gentleman."

Adams rose to his full height. Clarissa did not remember him being so tall. "And you look beautiful, Ms. Burden."

Clarissa thought that there was a rule somewhere that married women were not to accept compliments from young, handsome, single guys — especially single guys whose blue eyes were nearly black and whose brown hair fell in the sexiest little tendrils down a long, tan neck and whose jeans fit the way orange peels fit fruit. But she couldn't remember the details of said rule and therefore decided, given various other circumstances, she was under no ethical mandate to obey it.

"I'm sorry I missed your reading," she said, brushing an unruly curl off her face. "Today's just been" — she looked past his shoulder, trying to gather the right words, but soon realized that specificity in this instance was not in her best interest — "crazy."

"Ah, don't worry about it, baby. No big deal. I'm just happy to see you."

"Me too," Clarissa said, grinning, self-conscious, tugging at the spaghetti strap that had slipped down her shoulder. "I mean, I'm happy to see you."

He reached over and plucked something off her cheek. "Bug," he said.

Holy crap. She wanted to die. How long had it been there? Was spontaneous combustion due to embarrassment an option? Tingling from his touch, she had to do something and do it quick. She could not just stand there, grinning, nearly drooling, cockeyed as a drunken sparrow. Through the magic of self-preservation, she managed to sputter, "How was your trip?" but even as she spoke, she feared it was in Deepak's singsong lilt.

"Fine, just fine." He put a polite hand on her elbow and they drifted uphill, toward the bed-and-breakfast.

"The reading?"

"Not bad. I read from some new stuff. Maybe I'll let you take a look at it."

"I'd love that."

He put his arm around her, squeezed her shoulders, and said, "It's good to see you, Clarissa."

"It's good to see you, too."

He swung open the picket fence gate — the scent of those yellow roses mingled with the heavy intent of the jasmine — gestured for her to go in, and asked, "How's Iggy?"

"Fine. Busy. Working on a wire sculpture exhibit, other stuff. You know. He tried to make it but is" — she zipped through her mental Rolodex of excuses — "dealing with some sort of deadline." Clarissa flashed a big smile, trying to sell it. "Were there a lot of people at the reading?"

"A fair number. One writer — he's about to graduate from some junior college near here — he had a big family. That saved us all."

They gained the steps of the veranda. Clarissa coveted the wicker rockers and fern baskets. "And this was sponsored by the public library?"

"Yes indeed. Meet Florida's Up-and-Coming Writers. One of us was an eighty-two-year-old woman who wrote what she called 'cracker romances.' Brilliant stuff. She even gave me her business card. She has business cards. I don't have business cards."

Clarissa studied his face. He appeared bemused, not harsh. She liked that. The cracker romance writer, she thought, was probably smitten with him. "And I bet she sells the hell out of them."

Adams paused, his hand on the screen door of the old mansion. "You really do look pretty, Clarissa."

She felt herself sparkle, head to toe, and wondered if gravity weren't a law but a suggestion. She wanted to say something witty, sophisticated. But all she could get out was a giggle in a minor hysterical scale. Criminy, she thought, I am behaving like a wounded old waif in a Tennessee Williams play.

Adams held open the door. "After you, sweetheart."

Clarissa stepped into the house, her bangles melodious as they clinked one against the other. She stood just inside the doorway and was immediately struck by how much the interior also resembled her house, only larger and not as accomplished. The sweeping staircase with its carved newel post was nearly identical, except the carving was rough—hewn by an unsteady or untrained hand. In an ill-conceived remodel, someone had dropped the ceiling—probably to keep down heating and cooling costs—but it did the house no favors. Clarissa had admired the structure from the street, but now that she was inside, she felt claustrophobic. The dropped ceilings caused the space to feel smaller than it truly was, as if the weight of the house were pressing down on its inhabitants. She walked over to the wall nearest the entry and studied a gilt-framed photograph—an old studio shot, late nineteenth century, if she had to guess—of four men, dressed in suit coats, staring glum-faced at the camera. One of them was missing an arm, another an eye. Despite the suit coats, the men appeared rough, even violent. Clarissa felt the stir of an odd and distant fear.

"Nice, isn't it?" Adams said, looking around, picking up a porcelain whatnot. "A little froufrou for my tastes with the curtains and all, but real nice. Beats my apartment any day."

"It's a lot like my house," Clarissa said, looking around, trying not to feel creeped out. "But not, I don't know, as finished. You should come see it sometime. It's a grand old rambling example of..." Her voiced trailed away as her middle-aged station in life began to assert itself.

"I'm going to just go drop off these pages," Adams said, pulling a thin sheaf from his back pocket, "and then I'll be right back down. How about we go get a drink?"

"Sounds good."

Adams took the stairs two at a time. He seemed awfully fit. He must be working out. Clarissa imagined herself in a muumuu, slugging Geritol straight from the ugly brown bottle, but before her self-loathing fantasy could gain any air, a well-appointed sixty-something woman with a pretty cloud of silver white hair pattered in. "May I help you?"

"Oh, no. I'm just waiting. I'm visiting a guest of yours." Clarissa could feel her nerves gnawing away at the private maze of her intestines. She did not want this woman, whom she didn't know from a cornflake, thinking she was a floozy. "We're going out just as soon as he gets downstairs. If that's all right."

"Of course it's all right, dear." She reached for her glasses, which were on a golden chain around her neck, and perched them on the tip of her nose.

"This house, it's wonderful," Clarissa said. "It looks so much like my own."

"The Old Florida Magnolia Inn, circa 1845, is very special indeed," she said. "It has gone through many a delicate renovation, survived a fire, and is, simply put, a stunning example of early Florida architecture." The woman wafted her bejeweled hand through the air—a gesture designed to punctuate the house's grandeur. "I'm sure any similarities with your house are purely a result of region, dear." The woman seemed very certain and prideful and in no mood to learn anything about Clarissa's house, including that it predated the bed-and-breakfast by two decades.

Clarissa peered into the room to her right; it had been converted into a small dining area, complete with a reproduction Coca-Cola cooler and a new sign with an old message: MAN-

AGEMENT RESERVES THE RIGHT TO REFUSE SERVICE TO ANYONE. Funny how one person's nostalgia is another person's nightmare, thought Clarissa. "That sign in there," she said. "I realize it's a reproduction, but its original intent was to keep blacks out of white establishments. Don't your guests find it offensive?"

"Oh, that silly thing!" The woman again waved her hand, but this time in dismissal. "My nephew decorated in there and thought the sign was the cutest thing, and I haven't had the heart to take it down."

"But it sends a message that I'm not sure—"

"You look so familiar," the woman said, cutting Clarissa off. She readjusted her glasses. "Do I know you?"

"She's a famous writer," Adams said, jostling down the stairs, the thudding of his boots magnified by the vacant space of the stairwell. "Meet Clarissa Burden."

"Oh! The writer!" The woman beamed, and Clarissa turned red. "I read about you in the paper last spring. I cut it out, intending to buy the book. I just haven't done it yet. I'm sorry. But I will."

"Well, thank you." Clarissa looked at Adams, who was also beaming.

"You're much prettier than that picture they ran."

Clarissa shot the woman a polite smile and tried to remember the photo. "I'm afraid I'm just not very photogenic." The newspaper had sent out a staff photographer, but other than that, she came up blank.

The woman arched a penciled brow, and the perfection of it reminded her of Deepdeep. "A pretty thing like you! I'm sure that's not the case. It simply didn't reproduce well." The woman's hazel eyes took on a steel edge, as if this were a matter of deep consequence. "I'll run to the bookstore tomorrow. Will you sign it for me?"

"Books," Adams said. "She has several."

"Only two," Clarissa corrected, wanting her imaginary sinkhole to open up and save her.

"That's two more than most people, dear."

"Damn straight. In fact," Adams said to the proprietor, who seemed delighted by his use of profanity, "you should buy them all — multiple copies — one for each room."

"What a great idea, young man! You know, all my friends tell me I should write a book. Oh, the stories I could tell! Just about this house alone! Do you mind me asking, how long does it take you to write one? Start to finish?"

"Well, that depends," Clarissa said, a second wave of claustrophobia washing over her.

"Oh, right." The woman's face tightened as though she'd just received bad news. "Writer's block. Awful! I've heard of it. What a terrible thing for you."

How in the hell, Clarissa wondered, had the woman zeroed in so quickly? Was it that obvious? Or just a lucky, random jab? Payback for saying something about the sign? Clarissa felt a nearly irresistible urge to kick the old broad: one good blow to her shin. But instead, relying on her polite autopilot, she said, "I'd be happy to sign a book for you. Next time I'm in town, I'll stop by."

"Perfect!" On the strength of two simple syllables, the woman's sparkling demeanor returned.

"I hate to break this up," Adams said, taking Clarissa by the arm, "but somewhere in this town there is a bar stool with my name on it."

"Go, go! Didn't mean to keep you," the woman said, fluttering her hands. "You two have a good night. And it was so nice to meet you, Clarissa Burden. See? I remembered your name. I'm Mrs. Butler. Eunice Butler. I married the great-great-great-grandson of the man who built this house."

"Very nice to meet you, too, Mrs. Butler." Clarissa inched

toward the door. She could feel a story coming on. She could see in the woman's prideful smile that she *needed* to tell Clarissa all about it. And perhaps if Adams hadn't slipped a guiding hand around the small of her back, she would have been happy to listen. Listening, after all, was a writer's mandate. But the house gave her the creeps, and the sign had pissed her off, and the woman was spooky, and Adams was making her swoon ever so slightly, and even though the day was long, in all honesty, the night was young. The old woman's story would have to wait.

Clarissa and Adams stepped onto the porch and headed down the steps. Happy to be out of the uneasy house, Clarissa took a deep breath and held the steamy air in her lungs for five long counts.

"Good night!" Eunice Butler called from behind the screen door.

Clarissa breathed again and thought that the woman's vibrancy was weightless, like an image spun from the heated lens of a projector. She and Adams responded in unison, "Night!"

The woman closed the door—they heard the click of the lock—and Adams and Clarissa found themselves on the side lawn, standing by a fountain dappled with goldfish, staring up at the hot, hot sky, talking about things of little consequence, things Clarissa would soon forget; and as they conversed, the evening's first star pierced the solstice's deep sky.

⌐◠

They walked down a sidewalk buckled from the great roots of the oaks that lined the street, toward the Capitol and its nucleus of bars and lobbyist offices. Clarissa, slipping her hand around the suitable crook of Adams's arm, sensing this was a man who would appreciate her day's crowning jewel, said, "Okay, before we do anything else, you have to see what I bought today. It'll take just a second."

She steered him in the direction of her car, and when she stepped onto the cobblestone road, he glanced at her sky blue pumps and asked, "Uh-oh, should I carry you?"

She laughed but kept her focus. "You, unlike some people I know, will appreciate this." Avoiding the heel-trapping cracks, holding her arms away from her body for balance, Adams doing the same in childish solidarity, Clarissa led them one block over.

When they got back on the sidewalk, Adams paused in front of a house that had been converted to attorneys' offices. A trellis arching the walkway supported a climbing rose, its twisting branches supple, snakelike. Adams reached into the thicket, snapped a tight pink blossom, and said, "For you." He slipped it into her hair.

"Thank you," she said, resisting an urge to touch his hand, feeling as if she were slipping into someone else's life. She noticed that the vine had not given up the blossom without taking its weight in flesh. "You're bleeding."

"It's nothing." He readjusted the flower. "Perfect. Now, what is it that we've got to see?"

"It's not far. Follow me." She led him across the street, walked past the snaggled line of parked cars, stopped at the El Camino, dug into her silk clutch, lifted out her car keys, and jiggled them.

"This!" Adams said, his voice rising an octave and his navy blue eyes widening. "This is yours?" He shook his head as if in amazement. "No shit?"

"No shit." Clarissa swept her arm Vanna White style. Pride bubbled through her like a clear, untainted stream.

"Fantastic!" He walked the circumference of the vehicle. "This is a classic muscle car. And it's...oh, my God..."

"Cherry?"

He stopped at the left headlight, hands on hips. "Yeah!" He held out his hand. "Give me the keys."

"What?"

"Give me the keys."

"Why?"

"Because we're taking Yellow Bird for a spin."

"Yellow Bird. I love it!" Laughing, thinking, Why the hell not, she tossed them to him. The keys sparkled, end over end, under the glare of the streetlight. Adams grabbed them out of the sky, sure and confident. When he opened the passenger door, he offered her his hand—the one marked by the rosebush thorns. She took it and slid in, careful not to let her palm linger too long in his. As he walked to the driver's side, she touched the rose, her husband's recriminations growing ever more distant. In fact, she thought as Adams eased behind the wheel, she could barely hear them.

⁓

As Adams threaded Yellow Bird through the Tallahassee traffic, Clarissa looked in the side mirror, saw the city slipping away, and a memory from that long day surfaced: her husband touching Yvette's chin and tilting her face to the light. *You have beautiful skin, even when you sweat.*

"I like the tunes," Adams said, tapping his long fingers in time to the Tejano rhythms.

"What?" Clarissa pulled her gaze from the diminishing city.

"The tunes. They're great."

"Oh, right," Clarissa said. "Me too. Especially the stuff with the squeeze box."

"Exactly! Mexican polka!" Adams laughed as if he were deeply satisfied by the notion.

"What are we doing?"

"Don't know. Just driving." He turned left onto Monroe. "Do you realize that the earth's temperature is the highest it has been in four hundred years?"

"No kidding. Like that's breaking news," Clarissa said, grinning. "It was a hundred and seven degrees at my house."

"I don't mean just today. I mean, like, it's a trend."

"Oh, like we're totally screwed."

"Exactly."

"What do you think?"

"Of what?"

"Of Yellow Bird?"

"She's fantastic!"

They cut over to Crawfordville Highway, passed through the big intersection at Capitol Circle. The strip malls thinned, replaced by trailers and houses, which soon gave way to forest. Dirt roads splintered the darkness, east and west. "Where are we going?"

"Where do you want to go? Man, oh man, will you listen to that engine!" Adams stared straight ahead. He looked fearless. She loved that.

"I'm not sure." Clarissa shook her head; that old feeling of being in free fall, the Sears Tower slipping past, returned.

"How far to the coast?"

Clarissa glanced at the speedometer. The needle was pegged at seventy-five.

"From here, going this fast—maybe thirty minutes."

"What do you think?" He looked at her for a three count and then back at the road. Clarissa thought she'd not been glanced at that forthrightly by a man—not even Trash Man or Cracker Bandit or Raul or even that dwarf—in a good long time, even if it was only for three seconds.

The road through this part of the forest was narrow. Except

for the occasional oncoming vehicle, the El Camino and star shine were the only light sources. Anything could happen in a place like this, in a situation like this. Perhaps living a life full of possibility was a conscious choice. You either did or you didn't. Yes or no. Black or white. Sugar or salt. Bored and safe or thrilled and dangerous. She stared at the parallel universe of the double yellow lines. She thought she felt her heart beat: steady, with a fierce, calm intent, totally out of sync with her brain. Truth be told, she preferred the forest and the coast over the city and a bar, a cherry El Camino over a fucked-up Dodge, a man who just turned up the radio and sang off-key to a song whose words he didn't know over a husband who demanded her loyalty but eschewed her heart.

Adams took a curve, hard and fast. The centrifugal force pressed Clarissa against the seat. She enjoyed the feeling: earth's power sliding right through her.

"It's up to you." Adams pressed the accelerator, brought her up to near eighty. "Do we turn this baby around or head for the Gulf of Mexico?"

Clarissa looked at the blacktop, stretching, it seemed, into eternity. She'd been cautious all her life. But she'd already made the leap. She knew that. The only question left was where she would land.

"Let's do it. Let's head for the coast." She loved how confident she sounded, loved how the high beams illuminated just enough of the blacktop. Just enough.

"There's a town up here?"

"Yep. Crawfordville."

"They got a liquor store?"

"You bet."

Adams flashed the lights at an oncoming car, signaling them to turn off their brights.

"Adams?"

"Yes, baby?"

"I'm not writing anymore."

Adams whistled one low, steady note. He reached for the stereo knob, turned down the volume. "What do you mean?"

"I mean, I sit at the computer, day after day, and nothing comes. It's like the well dried up."

"You sure?"

"One hundred percent."

His mouth twitched in that way men have when they are trying to convey, man style, that they feel your pain. "That sucks."

"Yes. It does." She was unsure if she appreciated his candor or was offended by it.

"So what's going on?"

"I don't know. I mean, I start a sentence or two, and then I just end up deleting them because I can't see them leading to anything. Nothing lines up right." Clarissa felt a knot form in her throat, and she feared she might cry.

"What do you mean, 'nothing lines up right'?" He smiled at her.

"You know, like the alphabet. The freaking basics. A is supposed to precede B, and then comes C, and it's all supposed to add up to something." Clarissa barked the words.

Adams's grin collapsed into shock. Or was it pity? Confusion, maybe? Before she could figure it out, he started laughing. She glared at him, wanted to punch him.

"What the hell is wrong with you?" But even before she'd finished uttering the question, she realized that her popped-off response contained, at least, a dose of hysteria. Shit, she couldn't make B follow A? That was some sad business for someone who called herself a writer. Suddenly her anger seemed altogether silly, and she laughed with him, full-throated, the sound of their mirth mingling with a Mexican love song blaring from the radio (*mi corazón, mi amor*: Clarissa knew these words) and the thrum of the big tires. She slapped her knee and held her sides.

"Well, that's pretty fucking bad, darling," he said, his laughter slowly subsiding.

"I know!" She laughed some more and glanced away. For a moment, she thought that the night—its darkness and shadows—was just an idea and not real at all. "What am I going to do?"

He did not answer, and she wasn't sure if she had said it loudly enough for him to hear. Or perhaps she had not uttered the question but only thought it. Why was she unsure of even this? Again, the smoky fear: Was she going mad, or were his pheromones jamming her perception receptors? Should she repeat herself at the risk of sounding like a doddering twit? In the silence, she continued to stare into the forest, hoping for an answer to her uttered or unuttered query. When it came, she was not ready for it.

"Walk away."

She looked hard at Adams. His face was placid, as if he really believed he'd stumbled upon the solution. "Walk away?"

"Absolutely. Don't sit there trying to force yourself on the story. Go do something. Take a trip. Run away. Live life. You got more talent in that pretty little toe of yours than a lot of people have in their whole bodies. But stories aren't born in safe places."

Clarissa folded her hands in her lap. His advice, she knew, was mighty damn dangerous. If she followed it, the sum total of her life—cooking supper at five, paying bills at seven, watching TV at eight, waking up to an empty bed at midnight, putting on the coffee at six, staring at the computer two hours later while engulfed in spousal death scenarios—might be shot all to hell.

"Baby, I got four letters from the English alphabet for you."

Clarissa turned to him, studied his handsome, black Irish face.

"Just four. And if they line up right in your brain, you'll know what you need to do."

"Oh yeah?" In this dim light, his blue eyes had taken on a charcoal tinge. "What are they?"

"I'm not going to tell you yet."

"Why not?"

"Because first we need to get to the liquor store so we can toast my reading and your astounding purchase."

"Fine," she said. "But they'd better make sense or else I'll know you're just like all the rest of the men in my life—hot air and no action."

"Ha!" he said, reaching over and pinching her nose. "We'll just see about that, won't we?"

"Yes," she said, "we will." She giggled. Even to her, her laugh sounded wild, unhinged. She watched him. He appeared to be a happy man, a welcoming man. She liked that he was smiling. She liked that she felt comfortable sparring and joking with him. She liked that she was able to confess her writer's malady and not feel judged for it. As the small-town lights of Crawfordville smudged the gathering sky, she thought, I like.

⁓

Because Adams insisted that they could not go to the beach without something to sit on, they stopped at the Walmart Supercenter and bought the cheapest comforter they could find: twin-size with a Jetsons theme. At the liquor store, they bought two bottles of Cabernet, a pint of Jack Daniel's, paper cups, and a corkscrew.

"I don't drink hard liquor," she told Adams.

"Well then, I'm not going to let you have any," he said, sliding the JD across the counter, where the clerk who didn't appear old enough to work in a liquor store stood reading the fine print on a Maalox bottle.

"That stuff will kill you," Adams said.

"Maybe." The clerk, whose acne was blazing like a three-alarm fire, set down the Maalox and rang them up, avoiding eye contact, his face slack, bordering on utter despair.

"Also," Clarissa said, counting down in her head the many problems with the present scenario, her optimism—for reasons she could not identify—suddenly quivering in preparation for flight, "I don't think I should drink on an empty stomach."

Adams counted out some fresh bills and handed them to the sad-sack clerk. "What's open around here for some good eats?"

Without looking up, Sad Sack said, "Sonic. Just down the road. Milk shakes aren't as good as Myra Jean's, but she's closed."

Clarissa's stomach shuddered. She had, in her years since becoming a married woman, sworn off fast food and had willingly, wearing her palate on her sleeve, devoted herself to all local, all fresh, all the time. It was both a conceit and a cause she believed in.

"Oh, man!" Adams's rugged face melted into something akin to beatific as he said, "A burger, fries, and a shake. Now that's a holy trinity you can sink your teeth in." He looked at Clarissa. "How 'bout it, baby?"

From deep within the secret passages of her hypothalamus, Deepak said in his clipped, chimes-and-incense accent, "Yes, baby, how about it?"

Clarissa, drinking in Adams's enthusiasm as if she'd been wandering the desert without benefit of camel or canteen, her optimism settling back in, said, "Fantastic!"

Her ovarian shadow women, taking on the throaty maw of Broadway-bound chorus girls, doing their best Ethel Merman imitation, sang, "Maaaaad! You're going maaaaad!"

Adams slipped his wallet in his rear pocket. "You want us to bring you back anything, buddy?"

Sad Sack looked up, apparently taken off guard by the offer and Adams's random kindness. The kid had the prettiest brown eyes Clarissa thought she'd ever seen. A smile broke out across his pimply face, and Clarissa knew, just absolutely knew, that if there was a God, this kid's skin would clear up soon and his main trouble in life would be too many girls. "Oh, wow. I already ate. But thanks, man."

"Not a problem. You have a good night."

"Y'all too."

Adams and Clarissa headed to the door. She was well aware that the clerk had mistaken them as a couple. This pleased her.

"And remember," Adams said before stepping outside.

"This stuff will kill me!" the clerk said, holding up the Maalox, laughing.

Clarissa laughed, too, and, unaccustomed to casual happiness, followed Adams into the night.

———◦

*S*he had no choice. In order to read the menu, she was forced to lean in so close to Adams, they touched, repeatedly. Really. The contact was necessary, vital, demanded. It was a matter of sustenance and proximity versus starvation and propriety. This was Sonic, after all, a sanitized version of a 1950s carhop, where every parking space had its own bite-size, backlit, drive-through menu board replete with a call box and credit card swiper.

Seriously, touching could not be avoided. As she leaned in to get a better look at the delectable images of burgers, coneys, and frozen delights, her bare arm brushed his twice. Once, when she placed her right hand on the steering wheel in order to read the small print describing the ingredients in a SuperSonic Cheeseburger (only $6.29 for the combo), he traced the circumference of the third bangle on her left arm using only the tip of his right index finger. The fact that he smelled like Ivory soap thrilled her. Each time she moved—to brush her hair off her face, to adjust the strap of her chemise, to gesture in time to whatever point she was trying to make, to muse that the onion rings looked awfully good—her bangles chimed softly.

"Cream-pie milk shakes?" Clarissa murmured, seeking ballast.

"Doesn't seem right, does it?" Adams ran his hand through his beautiful ringlets and gazed at her as if he'd just said something important.

Clarissa looked away, tried to refocus on the menu. "Not at all." In her mind's eye, she imagined herself stuffing a giant pie down the throat of a blender. In her postsurgery days, back when she was wired shut for a month, she'd had to run everything through her Hamilton Beach. "Well, I'm going with tradition. A cheeseburger, fries, and a chocolate shake."

"Ditto," Adams said, and he reached his long arm out of the El Camino, pressed the talk button, and tripled the order.

"Wow. You must be—"

"I am. Famished. Those little cheese squares at the reading did not hit the spot. Speaking of which"—his eyes twinkled as they took her in—"where's the wine?"

Clarissa rummaged through their collection of sacks, then handed him a bottle and the corkscrew. She fiddled with the plastic cups and held two aloft. "So are you going to tell me the secret word now?"

"After we toast. Everything in the right order." He poured the wine.

"You know, I'd forgotten how obsessive-compulsive you are," she said, laughing.

"To our writing, baby. The future looks bright."

He started to tip his cup against hers, but Clarissa hesitated; she knew he meant no harm, but his words hurt. "I'm not so sure."

"Oh, come on now. You just hit a washout in the road, baby." With his free hand he touched a strand of her hair. "You'll start rolling again in no time."

His gaze was unblinking, leonine. Clarissa wanted desperately to believe him. "I hope so."

They tapped their cups and drank. The wine's dry, peppery bite surprised her. Adams took a second sip and then placed the cup gingerly on the dash. Without looking at her, he said, "Risk."

"What?"

"Risk. How do you spell it?"

"R-i-s-k. Why?"

"Did the letters line up?"

"Oh." Clarissa dug her hand into the upholstery. Smart-ass. The wine was looking like a better idea all the time. Maybe even the JD. "So, you're saying my block"—she hated that word—"is because I started playing it safe? That I've become just another boring, almost middle-aged, complacent, bloated cow of a woman with nothing to write about? That my past or my pain or my future doesn't count because I finally eked out an ounce or two of stability in my life?"

Adams shook his head, his curls bouncing, and said without a hint of reprisal, "Whoa, baby. I didn't say any of those things."

"Well, what are you trying to say?"

"I'm trying to say that you have to risk being scared again. Isn't that what you told that room full of wannabe writers the day we met? That writing wasn't for the faint of heart? That it was scary and it hurt and it welled up from the most dangerous and injured places in our fucking souls?"

Clarissa allowed herself to smile. "Gee, you were listening." She drank more wine. "I hear you." And although that was true, sitting there in the neon glare of the Sonic sign, she wasn't sure what to make of her words being tossed back at her.

"Good. Now, tell me about that big house you moved into."

"Well, funny you should bring that up," Clarissa said. Happy to be moving off the subject of her dysfunction, she reached for the dossier she'd stashed under the seat. "I'm discovering all sorts of amazing stuff about the place." She flipped open the file and fished out the photocopy of Olga Villada.

"Not only did this woman build my house, she owned about half the county."

"How? Y'all couldn't own property back then." Adams squinted at her, the great skeptic.

"Because Florida was controlled by Spain, and under their laws, women could be property owners."

He snapped his fingers. "Really? Wow. That's crazy good."

"Yes, sir. And she had a common-law husband, a black man, who was free because in 1811 Spain abolished slavery within its borders and all its territories except three in the Caribbean. Puerto Rico. Cuba. And I think Santo Domingo. Talk about crazy."

"Wait a minute." Adams reached for his wine. "So Florida was a slave-free zone while under Spanish rule, but right across the border in good ol' Georgia, U.S. of A., slavery was legal?"

"That's how I'm reading this."

"Damn." Adams shuffled through the copies. As the waitress arrived with their food, Clarissa reached for fresh pages. The scent of industrial beef caught her by surprise, but she wasn't going to not eat; she'd already committed.

"Look at this," Clarissa said. It was a pen drawing of a fiddle, replete with Amaziah's signature heron carvings, held with all the tenderness of a father presenting a baby for its first blessing. The subject's hands were both elegant (long fingers) and strong (wide with thick, callused palms). "These are Amaziah's hands—Olga Villada's husband. This fiddle—it's exquisite." Clarissa touched the drawing. "I think he was a magic man."

Adams looked up from his pile of papers, glanced at the drawing, and said, "Well, honey, listen to this." His bony index finger followed lines whose unevenness, complete with blurred-edged letters, was proof that the document had been pounded out on a manual typewriter. "'No doubt the fact that Olga Villada's beloved father was a great flamenco guitarist in Spain figured into her fierce, enduring love for Amaziah.'"

"What's that from?"

Adams turned the page over three times, studying it. "Not sure. Looks like somebody wrote a research paper on your place. It has two stamps—FAMU and the Aucilla County Historical Society."

"Oh, yeah. I read a little bit of that already. You know," Clarissa said, reaching for a French fry, "this might sound crazy, but I swear to you I've been hearing music in that house. At first I thought it was the wind blowing through the eaves, but I don't think so. I mean, sometimes it even wakes me in the middle of the night. Last time it happened, I stepped outside and was met with nothing but hot air—no wind, nada."

"What's it sound like?" He unwrapped a burger.

"Like my house is haunted." She popped the French fry in her mouth.

He laughed. "No, really."

"I'm serious."

He grinned at her, hamburger in one hand, red wine in the other. "What, Ms. Burden, does the music sound like?"

"I don't know. Outlaw love music or something." Clarissa averted her eyes, knowing she had not kept at bay the flirtatious lilt in her voice. She picked at a loose thread in the embroidered poppy that bloomed all along one leg of her jeans. "I think the energy is still in the house, so every now and then, a refrain rises up to a dimension I can hear. I swear." She looked at him; he had adorable dimples. "How's that for a theory?"

"Have another drink."

Clarissa ignored him. "The house is amazing, Adams. You've got to see it. I mean, the framing is pinned together with nearly foot-thick cypress beams. It's all dovetailed, solid as hell, like they thought they'd be there forever."

"You're amazing," he said.

She felt herself blush. She picked up fresh pages. He returned his attention to the thesis. They read in silence until Adams said, "Wow!"

"What?" Clarissa nibbled at what she decided was sawdust meat.

"This thing, this thesis, whatever, it's a danged gold mine, Clarabelle."

"What do you mean?"

His eyes scanned the page. "It's some heavy shit."

"Like what?"

"Want me to read it to you?"

"Yes."

"Now?"

"No, three years from now." She threw a fry at him.

"I love it when you're sassy."

He wiped his hands on his jeans, angled the page so that the light from the Sonic sign illuminated it, and began to read. "'Villada's fearless, optimistic nature—which made her alluring to powerful, corrupt men and talented, ethical ones—also made her particularly well suited to navigate and tame the dangerous times she lived in—that is, until a new world order, inflicted under the auspices of the United States government, descended upon them.'" He glanced up. "Want to hear more?"

"Absolutely." Clarissa turned so that she faced him directly. She studied his face—the strong cheekbones, the dimpled chin, the freckle that looked like a tear at the edge of his right eye.

"'The U.S. takeover of the Spanish territory could not have come as a surprise to someone as smart, as worldly, as land rich, as Villada.' God, this writer thinks he's freaking Shakespeare."

"She."

"What?"

"It's a she. The writer is a she."

"Whatever. Are you going to drink your shake?"

She handed it to him. "Read!"

He took a long draw off the straw, set the icy cup carefully between them, said, "Let's see here," ran his finger down the page, and started where he'd left off. "'The Florida Purchase Treaty of 1819 guaranteed that the United States would lay claim to Florida two years hence. Did Villada and Archer not understand the wholly brutal nature of U.S. law as it pertained to black people?'" Adams paused, reading ahead silently, and whispered, "Jesus Christ."

"Please," Clarissa said, her flirtatious streak obliterated, "keep going."

"It's not good."

"I don't care."

He nodded, his natural, happy-bordering-on-bravado demeanor replaced by a seriousness Clarissa had never seen in him. He sighed and plunged back in. "'Did they not know that surely, under this new regime, a man who had been free his entire life and his equally free mulatto son (a certain Heart Archer) could be, would be eventually—without recourse, no matter how much land was in the family's coffers and no matter what former Spanish governor Villada might have influence with—wrenched, using whatever means necessary, into slavery?'"

Clarissa's stomach cramped. The horror of the situation, the unadulterated evil, the legislative stroke-of-a-pen nonchalance, made her want to scream. "You know what's really upsetting?"

"What, baby?"

"Nobody cares. People say, Just get over it. How? I mean, Amaziah was a landowner, he had all his rights intact, and then a real estate deal took place. One day you're free, and voilà, the next day the law says they own you: Body and soul, you're suddenly just a piece of freaking property." She reached for her wine. Adams poured her a fresh glass. "So they had a child."

"Yep," he said. "A little boy. Heart Villada-Archer. Nice name."

"I knew it," Clarissa said, thinking back to the morning and the kerfuffled quilt, the buoyant laughter. "Yeah, it is a nice name." She leaned against the seat. "What else?"

Adams flipped through the pages. "You sure you want to hear more?"

"I'm sure."

She watched him out of the corner of her eye. He looked like a scribe reading an ancient text, his finger following that bumpy, typewritten trail. She could not tell if he was skipping over anything. She hoped not. "'Florida was deemed a U.S. territory in July of 1821, and by 1828 all the humane, logical, and sane tendencies that had been exhibited and practiced by Spain were obliterated. Free blacks were barred from entering Florida. What had been basic freedoms—assembly, speech, bearing arms—were stripped away. Head taxes were levied on free blacks. They were no longer allowed to sit on juries, testify against white men, or conduct commerce on Sundays. Interracial marriages were outlawed, and the children of such unions were not allowed to inherit their parents' estates. Free blacks were captured and enslaved. Lynching—while at that time still more commonly meted out to people of European ancestry—was nevertheless well on its way to becoming the favored mode of nineteenth- and early-twentieth-century American terrorism.'"

"Holy Christ," Clarissa said. She reached for the dossier. "Give me some pages."

Sitting at a burger joint called Sonic, in a 1970 Chevy El Camino SS, on the shortest night of the year, which was also, as luck would have it, the hottest (how could it not be, given the day's bludgeoning heat?), Clarissa and Adams read through the dossier, sometimes sharing information, sometimes not, each uncovering the secrets of Clarissa's house and the tragedy of the family who had first called it home.

"How do we know if all of this stuff is true?" Adams asked, rubbing his eyes. "Or what's true and what's been spun for money, politics, people covering up their own shit?"

"We don't," Clarissa said. "It's like religion—you either believe or you don't."

And Clarissa, for all of her struggles with writer's block, remained a devout and skilled believer. Each time the historical trail grew murky, her old knack for narrative kicked in. Before they had downed the last French fry or touched the second bottle of wine, Clarissa was certain she knew exactly what had happened to the Villada-Archers.

In the fall of 1825, a group of four brothers, last name Butler, set out from Flatbush, New York, with six flintlock rifles, ten horses, the clothes on their backs, two hundred dollars (most of which was willed to them by their father, who died from injuries sustained when he was trampled by a runaway stagecoach), a proclivity toward less talk and more violence, a shared determination to become rich men, and not much else. But at the end of the first quarter of the nineteenth century, those assets — along with a dose of luck and/or fate — were all that were needed to reinvent a life and destroy a host of others.

Having tested the abolitionist winds in New York and sensing that slavery would not be long-lived in that state, the Butler boys headed out. Florida had not been their firm intention. But as they traveled farther south (below Virginia, the whole world seemed to be on the move), everything they heard about the new territory and its possibilities (acres upon acres of cheap, fertile land, an abundant, no-end-in-sight free labor source, and no real lawmen of note) inspired them to push on.

By the time they crossed into Florida, all but one of the Butlers were bona fide killers. The middle boy, Bobby, had shot a man in the back because the man had beaten him, fair and square, in a poker game in a Beaufort saloon and Bobby didn't take well to losing. The man stumbled out of the saloon and fell facedown in the road that was mostly mud thanks to a recent downpour. Bobby turned him over and using nothing but his fingers dug out his left eyeball (gray-eyed son of a bitch), popped it in his mouth while the orb was still warm, chewed with the vigor and good manners of a starving dog, wiped his mouth with his sleeve, and said, "A tad chewy, but still, that there is some gooooood eating!"

His intent, of course, wasn't to satiate his need for protein or gore, but to inspire any bystanders who might have been considering taking him on to reconsider the wisdom of such a move.

Lawrence Butler, the baby and the only nonmurderer among them, broke six hearts—him with his long blond hair and sweet-talking ways—and lost two teeth along the journey.

Hazelton Butler, one year older than Lawrence, for the most part kept a lid on his violent nature because he wanted to store his rage—much of it stemming from a generalized disgust with human nature—until they got to where they were going, so it could be used to maximum benefit. He did, however, slit the throat of a black field hand in Virginia because he wanted to know what kind of force it took to cut through black skin. This particular crime could have landed him in serious trouble, because slaves—while supplying free labor—were not cheap, and slaveholders did not take kindly to losing their property. So the boys' time in Virginia was brief.

Maurice Butler, the oldest, fearing that his dreamtime fantasies involving trysts with young boys meant he was a homosexual, raped three women—one in a farmhouse in Pennsylvania (she was not quite a woman, being only fourteen), one in a barn in Maryland (her skin was so dark, he thought she might be mulatto; he carved an M into her cheek with his hunting knife so she would not forget him), and one in a pasture in south Georgia (she was well past her prime, maybe in her sixties, which was old in the 1820s, and, unable to put up much of a fight, she just whimpered and prayed, knobby word after knobby word uttered without effect, worry beads trapped in a bone-dry clutch, "no dear God no dear God no dear no God no").

Lawrence wasn't sure about all this violence, but because—given his birth order—he had no standing of any merit, he was impotent to do much about it. He did speak up about the rapes, however. The night of the Georgia assault, under the brilliant starlight afforded by a new moon, when they were camped in a field north of Thomasville, Lawrence protested gently. "I just don't understand why you have to rape them," he said, staring into his battered tin cup, which stank with the after-rise of stale whiskey.

"There's no rape going on, baby brother," Maurice said, a snake smile slipping across his face. "I could tell they wanted it. Every single one of them. That little pink bud between their legs twitched like crazy, a flesh-and-blood jumping bean. Stupid whores."

Lawrence shook his head; the kernel of morality that rolled loose and wild in the pit of his gut could not abide his brother's actions. "Bullshit," he said.

Maurice spit in the dirt and muttered, slow and soft and with the dead intent of a hangman who enjoys the wooden muffle of the trapdoor opening, "There is no such thing as rape. Plain and simple. We rule this earth, little brother. Everything out there"—he nodded his head to the vast blackness—"is ours for the taking. You got that?"

As they crossed into Florida, the boys had in their possession thirteen rifles, seven horses, and a modest herd of cattle that they had amassed by rustling one here, another there (in Cairo, Georgia, they stole six cows from Mrs. Whitaker Peacock, a woman who was recently widowed and had no idea how many cows she owned until her stock had dwindled to six).

When the four men gained the steps to Olga Villada's home and knocked on the door, she, in all likelihood, offered the men refreshments. And surely the conversation turned to land, and perhaps Olga Villada and Amaziah Archer were interested—now that Florida had been discovered and Amaziah and Heart were in ever greater danger of losing their freedom—in selling some, if not all, of her vast holdings. Finding a safe way out of Florida and to Spain, the most likely scenario to ensure the continued safety and prosperity of this family, would not be an easy, safe, or cheap proposition.

The archives held no clues as to the details of how the crime unfolded. Did Maurice rape Olga Villada? Did he harm the boy? Given the sadism the Butler boys had already exhibited, what heinous denigrations did they inflict upon Amaziah Archer? As one document suggested, did they force Amaziah Archer to play the fiddle while one or two of them harmed his common-law wife and son? Or was that simply a grotesque rumor spun in the aftermath of a terror so great that adding lies to the crime diminished its cruel reality?

Clarissa did not know. A goodly portion of her refused to know. Whatever prevented her from feeling like a whole woman with a future wild with possibilities also prevented her from fully imagining the god-awful last moments of Olga Villada, Amaziah Archer, and Heart Archer. When it came to understanding their deaths, at least while she sat in the neon glow of Sonic, Clarissa dared only to tangle herself in the facts as presented in the dog-eared, French fry–fingerprinted pages of the dossier.

According to documents attached to the coroner's report, on June 15, 1826, a little slave boy—name omitted, but age given as ten years old—discovered the family as he walked through the swampy forest on his way to the general store, a task assigned him by his mistress, a Mrs. Lucretius H. Ball. The boy was reported to have made this statement: "I was walking by Black Hole Slough on the north side of Jake's Hell when I heard something way high. I looked up and studied on that giant oak on the dead people's land. And there theys were, the three of them, just a-swinging, blowed by the wind."

The victims had been severely beaten. Amaziah Archer had been bullwhipped. All the bodies, to varying degrees, had been burned. "Evidence of torture is abundant," wrote the medical examiner in a right-leaning, elegant cursive script.

Cornelius Slidell, a reporter for the *Florida Intelligencer*, wrote in the June 30, 1826, edition:

Eyewitnesses report the beaten, burned corpses were found hanging from three separate nooses, yet their bodies were intertwined and from a distance appeared to be part of the tree. A thirty-four-year-old man who declined to be identified said, "They's was all of one piece, woven tight into each other—no sunlight a'tall shining through, just flesh-to-flesh, twisting, swaying like a muscle-bound vine from that big old oak out back the house. Looks like that family, they died clinging to each other, suffering themselves into one person. The mama and daddy managed to nestle the baby between them. I think they cradled that child straight to God.

The only other entry about the house or Olga Villada's real estate holdings was a listing in the September 14, 1826, *Intelligencer* in the "Land Acquisitions" section:

Butler and Butler, Incorporated, a family interest in Aucilla County, have acquired from the state tax agency, for a total sum of $3.95, one hundred acres, more or less, of land in said county. Included in the parcel is the former homestead of the recently deceased Olga Villada, who is thought to have been a Spanish-born citizen.

When Clarissa and Adams finished the final page, they sat for a good two minutes in silence. Adams reached for the Jack Daniel's. "I'm fucking glad I bought this," he said.

Clarissa held the dossier, her hands shaking, overwhelmed by the reminder of the human capacity for violence. She did not want the story to be true. She did not want the couple and their child to have suffered in any way. She did not want the image of their charred, beaten bodies swinging as one from a rope slung over a branch of the sentinel oak to be burned into her memory bank as if she herself had been a witness. She did not want — in the long, gravitational pull of history — to be stained with culpability. But she was. America was. She remembered the truck that belonged to the boys who had ice-picked her tires: the FORGET HELL bumper sticker and the vinyl wrap image of the Stars and Bars. "Ignorant, fucking little jerks," she said.

"What are you talking about, Ms. Burden?" Adams readjusted the rose in her hair.

"Nothing... I've just had quite the day. One-eyed men, quick mud cemeteries, pet rattlesnakes, and punks with ice picks."

"And you bought Yellow Bird."

Clarissa smiled. "Yes, indeed I did. Did you notice that the B and B has one of those old signs about management reserving the right to refuse service?"

"I did not see that."

"Well, they sure as hell have. It's hanging in the dining room. The old lady dismissed it as her nephew's poor attempt at interior decorating. How would she feel if the tables had been turned? If it had been her white relatives who were refused a seat at the table?"

"You know what I'm going to do?" Adams sipped his JD. She could tell by the set of his jaw that he was letting the liquor linger on his tongue.

"What?"

"When I get back there tonight, I'm going to steal that fucking sign. And the next time I see you? We're going to burn it."

"You serious?"

"One hundred percent."

Clarissa believed him. "You rock, Leo Adams."

He tapped the dossier. "This all sucks, what happened to them. What the hell is wrong with people?"

"You know, that old woman at the B and B said she was married to a Butler."

Adams swirled his JD. "Christ. She sure did."

"And that place looks like a cheap knockoff of my house." She recalled the fading, sepia-toned photo on the wall of the four men—one missing an arm, another an eye—and her unease.

"Those guys in the photo, Adams, I think they were the Butler boys. Jesus. Years later, they went on to become respected businessmen. They were murderers! Terrorists!"

Adams picked up the dossier. "Clarissa, this is it. This is what you ought to be writing."

She looked at him; his eyes appeared lit with a certainty that Clarissa could not bear. How could she explain that he had no idea what a dark and dangerous place her internal landscape really was? She wanted to agree with him. He would like that. It would make for nice chitchat. But she couldn't. She could not lie about her current capacity—which was zero—to immerse herself in horrors committed by monstrous men. What amounted to a hypersensitivity to torture and cruelty—born from being raised by a mother who stubbed out cigarettes on her arms and thighs while telling her that little boys hated little girls with buckteeth so much that they wanted to pee on them, that she should run if she was alone and a boy approached, because surely she was about to be pissed on (the cruelty of both word and deed)—prevented Clarissa from agreeing with Adams or admitting to herself that perhaps the story of Olga and Amaziah Archer was what the blank, mocking virtual pages of her word processor were waiting for. In her mind, the letters lined up: RISK. And then she revised the one-word directive, turning it into a two-word warning: TOO RISKY.

"Are you done?" she asked, erasing the words from her mental blackboard.

"Full up," he said.

She needed a change of both scenery and subject. "Well, the coast isn't too far now."

Adams leaned toward her, maybe a half inch. She could have sworn that the possibility of a kiss existed, stirred by shared sadness, twin yearnings. But then he turned away, his face betraying not a single drop of want, jammed the key in the ignition, and started the engine. As they pulled out of Sonic and headed south, he said, "Too bad Iggy isn't here. I would have liked to see him."

Clarissa, unsure if he was being cruel, sarcastic, or naively honest, balled up the waxed-paper wrappers and shoved them in the greasy Sonic bag, her silver bracelets chiming softly. They should have left the trash behind, but he'd taken off too suddenly. "I'm sure he feels likewise," she said, careful to avoid any note of remorse, regret, reality.

~

*T*he wind whipped and the temperature dropped as they approached the coast. Lightning illuminated storm clouds boiling up along the wide seam of the horizon. The change in the weather helped ameliorate the somber mood that had descended thanks to the hard blade of the dossier.

"Is there a beach around here?" Adams asked, slowing down as they entered the blinking-light hamlet of Ochlockonee Bay.

"Yep. Take a left at the light, just past the BP. Mashes Sands. I don't think they patrol down there."

"Are you going to get us arrested, baby?"

"That would make for good literary cocktail party gossip."

"Fuck 'em."

"Exactly."

Something darted across the road. Adams slammed the brakes. "What the hell was that?"

"Bobcat! How great!"

"Really? Maybe I should have bought some pepper spray at Walmart."

"Nah. That stuff only pisses them off."

"That's my girl. Anything else out here I ought to know about?"

"Don't feed the bears."

Adams laughed, and Clarissa felt the tension that had gripped her at Sonic ease. She was happy to slip into the safety zone of meaningless banter, happy to behave as though she did not live with a family of tragic ghosts and a holier-than-thou husband. She hoped Adams would not mention him again.

They wound their way down a deserted two-lane blacktop, a canopy of stars shining close and bright. Porch and dock lights flickered in the distance, giving shadowy form to fishing cabins and river houses. Piney woods thinned into wire-grass savannas and saltwater flats. Eventually, in graceful measure, all semblance of terra firma gave way to the gently arched hip of the Gulf of Mexico. When they could go no farther because they had reached land's end, Adams and Clarissa got out of the El Camino, slipped off their shoes, rolled up the hems of their jeans nearly to their knees, and — not touching — walked toward the sea.

"I like the sound of those bracelets," Adams said, marching, Clarissa thought, with undo but charming purpose.

"Me too." The wind whipped over them. Lightning, far out to sea, pulsed. The low-tide surf song unfurled to the cadence of the planets. The stars sparkled from the high dome of the sky all the way down to the warm and restless water.

Clarissa felt Adams's presence more acutely than ever. As the surf washed over their toes, feet, ankles, she said, "Look at all those stars."

"I've never seen a sky like this. Except in dreams. Never in person. No wonder the ancients decided it was crowded with gods."

"Sure beats TV."

"Look," Adams said, "those two stars—real close together—the ones whose light holds steady?"

Clarissa followed the invisible line—hand to sky.

"They aren't stars. It's Mars and Saturn. They were right near on top of each other a few nights ago. Now they're drifting apart again, like a planetary tango."

As Clarissa searched for the dancing planets, the rose Adams had placed in her hair fell silently into the water and ebbed away. Neither of them noticed.

Adams continued his sky search, pointing out Jupiter's waning light and "over there, way down low in the west? That's Mercury." When Clarissa wasn't actively engaged in his planetary tour, she was covertly studying Adams. He was so engrossed in the sky, she was sure he didn't notice. As he chattered, his Adam's apple wobbled and she thought it looked knobby, like an oak burl. It struck her as hilarious that someone named Adams would actually have an Adam's apple. Or maybe it was simply the wine.

"We got ourselves a balsamic moon," he said.

"What does that mean?" Clarissa asked, the surf surging up her calves. "I don't see any moon at all."

"It's the wishing moon. She shows up as a crescent predawn, just above the Pleiades and Venus." He glanced at her. "You're supposed to wish upon her."

He scanned the sky's zenith. She followed suit. "How come?"

"Because if you pay real close attention during the balsamic moon, you'll know what to wish for instead of blasting away shotgun style. That way, when the new moon arrives, you've got a clean slate and a pocket full of fresh dreams."

"You know a lot about the moon, Adams."

"I had a girlfriend who was an astrologer."

"I see."

He looked at her. "Is this okay?"

"What?"

Adams reached over and moved a blowing strand of hair out of her eyes. "Standing here, with you, looking at the stars. I mean, you're married and all."

"I know," Clarissa said, wondering if she would ever learn the names of all the constellations, the stars, the phases of the moon; wondering how warm and sweet his tongue was. "I sure do know."

They stood there, alone at the edge of the world, no one suspecting their whereabouts, gazing into each other's eyes, Clarissa fearful he would say something important and fearful that he would not. Just before they began to appear foolish, he stepped away and looked at the sea. "We could go for a dip."

"No way!" Clarissa kicked an incoming wave. "Sharks love the night, and white girls who wear too much perfume."

"Oh, come on," he said, laughing, the Milky Way sparkling a kajillion miles above his head. He was gorgeous. Clarissa was certain that every inch of him was gorgeous.

"No!" She could not, would not, take off her clothes, even if he didn't look. She wished she were that sort of woman — full of confidence, not caring what others thought of her body, comfortable in the opulent fact of her hips, breasts, and marital status. But that was not who she was. Not yet. She started laughing. "I am not skinny-dipping with you, Leo Adams."

"Why not?"

"Because my number one goal in life is to remain clothed at all times."

"Even in the shower?"

"Close. If God had wanted me to be naked, He would not have given me a passion for fashion."

Adams walked farther out into the water; holding up his jeans by the waist to avoid getting wet. He looked really funny, she thought; Ichabod Crane goes swimming. "I'm going to quote you on that one day."

"Be my guest. And when you do, not one centimeter of my body will be showing."

"Iggy must be thrilled," Adams said over his shoulder.

"Iggy doesn't care," Clarissa shot back.

"Ouch."

"Yeah, well..." Clarissa trailed off, dug a hole in the sand with her toe, wished she had kept her trap shut.

Adams turned around and, not speaking, sloshed back to shore and headed in the direction of the car.

Clarissa hurried to keep up. "Where we going?" she asked, trying to put the lilt back in her voice, hating that she'd said anything truthful about her husband. What was wrong with her? Adams was the last person to whom she wanted to air her dirty and discontent laundry.

He paused, held out his palm. "Give me your hand." She took it. Flesh on flesh: It felt real good, needed.

"Let's get the blanket. Lie down. Stare at the stars."

"Clothed?"

"Of course."

"You sure?"

"Are you?"

She looked away. He squeezed her hand but did not let go.

⌒◦

They sat hip to hip. Adams sipped Jack Daniel's. Clarissa stayed with wine. They talked about little things—her love for semicolons, his preference for dashes. He said he wanted to visit Florence one day and wear a cowboy hat to the Uffizi. Clarissa said she wanted to be queen of the Nile and wear thick black cat's-eye liner that extended from her lids to her temples to her hairline. She told him about how she'd grown up with teeth so wicked that everyone made fun of her but that when she was still in college, bartending at a local pub, a man walked in, ordered a Scotch and soda, and said, "You know, I can do something about those teeth."

"His name was King van den Berg."

Adams spit JD out of his nose. "His name was what?"

"King van den Berg," she said, giggling. "He was a maxillofacial surgeon, not long out of med school. I was good for his career."

"What do you mean, sweet thing?"

"I mean my lousy bartender's insurance wouldn't pay for everything, so he waived his fee. I had to pay the hospital and the orthodontist, but not him. Five years in braces, seven hours under the knife, and voilà, he created a Clarissa I didn't know, and he used my sad-assed case to build his practice." Clarissa didn't realize it, but she was smiling.

"Well, here's to King van den Berg, the good doctor."

"Here, here!"

Adams poured more drinks. He had very steady hands. "A Clarissa you didn't know?"

She watched him recork the wine. If she tried really hard, she could hear the wind offshore and inshore. Beyond the breakers, it sounded very much in charge. Out there, a person could die. Pull a Virginia Woolf: Just step into the surf, your pockets full of rocks, and walk, walk, walk, until the water is deeper than you are tall; just let the current pull you under; no more creepy husband to make you feel like a piece of shit. "In my mind, Adams, I'm still her. I look in the mirror and don't know the woman who stares back."

"Clarissa?"

"What?"

"Look at me."

"No."

"Please."

She focused on the silly images of the Jetsons flying through space. She wondered what it would feel like to be fire instead of stone. She tuned in a distant gale, the old catechism of family sin and regret bearing down: Some children had loving mothers; some children had fathers; some women had tender husbands; most women her age had their own families so that they could re-create the world into a kinder and better place, remap it all so that old cruelties were banished.

"Clarissa." She felt his hands cup her face, felt him tilt her head toward him. "Listen to me, Clarissa."

The wind blew harder, driven by the force of the offshore storm. The surf pounded. In the deep distance, night birds cried. The world at the edge of the sea was a noisy, busy place. But still, despite the cacophony inside and outside her mind, she heard him.

"She's beautiful, Clarissa. You're beautiful."

She searched his eyes, looking for a lie. *She's beautiful. You're beautiful.*

"Did you hear me? Do you believe me?"

Clarissa placed her hands on his. She tried to say yes but could not speak. She remembered what he'd said about a balsamic moon and managed a silent wish: Please, make it true.

He pulled her to him and whispered, "Clarissa. Clarissa. She's beautiful. You're beautiful."

They held each other for a long time under that changing sky—Mercury disappeared; Mars and Venus tangoed farther apart—until finally Clarissa said, her head on his shoulder, "What keeps them up there?"

"Keeps what where, sweetheart?"

"The stars. Why don't they fall down, fill up our shoes, get tangled in our hair?"

She felt him move against her. He placed his lips against her cheek. "Einstein, baby."

Clarissa laughed. Never in all her days had she heard those two words spoken jointly. *Einstein, baby.* "What do you mean?"

He held her by her shoulders. "Newton had it all wrong. None of us are going in a straight line. It's okay."

In her mind's eye, she saw herself tumbling through that starry sky, following a curving path, colliding with nebulae and novas and planets as yet unknown.

"Clarissa, I mean it."

"What?"

"I don't know what's going on with you and Iggy. All I know is that all of you—the old and the new and the one who doesn't even fucking exist yet—is beautiful. Whoever led you to believe otherwise is a goddamn asshole."

She had fought against it all day: when she was in the trash truck and lost in the swamp, when she nearly drowned in quick mud, when the kids ice-picked her tires, when her husband had laughed at her derisively, in essence dismissing her. But she couldn't hold back anymore. The whole of her life—its sadness and its promise—seemed suddenly necessary, and she began to cry.

Adams pulled her back into his arms. He stroked her hair, chanted, "Clarissa, Clarissa, Clarissa," over and over, the same three syllables, as if he were determined to weave her name into the wind. *Clarissa, Clarissa.* He wrapped his fingers around the charm necklace, lifted it over her head, set it in a gleaming swirl beside their feet... *Clarissa, Clarissa...* and then, one by one, he removed her silver bangles. He slipped them down her arms, over the thin ovals of her wrists, the gentle rise of her palms, her hard knuckles, her waiting fingertips...*Clarissa, Clarissa*...first her left arm, then her right, never two at a time; always with the sweet, slow ache a lover is supposed to take with his beloved, even though they were without shadow, until her skin was bare. He set each sterling circle on the comforter, beside the swirled necklace. Twenty bangles total, they formed their own constellation that shimmered gently in the star shine. When he was done, he again took her in his arms and cradled her the long distance to the earth. *Clarissa, Clarissa.*

On a small stretch of sand, in repose, they watched the heavens, and still he stroked her hair and whispered her name, and still she wept.

———

*W*ith the shedding of each tear, Clarissa felt the weight of her life shift. Her mother's madness, her husband's meanness, her battered past; small kindnesses abandoned behind slamming doors; benign passions left to fester in the hollow sound of an unfinished sentence; minor intimacies—a caress here, a glance there—circumvented daily; the babies she never birthed, even though in her waking moments they seemed so real that she had named them—Pearl Rose and William Isaac, little Rosie and Ike; the terrifying minutes, hours, years, she felt spurned by both her husband and God; all those broken moments as she stared out her kitchen window, watching Iggy worship yet another woman: Little wounds all, but she could no longer carry them. Their weight was too great. There was a continent of light lying before her called the future. As her stubborn bog of old grievances lifted, the entire little planet with her name on it began to spin more confidently, its orbit a rosette: circles upon circles of life hidden and revealed. Oh, how she loved being touched.

Clarissa. Clarissa.

⁓

*T*hey did not make love. They did not take off their clothes. They did not touch in places off-limits to friends and strangers. He interrupted the whispering of her name only twice: once to kiss her cheek, once to kiss her forehead. The innocent and long-craved intimacy was, for Clarissa, cataclysmic. No one would believe her: *A man touched my hair and whispered my name, and when he was finished, I knew I was going to leave my husband.*

⁓

*T*hey left the Gulf before the golden crescent of the balsamic moon had risen in the eastern sky.

"I have to get home," she whispered.

Adams touched her shoulder and the silk strap of the chemise and said, "I know you do, baby. But wouldn't it be great to stay out here all night?"

She sat up, feeling as if she were a ribbon unfurling from a good man's arms. "It sure would be," she said, "but look, the tide is coming in. It's going to get us." She gathered her jewelry and her blue shoes. She thought how wonderful it was that the cerulean boots came in all sorts of disguises.

"Let me help you with that." Adams slipped the necklace over her head, held up her hair so that it wouldn't get caught in the chain. And then he slid twenty bangles, one by one, reversing their journey, over her fingertips, palms, knuckles, wrists.

She watched him, how he held each one as if it were precious, how he moved them gently up the slope of her arms, how attentive he was. "Adams?"

"Yes, baby?"

"You're a magnificent man."

"Ah, girly"—he draped his arm over her shoulder—"you're the one with glitter on your toes." He kissed her forehead. "You just don't know it yet."

⟶

*T*he late hour and the three shots of JD took a toll on Adams; he slept most of the way to the Old Florida Magnolia Inn, his feet resting on the folded comforter, and that was okay with Clarissa. She needed the silence. Maybe it was simply because she hadn't been touched in a good long while, but she felt cleaved in two, as if her life had already changed but she wasn't yet sure of the details.

Traffic was light; forty-five minutes after leaving the coast, she arrived at the bed-and-breakfast. It was lit up with spotlights—even the trees—and she wondered how the guests slept with all that blaring light.

After having read the dossier, she got the creeps just from looking at the place. She was fully convinced that the murdering Butlers had built it and had based its layout and flourishes on the house whose owners they had butchered, the house she owned, the house where her husband was holed up doing only God knew what.

She shook Adams awake. He stretched his arms over his head and yawned. "Whew! I'm beat."

"You look tired, like you need a solid eight."

"I have to get on the road early. I've got a class to teach tomorrow night. Did I tell you I'm teaching?"

"I did not know that."

He looked at her, sleepy-eyed, and sighed. "You okay?"

"I am," she said. "Very, very okay."

He touched her face with two fingers and traced her jawline.

"I have to go home, Adams."

"I know."

"I don't want to."

"I don't want you to either."

He looked away, into the night, and she wished for a different life.

"You're going to start knocking out that novel. You'll see."

"I hope so."

He kissed her cheek. Clarissa's body ached and tingled in places she forgot she had. This made her happy.

"I'll call you tomorrow, Clarissa. Tell Iggy I said hello, but don't take any shit off him. I don't want to get between you two, but I'm on your side. You know that, right?"

She nodded yes.

"I'm serious. You need me, I'm there." He kissed her once more, again on the cheek, opened the door, and said, "I'm really glad I got to see you."

"Me too, Adams." He eased out of the car and shut the door, but before he could walk away, she said, "Adams?"

The streetlight illuminated his face; he looked content, as if zigzagging through life—holding someone when she needed to be held, whispering her name so many times it became an incantation, not asking for a single thing other than that she find her joy—were a good way to live.

"Thank you."

"Anytime, baby."

"No, I mean it."

"I do, too. And by the way, I'm going to go steal that fucking sign now."

She laughed. "Don't burn it without me."

"It's a date."

She put the El Camino in gear, and being a girl with a lead foot, as always, she pressed the gas with too much purpose, spinning the tires. Adams laughed and waved good-bye. She steered Yellow Bird out of downtown and toward home and understood something that heretofore had been a foreign concept: Everything else that would happen that night depended on her, and solely her.

$\sim$

She had just crossed the county line when the monsoon began. The thunderstorms—built on the energy of the day's heat— illuminated and nourished the swamp, prompting foxes, deer, possums, and various other animals along Clarissa's path to hunker down. The wipers ticked out of time to the Tejano beat, creating a dissonance that Clarissa found oddly comforting. The rain came down so hard, she could barely see out of Yellow Bird's wide windshield. She took a curve too fast, considering the wet road, and eased off the gas pedal. *Clarissa. Clarissa.* She could smell him on her. She had no desire to shower his scent away. It was as if Adams had, through a kind and innocent intimacy, changed the combinations on all her locks. Click, click, click. What would she do now, with an open heart?

She turned off of Tremble and Shout—the rain eased— and slowed to nearly a crawl as she passed the village green, which had been transformed into a small town of not just dwarfs, but (according to the signage) full-body-tattooed dwarfs and sword-swallowing, fire-breathing dwarfs and three-hundred-pound dwarfs (which even Clarissa found over the top) and bearded-lady dwarfs and, if the art on the side of one of the trailers was to be believed, Siamese-twin dwarfs. There was even the World's Smallest Dwarf dwarf, which made Clarissa laugh as she imagined a twelve-inch man running around, biting the ankles of all the other dwarfs. She felt ashamed for finding a dwarf village amusing, but weren't they, after all, making a living based on their size, and did that not leave them open to some level of bemusement? She stopped Yellow Bird and gazed at the trailers and the big white tent and the gigantic fire tower that loomed over the village. Random lights burned brightly—trailer to trailer—and red and white bulbs were strung like happy barbed wire along the green's perimeter. She noticed that the Rocket Dog trailer was lit brightly from within and saw a shadow pass by its curtained window. Perhaps the dwarf whose talent was being shot out of a cannon was an insomniac. Who could blame him? If she knew that come tomorrow she was going to be a human cannonball, she'd probably have a sleepless night, too.

And with that thought, her bemusement vanished. These were just folks, making a living, talented, brave, hungry, mischievous, petty, kind, gentle, good, mean, evil, silly, serious, tired, hopeful, scared, longing, confused, arrogant, jealous, wise: the human condition in all its frail and glorious fuckery. And what was a dwarf going to do in this world besides stick around with a bunch of other dwarfs, where no one but the interloping tall people took a second gander? And weren't the tall people the outnumbered outsiders and therefore members of a powerless minority? Was a freak show a freak show when everyone looked alike save the customers? She decided that no matter what, come morning she would visit the All-American Dynamite Dwarf Carnival, and she would try not to feel guilty or superior or inferior. She would try to just be. *Clarissa. Clarissa.*

She drove the three blocks to her house and turned in. The place was lit up stem to stern, as if electricity were free. Did everyone on the planet tonight, she wondered, need illumination? She hadn't counted on him being awake. Would he take one look at her and know that another man had held her? Would he smell the scent of want and abandon and fear and willfulness? Would he care? Or would he rage? What should be her stance? she wondered, turning off the wipers and then the headlights. She gazed at the old house—its clapboard siding, its wraparound porches, its beautiful old wavy glass windows—and understood that a terrible crime had been committed there. She'd woken up that morning naive. And now she was not. Now the world was a different place. And Iggy was going to have to catch up.

"Steady as she goes," she whispered as she got out of Yellow Bird and made her way past the salvia and bee balm to the porch, where an armadillo stood hunched in the shadows, considering upending the yarrow so that he could enjoy their tasty roots.

Her ovarian shadow women began to whimper, but Clarissa wasn't all that afraid. Rather, she was curious. She stepped into the chandelier room and tried to divine Iggy's whereabouts. Was he watching TV, in his office staring into the glow of the computer, or wrapped in a fetal knot in the far corner of their bed? She checked her cell phone—3:05 a.m.—and decided to try the bedroom first. Winding her way through the back hallway, her bangles chiming, announcing her arrival, she decided that thanks to some dogleg detour in love's reasoning, the chaste nature of her evening with Adams made the entire episode even more explosive.

The bedroom door was closed. She gripped the knob but hesitated. Should she feel guilty?

"Absolutely not," her old friend Deepak chimed. "You were only seeking your bliss. Bad situations prompt that, you know."

Deepdeep was right. She turned the knob and charged into the room as if she had every right to come home at three a.m., excuse-free. But even in the dark, she could tell that Iggy wasn't there. She walked over to the bed and felt the spread; it had not been slept in. For reasons she couldn't quite put her finger on, this pissed her off. Perhaps she was primed for a reckoning and needed him to show up for it. Otherwise, what was the point? She went into her closet, kicked off her pretty blue pumps, shimmied out of her jeans, pulled the chemise over her head, snapped off her bra, and left everything in a pile on the floor except for her jewelry. She kept that on, including all twenty bangles; she might need armament. She slipped on her robe and resumed her search.

As she wandered, finding nothing but one empty room after another, her mission to confront him became more urgent. When she approached the living room, she tuned her ears, trying to detect the gaspy sound of late night TV porn. She knew what he did in the wee hours. Many a morning, she checked the on-screen purchase history to find his late night proclivities spelled out in a list untainted by judgment (just the facts: film titles, purchase price, time ordered). Clarissa would read through the titles, searching for clues about why he preferred adult movies to her. She was just down the hall, after all; warm, alive, wanting. Perhaps she simply couldn't compete—even though she was in the flesh—with the girls in *Oral Ecstasy Three*.

She pressed her ear to the door. All was quiet. She walked in and searched for clues. The TV was off but still warm. An empty bottle of Heineken, its sweat leaving water trails on the coffee table, was still cold. He'd cleared the room in only the past few minutes, she decided; perhaps he'd heard her drive up and took his leave. A stack of contact sheets lay abandoned on the couch.

She shuffled through them. They were images shot that day, mostly in the barn: the two models together, acting like farm animals, mounting each other. How was this art? How did this uplift or inform the human condition? How was she supposed to live like this? He was sick, she decided, a fucking nutcase.

Clarissa tossed the contact sheets on the table, brought her robe more tightly about her. Perhaps he was in the darkroom. She'd sure as hell aim to find out. She threaded her way back through the hallways and empty rooms, calm yet fierce, out the back porch, and down the stairs. She marched through the wet grass, made a beeline for the building that was situated directly behind her studio, pounded on the door. No response. Fuck! Exasperated, she wandered past the rose garden, stood in the clearing, and stared at the heavens. Remnant storm clouds swept eastward, pushed by a fair, warm breeze that — even without the poisonous effect ghosts had on particularly annoying insects — kept the hypodermic needles known as mosquitoes grounded. The stars, while not as stunning as they were at the beach, still gleamed with an intensity unseen by city dwellers. The waning crescent moon — the wishing moon of witches — was just beginning to suggest its presence by a nearly imperceptible glow in the eastern sky. More storms approached from the west.

Clarissa's long hair hung thick and wild around her shoulders. She was barefoot but didn't care. She liked the feel of wet earth beneath her feet. There wasn't a worm in the world crazy enough to take her as its host — that's what she always thought whenever her mother's admonition of "You'll get worms if you go outside without shoes on, you little tramp!" swept through her memory bank. Little tramp: What a laughable arrow to aim at her. All those names her mother called her, all those secret scars from the whippings...Mother was mean and vicious and rotten. That's all there was to it.

The same armadillo that had watched her make her way into the house paused from his conscientious uprooting of the yarrow and studied her. It was impossible to know if the armadillo was sizing her up because he feared she might interrupt his late night tending or because she looked quite mad. Whatever the case, his beady eyes gleamed as they took her in.

Oblivious to his presence, Clarissa realized that she was backsliding. Hadn't she cried those old wounds away while lying in Adams's embrace? She sure as hell had tried. Watching the clouds race eastward, she veered into a Deepakesque scolding. Think nice thoughts, goddamn it. Think about the cosmos and the rivers flowing deep in your soul and the full-moon beauty of your ass and Eve's ancient wisdom nourishing your ovaries and how magnificently your hormones spin inside the uterine whole- ness of your feminine goddess and...oh, horseshit.

All the straps and rubber bands and cords and ropes and tie-downs and chains and duct tape and Band-Aids and Post-it notes Clarissa had used pretty much her entire life to hold her anxiety and emotions in place popped free — snip, snap, whiz, watch out! — in one great moment. Fists clenched, robe asunder, hair wild, breasts bared, Clarissa threw back her head, bangles up to her elbows, and screamed more loudly than she had thought humanly possible. It was a scream that endured, beginning in her neglected loins, swirling and gaining momentum in her belly and lungs and bellows of her heart, deepening in the protean cords of her voice box, breaking across her lips like an ocean unleashed, traveling through time and space with the grace and speed afforded solely to the good but fed-up women of this earth.

The armadillo jumped before scurrying behind the steps. The lover herons roosting in the sentinel oak raised their heads, tested the air, shared a glance that spoke volumes about what they thought of humans, and then went back to sleep. Larry

Dibble, having taken shelter in the barn, woke from a fevered, nightmare-riddled slumber, said, "Shut the hell up," and, for reasons he couldn't ascertain, began to weep. An owl on the prowl for rats and snakes blinked once before flying from his perch in a nearby cypress to a pine snag down the road. The rat family living in Clarissa's attic froze for a mere three seconds, determined they weren't in danger, and then continued on, chewing through a tart rectangle of luscious cotton-candy-pink insulation. An indigo snake, unseen in the night, slipped deeper into the brambles, its tongue alive with the vibrations Clarissa stirred. These vibrations tripped invisible and sure over the glossy tongues of magnolia leaves and the satin petulance of her rose garden. And as for the stars? A reasonable person could have easily imagined that the buckle in Orion's Belt and the bowl of the Big Dipper's ladle shook, their star shine blurred under the weight of that distant howl. In all of Clarissa's known world, only her husband—a man who had snuck past her when she was snooping at the contact sheets and then slipped without a sound into their bedroom, where he fell into an immediate and deep sleep—was left untouched, unaware.

Letting go so fully was exhausting. And although Clarissa did not grasp the magnitude of what was happening, hers was not so much a private, primal scream as it was a release of all the vicissitudes that all women through all time had ever experienced. And she also, thanks to how desensitized she'd become in her rabbit hole of a marriage, did not yet know that such belly-busting hollering was an important step in becoming (a) free, and (b) a full, card-carrying member in the army of women who—at great peril to their safety and ingrained comfort zone—acted upon the hard-won knowledge that subservience wasn't their game.

Having emptied herself, at least for the moment, of ancient burdens, she found room inside for further self-expression, which was the risk in finding your voice: You wanted never to be silent again. And so, as if possessed by the Holy Spirit, Clarissa began speaking in tongues. Except she wasn't full of the Spirit, and she wasn't uttering Aramaic or some other such nonsense. With her breasts aglow in the moonlight, her core immersed in the eternal, roiling river of female vexation, what flowed was a mighty torrent of soul-saving obscenities. "Goddamn motherfucker son-of-a-bitch asshole jerk-off bastard. You will not do this to me, motherfucker! Shithead son of a bitch!"

Feeling as if she were slipping from the grip of martyrdom—a condition she had co-opted and cultivated—Clarissa stomped inside the house with all the righteousness of Sherman marching to the sea. Instincts afire, she knew where to find the no-good, cheating, stomp-on-her-heart, slink-through-the-night bastard. Her robe hanging half off one shoulder, sweat beading translucent and pure along her hairline, she busted again into their bedroom. Blinded by the pitch blackness, she could smell him. She shut her eyes and counted to ten. When she opened them, she could make out things fairly well. Her husband—a sheet covering his torso—lay huddled in the far corner of the king-size bed. He was curled in on himself like an armored bug protecting his belly.

She kicked the bed. "Wake up!"

He moaned, curled tighter.

"I said, 'Wake the fuck up.'" Clarissa frightened herself, but she was also excited. Who knew where this new tack might land her?

He leaned on his elbows, shoulders slumped, eyes hooded. He looked drunk, but Clarissa suspected he was simply confused. She stood over him, her robe open, her body exposed.

"What the..." He shielded his eyes with his hand and fell against his pillow. "What's wrong with you?" His voice was clotted, thick with sleep.

"Look at me, you son of a bitch. Look at me! You don't even look at me anymore."

He rolled over, away from where she stood. "Jesus H. Christ." His words were muffled, tangled in the bedding. "*Voertsek! Scram!*"

Clarissa wanted to beat on him, scream at him, make him hurt, make him react as if he had some feeling—even hatred—toward her, anything but this all-abiding insouciance. "Get your fucking camera right now, asshole. Take my picture. If you're incapable of fucking me, at least photograph me."

He didn't move. He lay there, face in his pillow, belly down.

"You don't touch me. You don't look at me. You barely even talk to me." Clarissa spoke in a near whisper, which was appropriate given that she had just lifted the veil on the holy trinity of her discontent. "Talk to me. What is wrong with you? You haven't touched me since the freaking Clinton administration!"

She sat on the bed and batted down a desire to press her fingers into the small of his back. The ovarian shadow women whispered, "Don't say another word; you've gone too far already."

But she couldn't stop herself. Her entire future, in that one convulsive moment, seemed to depend on her asking what she had barely been able to ponder privately. She did not allow herself even a second or two of self-reflection so that she might consider whether blind rage or a reasonable need for truth propelled her forward. Clarissa Burden had come unhinged. Getting to the truth at any cost was suddenly the only thing in her life that mattered. She heard her voice scrape across the canvas of her husband's indifference: "Am I that revolting to you?"

In the silence that followed, she took note of little things. His inhalations and exhalations each lasted three seconds. The night-light in the bathroom cast a faint, milky path that stopped just short of the doorway. A dog—perhaps a quarter mile down the road—barked four times, paused, then barked again. She imagined him, a hound, satisfied that he'd run off his imaginary intruder, circling one tight revolution before settling down to sleep. Something lithe and small scurried in the attic. Rats. Always rats.

And in this silence, which was really quite pregnant with sound, she waited a long time for her husband to respond, long enough that she quit counting the intervals between his breaths, long enough for the hound to complete a dream in which he flushed a bevy of quail out of tall golden grass, long enough for the rats to lose interest in the copper wiring through which the house's electrical lifeblood flowed, long enough for her anger to subside, for it to be replaced by something hard and cold and on the move: an ice floe.

When the silence truly was pure, when the last ounce of warmth had drained from her fingers, she placed her hand on his spine. His shoulders, filmed in sweat, shook. The motion vibrated all the way up to her elbow and remained there, barbed, stinging cartilage, marrow, bone.

Uncertain as to whether he was laughing or crying, she gathered up her robe, covered herself, touched his neck, felt the moist warmth of his scalp, whispered, "I understand," and left the room.

$\sim$

She stood in the back hallway of their gigantic old house and once more felt the electric jolt of something imperfect, beautiful, terrifying. She knew it was Olga Villada, that her house was full of haunts, and that the family who'd suffered such a hideous end was still here, demanding what? Justice? Revenge? Peace? Clarissa leaned against the wall, wishing it would absorb her, steady her, certain that this sensation of being suspended in a lightning bolt was not because she had made an ass out of herself in front of her husband by essentially screaming that she needed to feel loved; or because she had, in her unhinged plea, reduced him to what she now presumed were tears; or because her marriage was hurtling toward the cliff's edge and the carriage had no brakes—but because she did not know how to help herself, much less the long-dead Villada-Archer family.

Slumped against the wall, Olga Villada's cold hand squeezing her shoulder, Clarissa felt herself collapse amid the ruins of her marriage. She wanted her husband to love her, to make her feel what she had felt when Adams held her—worthy, adored, no longer alone—or else she wanted out. By action and deed, her husband had left her to fend for herself in this godforsaken wilderness of a marriage while he surrounded himself with intimate strangers.

Maybe if she said, "Look, we started out loving each other and now we find ourselves separated by things and people we don't really want. Let's just get rid of them. Let's find a way back," he would understand that she was right, that the absence of loneliness was a worthy goal, that intimate strangers were expendable.

As Clarissa pushed away from the wall, Olga Villada spun toward the middle of the room, pulsing with both light and shadow. The old pain of not being released from this place had taken hold again. The solstice having passed but the night still intact, she wished for only one thing: to die completely. She began to whirl, faster and faster, tearing a hole in time's scrim, thinking, Surely this agony will ease; no one can survive eternity bearing a pain this great.

Clarissa closed the distance between herself and the bedroom. She had to tell him. Surely, after all she'd just said, he was lying in bed consumed with sadness, crying, possibly even repentant.

She cracked the door, peered in, and was met with the slumberous cacophony of her husband's contented snoring. He was no longer rolled up in a don't-touch-me ball but was on his back, legs and arms spread wide, as if claiming the entire bed, as if he somehow were the victor. Standing in the doorway, the darkness consuming her, Clarissa wondered how he could—after all that she revealed—roll over and go to sleep. In that moment, Clarissa's old world, the one where she had made certain assumptions about the goodness of her husband, exploded. He had been laughing at her. Did he have a humane or caring bone in his body? Were his actions calculated, or did dismissing her come naturally?

As her husband snored with the unstable ire of an old man, Clarissa admitted a truth she had been running from: Her husband really did not care. It wasn't an act or a conceit; his indifference was his heart. She could yell or beg or plead or dance a striptease from dawn to dusk, and it would not affect him. He lived in her house and ate her food and used her electricity and her water and spent her money to buy his clothes, and underwear, and paintbrushes, and canvases, and videocameras, and wine-soaked lunches for his intimate strangers. Living with her, putting up with her presence, she realized, was a small price to pay for a life without responsibility or duty. He lived a wholly separate existence. She was an insect to him: swat, swat.

She closed the door and spied in the shadows Olga Villada swirling, conjuring a dust devil composed of the debris of abandoned dreams. Surely after you have lost everything, even your life, in the most violent fashion possible, and you are spending eternity at the scene of the crime, what else is there to conjure other than dashed dreams?

"It's all over," Clarissa said, unshaken by the visage of the ghost. She had moved on. Her husband's disregard for her no longer bothered her. Anger? Sadness? Hopefulness? Nothing applied. She had transcended banal emotions. Truth was a great clarifier. As she watched the ghost spin with the manic religiosity of a dervish, a calm and steady Clarissa decided her husband was an unreconstructed Afrikaner who carried with him the malignant stain of his people's sins. She could not allow him to remain in her presence or even in the house. Olga Villada and her family deserved better. Hell, Clarissa deserved better. Yes, she decided, standing in the shadow of a whirling ghost, she had married an amoral and dangerous man. He would not leave willingly. He had, after all, a perfect life: no bills or responsibilities, a beautiful home, someone who cooked and cleaned for him, and a bevy of naked women with whom he shared, she was certain, a lot more than witty banter. She had no choice. She would kill the son of a bitch using the only gun in the house: the rifle that he claimed had taken the lives of thousands of Zulus at Blood River.

She walked through that labyrinth of a house in the pressing moments before dawn with a purpose and energy previously unknown to her. Olga Villada, fascinated by this newly confident Clarissa, slowed her spin and, skirts swishing, sadness intact, followed her.

Clarissa marched into the library, grabbed her machete off her bookshelf, walked into the chandelier room, stood before her husband's alleged ancestral rifle in its pink ivory wood shadow box, and swung. She hit it dead center, causing the glass to break in radiant spokes. She continued to strike strategically, turning her head and closing her eyes with each blow. A small shard hit her cheek. A rivulet of blood flowed darkly against her pale skin. She did not care. She was not in a hurry; she was not seized with panic. She was, she believed, in charge.

Olga Villada stood under the chandelier's dusty glow, wondering if she should intercede, sensing that a placid, insane fury had taken hold of Clarissa. She knew that women whose anger had grown so deep that it presented a smooth surface even as they reached for a rifle were capable of almost anything humans could dream. Perhaps she should fetch Amaziah.

The fly Clarissa had killed earlier that day lit on the ghost's shoulder. Olga Villada cast an annoyed glance but, recognizing that he had traveled a very far distance in a single day, allowed him to stay. The fly could not imagine why his killer, who was also the object of his affections, was swinging a machete, breaking glass, and doing so in a fashion so deliberate that she appeared to be in total control of her faculties.

Despite her careful approach, Clarissa cut the fatty rise of her palm when she removed the last shard. She took off her robe's cotton belt and wrapped her hand. She removed the rifle and retrieved the box of bullets from the rolltop desk. She wasn't sure if she would remember how to load the thing—it had been three years—much less shoot it; but clarity serves memory, and she slipped a bullet into the chamber, snapped the breechblock closed, and thought life must have been good if you were Annie Oakley.

She didn't know what type of rifle this was, other than it being a single-shot contraption. She didn't know its vintage or its provenance, but from the research she'd done regarding the 1838 massacre of Zulus at Blood River—the battle her husband was so proud of—he was obviously a lying sack of shit. The Boers had been armed with muskets, not single-shot rifles. They'd had to pour gunpowder down the barrels and, using rods, ram the weapons full of lead balls. The Zulus, armed with spears, never had a chance. And then the fuckers had the nerve to claim the victory was God's. I'll show the bastard victory, she thought; I'll show him what it means to lie. She hefted the rifle. One shot would have to do.

As she threaded her way through the broken glass—she cut her left foot but not her right—and then retraced her steps through the brightly lit house, the rat family in the attic scurried to the dormer to see what tantalizing possibilities dawn would bring. The armadillo, sensing daylight and danger, retreated to his den under the house. The love herons, just beginning to feel dawn's tug on the tender undersides of their wingtips, stretched their long necks skyward. Throughout the house and grounds, diurnal spiders were waking (an entire day of weaving and killing awaited them), while their nocturnal cousins were withdrawing into crevices alive with such sincere bursts of activity that they resembled a bug-life version of a bustling city. As the crescent moon rose in the east, tied to Venus's blatant diamond shine—and even as dolphins, manta rays, flying fish, and sharks anticipated the sun's ascent from African shores—Hope, Florida, teemed with creatures of disparate minds: those that sensed—even in slumber—that a new day was imminent and those that dealt with the reality of the solstice's short feeding night and thus began their journeys back into nooks and crannies far beyond the sun's deep reach.

Larry Dibble, wide awake in the barn, lay prostrate amid dirt and roach droppings. Finally, after nearly two centuries of fighting the truth, he began putting together bits and pieces of his hazy past, crying like a little bitch because he could not face what he had done.

Amid the change from dark to light, energy from the heat-driven storms still lurked.

Clarissa allowed herself, as she advanced through the house, to consider the possibility that she was temporarily insane. Her contemplative moment was cut short by a resounding *Nonsense!* When the judge asked her to plead, she would say, "Guilty by reason of pitch-perfect sanity."

The fly zoomed in spiraling circles, tracking her progress. Olga Villada whirled from room to room, in search of her husband. She found Heart where she had left him an hour earlier: asleep in the upstairs bedroom, one corner of the wedding ring quilt bunched in his tiny fist.

Clarissa held the rifle perpendicular to her body, the butt end tucked under her arm. Her hand bled through her robe's cloth belt. She didn't notice. Upon arriving at the closed bedroom door, she opened it with her free, uninjured hand, walked over to her snoring husband, put the cold nose of the rifle to his neck, and said calmly, "Wake up, Iggy. We're going to talk."

He opened a weary eye and then squinted at her as though she were an apparition composed of sandpaper.

She jabbed the rifle into his jugular. He made a gurgling noise, and his big baby blues widened. "And I mean now."

"Clarissa. *Skort.*"

"Don't tell me to be careful, you son of a bitch. In fact, don't even move until I tell you to." She raised the rifle, looked down its scope, kept him in her sight, took three steps back, and eased onto the big black trunk filled with old stuff — photos, newspaper clippings, her first fan letter, poems scrawled in the desperate light of a dying day and never to be seen or read by anyone.

"What the *fowking* hell do you think you're doing? That's a family heirloom!"

"Oh, stuff it. This rifle never saw action at Blood River. The Boers used muzzle-loading rifles in 1838. This baby here" — Clarissa patted the barrel with her bleeding hand — "is a single-shot, breech-loading motherfucker that didn't even exist for another, I don't know, let's say quarter century. You're such a liar."

"It did belong to my family. A distant uncle." Iggy pulled the sheet up to his chin. As if *that* were going to protect him.

"Great. Then why all the crap about Blood River?"

He shrugged. Getting caught in a lie didn't appear to faze him.

"You know what I think?"

He looked at her; his thick lips—abundant amid his beard—had begun to fold in on themselves, forming a long, thin, pink line. Maybe he wasn't breathing well.

"All your talk about renouncing your family and rejecting their colonial, racist ways is bullshit. You're just like them."

"*Skort!* I am not just like them, Clarissa."

"Oh, yeah? Liar. You trumped up a story about this fucking rifle and paid God knows how much money to display it. And you used pink ivory wood, no less. Talk about rubbing salt into an ancient wound! You're proud your family took part in a massacre. Or did you make that up, too?"

"My great-great—"

"Shut up. You don't get to talk yet. You think you're better than me. You walk around this house as if you own it. Well, you don't. I do. You don't own squat."

"Careful, Clarissa."

"Or what? I'm the one with the weapon."

"You don't even know how to use it."

"Are you really willing to risk that?"

"You are so stupid, Clarissa."

"I'll tell you what's stupid. Your paintings are stupid. Your sculptures are stupid. Your meaningless, gibberish-filled films are stupid. Your photographs are stupid. Your bimbo models are stupid. The way you treat me is worse than stupid."

He smoothed the sheet as if he were settling in for a nice cup of tea. "I treat you the way you deserve to be treated."

"What are you talking about?" Clarissa spit the words through gritted teeth. Her bleeding hand hurt. The rifle was heavy.

"You are a silly little fool, Clarissa. You write your silly books and talk to your silly friends and live your silly little life while I make art."

"And you fuck your models."

"So? They're prettier than you."

Clarissa stood, aimed the rifle, tried to keep her soul intact—the fly landed on the muzzle; in his fly heart, he hated Igor Pretoriun—and slipped her finger into the curved sweetness of the trigger. The belt-bandage slipped off her hand. It had started to rain again; she heard it coming down on the tin roof: ping! ping! ping! Iggy laughed. He laughed so hard that tears ran down his cheeks and moistened his beard. He was mocking her. Again. Her finger flexed twice, and then she began to squeeze. She wanted Igor Pretoriun dead, and if her spousal death scenarios weren't enough, perhaps a 150-year-old bullet to his nether regions would do the trick. She had to decide: Head or dick? Head or dick? Fuck! She couldn't make up her mind, so she aimed the rifle at his heart.

"You don't know anything, Clarissa. You don't know how much you bore me. How your little dinners with your little salads and your little garnishes and your little desserts make me want to puke. How your books about stupid women who struggle and overcome and who are full of female wonder make me embarrassed for you." He smiled—a big, grand, generous smile. "You, my dear, are my private joke."

The fly landed on Clarissa's shoulder. He felt the monumental breaking of her heart. He wished he were a cougar, not a fly, so that he could kill the man himself.

Clarissa, however, went through yet another transformation. With her heart shattered, it was easy for her to decide that she would not let him hurt her one more time. She refreshed her aim: his big, fat face. "Iggy, you're a sick, sick man, and I'm sorry I ever married you." Clarissa tilted the rifle to a point just above his head and fired. The kick knocked her back.

"You *fowking* bitch! *Jou teef!*" he yelled, leaping from the bed.

He lunged for her and wrapped his big hands around her throat. He slammed her against the wall. She felt her skull crack; her larynx, veins, and arteries began to constrict and fail.

The ghost fly couldn't take it anymore. He had to do something. So he buzzed through the hot and humid air of the bedroom, took dead aim, and landed on Iggy's big eye.

"Shit," Iggy said, shaking his head. The ghost fly, with those wonderful sticky ghost feet, held on. Iggy let go of Clarissa, stumbled backward, and cried, "Ahhhhhh," as he scratched at his eye.

Clarissa ran into the closet, locked it from the inside. Iggy roared. The ghost fly lost his grip, and Clarissa honestly wondered what she had ever seen in her lousy excuse of a husband. She threw on the clothes she'd worn that night as he pounded on the door. She needed her keys. She needed shoes. She needed to get into Yellow Bird and flee. She had barely pulled the chemise over her head when the door gave, splintering along a fault line in the wood.

Iggy pinned her to the floor and slapped her, his big ham-bone hand crashing into her cheek and top lip, which split open. "How dare you try to shoot me, you bitch!"

Clarissa had clearly shot over his head. He was ridiculous. Maybe he had been waiting for years for an excuse to murder her. "I didn't shoot you, you asshole!"

He lifted his hand again. Clarissa did not think she could take the blow. She reached wildly, found her blue spike pump under her coral chemise. Unbeknownst to Clarissa, her attempts to pull it out of the cobblestone had sharpened its steel edge. She gripped that shoe as if it were a cleaver and — with a strength that transcended a need to scream, Fwuk u u liho! — dug the spike heel into Iggy's soft, doughy, alabaster cheek. He screamed, and she scrambled from beneath him. The spike, she thought as she watched him tug, must have hit bone. She was only half-sorry that she hadn't gouged out his eye. He screamed louder as he extracted the heel from his face.

Clarissa ran. She tumbled barefoot into the yard, without her keys. In her panic, she could not remember where she'd left them. And she could not go back into the house. Surely he would kill her.

Cold rain pelted her skin, the armadillo watched her from behind a blind of daylilies, thunder rolled long and hard like a breaking wave. The ghost fly lit on the back porch screen, trying to determine if his spectral wings would carry him through the storm. Olga Villada, not knowing the whereabouts of the rifle-toting Clarissa (perhaps I influenced her a bit too much, she fretted) or her husband, scooped Heart out of bed. The little boy began to cry.

"Shh, baby, shh. We're going to go find your father."

Clarissa ran toward the rose garden; if nothing else, she would escape into Jake's Hell. She heard a huge commotion coming from the house. She looked over her shoulder and saw her vase—her beautiful, beautiful cut crystal vase full of roses—somersault through the air and shatter on the porch floor. Iggy, blood rushing down his face, slammed open the screen door, screaming, "You *fowking* bitch!" He held up her checkbook from her secret account and the keys to Yellow Bird. "You're the *fowking* liar, you *fowking* cunt!" He heaved the checkbook and keys through the rain. Clarissa watched them arc and tumble through the air and then land amid the thick chaos of the magnolia's fallen leaves.

Iggy ran after her. He was tall, and those long legs made quick work of the distance between them. She felt as if she were in that childhood nightmare, the one where she kept trying to run but her legs kept disintegrating into dust while the giant snake slithered closer and closer. She had barely made it to the center of the garden when he tackled her. She fell facedown in the dirt. He grabbed her hair and yanked. She thought, Oh, my God, he's pulling my hair out.

The ghost fly, his legs twitching, decided he had no choice. Invisible, he pushed through the screen and flew on wobbly wings — as if he were an unskilled aviator rather than the aerial acrobat of just hours ago — through the rain, toward his beloved, who he was sure was about to die.

Olga Villada, her son in her arms, having scoured the house for her husband, thought, He's not out there hacking away at the tree again, is he? Not at this hour, in this storm. She rushed onto the back porch, her son still crying, broken glass crunching beneath her boots. "Oh dear, no," she said as she saw Iggy snatch Clarissa by the hair and wrench her neck into a horribly unnatural angle.

"Olga! Hurry! Hurry!" Amaziah ran across the yard from the direction of the sentinel oak, an ax in his hand.

"Have you been hacking the tree again?" Olga Villada yelled. "In this weather!"

"Honey," he said, reaching her side, his eyes alight, "this might be it! Come on, let's go!"

Olga Villada, annoyed with her husband (how could he not break the family rule just this once?), jabbed her head in the direction of the raging couple. Clarissa screamed, "Please stop!"

"We have to do something! We can't let him kill her." Olga Villada brushed away her son's tears. "Shh, baby, shh."

"We're ghosts, honey. They're humans. And there's lightning in that storm cloud." Amaziah pointed skyward with the ax.

"Darling, you've been saying that same thing for nearly two hundred years." Olga Villada shifted the weight of the boy on her hip.

"I'm telling you, woman, this is it. I've got a feeling. Let's go!" He set the ax by the door, took Heart into his arms, grabbed her hand, and said, "Now!"

"And what about them?" Olga Villada said, gesturing toward the living.

"We leave them be." Amaziah's eyes were fierce.

Olga Villada thought about the unbearable burden of living forever in a state of twilight. She also thought about the terror of being beaten alive when you've done no harm. She squeezed his hand. Her beautiful lips began to tremble.

"We've got to try, honey."

Olga Villada looked into her husband's tortured but hopeful eyes and knew she had to let him do it his way; he had never stopped believing that a new world awaited them, one where even their son would be free. "Okay, my love. Let's do it."

Amaziah guided his family through the storm, past the struggling couple and the inflamed beauty of the rose garden, toward their crucible.

⁓

The first rays of dawn seared the approaching thunderhead with quicksilver light, but as the storm moved over the tiny village of Hope, the towering clouds obliterated the first moments of the new day.

According to old Mrs. Hickok's thermometer, just before the storm's arrival the temperature was ninety-eight degrees. When the hail began, the thermometer's mercury plummeted fifteen points. The wind howled, stirring up a tempest, and the hail forced both husband and wife to cover their heads, effectively pinning them to the earth.

The ghost fly, struggling, sought shelter beneath a blade of grass near Clarissa's left shoulder. The Villada-Archer family huddled beneath the canopy of the tree where they had lost their lives 180 years and 7 days prior. In the clearing, the skin shed by the black snake disintegrated in the pounding rain.

Curled up amid rodent and insect shit, Larry Dibble vomited. What he retched was not food—this angel rarely ate. It was his past, one that he had managed, despite his boss's best efforts, to keep buried deep in the convulsive impulse called his soul.

Larry Dibble had died in 1860 of snakebite near his shotgun shack in Capitola, a village twenty-some miles east of Tallahassee and about twenty-five miles west of Hope. He'd snuck into a neighbor's tomato patch, intending to steal the season's final bounty. Brimming with fallen and overripe fruit, the patch teemed with rats and, thus, also with rattlers. Two serpents struck him three times: hand, thigh, ankle. It was a painful death.

While the storm raged, pounding Clarissa Burden and Iggy Pretoriun into temporary submission and confounding the sweetest wishes of Olga Villada, Amaziah Archer, and Heart Archer as they sought a new way of being, it was Larry Dibble's life—not his death—that he remembered.

This thing, barely an angel, was not born Larry Dibble; that was a name assigned at ascension. Lawrence Butler had been the youngest brother in a group of four violent men. He was not of the same ilk as his brothers; though, lacking backbone and a sense of righteous anger, he went along far too often. When the Butler boys arrived at the Villada-Archer home on a clear, hot morning on June 15, 1826, Lawrence thought the purpose of the meeting was to negotiate the sale of the property. These were colored people with a colored child, and Florida was no longer a safe place for them. He did not know—how could he know, he wondered amid his waste—what Maurice would set into motion. Lawrence did not partake in the lynching, the torture, the murder. What he did do, which was what earned him those provisional wings, was to step in when Maurice tried to rape Olga Villada. He pulled his big brother off the screaming woman and the two men fought.

Maurice was strong, with a sadistic streak wilder than a herd of untamed horses. As they tumbled across the floor of what Clarissa Burden would call her chandelier room and out onto the back porch, both brothers spied an ax propped in the corner beside the door. Lawrence calculated the distance and knew that Maurice would get to it first. So, using his right thumb as a spike—he remembered full well what brother Bobby had done to the man in Beaufort who'd beat him fair and square in a card game—Lawrence gouged out Maurice's left eye. He dug deep and hard. He did not want that woman to get raped. Nobody deserved that. Nobody. Not even a pretty Spanish woman with a colored husband.

Maurice pushed Lawrence off him and—laughing, blood streaming—reached out his long arm, managed a good grip on the ax, reared back with the strength that comes of wrestling both man and bull, and hacked his baby brother's right arm clean off. Lawrence, yowling with the depth of the damned, writhed on the porch floor. Maurice, now blind in one eye, threw his brother's arm into the yard and aimed to finish what was left of these people.

Lying in a pool of blood, Lawrence managed to tie off an artery, thus saving his own life. Wounded as he was, he passed in and out, but fate forced him to be a witness. He saw his brothers lynch that family—even the little boy—and he heard the names and taunts, saw the whipping Amaziah took and the sheer pleasure his brothers derived in the crime; but right before he passed out for what would be three and a half days, the man chose to forget. And that was his problem; reconciliation of the soul doesn't occur without long and painful admissions of truth.

Until his death by snakebite, Lawrence Butler remained a man of compromised morals, stealing from his neighbors, sometimes stopping in to see Maurice in Tallahassee (his big brother had become a substantial landowner, parlaying Olga Villada and Amaziah Archer's land into valuable real estate near the Florida Capitol) to ask for money and various other favors. He never ratted out his brothers, although given the climate, justice was the province of the few and privileged. But right was right. Wrong was wrong. And he'd committed one brave and noble act, which had earned him not only a pass but a chance. Provisional wings were designed not for eternity, but to allow a flawed man the time and space to atone.

Larry Dibble sat up, whimpering, and wiped vomit off his mouth with the back of his hand. He'd gotten it wrong, so, so wrong. He stood—unsteady and ashamed—grabbed his rope, and wondered if there was still time to make anything good of his life, to even for one moment begin to make up for the hell he'd helped create on this earth.

⁓

A clap of thunder shook the ground, rattling the house's windows, buffeting the barn doors, sending swamp critters fleeing for deeper cover. Before the sound waves had settled, the hail stuttered to a stop, replaced by cold rain. Larry Dibble—finally attuned to the horrible fact that he'd been a lousy angel but an even worse man, that one decent act did not a good life make— ran into the yard. The family he had helped destroy (he should have, he knew, stopped Maurice before they ever crossed into Florida) stood huddled beneath the great arms of the tree where they had died. They were comforting one another. Rather than bitter, they seemed joyous that something wonderful might be imminent. He stood in the driving rain — the ants that had long made his hair home drowning, his long-nonexistent arm itching for the first time in a hundred years — and finally understood. It was too late for him, but they still had a chance.

He sprinted across the clearing and, relying on the agility he'd gained as an angel even though his wings were now useless, tossed the rope over a low-lying limb, climbed it as fast as he could, navigated the thick oak maze, past big branches and sharp twigs, smothering at times in impenetrable tangles of Spanish moss, ingesting dirt and fungus and leaf dander, his remaining arm aching as though venom-filled, until — with great effort — he ultimately reached the summit. Atop the tree, he hovered, truly angelic yet fully mortal, rising to his full and modest height, asking not for forgiveness because he realized he was not worthy of mercies tender or harsh, and then he turned himself — body and soul; present, past, unknowable, and immense — into a lightning rod.

The wind howled; the rain slashed horizontally. Olga Villada reached over to comfort and protect her son. Amaziah scanned the heavens, looking for God. Just as Olga Villada was about to say, "How long do you expect us to stand out here?" from a great height Amaziah's long-desired lightning bolt scarred the heavens, burning a jagged path from the dark and roiling cloud bank, sundering the clownish but sincere angel, incinerating the sentinel oak's green crown, and pulsing — full of fire — straight into the core of its ancient trunk.

Clarissa saw the flash from behind her closed lids. She forced open her eyes just in time to see the two heron lovebirds rise into the sky as the great tree cleaved in half. The scent of sulfur and wood soured the rain. The awful groan of old-growth wood giving way echoed through the swamp.

The rat family in the attic scurried for cover behind the stiff canvas of an old painter's drop cloth. The armadillo, sheltered under the house, behind a blind of lilies, did not move.

Clarissa began to cry—not because her husband had her pinned in the dirt she had tilled in the garden she loved, but because the tree was falling in two giant, slumberous halves, its crown taking forever to touch the earth. Oh, my God, she thought, oh, my God; the tree is dying.

"*Fowking* mother of Christ!" Iggy said. "The whole *fowking* thing is coming down."

"It's about time," Amaziah murmured, batting back tears. He hugged his wife even as he held on to his son, who patted his daddy's face and watched, wide-eyed, the big tree fall. For nearly two centuries, they had waited for this moment—the time when the suffering and cruelty would be rendered toothless. Their pain and the Butler boys' sparkling violence were spiraling on paths unseen, being absorbed by the fine, far-flung molecules of heaven and hell.

"It's over. It's finally over," Olga Villada said. She kissed her baby's cheek, held her husband, listened to the tree die, hoped Clarissa would survive her husband's attack, and that amid what might be a long and happy life, the young woman would one day write the story of the tragedy that unfolded on this very spot. June 15, 1826, had started out so beautifully, she thought: a clear sky, a fair breeze, her son's laughter, her husband's buoyant talk of things to come. Olga Villada pressed her face against Amaziah's chest and prayed that their murderers would not be treated well by history.

"I told you," Amaziah said.

"Yes. Yes, you did. And what's two hundred years"—Olga Villada smiled up at him, wiping away her ghost tears and reaching again for his hand—"when you've just been released from an eternity spent thinking about the moment we died?"

"You ready?"

"Yes. And you?"

"Absolutely."

The family gathered in a single knot—ghost to ghost to ghost—the little boy, as on the day they died, protected within the eternal cocoon of his parents' bodies.

Olga Villada said, "This is a good thing, baby. Do not be afraid."

Hidden in the grass, the ghost fly wondered if he should join them on their journey but decided he could not bear to leave Clarissa, his murderer, his beloved. So he remained there—in the tall reeds, Clarissa by his side—listening to the Villada-Archers whisper words he would never forget: *I love you, Mama. I love you, Papa. I love you, Olga. I love you, Amaziah. We love you, baby, we love you. Oh, how I love each one of you.*

The herons circled the dying oak, spiraling higher at each turn, their heron song sounding like plaintive weeping, but really it was simply the song of life changing, and for the length of one strong inhalation, even the wind did not stir. After 180 years of limbo, during the updraft of the herons' final spiral, Olga and Amaziah and Heart—a family entwined—left the old earth.

The storm edged eastward, toward the Atlantic. Daybreak unfurled like a dream, tinting red the few remaining stars. The angel named Larry Dibble, who had been as compromised in death as he had been in life, became a single speck of carbon, carried to far shores by a restless breeze.

Clarissa Burden, for the third time in less than an hour, escaped her husband's grip. She watched her ankle slip through his long Dutch fingers. She did not want to die this way, at the hands of her husband. She had nothing with her—no keys, no access to Yellow Bird, no money, no shoes. So she ran. This time she decided the swamp would kill her. Best to move toward people.

Her feet burned against the asphalt, which held the previous day's heat despite the rain. She would not let that stop her. She had never before wanted so deeply to live. The ovarian shadow women ran with her. The carnival was only three blocks away.

The ghost fly watched her flee. He tried his wings, but they were soaked through and useless. How could he, a ghost, be immobile? He had, he realized—his little heart aching under the weight of being unable to help his beloved—so much to learn.

Money Dog watched the final preparations for the carnival's opening day from the awning-covered stoop of his owner's trailer. Moments before, he had eaten a breakfast of scrambled eggs with chopped sausage, a luxury his owner shared with him at intervals he could not measure. He had consumed it in six fast bites, hoping for more, although more never came, at least not until some unknown point in his unknowable future that he, frankly, hadn't the ways or means to contemplate.

For now, he was focused on his most recent obsession. No longer content with being a sideshow, Money Dog yearned to take center stage. Show after show, his owner, a man named Nicolai, bedazzling in a tight silver suit, flew through the air after being shot out of a golden cannon. Sure, Money Dog, show after show, leapt on cue—his little doggy red cape flapping—into his triumphant owner's arms. And sure, using his stage name Rocket, he never failed to delight as he hopped and flipped and twirled on his tippy toes before making the required grateful leap. And no doubt the crowds—especially the children—adored him. But there was something about the visage of his owner flying through the sky that got to Money Dog, that made him ache to crawl into that golden cannon and see for himself what the ride was like.

As an early morning storm raged and as roustabouts, cursing the weather, continued with the business of preparing for opening day, Money Dog contemplated his desire to be the one who flew and also the fact that this was a carnival, after all, so nothing was as it appeared. Even the names were illusions. Nicolai—who sported a goatee and a fake Russian accent when speaking to fans—was actually from Toledo, Ohio, and his name was Glenn, and he had a sweetheart who was very tall named Rane.

And Rocket, who was known as Money Dog among the carnies because people seemed never to be able to get enough of the short little fox-tailed thing, was neither Rocket nor Money Dog in reality. Upon finding him scavenging for food after the show had gone dark, and seeing that he was a mess of sticker burrs and want, and assuming correctly that he'd been wandering for a good long time, Tom Brown (a clown known as Shorty) dubbed the dog Ulysses and brought him into the fold, where he was promptly won by Glenn in a poker game.

Ulysses was a curious dog, and like his namesake who traveled the Greek Isles for ten years, he enjoyed seeing the world. And what better way to do that than with a carnival? True, he preferred his given name to Rocket or Money Dog, which even he knew sounded crass and maybe a little dirty. But given that he was a dog, sometimes it was best to answer to what the humans called you. Wise dogs — of which Ulysses counted himself as one — knew when to walk away from a fight. And as for his stage name, that just went with the territory. Hell, even Petunia the Potbellied Pig preferred to be known as Alice.

He scratched behind his left ear, heard the sizzle of lightning making contact, caught the scent of something ancient singe the storm-scrubbed air, lifted his nose, and tested the wind. The echo of a dying tree passed over him. When the rain had all but stopped, he went in search of the cannon, peeing on every tent spike he passed.

⟋⟍

Clarissa was not of a mind to take in the sights. But if she had been, she would have seen the little mechanism — this clock's heart known as a carnival — begin the countdown to its day. The All-American Dynamite Dwarf Carnival opened its gates to the public in just three hours, and there was much to do. Costumes to be ironed. Beards to be waxed. Hair — depending on the person — to be straightened or curled. Bolts to be tightened, hinges oiled, signs dusted, apples candied, miniature horses and pygmy goats groomed, banners unfurled, bulbs changed, throats cleared.

Nearly every member of the carnival found comfort in the redundancy of his or her nominal predicaments. *The smallest this, the tiniest that*, provided a stable foundation from which to live, and even embroider, their lives.

Gloria, the World's Smallest Trapeze Artist, went for a couple of whirls naked — platform to somersault to rope to platform — for good luck before breakfast. Hiding behind a trash barrel, Krestar, the Tiny Fortune-Teller, watched, counting how many seconds she spun, resplendent and nude, in the hot, hot air.

Jack and Jill, the World's Only Married Dwarf Siamese Twins, who were not Siamese or twins or related in any way, had loud sex in the front room of their small trailer. Jill was also Contessa Alexandra, the Two-Pint Contortionist, so the sex was particularly exciting.

Out behind the bevy of food booths, Dick, the Universe's Smallest Dwarf—he stood only two feet tall and may well have deserved his carnival moniker—lifted weights (Ben Wa balls, a gift from an old girlfriend), while Vladimir, the World's Last Remaining Fire-Eating, Sword-Swallowing Dwarf, spotted him.

In the privacy of his darkened bedroom, Shorty the Clown stared at himself in a hand mirror. He dreaded this day, as he did every other day. He did not want to become even more hideous as he disappeared behind his whiteface makeup; he did not want to be the butt of the joke, the crowd laughing not because he was humorous, but because he was a freak; he did not want to be afraid to pick up the phone and call his son, who was a tall person, standing an astonishing five feet eight inches—his beautiful, beautiful, normal son. He hated living in a world of paradox and extremes. Nevertheless, in the still, dark room, using his real voice—not his clown voice—he said, "You are also a father. Freak, maybe. Father, definitely." So he set down the mirror, picked up his cell, dialed the number, and hoped against experience that this time, unlike the past forty-three attempts, his son would answer.

Happy, the Teensy Human Pincushion, busied himself with what he did every morning: He read. On June 22, 2006, he was thirty pages shy of finishing *Remembrance of Things Past*—his fifth time devouring Proust's masterwork. He loved this passage:

And I begin to ask myself what it could have been, this unre-membered state which brought with it no logical proof, but the indisputable evidence, of its felicity, its reality, and in whose presence other states of consciousness melted and vanished. I decide to attempt to make it reappear. I retrace my thoughts to the moment at which I drank the first spoonful of tea. I rediscover the same state, illuminated by no fresh light. I ask my mind to make one further effort, to bring back once more the fleeting sensation. And so that nothing may interrupt it in its course I shut out every obstacle, every extraneous idea, I stop my ears and inhibit all attention against the sound from the next room. And then, feeling that my mind is tiring itself without having any success to report, I compel it for a change to enjoy the distraction which I have just denied it, to think of other things, to refresh itself before making a final effort. And then for the second time I clear an empty space in front of it; I place in position before my mind's eye the still recent taste of that first mouthful, and I feel something start within me, something that leaves its resting-place and attempts to rise, something that has been embedded like an anchor at a great depth; I do not know yet what it is, but I can feel it mounting slowly; I can measure the resistance, I can hear the echo of great spaces traversed.

The supreme attempt; that was how this forty-two-year-old man—real name William Hunter—who held a PhD in literature but who, because of his stature, was denied a job in the academy, came to think of life as a human pincushion: consciousness melted, measured resistance, great spaces traversed with the entry of each pinpoint. He set aside the book, reached for a shortbread cookie—the closest he could get to a madeleine—and bit down.

The rain having passed, Ulysses sat three yards out from the base of the golden cannon, which Nicolai was polishing with car wax. The dog was waiting for his owner to become distracted.

Understanding human nature as he did, he doubted he would have to wait long for such a lapse in attention to occur—Gloria would traipse by in her ass-cheek leotard or someone would pause to tell a dirty joke or the guys would simply drift off into inane conversation about women, booze, or cars, and that would be Ulysses' chance.

While the roustabouts shouted, hammered, and tugged the final preparations into existence and as Nicolai polished the golden cannon to an eye-squinting gleam, the distraction that Ulysses was gifted with turned out to be of greater consequence than anything the diminutive dog had imagined.

The dwarfs parted when Clarissa busted through the front gate, screaming for help, with Iggy following twenty paces behind. The couple looked quite mad—both of them bleeding about the head, wild-eyed, and shouting curses the wind stole.

Well versed in the dangers of becoming involved in domestic disputes, no one attempted to outright stop Iggy or even shelter Clarissa. The Human Pincushion, however, worried that he was too late to catch a glimpse of Gloria swinging naked, hurried out of his trailer, leaving the last twenty-five pages of *Remembrance* unread, saw the disturbance, did not like Iggy at first glance, wasn't about to get trampled by the giant man, and decided that quick, decisive, unorthodox action was needed.

He closed his eyes and willed his mind to Proust's place of nothingness, which was where he went every time a pin punctured his skin. When his mental landscape was clear and he heard no sound—not the shouting of the roustabouts, not the giggling of the dwarf lovers next door, not the clang! clang! clang! of small motors and large egos—he imagined the bad man's giant feet and how difficult it was to traverse the earth's surface with such large appendages; he watched the spastic feet grow larger, more grotesque, saw how the man simply could not remain upright given the enormity of his problem. He watched the man go down, face first, in the carnival sawdust.

When Happy, the Teensy Human Pincushion, opened his eyes, the bad man was trying to scramble back to his giant feet. The woman he'd been chasing was nowhere to be seen.

—◦

*C*larissa knew where she would make her last stand: the fire tower. Iggy was afraid of heights. She wasn't. Having not run this fast and this long since she was fifteen was taking its toll, but she figured Iggy—who was probably also shoeless—wasn't faring much better. As for the carnies, she wasn't focused on them. All she wanted to do was survive, and in desperation decided the fire tower was her ticket.

She reached the base of the huge monolith and gazed upward. Its zigzag superstructure of steel stairs piercing the sky reminded her of an Escher nightmare. She looked at her wounded hand; the bleeding had nearly stopped. She glanced over her shoulder, remembering Adams saying that none of us were going in a straight line, and found his observation particularly prescient given her predicament. She saw Iggy round the corner of the corn dog stand. He yelled as if possessed by the literary ghost of Stanley Kowalski, "Clarissaaaaa!"

Clarissa. Clarissa. That was her cue. She ascended the tower, moving as quickly as she dared. But her left foot was bleeding, her skull was cracked, and the steel was wet. Twenty feet up and out of breath, she slipped and fell, hit her mouth, and split open what remained of her lip. She gripped the railing and, careful not to look at the ground, pulled herself to her feet. The ovarian shadow women, sensing catastrophe was at hand, yelled, "Faster! You have no choice!" And she moved on.

The higher she climbed, the closer he got, just like that freaking nightmare serpent. She was no match for him, no match. What had happened to his fear? Finally, when she could not climb one step more, when the ovarian shadow women were too exhausted to offer a single word of advice, much less encouragement, Clarissa thought, Holy crap, I haven't even finished my book; my agent is going to kill me.

She managed two additional steps and then felt his hands on her ankles, legs, shoulders. He grabbed her by her arms and began shaking her. "You stupid little bitch!"

"I do not want to die," she said, tears falling.

"I am not my father's son. His sins are not mine. Say it!"

Clarissa feared that her skeleton was coming unhinged one bone, one joint, one tendon and ligament at a time. As he shook her, she felt as though she had no choice but to measure the long distance from whence she'd come. She forced herself to look past her husband and to the earth below. People were gathering (they seemed even smaller from this great height), running and shouting, pointing and jostling. She made out what appeared to be a giant bug with human legs — very short legs — wobbling in one direction, then another. She and her husband were, evidently, creating a great commotion.

Her ovarian shadow women, terrified and speechless, were being jostled so violently, they felt as if they had been tossed into Satan's demonic washing machine.

"Say it!" he yelled, shaking her one final, violent time.

Clarissa looked at Iggy — the wound she had delivered to his cheek was gaping and oozing — and she knew the time for half-truths and lies was long past. "You are your father's son. We all carry the burdens of our ancestors' sins. But some of us try to rectify and rise above. You, you, you secretly wallow."

The hand she saw coming at her was huge — his hand — and this time she was more than willing to take it. And survive it. She heard her eardrum pop as he made contact.

"Let me go!" she screamed, but she did not hear the words. She tried to wrench out of his grip, and as she did she saw him — her hearing gone — mouth, "I love you. Don't do this, Clarissa."

She pulled away and ascended three more steps before she tripped and — with her equilibrium gone thanks to her busted eardrum — began her long fall over the edge of the tower rail.

Iggy shouted, "No!" and he reached out to her. She did not reach back. If she was going to die, she decided, it would be an independent act. He would not divert or delay the inevitable. She damn sure wasn't going to allow him to save her.

This is not to say she wanted to die. Over the past twenty-four hours, in fact, she had figured out that she very much wanted to live.

As she tumbled, weightless, time — as it is rumored to do — slowed to a glacial crawl. The wind whipped her hair, and she wondered where in this entire big world her father was and if he ever thought of her. Did he know she existed? Did he, perchance, stop by a bookstore and, simply out of paternal instinct, find her books? Was his soul stirred at all by guilt? Pride? Wonder? She saw her mother as a young woman, fresh and alive with desire for her father, and decided — just decided — that her mother had indeed loved her. Loved her with her whole heart. She saw herself as a little girl: Clarissa in the trailer, standing before the cracked mirror, pushing on those teeth, those hideous teeth. From her high, failing perch, Clarissa saw that the little girl was beautiful — just as Adams had insisted — radiant in full measure, deserving, like any other child, to be cherished. As she approached the earth and what she was sure would be her death, Clarissa, for the first time in her life, was filled with love for that little girl. And she fully understood—deep in the inner sanctum of her conscience—that the child never deserved to be beaten or called useless or stupid or ugly or even Bucky. As she saw the end near, Clarissa knew that all those things that happened to her as a child were not of her own making. And she knew that Iggy probably did love her but that he was a broken man, and she hoped he would rot in jail and she did not experience one moment of guilt over said hope. As she followed the earth's curvature, which took her slightly away from the zigzagging fire tower, she said to herself, in the quietude of her mind, I love myself. I love myself. I love myself. And of all the things that came to her—gifts of the dying—she knew one final thing: She did not want the landing to hurt.

She decided she wouldn't feel it—that her conscious self would end in tandem with the awful thud, and though she had lived a vicarious life through her characters and her superhero meanderings, the last few moments of her life would be spent fully aware. So, with her ovarian shadow women having retreated into the dim glow of her subconscious, Clarissa opened her eyes and her arms and her legs, and she felt the wind blow over the length and breadth of her. She looked at the sky—the astonishing blue sky—and the trees at the edge of the green. She was on her back, wishing for one more glimpse of the moon, when she hit. And all the air left her.

⁓

While Clarissa and Iggy fought on the tower, Ulysses jumped into the mouth of the cannon. Inside, it was warm and dark, and he could not crawl out because he could not get a foothold on its smooth, interior surface. He whimpered and barked for a time, but with all the excitement surrounding the presumed lovers' spat, no one heard him. So he curled up, nestled in the cannon's movable cylinder, ignorant as to the effects of compressed air, and took a nap.

Nicolai, unimpressed with the fighting couple, never suspecting the deadly turn the woman's run up the tower would take, made his way back through the gawking crowd. Being shot out of a cannon was a serious endeavor. He cleaned, and shined, and double-checked the cannon's integrity before each show. He also, always, because he was a superstitious man, tested the compressor.

People thought that human cannonballs were launched by gunpowder. Nonsense. Human cannonballs did not possess death wishes, and most of them, Nicolai knew from experience, were smarter than the average carnival act. So the boom and poof, supplied by firecrackers, not gunpowder, was just for show. What propelled him through the barrel and catapulted him through the sky was nothing more than pressurized air. A cylinder—a contraption that slid up and down the cannon's barrel—was, in essence, a human bullet casing. Nicolai would enter the cylinder, and his apprentice, a young wannabe from Wichita named Corey Smith, would flip the switch, blasting the barrel with one hundred pounds per square inch of the stuff we breathe. The cylinder never left the barrel. The human bullet always did.

Finding the right amount of pressure had been a scary process of trial and error. Full-size human cannonballs relied on at least 150 pounds per square inch to fling them to the sweet spot. But that would send a sixty-pound man into the next county. This cannonball business was all about physics—mass, trajectory, speed, that sort of thing. So Nicolai consulted Happy, the guy with the pincushion act, because he was the smartest person he knew.

Happy's initial calculations proved a little off, and Nicolai overshot the giant landing pad of an air mattress by a good twenty feet. The only thing that saved him? The big top tent. He hit and rolled and almost shit himself, but the canvas held.

The last thing Nicolai wanted, besides making a bad landing, which of course was how human cannonballs died, was for the compressor to fail as the drumroll hit its clichéd but required fever-pitch furl. So it was not superstition alone that led him, before every show, to test the compressor and visualize the flight: he in his fabulous silver suit and the safe landing on the air mattress (its location meticulously calculated) that was emblazoned with the likeness of himself and Money Dog.

Nicolai turned on the compressor and listened as the machine hummed to life. He loved the sound of the cylinder blasting — as if a hollow rocket ship — up the cannon's barrel. Everything occurred just as it was supposed to. He heard both the propulsion and the sudden halt of the cylinder. And then something truly terrible happened.

Out of the mouth of the cannon came Money Dog, blasting through the air, a look of profound surprise on his little doggy face.

Stunned, but a man of action, Nicholai made the sign of the cross and ran through the crowd of dwarfs who were now watching, horrified, both dog and woman fly through the early morning sky.

⌇

*U*lysses, it cannot be denied, was shocked when the blast came. But once he realized what had happened, that he was fulfilling his life's desire, he nearly enjoyed himself. He liked the way the wind and all the crazy scents — cooking oil and sugar and cookies and crotches and blood—rushed through him as he catapulted, ass over end. He managed to spy the air mattress (for some reason it had been moved farther out and rested nearly at the base of the fire tower), and he—being a dog—instinctively understood the trajectory.

But he had to stabilize, had to quit the ass-over-end thing. He did not witness his mother get run over by a lousy excuse for a human being, he did not drink swamp water for months on end while he wandered motherless through the world, he did not survive infected buckshot wounds (he never again bothered with that cat food on the back stoop of that stupid cat lover's porch), he did not escape that fucking rattlesnake, to die now, especially since he was fulfilling one of his deepest desires.

Becoming truly mighty, he stretched his foxlike tail long and even, and used it like a rudder, taming the turbulent air. As he flew, a furry arrow, his eyes bright, he knew with a certainty only dogs have that he was going to make it.

○

On June 22, 2006, at 6:33 a.m. in a place called Hope, Florida, a convergence of events took place that the locals and religious nuts would—for the rest of their lives—call a miracle.

Clarissa Burden, a middle-aged woman of faint confidence, had been pushed or jumped or perhaps she slipped (each witness had his or her own version) from the Hope fire tower. Her husband, an Afrikaner, was arrested. No one liked him, and his fate, in large part, would be left to the kindness of strangers.

What no one could have known was that Clarissa Burden, as she fell the fifty-two feet to her destiny, discovered during that long fall that she was a woman of immense potential, that she wasn't ready to die, that she had many books left to write, that she wasn't ugly or stupid or any of those other cruel things her mother and husband had accused her of, that she desired many more friends and at least three more lovers. She even discovered the secret to her mother's blackberry cobbler (this was one of the finest things about her mother, that cobbler), and as Clarissa fell, she cried over the prospect of possibly never knowing if she was right: It wasn't a cobbler at all, but a blackberry-and-dumpling divination.

No, the folks watching could not have known what was in Clarissa's mind as she fell. But here is why they whispered and shouted of miracles. Clarissa Burden landed nearly dead center on the World's Smallest Human Cannonball's air mattress — the very same mattress that required thirteen roustabouts to set it in place. The landing knocked the wind out of her, but her body broke the fall of the miniature chow chow, who — had the mattress not been moved in a peripatetic attempt to save Clarissa — would have overshot it and surely perished. And that was how he acquired among the carnies yet another moniker: Lucky Dog.

Out of either great appreciation or a sense of civic duty — Clarissa would never be sure which — the chow chow licked her face, brought the warmth back to her skin with his silky tongue; indeed, he revived her.

As Clarissa rose to full awareness, she knew she would never let this little dog go; he was hers now. And one other happy thing happened as she lay there, oxygen and freedom vanquishing the fuzz lining the interior pathways of her brain: All the letters of the alphabet lined up in a sacred order. Finally, after all these months, they made sense.

Lying on her back, the earth's good air slowly filling her lungs, the dog cleansing her wounds, Clarissa imagined the beginning of her long-sought novel. With her fingers moving along the keyboard of the sky, she remembered:

On June 21, 2006, at seven a.m. in a malarial crossroads named Hope, Florida, the thermometer old Mrs. Hickok had nailed to the WELCOME TO HOPE sign fifteen years prior read ninety-two degrees. It would get a lot hotter that day, and there was plenty of time for it to do so, this being the summer solstice. But Chase Baxter, a thirty-five-year-old woman who'd moved to Hope six months prior with her husband of seven years, trapped as she was in a haze of insecurities and self-doubt, was peculiarly unfazed by summer's pall. Indeed, as she gazed out the kitchen window into her backyard, she felt an undoing coming on that was totally unrelated to the heat. It was as if her brain stem, corpuscles, gallbladder, nail cuticles, the mole on her left shoulder, the scar on her knobby shin, the tender corpus of her womb—the whole shebang—were about to surrender. But to what, she did not know.

Acknowledgments

Using the creative license fiction affords, I rearranged the north Florida map, creating, among other things, a county that does not exist. Whenever the book was served by doing so, I moved highways and landmarks.

Writing is a courageous act committed by obsessed souls. Joy Harris and Deb Futter saw me through the process with wit, tenacity, and deeply appreciated honesty. My husband, Bill Hinson, brought me hot tea, rubbed my feet, tended my fears, checked facts, provided data, and never doubted. Michael McNally rebuilt my foundation metaphorically and otherwise. Rane Arroyo perceived in the first fifty pages the final three hundred. Mike and Zilpha Underwood offered sage and timely advice in addition to good cheer. Jerry Wayne Duncan reinforced my research and suggested roads not traveled. Baby Jalen taught me through the eyes of a child what pure joy truly is, inspiring Heart Archer to rise through the muse's murky depths. Olga-Villada Barnes's transcendent love for her husband, Al, even in his passing, helped shape her namesake's passion. Peter Ripley provided ballast, insight, and Mexican food that fueled the journey. Dianne Choie, Adam Reed, and Sarah Twombly meticulously guided me through the must-do's.

My writing students stirred up tiny dust devils full of miracles. Deidre, Phil, and Sean were there whenever I needed to feel solid earth beneath my feet. To all these people and their many gifts, and because they helped Clarissa fly, I am forever grateful.